Dark Enemy
REDEEMED

THE CHILDREN OF THE GODS
BOOK SIX

I. T. LUCAS

Contents

1. Amanda — 1
2. Andrew — 10
3. Amanda — 18
4. Syssi — 29
5. Amanda — 33
6. Syssi — 44
7. Andrew — 52
8. Amanda — 57
9. Dalhu — 73
10. Sebastian — 80
11. Kian — 85
12. Andrew — 91
13. Amanda — 95
14. Dalhu — 98
15. Kian — 102
16. Amanda — 113
17. Andrew — 121
18. Amanda — 133
19. Andrew — 141
20. Sebastian — 150
21. Amanda — 157
22. Kian — 166
23. Sebastian — 173
24. Amanda — 179
25. Dalhu — 190
26. Amanda — 197
27. Dalhu — 205
28. Amanda — 211
29. Sebastian — 217
30. Kian — 223

31. Sebastian	229
32. Kian	232
33. Syssi	238
34. Kian	248
35. Amanda	253
36. Anandur	262
37. Dalhu	271
38. Sebastian	279
39. Kian	282
40. Syssi	285
41. Andrew	293
42. Amanda	301
43. Kian	308
44. Dalhu	311
45. Amanda	315
46. Amanda	321
47. Dalhu	330
48. Amanda	337
49. Kian	341
50. Amanda	348
51. Syssi	355
52. Andrew	362
53. Anandur	370
54. Dalhu	379
55. Kian	389
56. Amanda	393
57. Syssi	398
58. Andrew	402
59. Amanda	416
Dark Warrior Mine	429
The Children of the Gods	459
The Perfect Match Series	467
Note	473
FOR EXCLUSIVE PEEKS	475

Amanda

"Are you sure? Not a single karaoke machine?"

Freaking Lana probably hadn't bothered to even look for it.

"*Niet*, I found one in a bar, but the owner not want to sell."

"How much did you offer?"

"Two thousand."

"You should've offered more."

"We buy the vodka and the fish you want, and this was all the money left from what you give me."

While the *Anna* moored for the night in Avalon harbor, Amanda had sent Lana and Sonia with instructions to buy supplies and find a karaoke—whatever the cost. Because c'mon, a party wasn't a party without one.

Especially since this one would be missing the most important element—hunky guys.

Regrettably, though, twenty-three hundred and some change in cash had been all she'd had on her, and the Russians had refused to take her credit card.

The obvious solution would've been to go with them, but she preferred to stay on board—not only because their company was such a dubious pleasure, but because she dreaded encountering horny males and their lustful, leering looks.

Which was sure to happen if she were to grace the streets of Avalon.

There was a price to be paid for beauty, and enduring leering glances from men wasn't even the worst of it—heck, most of the time she didn't mind.

Topping the list were the resentful looks from other females, followed closely by the presumption that all beautiful women were airheads.

Come to think of it, most people, males and females alike, found her looks intimidating.

So yeah, she had been enduring leering glances since she was scarcely a pubescent girl, but they hadn't bothered her before—on the contrary, most times she'd found them arousing.

But nothing was as it used to be.

She was horny, but at the same time felt nauseated by the prospect of a meaningless hookup. And earlier, during her afternoon *nap*, when she'd given self-pleasuring a halfhearted try, it had been more of the same.

Because there was only one male she was able to fantasize about, but the guilt and loathing associated with her attraction to Dalhu weren't exactly conducive to that particular activity.

Shit. It was hell, and it seemed she was going to be stuck in this purgatory for the foreseeable future.

Oh, well, there was nothing to be done about it, except giving it time.

Besides, as the *Anna* swayed gently on the pull and ebb of the tide, lying on a lounger on her top deck wasn't exactly a torment. And the fishy, salty smell of the murky waters wasn't all that bad either. Actually, it could have been quite pleasant if not for the diesel fumes wafting up from the boat's engines.

Fates, how she missed the era of old-fashioned sailboats. The experience had been completely different—the ocean had smelled wonderful—unpolluted.

On the other hand, there was something to be said for the speed, luxury, and modern amenities of the *Anna*.

This was the thing about life—nothing was ever perfect, and to gain one thing you often had to sacrifice another.

And wasn't that the inconvenient truth.

She'd found spending the day with a good book relaxing and would've loved to keep on reading, but the sun was getting low on the horizon, and even though the drop in temperature wasn't all that significant, it was getting too chilly for lounging in a string bikini.

With a sigh, Amanda closed her book and padded inside.

Back in her cabin, she eyed her laptop. Maybe she should check her e-mail to see if the design ideas for Syssi's wedding gown were ready.

Joann had been amazing, as always, and had contacted all of her designer friends, asking if they'd be willing to do a rush job. But with less than two weeks from idea to final fitting, only two had accepted the challenge of creating an original, breathtaking masterpiece for Amanda's best girl.

Nothing less than spectacular would do for Syssi.

With a frown, Amanda wondered if anyone had remembered Kian. After all, the groom also needed something new and fabulous for the event. Unless her brother was planning on showing up at the altar in his fancy Regent robe.

Yeah, right, she chuckled. In her opinion, he looked dashing in it, regal, but she was well aware that Kian detested the thing.

Maybe she should call him and suggest the robe. At first, Kian would blow up, but then he'd realize it was a joke and they would have a good laugh about it.

Or maybe not.

Amanda plopped down on the king-sized bed and crossed her arms over her eyes. She was dimly aware that the suntan oil she was covered with would leave a sticky imprint on the sheets, but she just didn't give a damn.

Who cared about bed linens when she was contemplating the depressing prospect of never regaining the easygoing, loving relationship she and Kian had enjoyed prior to this whole ugly mess.

Her hand reached for the phone, and she was tempted to hit his number.

But what would she say to him? Ask for his forgiveness?

If she believed it would mend things between them, she would've done it in a heartbeat. Pride, or who was right and who was wrong, was of no consequence when the stakes were so high.

Amanda just wanted her brother back.

Instead, she selected Syssi's number.

"Just a sec"—Syssi answered after the first ring—"let me get someone off the other line."

"Take your time."

Syssi came back after a few moments, puffing as if she'd been running. "I'm all yours."

"What's going on? You sound harried."

"You think? You try planning a wedding for six hundred guests. Neither your mother nor I have any experience in organizing events. And before you ask, no wedding coordinator worth her salt will take the job on such short notice. Ugh, it's going to be a disaster."

Amanda smiled. "Who's the drama queen now? Relax, it's going to be amazing. It shouldn't be all that difficult to arrange for good food, lively music, tasteful decorations, and most importantly—a gorgeous wedding dress."

"Yeah? The way things are going it seems Okidu will have to cook, decorate, and sew the dress. Because every caterer and florist I've called has practically laughed in my face. I had no idea these people are booked months in advance —some even years."

"This is actually a splendid idea. Between Okidu and Onidu and my mother's two, the Odus will have no problem pulling it off. All you need to do is give them a menu, including the recipes, show them pictures of how you want it to look, and they will take it from there."

"You must be kidding, right?"

"I'm dead serious. They can do all of it, except for the dress, which I've got covered."

"Oh, yeah? Do tell."

"Hold on, I'm checking my e-mail. Joann, bless her soul, found not one, but two designers who were willing to take on the challenge, and I'm waiting for the initial sketches." She quickly scrolled through her inbox, but there was nothing from Joann. "Nope... nothing yet. As soon as I have something, I'll forward it to you."

"That's wonderful, thank you. Joann has impeccable taste, I trust her completely."

"Good, I was afraid you'd hate me for not checking with you before talking to her."

"Nah, after outfitting me with an entire wardrobe of fabulous, I trust her to come up with something I can't even imagine. I'm all for letting the pros do their thing. One less item to worry about."

"Poor Syssi, you sound as excited about this wedding as if it was somebody else's."

"I know, right? I hate big events, and being at the center of one is my personal idea of hell. If it were up to me, it would've been just Kian and me, you, Andrew, and Annani. That's it."

"Really? What about your parents? And my sisters Sari and Alena? And the Guardians? And William and Bridget?"

"Okay, them too, but that's it, no one else."

"Oh, sweetie, don't you see? You might be happy with only our immediate families and the few people you know and care for witnessing your joining, but Kian wants, needs, each and every member of the clan to be there."

"I know. That's why I'm still here and not running off screaming." Syssi let out a huff.

"By the way, speaking of Kian, did anyone remember to get him fitted for a tux for the wedding? If you leave it up to him, he'll show up wearing one of his old business suits."

"You're right. God, I can't believe I didn't think of it." Syssi heaved a sigh. "Just another reminder of how little I know about the man I'm going to marry in thirteen days."

"You know everything that really matters, and you have endless time to learn the rest. So, stop fretting. Kian is a great guy—bad temper and all."

"Yeah, I know… but speaking of your brother's *sunny* disposition,",Syssi switched to a whisper, "Kian spent the entire evening with Dalhu and came back… well, I wouldn't say happy, but not enraged either. I think it's an encouraging sign."

Amanda chuckled. "I guess it is—by Kian's standards. Did you ask him what they talked about?" She wasn't curious, not at all…

"He gave me no chance, planting one hot kiss on my mouth and heading straight to his office to grab a file for his next meeting. But I'll grill him later tonight and report to you tomorrow."

In spite of herself, Amanda felt her heart give a little flutter. Kian must've been in at least a decent mood if the first thing he had done after spending hours with Dalhu was to kiss Syssi.

"Deal. First thing in the morning."

"Are you sure you want me to call you that early? You might be too hungover to talk after your drinking party with the Russians."

"Oh, please, I'll be fine. I'll have them drunk and singing in more ways than one before I'm even tipsy."

Syssi snorted. "If you say so."

"I've got it covered."

Well, almost. Without the karaoke, she would have to make a playlist on her phone and hook it up to the sound system in the grand salon, then hand out printouts of the lyrics to the girls.

Russian songs would have been the best, but unfortunately, although she spoke it with decent fluency, Amanda never bothered to learn to read the Cyrillic script—and mastering it in a span of a couple of hours was a feat that even she couldn't pull off.

Andrew

As Andrew knocked on the clinic's door, it crossed his mind that it was late and chances were that Dr. Bridget had already gone home.

Disappointed, he gave it one last go and knocked again, then waited. After all, he was already there, and it wasn't as if there was somewhere else he needed to be.

Calling it a night and heading back to his empty house was no more appealing than standing in this deserted corridor and waiting for a woman that might not even be there to let him in.

Kind of pathetic.

The life of a bachelor was not everything the married guys believed it to be.

True, he was free to shag whomever he was able to seduce —and there was no shortage of those—but most nights it just meant that he ended up going home alone.

That's why Syssi's news about the wedding hadn't been such a big surprise—not for him anyway—he'd been expecting it. Though maybe not so soon. He could empathize with Kian's desire to end his lonely bachelor life the moment he'd found the right woman to spend eternity with.

Andrew couldn't even imagine what it must have been like for the guy, spending endless years without someone to share his life with.

He was happy for them, he really was, but he couldn't help feeling a little jealous—even though his single status wasn't anybody's fault but his. And the excuse of his chosen occupation precluding meaningful relationships was just that—an excuse. Somehow it hadn't stopped his comrades from tying the knot.

Problem was, he'd never dated a woman he could imagine spending his life with, and not because none were good enough. Andrew suspected that the flaw was within him —he was either emotionally stunted or just too picky.

Another minute passed, and he was about to turn on his heel and head back when the door finally opened to reveal a surprised Dr. Bridget—the red handbag clutched under her arm betokening that she was on her way out.

Wow! Can you say sexy?

Gone was the conservative doctor, and the woman that had taken her place was hot. Bridget looked ready for action—with her wavy red hair loose around her shoulders and her curvy figure encased in a pair of skin-tight jeans and a clingy red T-shirt. But what had really done it for him were the red, fuck-me heels.

Evidently, Bridget loved to flaunt her red.

Trying hard to look into her pretty eyes and not glance down to peer at her ample cleavage, Andrew ran his hand over his mouth. Who could've guessed the petite physician had been hiding all of this under her doctor's coat?

"I'm sorry, I should have realized it was late. I'll stop by some other time, earlier in the day."

Her eyes widened, and she grabbed his hand, giving a strong tug. "Nonsense, you are coming with me." She pulled him behind her as she went inside and flipped the lights back on. There was a sly little smile on her lovely face as she turned around and looked up. "I'm not going to waste the opportunity of you coming to see me of your own volition. I thought I'd have to drag you here by force."

Andrew was about to snort at the ridiculous idea of her forcing him to do anything when it occurred to him that although tiny, she might be stronger than him. He hadn't resisted when she'd pulled, but still, it had been one hell of a tug.

Did it make her any less appealing? Hell, no, quite the opposite. "You underestimate your charms, Dr. Bridget. There is nowhere I'd rather be than here, with you."

A lovely blush blossomed over her pale porcelain cheeks, and she glanced away. But that sly smile was still there when she returned her eyes to his face. "Quite the charmer, aren't you? I bet you make all the ladies swoon."

Andrew chuckled. "Hardly." He let her lead him to an examination table and sat down.

"Take off your jacket and your shirt," she said and reached for her stethoscope.

"What? Already? I was hoping for a nice dinner and a pleasant conversation before you got me to undress for you," he teased as he shrugged off his jacket, folded it, and put it beside him on the table, then tackled the buttons on his shirt.

Bridget smiled, the pink blush refusing to abandon her face. "I'll take you up on the offer of dinner and flirtatious chitchat, but first, I'm going to check you out." She winked, her blue eyes sparkling with mischief.

"I'm all yours, Doctor." Andrew shrugged his shirt off, making sure to suck in his gut and flex as he exposed his torso to her gaze. He was in good shape and carried no excess fat. Nevertheless, he didn't have the body of a twenty-year-old either. Not to mention the many scars—some small, some large—scattered over his chest and abdomen as well as his back. And the sparse hair on his chest wasn't enough to hide even the smaller ones.

Bridget let go of the stethoscope and let it hang around her neck. Getting closer, she reached with gentle fingers to touch an old bullet scar. "You lived dangerously, didn't you?" she whispered, trailing her fingers over some of the others.

Thank God, it hadn't been pity that he'd heard in her voice, more like admiration. Or at least he hoped it was the latter. "You could say so."

"You know, once you turn, your body would probably heal these, even the older ones." She let her hand drop, but her eyes trailed over his front, making a tally, and she glanced behind him to look at the scars on his back.

"Would you like me better without them?" he teased, her scrutiny making him uncomfortable.

"I like you either way, with or without, how about that?" She plugged her ears and palmed the chest piece of the stethoscope. "Okay, breathe in… breathe out…"

He did as instructed, using the opportunity to sniff her hair as she leaned over him. Nice, some mild flowery scent, sweet and feminine, like Bridget herself. There was something very attractive about a soft, small woman that at the same time was a capable physician with a no-nonsense attitude and a strong personality.

"Perfect." She took the earpieces out and put the stethoscope away. "Okay, now shuck the pants."

"What? Why?" If Bridget was thinking about administering a prostate exam, she should think again.

"Got you!" She giggled. "You should have seen your face… the sheer horror… Though come on, it's not like you have something I haven't seen before."

Devilish woman. "First of all, how do you know I don't?" He cocked a brow.

"Yeah, yeah, I'm sure you're hung like a horse..." Bridget pushed at his chest to have him lie down. "And what's the second thing?"

"If I'm to let you poke me where the sun doesn't shine, it would only be after I've been naked in your bed first and have done some poking of my own."

Her cheeks pinked again. "My, oh my, what a naughty boy you are...," she murmured as she palpated his abdomen.

"You have no idea." He caught her hand and gave a tug, pulling her down on top of him. "Permission to kiss the doctor," he breathed a fraction of an inch away from her mouth.

"Permission granted," she said against his lips, then kissed him.

Tentative at first, it was no more than a brush of her lush lips against his, but as he closed his palm around her nape and drew her closer, she let out a moan and licked into his mouth.

His hands gentle as he caressed her back, Andrew wrestled with the urge to grab hold of Bridget and flip her under him. But she was so tiny compared to him, and he was afraid that letting out his hunger might overwhelm her.

Better let her set the pace.

Except, he wasn't sure how long his restraint would hold under Bridget's onslaught. She was kissing him and writhing on top of him with the abandon and urgency of a woman who knew exactly what she wanted and was starved of it. Her fingers seeking purchase on his short hair, she held him as she kissed him, her hips rocking over his hard shaft, setting him on fire.

"God, Bridget, I need you naked," he heard himself murmur against her lips as his arms tightened around her.

Fuck, he hadn't meant to say it out loud, and he hadn't meant to squash her to him either. But damn, it felt good — feeling her sweet little nipples getting so hard that they rubbed at his bare chest through her clothes. With a herculean effort, he eased his hold.

"Your wish is my command," she purred and reared up to her knees. Straddling his hips—her seductive smirk promised anything but demure obedience. She grabbed the hem of her red T-shirt and tugged it over her head, revealing creamy breasts covered by a sheer red bra that left nothing to the imagination. A moment later, it joined the shirt on the floor.

As if possessing a mind of their own, his hands reached and palmed the perky beauties.

"You're gorgeous."

She leaned into his touch, her eyes hooded. "Hold nothing back, Andrew, I'm a lot tougher than I look."

Okay...

She was under him in a flash.

"Better?" He smiled down at her before dipping his head to nuzzle her neck.

"Yes…" She arched into him, rubbing her breasts against his chest. "Oh, yes…just like that," she groaned as he slid down and licked around one nipple, then gasped as he sucked it in. "But it would be even better without the pants."

"Under one condition." He blew on her swollen, wet peak.

She arched a brow.

"The fuck-me red shoes stay on."

Amanda

"*Salute!*" Geneva raised her glass with an annoyingly steady hand.

Not quite drunk yet, Amanda might've been in better shape than her drinking buddies, but she was on her way to seriously tipsy. It was all good, though. Her plan was working—the atmosphere in the grand salon was becoming decidedly cheerful.

Situated on the main deck, the place was truly grand—in size as well as luxury. The sleek sofa in winter-white-colored leather was a custom-built beauty that could easily seat six, and it faced a glass coffee table of enormous proportions. Two brown overstuffed leather chairs completed the sitting area.

An oblong milky glass top and a wooden pedestal shaped like a tree trunk with sinewy branches comprised the dining table. Fourteen chairs, done in the same winter-white leather as the sofa, surrounded it.

The party had started with dinner, and the crew's mood had been steadily improving thanks to the bottle and a half of vodka she and her new friends had gone through—each.

Amanda could've enjoyed herself for real, if not for the stink coming off the grilled fish. The requisite butter-smothered potatoes didn't smell good, but not as bad.

As for her own culinary preferences, she'd been served a dish of string beans along with Renata's disgusted sneer. Apparently, green wasn't a color the crew appreciated anywhere near their plates. Renata's grilled tilapia, however, had been a big success with the girls.

A vegetarian hanging out with a bunch of Russians was like a nun in a bikers' bar—a page out of a find-the-one-thing-that-doesn't-belong game.

After dinner, they moved to the sitting area for the entertainment portion of the evening, and the girls humored her by giving a couple of the songs she'd prepared a half-hearted try. But then Sonia dropped the printed page on the glass table and began bellowing an old Russian Red Army song. Kristina and Lana joined her, and the three tried to harmonize.

They were either drunker than they looked or tone deaf. Except, it seemed that the painful cacophony didn't bother anyone but Amanda—the girls were having fun.

The only one who remained somber was Marta, a stocky woman with thick arms and wide shoulders and a scowl that was impressive even for a Russian. Her bushy brows, which looked like they'd never been touched by a pair of tweezers, were drawn tight despite the amount of alcohol she'd poured into her belly.

"Salute!" Amanda tossed back another shot, schooling her face not to show a grimace. The fact that she could handle a lot of vodka didn't mean she liked it—not unless it was mixed with something sweet and fruity. But to gain the Russians' respect, she had to drink it the way they did —straight up.

Pushing up to her feet, Amanda held onto the table as she refilled her glass—more for show than any real need. Her balance was still fine, thank you very much.

"To Alex! A great boss!" *Let's see what they think of their employer.*

"To Alexander!" The women all stood up for this one and tapped each other's glasses with loud clinks.

Interesting, they seem to like him.

Amanda plopped down on her chair, exaggerating her movements only a little—after all, good acting required subtlety. "So, tell me, Geneva, how did the bunch of you end up working for my cousin?"

"You are Alexander's cousin? He didn't tell me." Geneva eyed her with suspicion.

"What did he tell you then? That I'm his girlfriend?" Amanda snorted.

"No, just that you are an important guest and to be nice to you."

"Don't tell me you treat his other guests even worse. Because if that's the best you can do, well..."

Lana harrumphed which earned her a scowl from Geneva.

Amanda pretended not to notice. But c'mon, were they supposed to be nasty to Alex's guests?

Geneva waved a dismissive hand. "Alexander doesn't have guests."

"What, not even girlfriends?" That was weird. What was the point of having a luxury yacht if not to impress others? Especially women?

Kristina giggled, Sonia snorted, and even Geneva was trying to hide a smile.

"What? I know he isn't gay. I've seen him with enough females to fill a stadium, so there is no way."

That statement seemed to sour their good mood. "No, Alexander is definitely not gay," Geneva bit out, then reached for her bottle, refilled her glass, and tossed it back without a salute.

Holy Fates, Alex must've really meant it when he'd said they were his girls. He was really screwing his crew, and not out of wages.

Amanda narrowed her eyes and looked from one face to another, but none would meet her gaze. "So, which one of you is he shagging, or is it all of you?"

"Why? What do you care? You're supposed to be his cousin, not his girlfriend." Geneva crossed her muscular arms over her chest, leveling a pair of intense gray eyes on Amanda.

Tough cookie, and quite pretty if one looked past the scowl, the very short hair, and the lack of makeup. Like those of a lot of Russians, her lips were full and fleshy. High, defined cheekbones hinted at some Asian genes in the mix, as did the almost pure black of her hair and the lack of a defined separation between the lower and upper lid. The rest was typical Slavic though—the very pale skin and big gray eyes, as well as the large breasts and the narrow hips.

"I don't. As far as I'm concerned, you can all be having big, multi-limb orgies. It's just that I thought you girls were into other girls, not guys, or a particular guy as it seems to be the case here."

Geneva snorted, then her wide shoulders began shaking, and she burst out laughing. Soon, the whole table was shaking as the other women joined in, laughing and banging their hands on the table.

"You think we lesbians?" Lana managed between giggles. "Why?"

"Duh, the buzz cuts, the big muscles…"

"Ah…" Lana exchanged smug looks with her shipmates. "Is because we are wrestlers." She banged her fist on her chest. "Strong muscles for fighting, and no long hair to grab…*Dah*?"

"Like in the Olympics? I didn't know they had women wrestling."

"Not in the Olympics"—Geneva chuckled—"in the mud."

"Mud wrestling? Get out of here!"

"Mud wrestling good money in Russia," Marta said with a heavy accent—her first words ever to Amanda.

"How did a team of Russian mud-wrestlers end up as crew on an American yacht?"

"Russian yacht. Alexander bought her in St. Petersburg."

"And?"

"We were working in a club, and Alexander came to watch," Kristina said with a quick glance at Geneva.

The captain lifted her palm to reassure her no harm was done. "It's okay. I'll tell the story."

"We were working nights in the club. A lot of men come to watch—Russians and foreigners. It is a very popular thing, more popular than strip clubs, better money too. The men think it's hot—strong women, practically naked in the mud, fighting each other, not just for show, but for real. They place bets, and some pay for private services later on."

"Just say it," Lana interfered. "They pay for sex. It's really good money, and working as a *prostitutka* is not a big deal in Russia. No shame."

Geneva shrugged. "Alexander came to watch one evening and paid for all of us to come to his hotel suite after we were done. We laughed on our way there. Crazy American, what was he going to do with the six of us? Sonia thought that he might want to watch us with each other. Some men do, you know..." She glanced at Amanda.

"Sure." Amanda nodded, stifling a smile. She could just imagine their surprise when Alex had shagged each and every one of them and then had gone for seconds.

"But Alexander is not an ordinary man—" Geneva shook her head.

You have no idea...

Renata harrumphed, "A sex machine..."

"Yes, so after he pleasured us, one at a time, two at a time, then again and again, he let us sleep over at his luxurious suite. It was the largest one in the hotel, top floor, two bedrooms, two bathrooms, a living room, kitchen, dining room, everything. In the morning, when he had breakfast delivered to us, we were ready to worship him as God." Geneva smirked.

"And sing ballads to his glorious manhood." Lana saluted with another drink.

"Over breakfast, he said he would like us to come work for him on his yacht. I asked as what? Prostitutes for his guests? I thought he planned to have a floating brothel. Not a bad idea, by the way. But he said he wasn't going to offer us to any other men, we were to operate his new yacht and serve only him. I asked how much he would pay. His offer was good, especially since he promised to take care of our legal status in the United States." Geneva ended her tale with another shrug. "And here we are."

Obviously, this wasn't the whole story. Alex had no need for a personal harem. There were plenty of readily available females at the club who were more than willing to share his bed. And besides, he was not known as a generous employer. For his offer to be good enough to cover what the women had been making from prostitution, he must've expected more than sex from them—and running the yacht as an added bonus wasn't it, or at least not entirely.

The question was what? And how to get them to spill? Geneva was still perfectly lucid despite the second bottle of vodka.

"I don't understand, though. It's not like being a captain of a vessel this size is something one learns in a day."

"No, I already had a license, and the club owner must've told Alexander. Not that it was a big secret or anything; everybody knew I was saving up to buy a small cruiser. I was planning to run dinner tours out of St. Petersburg. That's why I was working at the club. It was the only way to make enough money for it. Renata was saving up too. She was going to be my partner and the chef."

"Then Alex's offer must have seemed like a godsend to you guys."

"Exactly."

Geneva's choice of adjective indicated certainty, but her tone didn't, and a barely perceptible shadow of regret crossed her impassive face.

But why?

This job was a big step up from her previous one, and several steps closer to her dream.

Perhaps she resented having to sleep with Alex as part of her new job description. Except, the woman seemed genuinely impressed with the guy's bedroom skills.

"Is sharing him okay with you, though?"

Geneva shrugged again. "It's not as if any of us has fallen in love with him or anything. And none of us is in a big hurry to find a decent man of her own—if such a creature even exists. It's just business. Just until we make enough money to make a new life for ourselves here. We like it in America. We want to stay. But with a fresh start—leave our old lives behind and start over clean."

Amanda nodded and poured another shot. "To new beginnings!" She saluted, and the women joined her with an enthusiastic one of their own.

Fascinating story, but what did it hint at? Other than Alex's fetish for mud-covered females, that is?

The most likely scenario she could think of was that he was using the yacht to smuggle drugs. Alex must've figured that an all female crew would be less suspicious—or, that as females with a shady past and questionable legal status the Russians would be easier to control.

And in case the *Anna* ran into trouble, they were certainly not helpless either.

But for some reason, she had a nagging suspicion that it wasn't about drugs, at least not exclusively. There were much easier ways, not to mention less costly, to smuggle illegal substances.

Then what?

Maybe illegal aliens?

Except, she was pretty sure that smuggling illegals wasn't all that profitable.

Unless, the illegal aliens were the big money types, who liked to travel in style.

Drug lords? Mafiosi?

Recalling her conversation with Syssi, Amanda chuckled. *Kian a mafioso, really...* as if her uptight, do-gooder brother fit the profile. But Alex kind of did. And although Amanda thought he was okay, Syssi's opinion of the guy differed—she thought he was a major creep.

So yeah, that must've been the story behind the *Anna* and her peculiar crew. Alex was using the boat to smuggle wealthy criminals in and out of the United States, and probably drugs too.

She had no proof, though.

Unlike Kian, Amanda wasn't a do-gooder and, therefore, didn't feel morally outraged at Alex's alleged criminal activity. Not that she condoned it, but still, Alex was a friend who'd graciously loaned her the use of his boat.

Should she share her suspicions with Kian? Or should she keep them to herself—at least until she uncovered some solid evidence?

After all, to add fuel to her brother's antipathy toward Alex—based on a mere hunch—wouldn't be the right thing to do either.

Or would it?

To tattle on Alex without proof was bad. Except, how on earth was she going to get it? And even if she looked and failed to find any incriminating evidence, it wouldn't necessarily mean that there was none. After all, she was not an investigator.

If she chose not to confide in Kian because she had no proof, no one would even know that there was something fishy going on that required further looking into.

Damn, once again she was torn between two options—neither of them good.

Not that telling or not telling on Alex was in the same category as her other dilemma—it was like comparing shoplifting to armed robbery. Because craving the man who had ordered her nephew's murder was worse than any alleged smuggling. It was disgraceful, even revolting, but on the other hand, keeping away from him was hell.

Syssi

Damn, the man is fine, Syssi thought for the umpteenth time as she watched Kian walk into the bedroom with nothing but a towel wrapped around his hips. From the harsh lines of his gorgeous face to the ripple of his muscles, as he moved with that unnatural fluidity of his, he was so sexy that he took her breath away.

With all this glorious, male perfection scrambling her brain into a horny mush, her plan to ask about his meeting with Dalhu was shoved aside.

After all, a girl had to have her priorities straight, and as a blast of desire hit her breasts and landed between her thighs, guess what made it to the top of the list?

"Come here," she breathed, beckoning him to her with a crooked finger.

Kian dropped the towel. "Like what you see, sweet girl?"

Oh, yes, she liked.

Fully erect and ready for action, her man was magnificent. "You know I do. You are such a show-off," she teased.

"And you're not naked." Kian stalked closer.

"That could be easily remedied." She pulled her nightshirt over her head and tossed it to the floor, then shimmied out of her panties. "Catch." She aimed at his smirking face.

He caught them, shaking his head at the simple undergarment dangling from his fingers. "Cotton?"

What's wrong with that? Did he expect her to sleep in a lacy thong?

Not this girl.

"Cotton is breathable and comfortable."

With a wicked smile, he mounted her, his hands pinning her wrists over her head. "But not as breathable as having nothing on at all. If I can't have you naked all of the time, I want you to at least sleep in the nude."

She parted her legs to cradle him between her thighs. "If I wear nothing to bed, you wouldn't let me sleep at all."

"True, that." He pressed a kiss to the side of her neck, then licked the same spot.

As his hot shaft rubbed against her mound, his hips surging and retreating, Syssi closed her eyes and let herself slide into submission—her body liquefying under his. She no longer had to struggle to find that special place inside her head that allowed her to let go. Like a meditative state, once attained, she could now ease into it effortlessly.

The effect was almost euphoric.

"My sweet Syssi," Kian breathed, his tender, loving voice prompting her to lift her lids and look at him.

His beautiful eyes were glowing, but even their otherworldly luminescence wasn't as breathtaking as the love shining through.

"I love you," she whispered, wishing there was a word not as overused to express the magnitude of what was in her heart. Like an all-consuming fire, it was more than the physical attraction, more than appreciation for this amazing man, more than her need to be with him—begrudging every moment of his time away from her—and even more than his feelings for her that ran just as deep.

It was like the sum was greater than the parts. And what's more, the maelstrom of emotion no longer terrified her.

Maybe it was the upcoming wedding that had finally put her fears and insecurities to rest—their bond solidifying once the decision to have their commitment to each other witnessed and confirmed had been made.

But why?

What power did a piece of paper have? One that she was pretty sure wouldn't even be deemed legal in any mortal court?

Shouldn't their pledge to each other be enough? What additional validation did a marriage ceremony provide?

She used to believe that marriage was about a legal contract spelling out the obligations and responsibilities of two people engaged in the business of raising a family and sharing a household. But apparently, there was some metaphysical aspect to this age-old tradition as well.

And yet, observing the many corrosive relationships and failed marriages, she had to wonder if this elusive aspect had been either absent from them to begin with or just too easily broken.

She and Kian must be among the uniquely blessed—those who God or fate or dumb luck joined in a true love match.

Yeah, she was one lucky girl.

"What is this secretive smile all about, my love?"

"I'm happy that we are getting married."

"Yeah? What brought that about? Seeing my sexy body? My impressive size?" he teased, giving his hips a wicked twist that had the aforementioned sizable part rub her just the right way.

She arched into him. "All of the above and more. I'm just glad you are mine to keep."

"And you are mine." He nuzzled her neck. "To keep." His mouth trailed south. "To love." He licked at her nipple. "And to hold." He licked the other one. "And to make love to, again, and again…"

Amanda

"*O bo'ze moy, o bo'ze moy, o bo'ze moy, ya ydu hority v pekli...*"—Oh my God, oh my God, oh my God, I'm going to burn in hell—Marta was chanting over and over in Ukrainian, clutching her knees and rocking back and forth on the floor. Early into her third bottle, the woman had broken down, scooting into a corner to sob her heart out.

Renata had gone to sit with her, whispering calming words into her ear until the tears had dried out, but the chanting hadn't ceased.

Was Marta lamenting her whoring days? Or fearing her god's punishment for participating in drug trafficking?

Geneva ignored her fallen comrade. "You are going to lose, American," she said and pounded back another shot.

"Not a chance, Ruska." Amanda followed with her own.

She had been pretending to be wasted for the past hour or so, as she and Geneva—the last two standing, or rather sprawling as it were—had gone one to one on their third bottle of vodka.

Not that she had remained unaffected, but with her higher tolerance for alcohol and lesser need for sleep, there had been no doubt in her mind that the mortal would succumb first to the powerful combination of alcohol and exhaustion.

Mercifully, the chanting stopped, and Marta's head fell on Renata's shoulder.

Only two more shots to go. Amanda eyed her nearly empty bottle.

She had been sure Geneva would pass out by now, but the woman was proving to be stubbornly resilient.

"I finish first." Geneva's mumble was barely audible as her last empty glass clunked against the table.

Amanda emptied hers as well. "It's a draw," she slurred.

Closing her eyes and pretending to sleep, she waited until the captain slumped against Lana, joining her friend in a snoring duet.

With the crew finally asleep, passed out over sofas and chairs and the floor of the grand salon, Amanda was presented with a perfect opportunity to search for proof of Alex's illicit endeavors.

Trouble was, by now she was way beyond tipsy and into really drunk territory, not to mention exhausted. It was nearly morning, and outside the main deck's windows the sky was already pinking with the rising sun.

Okay, Mata Hari, time to investigate.

Amanda pushed to her feet and stood on legs that felt like two rubber noodles. Carefully, she took the stairs down, holding on to the banister as she placed one bare foot in front of the other. Her head was spinning, and the sway of the boat was not helping with her rising nausea. Still, she somehow made it to the lower deck without puking all over the pretty glass staircase.

Since Amanda had appropriated Alex's cabin—the large and luxurious master suite on the main deck—she'd been down to the lower deck only once to check out the fitness room that was right by the staircase. But she remembered Geneva telling her that the four guest cabins were in the front and the three crew cabins were in the back, or stern—if she remembered her boating terminology.

She decided to investigate the guest cabins first. Two were outfitted with queen beds and the other two with two twins each, but from the looks of things no one had slept in either of them since the yacht had been bought and redecorated. There were no towels or even toilet paper in the bathrooms, and although the beds were made with clean bedding and elegant duvets, it was obvious that the things were brand new and had never been washed. The sheets and pillowcases still had creases from the original packaging and stank of the formaldehyde the fabrics had been treated with.

After checking the closets and banging on the walls, the floors, and the ceilings, she had to accept that there was nothing hidden in the guest portion of the lower deck, and moved on to the crew cabins. Naturally, those looked lived in, and though a far cry from the fancy guest rooms, they were nonetheless comfortable. Each cabin had an adjacent bathroom. Those were small, with just a shower stall, a sink and a toilet.

Two of the rooms were shared, and one was a single. Recognizing the particular scent of each woman, Amanda had no trouble figuring out who slept where. Renata and Marta shared one, Sonia and Kristina the second, and surly Lana had a cabin of her own—probably because no one wanted to room with her and her attitude.

Unfortunately, Amanda's snoop of the crew cabins didn't produce any hidden compartments either.

Going for another round, she checked that the dividing walls corresponded to the cabin sizes with no significant gaps in between them.

But everything seemed kosher.

There was no space that could accommodate a hiding place big enough for one person, let alone several.

Geneva's captain cabin was on the upper deck next to the wheelhouse, but there was little chance Amanda would find what she was looking for up there—too public.

It didn't make sense.

Not unless she was wrong and Alex didn't smuggle people. Because even if there was a small secret compartment she hadn't discovered yet, it would have been used only in the rare occurrence of the yacht being boarded for inspection. At all other times, the guest or guests would have been staying in the cabins, which they obviously hadn't.

Unless they were staying with Alex at his master cabin. Which was ludicrous. Wealthy master criminals were almost exclusively male, and Alex didn't swing that way.

That left only the under deck.

Taking the narrow stairs down to the service area, Amanda ducked into the engine room, then continued to survey everything from the stabilizer fins, bow-thrusters, and other machinery, to the washers, dryers, refrigerators, and she even poked her head into the large double door freezer.

Nothing.

Shit.

She climbed the stairs back to the main deck, bypassing the salon where her drinking buddies were still sprawled out, and heading straight for her cabin. Maybe a shower would clear her head and lift the drunken fog, because there was no doubt in her mind that she was missing something.

Shimmying out of her jeans and thong, she dropped them in the pullout laundry bin. Her T-shirt was next.

Cold water would have been best, but Amanda was in no shape for self-inflicted torture. A warm shower would have to do. The hot spray was divine, and she braced her arms against the marble wall, dipping her head and letting the water pound her spine.

If Alex had been smuggling people, they must've stayed in the master cabin...

Of course, she slapped her hand on her forehead. It was so simple that she must have been really drunk not to figure it out right away.

While a guest stayed in Alex's cabin, Alex stayed with Geneva at hers. It probably wasn't as luxurious as this one, but it was most likely just as spacious and elegant as the guest cabin—captain's quarters on a boat this size usually were. Or, he might have even taken over her cabin and sent her down to room with Lana. There was a spare bed in her cabin.

That way, if the yacht were boarded for inspection, it would look as if no one aside from the owner and his crew were aboard. The guest would be rushed into some hiding nook—without the need for a mad shuffle to clean up his cabin and eliminate all evidence of him ever being there.

Simple and smart.

Except, she still had no evidence one way or the other, and this whole mental exercise could be nothing more than an interesting hypothesis.

If she wanted proof, she needed to find that hidden compartment.

Amanda was pretty certain it wasn't on the lower deck or the under deck. She had been quite thorough in searching those. Which left the main and upper decks.

The main deck housed the master cabin she was occupying and the grand salon. The salon wasn't accessible at the moment and the master cabin she could search later at her leisure.

Shit, she should hurry and check out the upper deck before the crew woke up.

Problem was, she was operating on fumes. Between the alcohol, the lack of sleep, and the effect of the hot shower, she was barely able to keep her eyes open.

With a hard resolve and a wince, Amanda turned the temperature dial all the way down, cringing as she waited for the cold water to hit her.

But the water wasn't just cold, it was freezing.

Damn, this is awful!

Unable to tolerate more than a few seconds, she jumped out and grabbed a towel, wrapped it tightly around herself first, and only then reached to turn the water off.

She was miserably cold and shivering, her teeth rattling like a pair of castanets, but hey, she was fully awake.

Eyeing the thick terry bathrobe hanging from a hook behind the bathroom's door, she hesitated for about a second. The thing must've belonged to Alex. It was an ugly mushroom color, and the idea of putting on something that had touched Alex's naked body was gross. But style and even personal hygiene be damned—she needed to get warm.

Wrapped in the double layer of bathrobe and towel, her teeth no longer banging against each other, she plodded back to the cabin and glanced at the bed with longing.

Hell, do I really need to be doing this? I'm no Mata Hari... More than anything, she wanted to crawl under the warm duvet and let sleep claim her.

Come on, Amanda, don't be a wuss.

With a sigh, she said goodbye to the lovely bed and stepped inside the large walk-in closet. After pulling on a pair of yoga pants, both towel and bathrobe still on, she grabbed the only long-sleeve warm top she had with her—a black, lightweight cashmere turtleneck. It required some acrobatic-level twisting to manage to get it over her head, while holding onto the towel until it was fully on.

A pair of red Uggs warming her feet, she left the cabin and tiptoed past the salon, counting the heads to make sure that they were all still there, before climbing the stairs to the upper deck.

Emerging up in the top grand salon, she passed the sitting area and the bar, disregarding them as potential hiding places, and headed straight for Geneva's cabin.

It was unlocked.

Size wise, it was similar to the smaller guest cabins, but the furnishings and their placement had been chosen for utility, not style. The queen-sized bed was covered with a generic, purple comforter and pushed against the side wall to make room for an oak desk and a small bookcase. Both pieces looked like something one would find discarded on a street of a shitty neighborhood or pay a buck and a half for at a Goodwill store.

Next to the bed, instead of a nightstand, a tall cherry wood dresser provided extra storage space. Inside, there were the standard panties and a couple of bras, socks, a few T-shirts, a beanie and some scarves, but not a shred of the personal memorabilia Amanda had hoped would shed light on the kind of person Geneva was.

Over at the bookcase, she flipped through a few of Geneva's books and shuffled through the disk cases that were stacked one on top of the other. Most were related either to boating or the mastering of American English—which explained her fluency and good accent compared to the rest of the crew. A few disks even tackled basic, spoken Spanish. Other than that, there were several Russian titles that seemed to be novels, but lacking the ability to read Cyrillic script, Amanda couldn't tell for sure. She flipped through them nonetheless, searching for photos or other documents that might have been hiding between the pages.

Nada, zilch.

The utilitarian theme continued inside the small clothes closet: A few pairs of jeans and khakis, some long, some short; four polo shirts; three button-downs; two jackets—one light and one warm; two pairs of shoes, one pair of boots, and no heel in sight.

How boring.

In the bathroom, Amanda finally found some small concessions to femininity; a lavender-scented soap, shampoo and conditioner, and lo and behold—a brown pencil eyeliner and black mascara.

There was only one toothbrush, and no razor, which meant first and foremost that Geneva's bare legs and armpits were laser-treated or waxed—shocking for a Russian—though it might have been a requirement of her mud wrestling job. And secondly, no male had shared her bathroom recently.

Not that there was even a sliver of a chance that Alex would have deigned to grace Geneva's spartan cabin, but neither had any other male.

Just to make sure, Amanda gave the bedding a thorough sniffing.

There was nothing besides the lavender soap scent, Geneva, and a laundry detergent. So unless the bedding was brand new, the woman had been sleeping alone.

Bummer. Yet another dead end.

Oh, well, she must've been wrong, inventing a whole bogus scenario built on nothing more than suspicion and conjecture.

Trouble was, she knew she wasn't. For Alex to make the kind of money needed to buy and run this yacht, he must've been doing a lot more than running a club and selling some drugs.

But if indeed that was all, then he must have been a major distributor.

Whatever.

She was too tired to think straight. Her investigation would have to wait for another day, or better yet, the proper authorities.

Syssi

"Last night, before I got distracted by your sexy body and impressive size." Syssi leaned against the bathroom's doorframe and ogled Kian as he brushed his teeth, naked. "I wanted to ask you how your meeting with Dalhu went."

Even though they'd just made love, watching the interplay of muscles on his sculpted back, she felt her nipples pebble.

Down, girls. She crossed her arms over her chest. But as he dipped his head to spit out the toothpaste, his strong thigh muscles flexing, she dropped her arms in surrender and let out a soft sigh. "You're doing it again..."

"What?"

"Distracting me."

"It's not going to work."

"What's not going to work?"

"I'm not going back to bed to satisfy your insatiable appetite. I have work to do, woman." Kian was trying for a severe tone, but was losing the battle to the twitch in his lip and the smile that was threatening to foil his show.

"What? Is there anything more important than taking care of your fiancée's needs?" Syssi taunted.

Kian was on her between one heartbeat and another. "Absolutely nothing," he whispered in her ear, then caught the soft flesh of her earlobe between his teeth and pressed.

She shivered and he picked her up, then carried her back to their bed.

"How about you take this off?" He tugged at the hem of her nightshirt.

"Seriously? Even my new and improved physique is not up to a third time. It's just that you're so sexy I can't take my eyes off you, you big, arrogant oaf."

"Is that so?" He kissed her nose.

"It is. You know you're gorgeous."

"As long as you think so, I'm good." He pressed another kiss to her forehead and pushed off the bed. "Regretfully, I need to get going. But you're welcome to join me in the closet. You can admire my body to your heart's content while I'm getting dressed."

Following after him, she did just that.

"So? How did it go?" Inside the walk-in closet, Syssi pulled out a footstool and sat down, straddling it.

"The Doomer didn't lie, but he didn't know much either. Apparently, he was just a lowly commander of a small unit. Leave it to Amanda to aim lower than low, falling for a Doomer that isn't even an important one. The girl needs to work on her self-esteem."

Curiously, Syssi didn't detect much bite in Kian's tone. He sounded almost conversational. Was he losing some of his animosity toward Dalhu? Or was it just the effect of postcoital bliss?

"Did you learn anything new, though?" she probed, not sure which direction her questions should take.

"A little." Kian shrugged as he buttoned his shirt.

Now, she knew for sure that there was something he wasn't telling her. "Come on, do I have to beg for crumbs?"

Kian paused with his fingers hovering over the top button of his shirt. "Wait here," he said and walked out of the closet in a pair of gray socks, a pale blue dress shirt, and no pants—no doubt the only man on the planet who could pull off that look with such tremendous success.

After a quick visit to the bathroom, he came back with a folded piece of green paper in his hand. "Take a look." He handed it to her.

Curious, she unfolded what looked like a flyer for a rock band concert and arched a brow.

"Turn it over."

She did and gasped. "Oh my God, this is amazing. Who drew it?"

"Dalhu."

Her eyes shot up to Kian's. "He is good, very good."

"I know. Not that I'm an expert on art or even know what to look for, but it's quite evident. And it took him no more than a minute or two."

"How did it come about? I don't suppose that just out of the blue he decided to draw Amanda's picture for you?"

"The Doomer was trying to prove he can sketch. Andrew suggested that we compile files on the top players in Navuh's camp. Dalhu offered to supply the information and even to draw their portraits for us. When we sneered at him, with Andrew saying that this was a job for a forensic artist, Dalhu drew the picture to show off his skill."

Kian walked over to the suit section of his closet and removed a pair of slacks off a hanger.

A suit, right. She'd almost forgotten. "Are your suits custom made?"

"Yes, why?"

"You need a nice one for the wedding, maybe a tuxedo?"

"Not a chance."

Syssi let out a soft chuckle. "Why am I not surprised... but anyway, do you go to a tailor or does he come to you? I want to arrange a fitting. We don't have much time." Now was not the time to argue about the tux. She would approach that subject again later.

"You have enough on your plate. I'll have Shai do it. He is the one who decides when I need new clothes and either buys them himself or invites Mr. Fentony to measure me for suits and dress shirts." Kian grimaced at a blemish he'd noticed on the pair of slacks he was holding and cast them aside, then reached for a different pair. "Though I have no idea why he needs to come, it's not as if my measurements change from one fitting to another. He probably does it just to justify his inflated prices." Kian chuckled.

Syssi felt her cheeks heat up though this time the cause wasn't embarrassment. Shai would not fight Kian over the tux. He would just do whatever Kian told him to. But there was more to it than that.

She was angry.

Why had such a trivial thing upset her so? Was it because Kian should've realized it was no longer his secretary's job to take care of him?

Don't be an idiot. The man has been on his own for literally forever, and you want him to adapt just like that? "I'll get Mr. Fentony's number from Shai and call him myself."

"Why?" Kian cast her a quizzical look.

"Because I want to." *Let him figure out the why himself.*

"Okay." He shrugged as if it was a nonissue.

Not that he was wrong, necessarily. It was just that she wanted to take care of him in any way she could, needed to, and there was so little she could do for him.

Someone else made sure Kian had new clothes and kept him company in the office; another cooked his meals and did his laundry. Not that she wasn't grateful for Okidu. She was so busy with the wedding plans that preparing a meal or stuffing the washer would've been all she could've managed.

And as for joining Kian in the office and learning about the conglomerate he was running, so she could eventually be of some help, it would have to wait until after the party.

Trouble was, Amanda wanted her back in the lab. But even though Syssi enjoyed the research, she hated the idea of being away from Kian for so many hours a day. Neuroscience was more exciting than administrative work, but sharing Kian's office and easing some of his load was more appealing to her.

Why?

Because she loved him, and people who loved each other wanted to be together and take care of each other.

It was as simple as that.

Syssi looked down at the crumpled piece of green paper she was still holding. Smoothing out the creases, she ran her fingers over the outline of Amanda's face. There was so much feeling in the eyes staring at her from the picture, and she wondered if Amanda had truly gazed at Dalhu like this, or had he drawn what he was yearning for.

But one thing was certain, only a man in love could've captured the beauty of Amanda's spirit, shining through the breathtaking perfection of her face, the way Dalhu had done in his sketch.

"He loves her... you realize that, don't you?" she murmured.

"Yeah, so what?"

"And she loves him back..."

"No, she doesn't."

"How can you say that? You haven't talked to her even once since the rescue. How would you know if she does or does not?"

"Because it's Amanda." Kian pulled on the pair of dark gray slacks and tucked the shirt inside. "She is frivolous, and like a succubus for drama, she feeds on it—the more, the better—but even she must realize that the Doomer is beneath her." He zipped up his pants, then moved over to the dresser and pulled out the top drawer—the one with his favorite ties. There were many more, taking up that whole bank of drawers. And yet, looking at his many options, Kian's brows dipped. He couldn't decide, or perhaps for some reason, none of them met with his approval this morning.

"Here, let me." Syssi shooed him over, looking through the tie selection for the one that would match the colors of what he was wearing. "I don't think social status has anything to do with love. Why is he beneath her? Is he stupid? Uneducated? Uncouth?" She held up a gray-and-blue-striped tie to Kian's pale blue shirt.

"I don't think he is educated, Doomers typically aren't, but it's not about that. I'm not educated either. But even though he seems intelligent and is well spoken, he is tainted by his past, and there is nothing he or she can do about it."

"Not a great believer in redemption, are you?" Syssi looped the tie around Kian's neck.

"Nope."

"You realize that it's not really up to you. You can huff, and you can puff, and still, when all is said and done, Amanda will do as she pleases." Syssi finished the knot and smoothed the tie over Kian's shirt, then placed her palms over his hard pecs.

He covered her hands with his and held them against his chest. "It is true that I have little control over Amanda, but I have complete control over the Doomer. And I'm not letting him out of that cell."

Andrew

"I'll have a double espresso and these." Andrew handed the tuna sandwich and the cup of fruit to the Starbucks barista.

Since he'd started the new desk job, he'd been having his breakfast at this same Starbucks every morning on his way to work. He knew everyone there by name, but this one was new. Brea—it said on her name tag—a slightly chubby girl with a pretty face and lots of makeup.

"Sure, will there be anything else, sir?" She smiled, revealing a set of small white teeth covered with shiny metal braces.

Damn, they were getting younger and younger, while he was getting older and older. And this morning in particular, his body felt like a used and abused forty-year-old truck. "No, thank you, Brea." Like some old fart, he'd been tempted to substitute *honey* for her name.

Not yet, buddy. He managed a tight smile as she swiped his credit card.

The place was packed with the morning crowd, but as most of the patrons were either standing in line to order their coffee or hovering around the other side to collect it once it was ready, he found an empty stool at the counter facing the window—his favorite spot. Unwrapping his sandwich, he listened for his name to be called out.

Hell, after last night, that double shot of espresso should be classified as medicinal. Andrew needed the stimulant to get his tired old ass in gear.

A sly smirk tugged at his lips as he thought back to his eventful visit to the good doctor. Bridget had introduced him to sex like he had never experienced before—mind-blowing intensity, insatiable, and the endurance to match.

It had been humbling.

While he had felt like he'd been through a marathon after climaxing for the fourth time—which was quite impressive for any male over twenty thank-you-very-much, though potentially life threatening for someone his age—Bridget had tried to hide her disappointment.

Her apology had made it worse. As if admitting that she hadn't been with a man for a while and then explaining the sexual appetite of immortal females was supposed to make him feel better.

With a smirk, he wondered if by literally sucking the life out of him the doctor had been violating her Hippocratic Oath to do no harm.

But hey, what was he complaining about? As if there was a better way to go than croaking from too much sex—he would have arrived on the other side with a big smile on his face.

Tonight, he was going back for seconds, but not before taking a nap and chugging an energy drink or two. Having a decent bed instead of the hard, narrow exam table would no doubt help matters as well. That bloody table must've been the source of most of his aches and pains.

Yeah, keep telling yourself that...

Should he bring flowers?

Bridget had invited him to dinner at her place, and showing up empty-handed seemed rude. On the other hand, neither of them had any illusions as to what this was all about, so flowers might not be appropriate—too romantic. God knew there was no romance involved, and chances were good that they would skip the meal altogether and jump straight into bed.

Wine would be a better choice.

Pulling out his phone, Andrew added it to his shopping list. But then, wine seemed like not enough for a woman that had rocked his world.

He added a box of Godiva chocolates to the list.

Not that this was enough either, but again, anything more would imply feelings that just weren't there, and might send Bridget running. After all, the woman made it clear she was just after his body.

Which was perfectly fine with him, she was welcome to use him for as long as he wished to be used.

"Double espresso for Andrew," he heard the barista call out.

On his way to collect his double shot of energy, he passed by several young women—mostly college students—sitting around the small tables with their laptops and their coffees.

They had no idea how lucky they were, and how inconsequential their troubles were compared to those of women their age in other parts of the world.

That thought pulled him away from the pleasant subject of Bridget and flowers to the disturbing one of Passion Island and the women imprisoned there. To do nothing about it went against everything he stood for, but the hard truth was that the idea of invading the island was indeed ludicrous.

Even if he succeeded in convincing someone in the government that something must be done about it, no one in their right mind would consider attacking a foreign country to free a bunch of women. And even if anyone did, there was the issue of an army of immortal warriors to contend with.

The sad reality was that as miserable as the lives of those women were, they were not worth the lost lives of thousands of soldiers or the havoc an international incident like that would cause.

The only thing to do was to make it damn hard for the Doomers to collect new flesh for their bazaar—at least from the States. And he could talk to a buddy of his on the Russian side about doing something about it on their front.

In truth, though, Andrew was well aware that he was indulging in mental masturbation. Nothing could stop the worldwide plague of kidnapping and sexual enslavement of women and girls—not as long as there was demand and big money could be made from the trade.

Regrettably, he had a hard time envisioning a future in which this age-old, loathsome market had been eradicated.

Amanda

"Hey, American! You alive in there?"

"Go away!" Amanda barked and covered her head with a pillow.

What the hell possessed Lana to bang on her door at this ungodly hour? And as far as she was concerned, it was an ungodly hour, even if it was two in the afternoon.

"Geneva said to check on you, so I did."

"Grrr..." Amanda tightened the pillow over her ears.

Shit.

Now that she had been so rudely awakened, the effects of last night's binge were making themselves known. Her head felt like it had doubled in size and was filled with sharp needles that were poking at her temples and her eye sockets from the inside.

I'm going to strangle her. Though, which her? Geneva for sending Lana? Or Lana for making a racket?

I'll strangle them both; problem solved.

With a grunt, Amanda threw the pillow at the door and shoved off the bed. Assessing the damage as she got vertical, she found that the dizziness had passed, and only a faint echo of nausea remained.

The headache was a bitch, though, and a glance at the time explained why she was still suffering from last night's drinking fest effects.

Are these fucking Russians insane? Seven-thirty in the morning? Really? She'd just gotten into bed a couple of hours ago for heaven's sake.

She'd better take something for that pounding headache before she went postal on the bunch. Maybe Alex kept some painkillers in his bathroom. Though why he would, she couldn't imagine. It wasn't as if immortals needed to have them on hand.

And yet, as she shuffled over to the vanity, she had her hopes up.

Catching her reflection in the mirror, Amanda winced. Since when did she wake up with dark shadows under her eyes? And what was with that hair? Her normally sleek, short hair, looked like a frizzy, messy nest.

She'd need to shower again just so it would dry properly. But first, a comb and a splash of water on her face were in order.

Done taking care of the necessities, she turned to search the drawers for something to relieve her headache. She found several brand new bottles of Tom Ford and Kilian perfumes for men, a few tubes of toothpaste, and several bars of soap, but no painkillers.

Damn, she'd have to ask the mortals for it, or just tough it out.

Or better yet, go home.

But she wasn't ready to face what she had run away from. Not yet. With no new insight or brilliant inspiration, she was exactly at the same place she had been before fleeing.

So what was the point?

With her hands on the counter, Amanda leaned and dropped her head. It had been fun to play detective, but with no evidence, she could no longer justify the distraction. It was time to do some hard thinking.

And as a last resort, maybe ring her mother.

Heaving a sigh, she pushed herself off the vanity and trudged back to the cabin. Inside the walk-in closet, the few remaining clean items of clothing out of all that she'd brought with her took up a tiny section at the front of it. And as she was in no mood to lounge on deck in a bikini or a sundress, her options were limited to one clean pair of jeans, one skirt, and two T-shirts.

Another reason to go home.

A sudden impulse had her look at the back of the closet, where Alex's incredible selection of designer clothes was either hanging from luxury hangers or folded neatly on shelves. Separated into casual and dressy, each section was color coordinated, with matching footwear on the lower shelves.

Considering Alex's metrosexual style, some of it might even look good on her. He might be a couple of inches taller, but then her legs were longer.

Not that she was going to put on something that he had already worn—even laundered, it would be gross. She still cringed thinking about that bathrobe of his she had been desperate enough to borrow. But knowing Alex, half of the stuff was probably brand new with the tags still attached.

The man was a major clotheswhore.

Amanda let out a chuckle as she sifted through the hanging garments, most of which had either a store tag dangling from a sleeve or a label or a tailor's note pinned on.

Taking into account the fact that Alex didn't spend all of his time cruising, the size of the wardrobe he kept on his yacht was impressive even by her standards. The guy was totally obsessed if he kept the one at his Malibu estate as fully stocked as this one.

Wondering if that included his extensive jewelry collection, she pushed aside the clothes to peek at the back wall in search of a safe.

The wall was decorated with fabric-covered padded panels in a nice beige and burgundy paisley design, each about thirty inches wide.

Running her palms over the fabric, Amanda patted the padded panels from top to bottom, squeezing herself between the wall and the hanging garments as she kept going from one panel to the next. But from one end to the other, her patting didn't discover any hard surface in the shape of a safe.

She repeated the process on the side walls with the same results. Or rather lack thereof.

Come on, open sesame. She pressed on each of the panels' sides as well as other random places, but none clicked open or even hinted at being anything but glued to the wall.

Back at the section that she had cleared of clothes, Amanda stood with arms akimbo and glared at the wall.

It wasn't about finding the safe anymore. It was about her instincts firing hot, hot, hot as she faced the wall, and cold, cold, cold as she took a step back.

Okay, Amanda, calm down, close your eyes and focus on your other senses, because they are trying to tell you something.

It wasn't easy with a pounding headache still drilling holes inside her head, but she closed her eyes and breathed in, slowly.

Then again, and again.

She caught a very faint scent, which was what must've alerted her subconscious in the first place. Feminine, a trace of perfume or body lotion... no... not one...Now that she was focusing, she was able to detect several different barely there scents coming from behind the paneled wall.

Straining, she tried and failed to catch any residual whiff of emotions. Unfortunately, even though her sense of smell was much better than that of a human, it wasn't as strong as an immortal male's. Still, something feminine had been stashed in there at some point in time.

Except, from this side of the wall, she couldn't tell whether it had been actual women or just their belongings that had left that scent behind.

Sesame open?

Hey, it was worth a try, maybe the magic words worked in reverse order.

Nepo emases? Emases nepo?

Backward didn't seem to work either.

Come on, Amanda, stop fooling around and think!

Trouble was, her brain was still kind of fuzzy.

Okay, it's probably not a pressure mechanism if pressing didn't work. How about prying it open?

The problem with this idea was that she had no tools. Going to look for one would, first of all, alert the crew to the fact that she was awake but hadn't gone out to sit on one of the decks—which by now they would know was not like her—and second, would raise suspicion as to why she needed it.

With one last sad look at her manicured nails, she attacked the panels with her fingers, or rather her long nails, barely managing to wedge them in the tiny grooves between the panels. Pulling was out of the question, as they would just break off. Instead, she tried to wiggle the panel a little to see if there was any give.

There was none.

But then, she couldn't apply much force. She needed a tool—something that was thin enough to fit in the grooves, but strong enough not to bend or break.

About to leave the closet and go search the cabin for a letter opener, she stopped as her eyes landed on something better. Down on the bottom shelf, a metal shoehorn was sticking from one of Alex's shoes.

Perfect.

It worked like a charm, and the first panel she tried popped out quite easily. But what she discovered behind it was nothing nefarious, just more shelf space.

Weird. Unless this hidden part of the closet was used to store the drugs she suspected Alex of smuggling. But after a few sniffs, she had to discard that hypothesis. The only scents lingering on the empty, padded shelves were those faint traces of feminine products.

No drug residue.

She pried open another panel just to make sure there wasn't anything else hiding there.

It was just more shelf space.

Come to think of it, the shelving was kind of peculiar, and not just because it was hidden behind a cleverly constructed false wall. It was deeper than standard, about the width of the panels, and peeking farther inside she saw no dividers, just long, deep shelves, padded and covered in the same fabric as the wall panels. In fact, it looked as if the same panels that made the wall were used to construct the shelves.

With not a lot of vertical space between them, the height of the wall allowed for five levels, and it seemed like they ran the length of the closet wall.

Kind of reminded her of the crypt underneath the keep. Except, the crypt's stone shelves were much deeper and spaced farther apart vertically to accommodate the bulky sarcophagi.

Amanda snorted. *So that must be it; Alex is smuggling dead bodies.*

Seriously, though, was this hidden compartment used to smuggle rich criminals from south of the border into the United States?

Female rich criminals?

Amanda took a step closer and sniffed again, making sure she hadn't missed anything, but the only scent was still female, and there was no residual scent of emotions. Which again didn't mesh with her hypothesis. If people had been hiding there while the yacht was being inspected, by whatever agency did those things, they would've felt fear or at least stress, and both emotions produced strong scents that would've lingered long after they were gone.

Unless they'd been dead...which would explain the lack of emotions, but then she was pretty sure that there was no profit to be made from transporting dead bodies.

As it was, it seemed that only inanimate objects had ever graced those shelves, which made perfect sense considering the fact that this was a closet.

Possibly, Alex didn't like how the yacht's previous owners designed the space and blocked off that rear section to square it off. Or he might have even bought it like this and wasn't aware that there was anything behind the closet's back wall.

Oh, well. So much for my conspiracy theory. Amanda shrugged and picked up one of the two panels she had pried off their metal guides. Pushing it back in place took some effort, and she had to lean on it to force it in. It wasn't perfectly aligned with its neighbor, but she decided to wait with the final adjustments until the other one was back in place as well.

Banging on the panel sides with the heel of her palm was painful, but that was the least of her worries. She was making such a racket that there was no way the crew didn't hear it, and at any moment someone might burst in, demanding to know what the hell was going on.

Exercising—and she was going to stick to it—kickboxing.

The panels must've warped a bit from her prying them out with the shoehorn because nothing she did managed to restore the wall to its former condition. The tight seams between those she had taken out were no longer as uniform as those between the others.

The best she could do was to slide the hangers over and hide the incriminating evidence behind the clothes.

Hopefully, Alex wouldn't notice.

Whatever, plausible deniability was the name of the game. If he asked, she would play dumb and say she had no idea what he was talking about.

Amanda returned the shoehorn to the same shoe she had found it in, and wiped her sweaty, throbbing palms on her yoga pants.

Oh, well, she had been so certain she would find something, but on the other hand, it was also a relief to find nothing incriminating about Alex. He was, after all, her friend.

Back in the cabin, she added her sweaty clothes to the pile of dirties in her carry-on and headed for the bathroom.

Surprisingly, no one came banging on her door.

After a quick shower, she put on her last clean pair of jeans and a red T-shirt. As she left her cabin and headed for the grand salon, she hoped Renata had left coffee and breakfast for her.

Thank heavens it wasn't ten yet. Otherwise the woman would've cleared the table already.

As it was, Amanda found the thermal carafe full and the coffee still hot. "I love you, Renata," she murmured, promising herself to be nicer to the cook from now on.

Watching the ocean while drinking coffee never got old, but it wasn't as relaxing as it had been the last time she sat here alone. She just couldn't shake the uncomfortable feeling that she was missing some important clue, or rather the insight to piece all the clues she had gathered into a cohesive picture.

Oh, heck, enough of that. She pulled her phone from her front pocket and called Syssi.

"Hi," Syssi chirped, then added in a whisper, "Sorry, forgot you're probably nursing a hangover."

"Just a pounding headache, but I'm drinking coffee and gazing at the ocean, so it's all good. How about you?"

Syssi snorted. "I'm fine, I'm not the one who has been drinking all night with a bunch of Russians. How did it go? Learn anything interesting?"

"Lots, but I'll tell you all about it when I come home."

"When?"

Amanda sighed. "Hopefully this evening."

"That's wonderful! But I thought you planned on staying longer, what happened?"

"I ran out of clothes."

"No, seriously."

"I'm very serious. I'm on my last clean pair of jeans. And you know me. Laundry is not something I do."

"Okay, be like that. If you don't want to tell me anything, it's fine, but I have something for you."

Syssi sounded eager to share the news. Must be something good. "Yeah? What is it?"

"I had to practically squeeze it out of him, but I got Kian to tell me about his meeting with Dalhu."

Excitement swirled through Amanda's gut. "And?"

"And, I have a feeling that Kian is softening toward Dalhu or at least easing up on the hostility. He even referred to him by name a couple of times instead of spitting out 'The Doomer' with murder in his eyes."

"Wow, miracles never cease."

"I know, right? But that's not all... Did you know that your Dalhu is a talented artist?"

My Dalhu... go ahead, twist the knife in my bleeding heart, why don't you?

"First of all, he's not mine, and second, what the hell are you talking about? To the best of my knowledge, killing is his only skill." She couldn't keep the bitterness out of her voice.

"Nope, not the only one. He draws, really well. He sketched your portrait and it is stunning. Want to see?"

Duh, of course she wanted to see it... "Show me."

"Hold on..." She heard Syssi take a few steps. "Okay, here it is. I'm going to switch to camera for a moment and send it to you... I'm adjusting the zoom... here, perfect." There was a click. "Go ahead, check your messages. I'm waiting."

At first glance, Amanda was impressed, then zooming in, her eyes teared. Not only because Dalhu's sketch was beautifully done, and not only because it was achingly obvious that he'd gotten to know her better than most—despite the short time they'd had together. But because the face staring at her from the small screen looked happy —excited, hopeful, and maybe even a little in love. It was a reminder of the one time she hadn't been faking it, but had actually felt this way.

"Are you crying?" Syssi asked softly.

"Just a little..." She must've sniffled.

Oh, what the hell, just go with it. Amanda let out a few louder ones, then blew her nose in the cloth napkin.

Gross, I need to remember to throw it in the trash.

"Are those sad tears? Or happy tears?"

"Happy-sad tears."

"Huh?"

"I don't know. It's lovely... I look so... happy. And Dalhu... well, I knew how he felt about me, but this just drove it home. And I've realized that I might've been falling in love with him as well." The waterworks started again.

Shit.

"So why sad?"

"Because it's all in the past, gone, kaput." She had to blow her nose again.

"It doesn't have to be...," Syssi said so softly it came out in a whisper. Then she added with more passion, "It's obvious that he loves you, and you feel strongly about him, maybe even love him... the rest is just background noise."

Amanda snorted. "More like a marching band parade."

"Ignore it... get out of your head for a moment and listen to your gut. A wise woman once told me that she always lets her instinct guide her because it's smarter than her."

"Yeah? And how did it work out for her?"

"Ask her yourself, it was your mother."

"First, I need to figure out what to do. I feel like I'm in a maze of one-way-street turns and can't get anywhere no matter which route I take. I'm going in never-ending circles in my head."

"See? You just reinforced what I said. You need to get out of that loop altogether. Stop thinking and just feel. What do you have to lose? Dalhu wouldn't harm you even if he could, which he can't because he is imprisoned in your stronghold. He can't leave you either. Again, because he is not free to go. And if you're thinking about Kian, don't. He'll come around if he has to. He loves you too much to stay mad forever. So, the way I see it, you hold all the cards in your hands."

"And what about my heart?" Amanda placed her hand on her chest. "What if I fall for him but then realize that I can never forget or forgive?"

"So you're telling me you'd rather play chicken? That doesn't sound like you."

Syssi was right, and what's worse, it reminded Amanda of a similar conversation she'd had with Kian. Only then, Kian had been the one who was afraid to take the plunge, and she the one giving advice and pushing him to jump off that proverbial diving board.

Hypocrite, anyone?

"You're right. It's about time I stopped being a chicken and unleashed the cougar."

"You go, girl! Sharpen those claws!"

"Grrourr..."

"I'll see you tonight, cat woman."

"Wait, don't tell Kian I'm coming home."

"Sure, but why not?"

"It will be hard enough to face Dalhu, and I'd rather save the inevitable confrontation with Kian for another day. One battle at a time is all I can handle right now." Amanda chuckled. "I guess this cougar is just a little one, with itsy bitsy claws."

"I've seen those claws, and they looked damn lethal to me."

Dalhu

"I come bearing gifts." Anandur waltzed in with a big cardboard box under each arm. "Something to keep you busy, frog." He dropped them on the coffee table.

"What's in there?"

Anandur dipped his hand inside the smaller one and pulled out a laptop. "This is for your memoirs. And as you naturally have no Internet access, William, our tech guy, has already downloaded a dictionary and an encyclopedia for your use. So no excuses for sloppy work." He handed Dalhu the device, then pulled a long, white cord from the box. "And here is the charger."

"Thank you." Dalhu lifted the incredibly thin laptop, weighing it in his hand. "This is really light."

Anandur grinned. "Yeah, the newest something-air. Only the best for our resident frog."

"This frog thing is getting old. Why not mix things up? Make it interesting with a couple of new derogatory nicknames for me." Dalhu connected the charger to the laptop, then plugged it into the wall socket.

"Nah, this one is so clever it's perfect, if I may say so myself. And it's not meant as an insult. On the contrary, it means you've got potential."

"I don't understand."

Anandur sat on the couch and started pulling out smaller boxes from the larger one. "Of course you don't. This fairy tale didn't exist when your poor mama was reading you bedtime stories."

"My mother was illiterate," Dalhu grated.

Anandur cast him a sad look, then shrugged. "Yeah... I forgot how old you are. Hardly anyone was literate back then."

Nice save.

Except, Dalhu had no doubt that Anandur and the others had been taught to read and write as children, and probably much more, regardless of when they had been born. And what's more, the guy's mother was probably still around, pretty and healthy, and not rotting in some unmarked grave after aging prematurely from hard use and then dying a broken woman.

That thought brought about a bitter dose of jealousy, which in turn supercharged the rage he had so far managed to control.

Get a grip, it's not the guy's fault that he had it better than you.

Fisting his hands, Dalhu forced his tone to what he hoped sounded bored, if not conversational. "If you insist on calling me a frog, at least tell me that damn fairy tale you keep alluding to."

Anandur's grin spread wide. "The princess and the frog... I may botch the story a little because I don't remember exactly how it goes, but you'll get why I think of you as the frog, and Amanda as the princess, obviously."

"Obviously..."

"Once upon a time... just so you know, all fairy tales start like that... a beautiful princess was playing with her favorite ball by a pond, but then it slipped from her hand and fell into the water, sinking fast. She tried to reach it, but the pond was too deep. 'Please, I'll give all my riches to have my ball back,' she cried." With a hand over his heart, Anandur enacted the princess in a high-pitched voice while batting his eyelashes.

Dalhu chuckled. "You missed your calling, my man."

"I know. But back to the story. Then the princess heard a tiny voice. 'I don't want your riches, but if you take me home and let me eat from your plate and sleep on your pillow, I'll get the ball back for you,' was the promise the ugly, slimy frog made to her."

Dalhu grimaced. "Now I get it. I'm the ugly frog who tricked the princess into taking him home with her."

"Would you let me finish?" Anandur rolled his eyes.

"Please, I can't wait to hear the end."

"The princess wanted her ball back, so, even though she was disgusted by the creature, she agreed and took the frog home. For three days the frog ate from her plate, and for three nights he slept on her pillow. And during that time, as they talked and played together, the princess grew fond of the frog. So much so that on the last night she kissed him good night on his ugly, slimy, green cheek. Then the following morning, in place of the frog the princess found a handsome prince sleeping next to her."

Dalhu snorted. "Then the beautiful princess screamed for her guards who rushed in and hastily killed the presumptuous prince. The end."

Anandur frowned. "Maybe in the story's adaptation for Doomers—"

Dalhu harrumphed and crossed his arms over his chest. "As if any woman who went to sleep with a pet and woke up with a man next to her wouldn't have screamed murder."

"Hello? A talking frog? Fairy tale?"

"Okay, go on…"

"The prince told her that he had been cursed by an evil witch and only the kindness of a good-hearted maiden who would let a frog eat from her plate and sleep on her pillow could've broken the curse."

"And?"

"And what?"

"What did she say?"

"At this point, the fairy tale ends with the unlikely couple getting married and riding off into the sunset to live happily ever after."

"I don't get it. So what's the moral of the story? Show kindness to a frog and it will turn into a prince?"

Anandur rolled his eyes again. "I can't believe I'm explaining a fairytale—to a Doomer. It depends on how you want to look at it. The moral could be that you should be kind to everyone, even to a lowly creature, because it might be more than it seems. Or, be careful what you wish for and who you make promises to because rarely anyone turns out to be a prince, and most times you'll end up stuck with a frog."

"I see..." Not really, though. What was Anandur trying to say? That Dalhu might be a cursed prince? Not likely. Probably more along the lines of Amanda wishing for a prince, but getting stuck with a frog. Which was true, but an insult nonetheless, and Anandur had claimed it wasn't.

Still, Dalhu wasn't about to ask Anandur for further clarification. As it was, the guy already thought him ignorant. He didn't want to add stupid to the impression.

"Here, frog, your chance to morph into a prince." Anandur handed him the largest notebook Dalhu had ever seen. The thing looked to be a foot and a half wide and two feet long.

"What is this?" He took it and read the cover—*Drawing* —which made his question sound stupid.

"I also got you charcoal sticks, charcoal pencils, drawing pencils, erasers, sharpeners—in other words, the works." Anandur piled the boxes one on top of the other as he listed what was inside them. "And if you want to dabble in acrylics or oil paints, I would gladly take another trip to that art store for you. They have very helpful staff if you know what I mean." Anandur winked.

Dalhu was rendered momentarily speechless, expressing his amazement with a whistle. "When Kian said he would bring me sketching supplies, I imagined a few sheets of paper and some pencils."

Anandur harrumphed. "I bet he did as well. I went wild in that store. You see..." He shifted to get closer and glanced both ways as if to check for eavesdroppers— strange, because they both knew that the place was bugged—then continued in a hushed voice. "The salesgirl had an incredible ass, and I made her run all over the store —following closely behind of course. It would've been rude not to buy all the things that she worked so hard on fetching."

Yeah, good story, but for whose benefit? Dalhu's or Anandur's? Was the guy reluctant to admit his kindness? Maybe he sought to protect his tough-guy reputation. Or, maybe he attempted to make it easier on Dalhu to accept the thoughtful gift and not feel weird about it or obligated in any way.

In either case, Anandur had proven himself to be one hell of a guy, a true prince among men.

"Thank you. I appreciate it." Dalhu offered his hand.

Anandur shook it. "You're welcome. I'll collect the payment later."

What the hell?

"Payment? I have no money."

"I'll take it in the form of marketable goods. A signed drawing would do, preferably of a nude female…just make sure that she doesn't resemble Amanda in any way." He winked and clapped Dalhu's shoulder. "Go, knock yourself out. I expect to see some production when I come back."

"You've got yourself a deal."

Sebastian

"Mr. Shar, would you please sign here." The driver of the delivery truck handed Sebastian a clipboard.

The fixtures for the upstairs bathrooms had arrived later than promised, but it was all good. Despite the slight delay, the additional crews he'd hired would help install everything by tonight.

Any other day, the two hours of pay for the workmen to just sit and wait would have chafed even though it wasn't money out of his pocket, but Sebastian was in a good mood. And not only because the first shipment of weapons had arrived on schedule in the early hours of the morning and was now stored safely in the outbuilding he'd dedicated as an armory.

Well, maybe in part it was. The quality of the few items he had inspected had exceeded his expectations. But mainly, his good mood had to do with the uniquely pleasing evening that he'd spent at his club—with a particularly loud sub.

The woman had not been a beauty by any stretch of the imagination, or even as young as he usually liked them, but she had been an excellent screamer. And the begging... beautiful, it had been music to his ears. He should thank the club owner personally for the suggestion. Without it, he could've overlooked a very pleasing sub in favor of a better-looking one.

How did the American saying go? Never judge the book by its binding? Or something to that effect.

He might even schedule another round with her. If she was up to it...

Maybe in a couple of days.

Or sooner.

The woman must've been amazed at how little damage she had actually sustained. Sebastian had been very careful to leave the memories of pain and humiliation intact, submerging only the memory of his bite.

For a masochist like her, a sadist like him must've seemed like a godsend.

Sebastian chuckled. Now, this was a term he had never expected a woman to associate with him. And yet, it was true. Who else could've healed the damage he'd caused so she could indulge in her kink much sooner than she normally would?

The novelty of having an enthusiastic partner—one that was up to almost all that he liked to dish out, and not because it was part of her job, but out of her own free will—had been unexpectedly pleasing, even satisfying.

For a moment, Sebastian entertained the idea of keeping her for himself, making her the first occupant of his dungeon.

He would not share her, though. A woman of that caliber was too good for the others.

He had even enjoyed her quick mind and, surprisingly, her sense of humor during the pre-assignation negotiations. The woman was intelligent, a lawyer by occupation, and had very few hard limits.

Still, had he enjoyed this new experience enough to shift his preference to willing partners?

Only one way to find out—follow up with his usual fare of victims. There were pros and cons to both, and he was curious which way the scale tilted.

Regrettably, he had to concede that even if the masochist won, his partner from last night wasn't right for his dungeon. She didn't fit the profile of an easy abductee—one with no family, friends, or coworkers who would notice her missing and report to the authorities.

The lawyer was a partner in a large firm, and her absence would be noted immediately. And anyway, a smart cookie like her might figure a way to escape.

Too risky.

In his experience, the prudent approach was to stick to what had been tested and proven to work well, and not gamble on something new unless it was absolutely necessary.

"Robert." Sebastian turned to his assistant.

"Yes, sir." The man's spine snapped into a straight line, but he managed to check himself at the last moment before adding a salute.

"Sorry, Se... bastian."

The man was a lost cause. "Did you call the commander of the other team? What was his name?"

"Dalhu, sir."

"Robert, Robert, Robert, whatever shall we do with you..."

"I'm sorry, I'll try harder."

"Don't try, just do."

"Yes..." The man swallowed hard, choking down the compulsion to finish with the requisite sir. "I've talked with his second. Apparently, Dalhu was one of the warriors who were taken out by the Guardians. But I forwarded your instructions to the second, and he was happy to hear that they were going home."

"What about the house they've been renting?"

"Tom already took care of it. The whole deal has been brokered from the start through our trade partners here in Los Angeles, so there was no paperwork to bother with. All it took was letting them know the men will be vacating the place by tomorrow."

"Good, well done, Robert."

Sebastian was glad to be rid of that team. The men he had chosen to join him were loyal to him, and he knew they were the right ones for the job. He had no intention of bringing in outsiders whom he hadn't personally vetted.

Still, he'd decided to wait a few days after arrival before arranging for their transport back to base.

He wasn't worried about anyone questioning his decision to send the other team home. But impressions mattered, and it was important not to look as if he feared outsiders. It might raise unnecessary suspicions when, in fact, he had nothing to hide. So he took his time.

His grandfather—the exalted leader of the Brotherhood of the Devout Order Of Mortdh—was brilliant, but unfortunately, he was also paranoid. And although Sebastian was loyal to the core, there was no convincing Navuh of that.

The man trusted no one.

Kian

Kian's phone chimed with the sound of bells—the ringtone he'd assigned to his mother.

"Good afternoon, Mother."

"Indeed, it is a splendid afternoon. I have just convinced Gerard to help. He is going to design a menu and even prepare part of it in his restaurant. The rest he will give Okidu the recipes for—provided in strict confidentiality, of course."

"You sure the Odus will be able to handle Gerard's elaborate creations for such a big dinner? What works for his restaurant might not work for a large scale production."

"I am sure an experienced chef like him will take it into consideration. But I did not call you to discuss the wedding menu. There was something important I wanted to ask you but had to wait until your lovely bride excused herself to go powder her nose."

Kian smiled, wondering if he should tell Annani that no one powdered their nose anymore.

Nah... "Ask away."

"Did you buy a wedding ring for Syssi? Or even an engagement ring?"

Fuck, how could he have forgotten an important thing like that? "No, I didn't."

"Just as I thought. Hurry up and buy both. And may I offer a suggestion?"

A suggestion, right. Kian rolled his eyes. Annani didn't offer suggestions, she issued diktats. "Yes, of course, Mother."

"Take your sweet fiancée out to dinner and present her with the ring in a romantic setting. I would think the girl deserves at least one date as your fiancée before becoming your wife."

"Can't argue with that logic." Did he feel like an ass or what? What was he? Twelve? That he needed his mother to point out the obvious?

"Do not forget that you need an appointment if you want a high caliber jeweler, which I am sure you do."

Hell, how was he supposed to know that? "Can you suggest one? I'm really out of my element here."

"But of course. I will do better than that. I will call the one I use and arrange for an appointment within an hour. Without my influence, any respectable establishment would demand at least a fortnight's notice to see you."

"Thank you, you're a lifesaver."

"No need to thank me. That is what mothers are for."

"How about, I love you."

There was a sniffle. "That is perfect."

Kian chuckled. "So why are you crying?"

"Because it has been ages since the last time you said you love me."

That can't be—

Actually, he couldn't remember telling her he loved her ever since he was a boy.

Regardless of how many times Annani had referred to herself as a mother, in his mind she was first and foremost the head of their clan, and, as such, deserving of his respect and deference. But her station aside, Annani was pure heart and valued love above all.

He should've been mindful of that.

"I'm sorry I've neglected to tell you I love you. I promise that from now on you will hear it more often from me."

Annani chuckled. "Do not make promises you are not going to keep, Kian. And I do not need daily affirmations to know that you love me. But once in a while, it is nice to hear."

And... the head of the clan was back. "As you wish."

"Call Syssi and tell her you are taking her out. Make it late evening in case the purchase takes longer than expected."

"Yes, she who must be obeyed."

Annani laughed, the chiming sound more beautiful than anything ever recorded. "Indeed," she said before disconnecting.

Kian swiveled his chair to face Shai.

The guy sighed. "I know, reschedule all your phone conferences and e-mail everyone waiting for a response from you to let them know they will have to wait a little longer."

"You read my mind."

"Don't I always?"

"Yes, you do."

"But before you go, there are a few quick items Onegus asked me to run by you. All I need is a couple of minutes."

"Shoot."

"He wanted to let you know that everyone who received the warning e-mail that he sent out confirmed that they got it and are going to take precautions." Shai chuckled. "He said that judging by the panicky responses, escort services are going to see an unprecedented spike in business. There were even a few who suggested that we should have our own private brothel..." He lifted a brow in question.

As if Kian was going to stoop to the fucking Doomers' level. "Not going to happen. Next."

"The first self-defense class is scheduled for seven this evening, and Onegus wondered if you'd like to come and say a few words. But obviously that's not going to happen either."

"No. But I'll try to make it to the next one."

"I'll let him know. And lastly, which left me somewhat puzzled, Onegus wants me to schedule a mandatory class for all our boys between the ages of thirteen and eighteen about sex and consent. And he wants Bhathian to teach it?"

"Yeah, after the fiasco with Jackson got resolved, we've decided it's a good idea. And Bhathian is just the right guy to scare the shit out of them."

"I thought Jackson was found innocent."

"He was. But the whole thing stunk. First, we got the accusation, then after Onegus e-mailed the accuser back and explained the consequences, the little chickenshit e-mailed an apology saying he misunderstood and that the blow job was consensual. Onegus decided to investigate anyway, but although he confirmed that Jackson was indeed innocent, he was alarmed by the boys' cavalier attitude. Hence the class."

"Okay... But did anyone ask Bhathian if he's willing to teach it?"

Kian smirked. "He can't wait to terrorize a bunch of boys out of their self-entitled attitude."

Shai nodded. "Good, I didn't want to be the one to ask the grouch."

"Is that all?"

"You want more? I have plenty…"

Kian swiveled his chair away from his assistant, letting him know he was done, and pulled out his phone to call Syssi. But looking at the picture of her beautiful, smiling face on his home screen, he opted for a more personal delivery.

The girl was a saint for putting up with him and all his blunders, and topping that long list was forgetting to buy her a ring.

He hoped to atone for his lack of finesse with some sinful kisses and a really big diamond.

Andrew

Andrew closed yet another airport employee file and stretched his arms over his head to release some of the tension that had accumulated in his shoulders. He'd been hunched over his desk since morning, but at four in the afternoon the big stack was only marginally shorter than it had been at the start of his day. And he hadn't even taken a lunch break. Instead, he'd grabbed a sandwich from the vending machine.

Blah. He could still taste the eggs on his tongue.

Damn, on a day like this, the idea of quitting and going to work for Kian looked better than ever.

If there was a way to tap into the government data without working for Uncle Sam, he would do it in a heartbeat. Nearly twenty years of dedicated service was more than enough to do for one's country. True?

Definitely.

Not that he had regrets, he'd loved his job up until the powers that be had decided to chain him to a desk.

Pushing away from the damned thing, Andrew got up to get himself coffee.

There was a new caricature taped to the wall above the counter in the break room, this time of Rick, and Andrew wondered when Tim would get around to his. Not that he was looking forward to it. The guy was vicious, blowing up each and every flaw—from yellowing teeth to a double chin and thinning hair.

And Tim didn't spare the female agents either. Nothing was off limits, wrinkles and sagging breasts included. One day they were going to gang up on him and take their revenge.

Andrew's lip curled in a smirk. He'd better hurry up and ask the guy to make a forensic sketch of Bhathian's long-lost lover before someone arranged an unfortunate accident for Tim. And considering the background of Tim's many slighted coworkers, it wasn't such a far-flung scenario.

Coffee mug in hand, Andrew wended his way through the maze of cubicles looking for Tim's—the one with pages upon pages of black and white caricatures pinned to every surface of the divider panels delineating his space.

The guy had definitely too much free time on his hands.

"Andrew, my man, what brings you to my humble little cube?" Tim begrudged Andrew his spacious office, even though he was sharing it with three other agents—or analysts according to what it said on the plaque on the door. Thank God. If he were forced to work out of a cubicle, Andrew would have gone insane.

"I have a favor to ask."

"It would be my pleasure to draw your portrait." There was an evil gleam in Tim's eyes.

"Not if you want to keep your nimble fingers in one piece. It's not for me. I need you to make a forensic sketch for a friend of mine."

"What's in it for me?"

"Helping a guy to find his long-lost love out of the goodness of your heart?"

"Nope."

"A couple of beers?"

"You've got a deal." Tim offered his hand, then quickly withdrew it. "These babies are too important to be squashed in your paw." He wiggled his long, elegant fingers.

"Tomorrow? Barney's at seven?"

"Fine, but I also want their grande nachos and pizza to go with my beers."

Andrew rolled his eyes. He had no doubt that before the evening was out Tim would renegotiate the deal. "No problem."

It wasn't as if it was coming out of his pocket. And spending a few bucks was a good deal for Bhathian even if nothing came out of the search. At the very least, the guy would have a picture of the alleged mother of his child.

Back at his desk, Andrew texted Bhathian the time and place.

Damn, he was itching to do a little preliminary investigation based on the woman's fake social. But knowing himself, chances were that he would get sucked into it, and hours would pass with him glued to the monitor before he realized six had come and gone.

Not something he should do while on the clock.

A quick look was one thing, spending hours working on a private investigation was another—it was unethical.

Better to wait for the forensic sketch, and once it was done dedicate an evening to the search—maybe even a weekend.

No big deal, he was used to working evenings and weekends.

But today, he was going to leave early, well, early for him. He needed to stop by the supermarket and buy wine and chocolates for Bridget before heading home to shower and change. And chug those energy drinks...

Unfortunately, there would be no time for a nap.

Amanda

The *Anna* had left Avalon an hour ago, but at her current speed, she was still at least an hour away from the mainland marina. Supposedly, plenty of time to think and plan—if one wasn't running in mental circles, that is.

Drinking coffee and snacking on pieces of cut fruit, Amanda appeared calm and collected when she was anything but. The Russians were suspicious enough as it was, and looking distraught might give them ideas.

Besides, projecting a façade was her default state.

There were the nagging suspicions about Alex—his lavish lifestyle that couldn't be reconciled with his legitimate finances, the unusual choice of crew, and the hidden section of the closet. Nothing added up, but she was no closer to solving this mystery than she had been yesterday—and not ready to chuck the whole thing as a product of her overactive imagination either.

Maybe she could've done better if her brain had stayed focused on solving the puzzle instead of constantly wandering to a towering hunk of a man with warm brown eyes and big gentle hands.

What was she going to say to him when she returned? *Hi, I'm back, let's pick up where we left off?*

Not likely.

Some form of heart-to-heart was in order. Trouble was, she didn't know what to think, let alone what to say. Seven years of intense academic study and she was fumbling for words like a high-school girl.

Perhaps she should see her mother first and listen to some words of wisdom before trying to organize the jumble of thoughts that were bouncing around in her head like a bunch of agitated molecules.

Like, how could she consider a murderer as her perfect mate? And what did it say about her? That she was insane? Insecure? Desperate?

But how could she deny her gut—the instinct that was relentlessly tugging at her to return to Dalhu?

Then again, maybe it wasn't her gut or her instinct at all that was doing the talking, but her hormones. If there was one thing that was beyond contestation, one thing that was perfect between them, it was the sex.

Fates, the sex.

Even not fully consummated, it had been the best she'd ever had. Amanda wanted more of that.

Heck, she was starved for it, would never have enough.

If only she could turn off her brain and forget all about Dalhu's rotten baggage—his sordid past that was stinking up what could've been as close to perfect as she was ever going to get.

But how?

How could she forget about Mark? Dishonor his memory by joining with the one who had ordered his murder?

Apparently, sleeping with the enemy wasn't the lower than low she had believed it to be: falling for the murderer of her nephew was worse—way worse.

Help!

She felt like taking a page from Marta's book—finding a corner and rocking back and forth on the floor while chanting, *oh my God, oh my God, I'm going to burn in hell*.

Trouble was, Amanda didn't believe in Marta's God or her biblical hell.

But then, the hell of her own making—the one burning her gut, cutting her heart, and incinerating her brain—was bad enough.

Dalhu

As he scanned the room for an empty spot for the drawing he'd just finished, Dalhu rubbed a charcoal-stained palm over his mouth.

Ever since Anandur had left him with the supplies, he'd been drawing like a man possessed. The black and white sketches were spread out over every available surface of the small living room.

It started with the various pencils and charcoals, tempting him to give them a try. But then one stroke had led to another, and before long Amanda's eyes were gazing at him from a dozen or so drawings—smiling, deep in thought, sitting in a chair, reclining on a sofa, dressed, and undressed...That one, though, he'd stashed under his bed.

As it was, by neglecting to work on the profiles he'd promised to compile, he was already courting Kian's wrath. To add a nude depiction of Amanda's perfection on top of that had the potential of pushing her brother into a full-blown murderous rage.

Hopefully, the guys watching the feed from the security cameras hadn't been paying close attention to what he'd been sketching. Though if they had, so be it. There was nothing he could do about it now.

Propping his latest creation against the wall, Dalhu stepped back to admire his work.

Damn, he needed some sticky tape or some pushpins to tack his drawings onto the wall. Save for the woman herself, there was nothing else Dalhu would rather stare at.

Though not as good as an actual photograph, he believed he'd managed to do justice to Amanda's beauty. But was he really as talented as the men had claimed he was? Or had they been simply impressed by his impeccable memory and his ability to reproduce on paper the snapshots that he'd taken with his visual cortex?

But then, producing an accurate rendition was more of a skill than an art, and he had no idea what that special something extra was that differentiated between the two.

He cast a guilty glance at the bar where the laptop sat still unopened on top of the counter. It wasn't smart to delay the profiles he'd promised Kian. He'd better stop with the drawing and get to work on those.

And yet, clutching the charcoal pencil in his hand, he couldn't bring himself to let go of it.

Hell, he didn't want to.

For those couple of hours or so that he'd been consumed by the sketching frenzy, he'd felt alive, and to open that laptop would be like dying again. Because the only way he could deal with diving back into the cesspool that had been his life over the hundreds of years of service in the Brotherhood was to get back to feeling nothing—numb—dead on the inside.

On the other hand, as gratifying as it had been to immerse himself in creating them, dozens of Amanda's portraits would get him nowhere. If he were right to assume that she'd abandoned him on her brother's orders, and not of her own free will, then Dalhu's first priority should be gaining favor with Kian. And he sure as hell wasn't going to achieve this by producing even more sketches of Amanda.

True, Kian had been impressed with that first sketch, and subsequently his attitude toward Dalhu had improved somewhat. But it wasn't enough to overcome the guy's hatred, or to influence his decision to disallow contact between Dalhu and Amanda.

As much as he loathed having to do it, Dalhu had to prove himself to the sanctimonious prick. And the only way he could attempt it in his current situation was to compile the fucking portfolios and sketch the goddamned portraits of Navuh's army's top commanders.

He'd better do an outstanding job on those and impress the hell out of the asshole. Perhaps this would convince Kian that Dalhu could be trusted.

Yeah, as if there is a chance in hell that's going to happen.

Still, there was nothing else he could do to improve his position, and it was worth the effort even for the less than slim chance that it might make a difference.

Closing his fist around the piece of charcoal, he crushed it to dust, then headed to the bathroom to wash his hands.

Kian

"You want to take me out tonight?" Syssi asked, her voice sounding a little panicky.

Kian shifted the phone to his other ear as he turned on the ignition of the Lexus and shifted into gear. "Why? Is that a problem? I figured that I still owe you a date." It was a shame he couldn't ask her in person like he'd wanted to, but there was a jeweler waiting for him behind an unmarked storefront in Beverly Hills.

According to Annani, those interested in the best jewels in the world were referred to LaBurg Jewelers by other distinguished clients. No signage identified the place.

Syssi chuckled. "Yeah, I guess we should go on at least one before getting married. It's just that I'm drowning in work with all the preparations for the wedding. But I'll make time for this. When do you want to go, and where?"

"I made a reservation for eight at *By Invitation Only.*"

"Oh, that's actually perfect. We can sample Gerard's creations before he finalizes the menu—an opportunity to make last minute changes if we find something we really like or conversely do not."

"Hey, that's great, that way no one can claim that I haven't taken part in the planning. Correct?"

Syssi hadn't asked for his help, but he had a feeling that it wasn't because she had no need, but because she'd known what his answer would be. And it wasn't only on account of his busy schedule. Truth was, he had nothing to contribute, and didn't really care about the details. Whatever made Syssi happy was fine with him. Well, that wasn't entirely true—eloping and skipping the big party altogether would've made her happier.

"Your only job is to show up looking handsome. Which reminds me, Mr. Fentony will be here tomorrow at twelve. I figured that scheduling him for lunchtime will work best for you, but if it's a problem, I can call him and move the appointment. For you, the guy would reschedule the president."

"It's fine. Noon tomorrow works for me."

"I love you."

"Love you more. Be ready by seven thirty." Smiling, Kian ended the call before Syssi had a chance to respond with an I-love-you-more of her own.

It was silly, competing for who said it last and won. But it was fun, and if it made him feel like a stupid teenager, it wasn't necessarily a bad thing for a two-thousand-year-old fart.

As he rolled down the freeway at a snail's pace, he tried to imagine the perfect ring for Syssi and drew a blank. Perhaps he should not have kept it a secret and asked her to come with him? Let her choose what she liked best?

Except, knowing his sweet, unassuming Syssi and her frugal disposition, she would've chosen something simple and argued with him endlessly about spending too much money on a proper ring.

Hell, she would've never agreed, and the outing would've ended in a big fight. Because there was no way he would've compromised on that one. His girl deserved only the best—even if she didn't want it—and he certainly could afford to give it to her.

Some impatient idiot honked the horn, interrupting Kian's musing. Where did the moron think he could go? He fought the urge to open the window and flip the guy off. They were all stuck on this endless ribbon of asphalt-covered concrete, and the only way off was to find an exit. Trouble was, the surface streets were just as clogged.

Kian sighed and turned on the radio, which was tuned to his favorite classical station. As Mozart's Concerto Number 21 filled the Lexus's interior with its timeless sound, Kian relaxed into his seat, his grip on the steering wheel relaxing.

If Amanda were back home, he would've brought her along to help with the selection. Except, he doubted she would've gone anywhere with him after the way he'd treated her. And frankly, he wasn't sure he was ready for her company either. It was so damn difficult to get rid of that bitter feeling he'd come to associate with her.

Disappointment. Betrayal. Taint.

The steering wheel groaned as Kian's grip tightened again.

On some level, he was aware that his lingering resentment toward Amanda no longer made sense. After spending time with the Doomer, Kian had to concede, albeit grudgingly, that he wasn't pure evil. Not to mention that it was glaringly obvious the guy was in love with Amanda and would do anything and everything for her.

Same way I would for Syssi.

Damn, where did this come from? Kian hated that his brain had spewed out such nonsense. Comparing his feelings for Syssi to what the Doomer felt for Amanda? Ludicrous.

But was it?

Kian's gut, or perhaps it was his conscience, insisted that the difference existed only in his head, tinted by his perception of who and what Dalhu was.

An enemy. A killer. A heartless, cruel creature with no conscience or morality. A self-centered, self-absorbed opportunist.

Or was he?

Casting a glance at Brundar's stoic face, Kian shook his head. There would be no words of wisdom coming from that direction. The guy was there only because Kian had promised his mother he'd go nowhere without his bodyguards, and not because he needed the guy's advice or his opinion. And it wasn't as if he would've gotten any if he asked. Brundar would've just arched his blond brows and returned to staring ahead.

It was easy to forget that he was even there.

Weird guy. But a goddamned excellent fighter. If Kian ended up buying a million dollar ring for Syssi, which was his intention, he wanted an extra pair of capable hands to guard it on the way home. And besides, having a passenger allowed him to make use of the carpool lane if one was available.

The drive that should've taken no more than ten minutes stretched to double that, and as he left the SUV with the valet, he was already five minutes late for his appointment with the renowned Mrs. LaBurg. A few seconds later, the reinforced glass door was opened by a courteous employee in a three-piece suit who introduced himself as Pierre. Kian wondered if the French names were real. Probably not. More likely a sly attempt to add a flair of sophistication meant to impress the high-class patrons of the place.

"Please, follow me. Mrs. LaBurg will see you in the private viewing room." Pierre dipped his head in a perfunctory bow and motioned for them to follow through a cleverly concealed metal detector. The main showroom was not as large as Kian had expected, but it was classy and understated. A pale Aubusson rug covered the hardwood floor, and several small oil paintings in substantial, yet minimally adorned, wooden frames hung on the walls. Small light fixtures cast soft illumination on the surfaces of the paintings, but little else.

The lack of bright light was a peculiar choice for a place that was supposed to showcase diamonds. But what did he know, perhaps this was the standard for jewelry stores.

As Pierre opened the door to the back room, an older lady rose to greet them. She was wearing a conservative beige suit that even Kian recognized as signature Chanel, and her small stature was aided by a pair of high-heeled shoes that seemed too tall for a woman who looked like somebody's grandma.

Her intake of breath as she got a good look at him was audible, but then her eyes drifted to Brundar and a tiny smirk lifted her thin lips. "Welcome, Mr. Kian." She offered her slightly wrinkled hand.

"Just Kian." He shook it. Damn, he really needed to come up with a last name for situations like these. He hated the generic "Smith" Shai had used for his driver's license and other official documents.

"And you are?" She offered Brundar a warm smile as he took her offered hand.

Fuck. Obviously, she thought Brundar was the one Kian was purchasing the ring for. Not that he could blame the old girl for her misconception. With the guy's smooth-shaven pretty face, and his fucking blond hair reaching his mid back, it was no wonder she assumed he was the fiancé. After all, this was Los Angeles.

"His bodyguard," Brundar clarified.

"Oh, yes, but of course. Very prudent of you, Mr. Kian." She quickly recovered like the pro she was.

"Though we would've gladly delivered your purchases to your home ourselves. Most of our clients opt to have it done this way. No need to take unnecessary risks. Unfortunately, it's not unheard of for criminals to observe an establishment such as ours and follow a client home." She was looking Brundar over from head to toe, no doubt searching for a concealed weapon—something that the metal detector up front had missed.

But heeding Annani's advice, Brundar had left his daggers stashed under the Lexus's back seat instead of surrendering them to Pierre upon entering the store. Even unarmed, however, Brundar was a deadly weapon—the daggers just one more accessory in his arsenal.

"It's very kind of you to offer, but as you can see, there will be no need. Can we please move on to the selection? I'm somewhat in a rush." Kian sat down and motioned for Brundar to do the same.

"Yes, right away, sir." She took a seat across from them. "Pierre? Could you please bring the selection for Mr. Kian?"

He'd wondered about that. There were no display cases in the private viewing room. It was set up as a parlor—with a thick Persian rug covering the hardwood floor, and a sitting arrangement comprised of a dainty sofa, two matching armchairs, and a dark-mahogany coffee table. A few pictures hung on the fabric-covered walls, the largest one a portrait, no doubt of the late Mr. LaBurg—the proud founder of LaBurg Jewelers.

Only the microscope and the powerful LED lamp sitting on top of the coffee table hinted at the type of business taking place in this room. To the side, a cart stood on two short legs in front and two large wheels in the back and held an ice bucket with a wine bottle chilling inside it. Kian wondered if the two crystal glasses on the tray next to the bucket were there for Mrs. LaBurg and him, or for the happy couple.

Pierre got busy at the sizable wall safe that was hidden behind Mr. LaBurg's portrait, pulling out a velvet-covered tray. His steps were small and measured as he brought the tray over and gently placed it on the coffee table. There were only four simple rings on top of that tray, but each held a diamond that was anything but, and as Mrs. LaBurg flicked on the LED lamp, the light reflecting off those stones was blinding.

Kian was impressed. The lady had asked for his preferences over the phone and had delivered exactly what he had in mind—a simple, elegantly designed ring with one extraordinary stone.

The modest design was the only concession he was willing to make on account of Syssi's aversion to extravagance—but the stone would be the best this jeweler had to offer. And as this was the most prominent establishment of its kind on the West Coast, it meant that it was the best there was.

"Can I pour you some wine while you examine the selection?" She pulled out the bottle from the ice bucket and presented it to him.

As if he was going to check the label. "No, thank you."

Kian lifted each of the rings one at a time, examining them under the LED light and then returning them to the tray before checking out the next. They were all equally beautiful.

"These are the best we have and, naturally, each diamond is certified by the two leading grading agencies. The GIA, the Gemological Institute of America. And the AGS, the American Gemological Society," Mrs. LaBurg whispered with reverence. "You will not find diamonds of this size and quality anywhere else on the West Coast, you have my word. At least not from a reputable establishment."

Did he believe her? Perhaps. But that wasn't important for him to have the absolute best. The best available, with certificates, would have to do because he was out of time. Besides, he knew next to nothing about diamonds.

"They are all beautiful. Which one would you say is the best?"

Mrs. LaBurg picked up the one he had his eye on. It seemed to be slightly larger than the others, but it wasn't the only reason he gravitated toward it. There was something about the ring's design and the stone itself. It just seemed like the one. "This is a flawless, nine-point-five-carat emerald-cut, D color. I think it's the most beautiful of the four."

He had to agree. "How much?"

"The best I can do is one million seven hundred and fifty thousand."

Not too bad. From what his mother had told him, he'd expected it to be more than two million. But that didn't mean he wasn't going to negotiate. If for no other reason than to tell Syssi that he got it at a bargain price without having to lie.

"If I have the money transferred to your account right now, can you do one and a half?"

Mrs. LaBurg didn't even blink. Evidently, he wasn't the first client to offer cash payment. She smiled, her veneered teeth gleaming. "You've got yourself a deal, Mr. Kian." She offered her hand.

From there it was a matter of getting her banking information to Shai and having him wire the money directly there.

Pierre produced a fancy box to house the even fancier little box he'd put the ring in, then wrapped everything and placed it in a small, black fabric bag together with the certificates the diamond came with. There was no logo or any other indication that the bag came from a store. Discreet.

"Of course, if there is any problem with the sizing, we will do all of the necessary adjustments." She handed Kian the little bag. "I hope your fiancée loves it, but if she is not happy with the ring for some reason, we would gladly exchange it."

"Thank you, I'm sure there will be no need."

The ring was stunning, and the only problem Syssi would have with it was its price. Kian was prepared for a long and hard argument.

Funny, here he was with a beautiful engagement ring, and instead of expecting a big thank-you he was worried that his fiancée would march him back to the store to return it because it was too extravagant.

Still, if this was all they would ever fight about, they were good.

When he stood up, Mrs. LaBurg offered her hand again.

"It was a pleasure doing business with you, Mr. Kian. Is there anything else I can interest you in? Maybe a set of matching earrings? Or a necklace?"

Well, in fact, there was. After all, his *pervy* proposal included a diamond choker to go with the ring, right?

Amanda

Standing on the top deck of the *Anna*, Amanda watched the sunset as the massive boat glided into Marina del Rey.

It wouldn't be long now before she docked in her spot. Not long enough, anyway. Amanda wasn't ready to face Dalhu yet.

Hell, she would probably never be.

For the past two hours, she'd been mulling over what to say to him—the thoughts running in circles in her head. Problem was, she still didn't know how she felt about him.

Liar... Her subconscious whispered.

If you're so smart, then you tell me.

Simple, you want him.

Simple? He's responsible for Mark's murder. There is nothing simple about it.

Great, now she was talking to herself as if her subconscious was a separate entity.

Okay, girl, you are a scientist, and scientists search for solutions to problems instead of dwelling endlessly on the unfairness of them.

First, for the sake of clarity, she needed to define the problem from a rational standpoint rather than an emotional one. Perhaps it would be better to write it down.

The *Anna* would be mooring soon, but no one said Amanda needed to leave right away. And if Geneva had a problem with that, so be it. Amanda had paid the crew a hefty sum, a whole week of double wages, and had used only three days.

Fates, it felt as if she'd been gone for weeks.

Her tablet was in her purse and she pulled it out, then settled on the chaise lounge to write her *paper* on Dalhu. Staring into the color-infused ocean, she gathered her thoughts.

Dalhu was an ex-Doomer, who had decided to leave his old life behind and turn a new page on her account. He had kidnapped her only because she would've never given him a chance and gotten to know him otherwise.

The little time they had spent together had been the best she had ever experienced—and that was saying a lot considering that half of the time she'd been either terrified of him or plotting to clobber him over the head with a shovel and run.

He'd treated her with respect—more like reverence—and she had no doubt that he'd fallen in love with her. He'd been mostly honest with her and had told her about his past without trying to portray himself as a better man.

Not telling her about Mark qualified more as an omission than an outright lie. Except, if he'd omitted one thing, he might have omitted other incriminating stuff. On the other hand, the list of his crimes was probably too long for him to mention each one separately. After all, he'd been a mercenary—a killer.

His past wouldn't have troubled her so if not for Mark. There was a big difference between thinking of Dalhu's kills as casualties of war, and regarding his part in her nephew's murder the same way.

And yet, she had to concede that there were mitigating circumstances.

When he'd issued the order to kill Mark, Dalhu hadn't known she even existed, or that Mark was an immortal. In his eyes, his intent, this was another casualty of war.

Except, Mark had been a programmer, not a warrior.

Then again, if Mark hadn't been a relative, it would've bothered her to a much lesser extent.

What did it say about her, though? What kind of woman was willing to accept a killer as her mate?

Why couldn't Dalhu have been a professor? Heck, anyone would've been better than a killer. Even an accountant.

Amanda chuckled. As if she would've ever been attracted to a boring number cruncher.

The embarrassing truth was that she liked dangerous boys, and mellow males left her indifferent. It was utterly stupid, especially since she was supposed to be this sophisticated woman and to know better. She was a professor, for heaven's sake.

Yeah, the sadistic Fates were probably cackling with glee at the havoc their machinations were wreaking. Why pair her with a nice guy, when an ex-Doomer provided so much more entertainment for them?

The Fates had been kind to Kian, though. Amanda couldn't imagine a better partner for him than his sweet Syssi. The girl was simply the best. But to be fair, Kian had waited an awfully long time for his fated mate. And while he'd waited, he'd been earning a shitload of points by impressing the Fates with all the sacrifices he'd made—always putting the welfare of the clan before his own.

So yeah, Kian was definitely deserving of their benevolence. Amanda, on the other hand, had partied for most of her life, and when she'd finally decided to take herself more seriously and dedicate her time to solving her clan's most pressing problem—finding Dormants of other lines—it hadn't been an entirely selfless move. She'd sought recognition and respect.

And anyway, it wasn't as if nice, eligible, immortal bachelors were lined up for her. Except for Andrew, that is. But first of all, Andrew wasn't an immortal, yet, and second, he wasn't an innocent lamb either—hence the initial attraction. But that attraction paled in comparison to what she felt for Dalhu.

"American, we've docked. Don't you want to go home?" Geneva's wide shoulders blocked the view.

"I need a few minutes. Half an hour tops. Why? Are you in a hurry, Ruska?"

"No, I let the crew off for the evening, but I'm staying. Care for some vodka while you stare at the blank screen of your tablet? You look like you need it."

"Actually, that's a splendid idea, though coming from you, somewhat suspicious. Why so nice all of a sudden?"

Geneva shrugged. "I don't like drinking alone."

"Fine, but mix mine with orange juice."

Geneva arched a brow. "That's a pussy drink, American. Good vodka should be drunk straight up."

"Yeah, yeah, whatever, I want a screwdriver."

"As you wish, pussycat."

Amanda flipped her the bird. It had been on the tip of her tongue to tell Geneva to go get drunk on engine oil, but it was never smart to offend someone who was bringing you food or drink—lest they spit in it.

Geneva flipped her back before taking the stairs down to the upper grand salon.

Okay, where was I?

Dalhu. Bad boy attraction. Fated mate. That about summed it up. Especially the fated mate part.

Was he, though? Her gut was saying yes, but her brain was refusing to accept it. Because if he were her fated mate, then she was screwed big time. She wouldn't be able to resist the pull, but her relationship with Dalhu would forever be tainted by Mark's blood.

"Here's your juice, American." Geneva handed her the tall glass, then walked over to the other side and sat down with the vodka bottle in hand.

Apparently, Amanda wasn't the only one having a tough time.

"What's wrong, Captain?"

"Everything. Nothing. Just life, you know, it sucks." She chugged an impressive quantity on a oner.

"Want to talk about it?"

"That's the problem with you, Americans—talk and talk and more talk. We Russians, we do not talk."

"Yeah? And what do you have to show for it? The last time I checked, nobody is rushing to your borders in hopes of a better life, chasing the *Russian* dream. While we can't keep them away."

"That is true. But the people who came here first and started your great country, they didn't spend their time talking, they were too busy building."

"Ha, but they came because they wanted to be free, and freedom is an idea, so they had to talk about it."

"Whatever, I'm not in the mood for a political discussion."

"You started it..."

"Just go back to staring at your tablet." Geneva waved with the almost empty bottle.

That's what I get for trying to be nice to a surly Russian. Amanda harrumphed.

But Geneva hadn't been entirely wrong. It was time to stop overanalyzing and overthinking. It was time for doing. Chickening out was the only reason Amanda was still on board instead of in a taxi on the way to the keep. And her sitting on her butt and pondering would resolve nothing.

She swung her legs over the side of the chaise and pushed up, then headed for the staircase, but stopped before descending and turned around.

"I'm leaving now. Come, give me a hug goodbye," she told Geneva.

As the woman regarded Amanda, her expression changed from her usual pissed one to something that approximated fondness. She got to her feet and pulled Amanda into a bear hug that would've crushed her ribs if she were a human. "You're okay, American. I like you." She let go with a slap on Amanda's shoulder.

"If that's how you are when you like someone, I wonder what you're like when you don't."

"You don't want to know."

"No, I guess I don't."

Andrew

The gate to the clan's private garage was on the lowest level of the high-rise underground parking structure, and Andrew slowed his car before coming to a full stop in front of it. The sensor read the sticker on his windshield, and the thing slid open.

Kind of made a guy feel like he was part of the family. Except, as the only mortal among them, he was still an outsider, albeit one with a key to the front door—but no room of his own.

He eased into a vacant spot between Kian's SUV and someone's black Porsche. Hopefully, he wasn't taking somebody's parking space. But there were no markings on the concrete aside from those delineating the spots.

He was curious about whom the Porsche belonged to.

Perhaps Bridget? He wouldn't be surprised if it were hers. Last night, he'd found out that the doctor had an adventurous streak. A fast car suited her.

Reaching over to the passenger seat, he grabbed the grocery bag with the wine and Godiva chocolates box he'd bought for Bridget. It wasn't that he hadn't thought of buying a gift bag, or skimped on the few bucks it would've cost. It's just that he wasn't sure if Bridget wished for their relationship, or rather hookup, to become common knowledge.

That was also why he hadn't brought flowers. Nothing like a guy walking in with a bouquet to advertise that he was coming to see the woman and not the doctor for some medical advice.

As he walked toward the bank of elevators, he had the impulse to check whether his thumbprint would work on the one dedicated to the use of the penthouse occupants, namely Kian and Amanda. Obviously, they weren't the only ones with access to the thing. Their mother, the two butlers, and the Guardians had to have access too. But there was no reason for him to be granted that privilege, unless, as Syssi's brother and Amanda's rescuer, William considered him worthy of the honor.

Why not check it out? After all, he wasn't due at Bridget's for another twenty minutes.

As was his habit, Andrew had arrived early for his dinner date, but he had no intention of knocking on her door before it was time. It wouldn't be polite. He'd intended to check out the underground gym, but he could spare a few minutes for a quick ride up to the penthouse and then take the elevator down to the basement—if his thumbprint worked, that is.

By now, he had ridden up and down enough times to figure out the clever configuration of the private and public elevator banks. There were three doors that opened to the lobby, one of them serving the penthouse and the other two serving the guests of the rental floors. Three additional doors opened on the other side and served the clan. The two general use public elevators were back to back to two private ones while the penthouse had only one, but it opened both to the lobby and to the back. Of course, one needed a key or a thumbprint to be able to use it.

Andrew pressed his thumb to the reader, and a split second later the light turned on.

Nice, he was impressed. Well, too early to pound his chest and declare himself king of the elevators. He still needed to see if the thing would go where he told it to.

When the doors swished open, he stepped inside and glanced up—showing his face to the surveillance camera. If he were overstepping his bounds, the guys in security would tell him to get out.

The loudspeakers remained silent.

Still, he didn't want to appear as if he was snooping around uninvited. Maybe he should stop by the lobby and check with the guys if it was okay.

But as he was about to press his thumb to the L button, the elevator lurched into motion, and a moment later it came to a stop right where he wanted to go.

Probably the security guys' work—overriding the elevator's commands and bringing him up for a polite yet stern explanation of why he shouldn't be using the thing without an invitation from one of the penthouse occupants.

Damn, they'd think he was spying, and this little joyride would cause an incident.

The doors slid open.

"Oh, it's you..." Amanda's hand flew to her chest. "I'm sorry, Andrew, for a moment there, I thought you were Kian." She blew out a breath and stepped in, pulling behind her a carry-on. A matching duffle bag was slung over her shoulder. "Are you going up to Kian and Syssi's? Or going down to the underground? I must've hijacked you."

Hell, this was awkward. What was he going to tell her?

"That's okay, I just wanted to check if my thumbprint works on the penthouse elevator, but you beat me to it."

Amanda smiled. "I don't see why it wouldn't, but go ahead, press away." She moved aside.

"Thank you. Going up?"

"Where else? I just hope I can sneak into my apartment without bumping into Kian."

Andrew arched a brow and leaned to press the button for the penthouse level.

"Here, give me your bag." He lifted the thing off her shoulder and slung it over his. "So, you're still avoiding him?"

Amanda sighed. "Yeah, I don't want to see him, not yet."

"No worries, he's not here. He and Syssi are on a date—the same one they were supposed to go on the day her transition started and you got snagged—some fancy restaurant that one of your nephews runs. Syssi said he is going to help with the wedding menu. She wants to sample the dishes he suggested before finalizing it."

"Well, good for them."

Andrew detected the slight undertone of bitterness that she was working hard to hide. "Want to tell me what's going on with you?"

"It's complicated, and explaining would take a little longer than this ride." She looked away, but he caught her grimace reflected in the mirror.

"How about we go to your place, sit down, and you tell me what's on your mind? Sometimes, talking about it helps." He held the elevator door from closing as Amanda rolled out her carry-on.

He still had time before he was supposed to show up at Bridget's. Besides, if he arrived a little late, she'd understand—one of the advantages of dating a woman who wasn't ruled by emotions.

As Amanda regarded him, her pinched brows and the tight line of her lips implied that it was a no. Perhaps she didn't want to talk about it—with him—but didn't want to offend him by refusing.

"I see that you're not in the mood. We can catch up some other time." He moved to step back inside the elevator.

"No, wait." Amanda's hand closed around his bicep. "It's not that. It's just that my mother is staying at my place and I'd rather have this talk without her running commentary. I love her dearly, but sometimes she's just too much."

Amanda was right, the Goddess's overwhelming presence wasn't conducive to a heart-to-heart convo that didn't include her. "I know what you mean."

"We can sneak into Kian's."

"You think he'll be okay with us invading his home? And anyway, do you have a key?"

Amanda was already pulling the carry-on in a big arc as she turned toward the other door. "Okidu is probably home, and he won't mind. But even if he isn't, Kian leaves the door unlocked. It's not like there is any chance of thieves making it up here unnoticed."

She knocked once, then tried the handle. Just as she'd anticipated, the door swung open.

"Come on." She crossed into the living room, leaving her rolling suitcase by the door and heading for the bar.

Following Amanda's example, Andrew dropped her shoulder bag next to the luggage.

"I'm mixing myself a screwdriver. What would you like?"

"Same."

Amanda chuckled. "Earlier today, I was told by a surly Russian that a screwdriver is a pussy drink. I doubt she would've dared to say it to you."

"Why? Do I look so tough?" Andrew took the drink Amanda handed him.

"Very." She walked over to the sofa and plopped down—by some miracle not a drop of her drink spilling over.

"I'm not sure if I should be flattered or offended."

Definitely flattered.

Especially since his manliness had been put to the test by a tiny redhead and been found wanting.

Amanda shrugged. "I have a thing for tough guys, so coming from me it's a compliment."

Was she coming on to him? And if she was, what was he supposed to say? Thank you? Instead, he took a big gulp from his drink and avoided her eyes.

"Everything okay? You seem... well, uncomfortable—for lack of a better word—like something is bothering you."

Yeah, time to fess up.

"You haven't asked me what I'm doing here."

Coward, just come out and say it.

Amanda arched a brow. "Okay... What are you doing here, Andrew?"

"Bridget invited me to a dinner date at her place."

"Our Bridget? Oh, Andrew, that's fantastic." Amanda put her drink on the coffee table and clapped her hands. "Tell me all about it. I want to hear all the juicy, romantic details."

Her eyes were sparkling with excitement as if he'd just told her the best of news as opposed to informing her that he was no longer vying for her affection.

Though truth be told, except for that first time they'd met in the restaurant, Amanda hadn't responded to any of his suggestive hints. Since hooking up with the Doomer, she simply hadn't been interested.

For a moment, Andrew experienced an ugly flare of jealousy. He was just too damn competitive to accept that he'd lost so handily to another man. Never mind that he already had come to the realization that Amanda wasn't the one for him.

He shrugged. "Nothing to tell, really. One thing led to another, and she invited me to a home-cooked dinner. So, here I am, bearing gifts of chocolates and wine." He lifted the grocery bag off the floor.

Amanda shook her head. "You men are hopeless. You can't show up for a date with a brown bag from a supermarket." She pushed up to her feet. "I'll go check if Kian has something you can use. Though I doubt he does.

Worst case, you can ditch the bag and just hold the stuff in your hands."

He grabbed her hand and pulled her back. "Sit down, Amanda. I don't need anything fancy. It's not that kind of a date."

"Oh." Her face fell. She sat on the sofa and reached for her drink.

"So, tell me, where did you run off to?"

"I borrowed a boat from a friend." She snorted at his surprised expression. "Not a fishing boat, a yacht with a crew."

He chuckled. "That's more like you."

"I needed time to figure things out. Sort my feelings for Dalhu." She sighed. "Not that it helped, much. I'm still having trouble deciding what I'm going to do about it."

"Lay it on me."

She scrunched her nose. "You sure? I know that you have something going on with Bridget now, but for a time you seemed interested in me, and I don't know if you're up to hearing about Dalhu and me. I don't want you to feel awkward."

"I was. Interested, that is. In fact, I was more than interested." He chuckled nervously. It wasn't something he was comfortable admitting. But if he expected her to open up and tell him private things, it was only fair for him to do the same—even if it came at the expense of his macho image.

"You are an exquisite woman, Amanda, but I'm ashamed to admit that this wasn't the only reason I was obsessed with you." He rubbed his palm over the back of his neck. "The truth is that I am an extremely competitive guy, and I just couldn't bear to lose you to Dalhu. Especially since I truly believed I was the better choice for you. I couldn't understand your infatuation with him. I thought, same as everyone else did, that your feelings weren't real, that they were the result of a stressful situation and your survival instinct prompting you to gain the affection of your kidnapper."

"What caused you to change your mind?"

"Dalhu." Andrew finished his drink and got up to refill his glass.

"What do you mean?"

Andrew poured himself more vodka, omitting the orange juice this time. "You want the short version or the long one?"

"What do you think? Of course, I want the long one."

He sat down next to her. "Kian wanted me to be there while he interrogated Dalhu—mainly because of my lie-detecting skills, but also to help with the questioning." Andrew took a small sip of the vodka. Not very manly, true, but showing up drunk for a date was even less so. "Don't get me wrong, it's not that I think your guy is good, or even decent. He is a cold-blooded killer that doesn't give a damn about anybody or anything. Except you."

What he was going to tell her next was the toughest part, and Andrew took a more substantial sip this time. "I realized that his love for you wasn't a temporary flare, but a fire that burned bright and hot and steady, and I had no choice but to accept that my feelings for you were just a pale approximation in comparison. And while he would always choose you, not only over other women but over anything and everything else, I had to admit that it wasn't true for me. Not the other women part, because c'mon, none could compare, but I knew that there were things I would love to do even more than be with you." He braved a quick glance at her face and was relieved to find a small knowing smile and not a sad or disappointed one. In fact, her sagely benevolent expression made her look a lot like her mother.

But then, the mischievous spark that he was familiar with reappeared, combined with a heart-stopping grin. "Oh, yeah? Like what? What on earth could be more satisfying than worshiping at my feet?"

"For Dalhu? Apparently nothing. But give me a mission no one in his right mind would take and I'd be on it like there is no tomorrow." Andrew snorted. "I guess Kian wasn't wrong when he accused me of being an adrenaline junkie."

Amanda's brows shot up. "Really? You'd take on a deadly mission over me? I wasn't offended before, but now..."

Taking her hand, Andrew looked into her eyes. "Don't. You are beyond gorgeous and hot as hell, and to be frank, I think I'm a better man than your Doomer. But I would be deceiving myself as well as you if I pretend that you've touched my soul the way you've obviously touched Dalhu's. After witnessing the powerful connection between Kian and Syssi and then recognizing the same in Dalhu, I couldn't in good conscience dismiss him as unworthy of you. The enormity of his love proves him as worthy, and condemns me as not."

There were tears glistening in Amanda's eyes, and the hand he was holding was trembling.

She whispered, "What are you saying, Andrew?"

"When I had this epiphany, I wondered if your feelings for Dalhu were as strong as his were for you, and I made a wish."

"What was it?"

He leaned and kissed her cheek. "May you find the wisdom to realize your true heart's desire, the strength to acknowledge it, and the courage to pursue it."

Amanda's lip quivered, and tears glistened on her long, dark lashes. "That's so beautiful"—she sniffled—"but unfortunately, far from simple."

Amanda

Sweet, sweet, Andrew. I wish that things were so straightforward.

But Dalhu's love wasn't enough to overcome his murderous past, or rather one specific murder.

"You're wrong," Andrew said.

With indignation drying her tears, fast, she crossed her arms over her chest and lifted her chin. "What? Am I supposed to forget and forgive the murder of my nephew?"

"No. But you shouldn't punish and torture yourself for it either. It had nothing to do with you."

Now, that was a convoluted way to look at it. Leave it to a male to try to simplify things to the level of absurdity.

Amanda chuckled. "Your interpretation of the situation is the equivalent of applying quantum physics to emotions and feelings."

"Huh?" Poor Andrew tilted his head like a dog trying to understand verbal communication.

Sliding into her teacher mode, Amanda put on a smile. "Our everyday reality, or the physics we are all familiar with, disintegrates at the quantum level—the level of elementary particles—where nothing makes straightforward sense. Einstein coined the phrase *spooky action at a distance* about what he thought was the improbability of quantum phenomena as presented by other scientists of his time. He also said that things should be made as simple as possible, but not any simpler."

"I must be dense because I'm not following."

"You are breaking it into its basic components while ignoring other relevant and limiting factors. The way you present it, all I need to do is figure out what I want, accept that this is indeed what I want, and go for it. As if nothing aside from my needs and wants matters."

"Because in the final analysis, nothing does. You cannot deny the powerful connection you have with Dalhu, one that even a dense guy like me has no choice but to acknowledge, and in the end, you are going to accept that there is no way you could go on without him. All you're doing in the meantime is suffering. God, or fate, or whatever you want to call it has decided that the two of you belong together, and to fight destiny is futile."

"Says Andrew the wise. How can you claim with such confidence that this is my fate or my destiny? How can anyone?"

Andrew shrugged. "Sometimes you just have to trust your gut."

"You sound like my mother."

"Who is very wise—a goddess, no less—with more than five thousand years of experience. I would listen to her if I were you."

He had a point. This was what she'd been planning to do anyway before he'd intercepted her and offered to play shrink.

"You're right, I will."

Andrew lifted his grocery bag and pushed to his feet. "Good luck," he said, offering his hand.

She pulled him into her arms and squeezed. "You're a great guy, Andrew. And I'm so lucky to have you as a brother-in-law. In fact, I consider Syssi a sister without the in-law and the same goes for you. From now on, for better or worse, you're my brother."

He grinned. "I never thought the day would come when I'd be glad that a stunning woman has sisterly feelings for me, but here I am—happy as can be to have gained another sister."

As she reached for her carry-on, Andrew lifted her bag and slung it over his shoulder. He carried it the short distance across the vestibule. She didn't need his help; the bag was bulky but not that heavy, and by now he must've been aware that, as an immortal female, she was at least equal in strength if not stronger than him. But it seemed to be something he did without thinking, a behavior so ingrained that it was on autopilot.

Such a gentleman.

"Thank you." Amanda kissed his cheek before taking it from him.

"My pleasure."

"Say hi to Bridget for me."

Andrew grimaced. "I'm not sure she wants anyone to know about us."

"Why on earth not? If you were my boyfriend, I would've paraded you around, showing you off."

"That's the thing. I'm not sure she thinks of me as her boyfriend. It's, you know, more of a short-term thing. I think…"

"You mean a hookup?"

Andrew's ears got a shade darker, and he looked away. "Yeah, kind of."

He was probably reading Bridget's signals all wrong. The doctor would be insane not to sink her hooks into this yummy piece of a potential immortal male. The problem must've been with him.

"Well, I'm sure you're wrong about this. But whatever makes you comfortable. If you want me to keep this a secret, for now, I will."

"I'd appreciate it."

"Goodbye, Andrew." She waved her hand as he stepped into the elevator.

Okay, deep breath, big smile, and go... Amanda depressed the handle and pushed open the door. But Annani wasn't there.

"Ninni? Where are you?"

"I am outside," her mother called from the terrace. The sliding doors were closed, and the curtains were only partially parted to admit the weak moonlight.

Onidu rushed out from the kitchen, a big smile plastered on his face. "Mistress, you are back. Let me take care of your luggage."

She pulled him into a hug before he had a chance to grab her things and scurry away to unpack.

As always, he stood motionless without returning her hug. The poor thing's programming didn't include the proper response. Maybe she should teach him what to do when someone embraced him. On the other hand, his response—or lack thereof—was so familiar that she would've most likely found it disturbing if he ever hugged her back. Never mind that it was silly of her to do so in the first place. But there was something comforting about the peculiar feel of his hybrid too-solid body. Perhaps it was just that he'd been with her since she was a little girl, and in her subconscious his presence represented security and being cared for. Was it a wonder then that she often thought of him as family?

Letting go, she handed him her purse. "Please put it in my bedroom. When you unpack the luggage, take the clothes to the laundry. Everything is dirty and needs to be washed or dry-cleaned."

He bowed. "It will be done immediately, mistress."

Of course, it would.

As she made her way out to greet her mother, Amanda shook her head. Annani was probably lounging outside and hadn't felt like getting up to welcome her daughter home. And it had nothing to do with her being pissed at Amanda for leaving the way she had. It was just Annani's normal diva attitude.

Having a goddess for a mother had its advantages and disadvantages.

Not that Amanda had ever questioned her mother's love. Annani was very generous with her affections, both verbal and physical. It was just that sometimes, not often, Amanda secretly wished for a mother that wasn't so grand—one that would go shopping with her, or out for coffee, or just call to chitchat about things of no particular importance.

Would've been nice—would've alleviated some of Amanda's loneliness.

It was dark outside, but Amanda found Annani sprawled on a lounger as if she was sunbathing in the middle of the day. Her mother was holding a book, her own glow providing the illumination.

"Good evening, Mother, what are you reading?"

Annani lifted the book and turned it so Amanda could see the cover—*The Abbreviated History of Humankind.*

Amanda chuckled. "As someone who has witnessed humanity's formative years in person, you could write one yourself."

"Perhaps one day I will." Annani shook the book. "This one contains so many untruths and misconceptions while omitting some of the most critical events that changed the course of history, that I suspect no one would believe an account of how things really happened. They would think it was all fictional."

Amanda pulled out a chair and turned it to face Annani. "I bet." She sat down and leaned forward, bracing her elbows on her knees. "How mad are you at me? For running off on you?"

Annani put the book down and sighed. "You were not running away from me, my dear child. You were trying to run away from yourself. One cannot do that, you know."

Amanda snorted. "Tell me about it."

Annani lifted one red brow. "I thought I did."

"It's just an expression, it means that I know you are right."

"Of course, I am. I am never wrong."

This conversation was going nowhere fast. She'd better get to the point.

"If you're so wise, tell me what to do about Dalhu."

"I cannot. It is not my place to decide matters of the heart for you. Only you can do it."

Annani could be so frustrating at times.

"Can you at least help me figure things out?"

Annani inclined her head. "Certainly." In one fluid motion, she lifted her legs and swung them around to sit sideways, facing Amanda. "Would you care for some sparkling water?" She poured some from a carafe.

"Yes, thank you."

Annani filled another glass and handed it to Amanda, then took a few small sips before putting her glass down. She then leaned forward and rubbed her palms. "Let us figure out things together, my dear."

Andrew

"Is this for me?" Bridget took the grocery bag from Andrew.

"My modest contribution to a meal that"—he inhaled deeply—"smells delicious."

"Thank you." Bridget stretched to plant a kiss on his cheek. "Please, come in." She pivoted on a very spiky high heel.

Damn, the same red fuck-me shoes from last night.

In response, his shaft punched out an erection that was about to pop his zipper. Apparently, he was like those Pavlov's dogs that salivated when the bell rang even when it no longer coincided with their meal delivery. Though in his case, it wasn't food, but a pair of spiky red heels on the feet of a deliciously compact female. They made her ass look so good that he felt like giving it a little love bite.

With an effort, Andrew managed to tear his eyes away from Bridget's sexy butt and take a look at the table that was set for a romantic dinner for two—including a fancy tablecloth, two crystal wine goblets, two lighted tapers, and a vase of fresh flowers.

Oh, hell, this doesn't look like a setup for a hookup.

Bridget had obviously put a lot of work into this dinner, and he was starting to think that maybe Amanda was right and he had somehow misjudged the doctor's intentions.

"Everything looks so nice," he mumbled, suddenly deeply embarrassed about the brown paper bag his gifts had arrived in.

Always listen to a woman's advice on matters like that.

Bridget's cheeks reddened. "I know that I went a little overboard with this. It's just that I've never had an opportunity to entertain a guy in my apartment before. Other than my son, that is. But he doesn't count." She took out the wine bottle from the bag and put it on the table. "Thank you for the wine." Next were the chocolates. "Ah, Godiva." She turned to Andrew. "You certainly know the way to a girl's heart." She licked her lips in a way that had his shaft pulsate—reminding him that it was still extremely uncomfortable and waiting to be taken care of.

But then what she'd said registered in his blood-deprived brain. "You have a son?"

And where was that son of hers? Sleeping soundly in one of the bedrooms? Damn, he hated hooking up with a mother—at her home. It was like having guerrilla sex, stealthy and rushed. Major bummer.

"Yes, Julian. He is a student at Johns Hopkins University School of Medicine. In fact, he's about to graduate."

For a moment, he was taken aback. It was hard to reconcile a woman that appeared to be in her late twenties with someone who had a son in medical school. But for all he knew, Bridget could've been hundreds of years old...

How was that for weird?

"Like mother, like son. You must be proud." He managed to sound conversational.

She beamed. "Very. And he is graduating at the top of his class. Though I'll be damned if I know how he pulled it off."

"Really?"

The boy must've been a genius to be at the top of a graduating class of a school that admitted only the best of the best.

"Julian still gets light-headed if I approach him with a needle in hand. He is like a baby when it comes to his own blood. But it seems that he is unaffected when it's someone else's."

"Do you visit him often?"

"Not really. It's hard to explain a mother that looks like me. We figured it would be best for him to come home when he can. But between the schoolwork, the lab work, and having a semblance of a social life, he doesn't have time—just the commute from Baltimore to LA takes half a day. Not to mention that he can't afford being jetlagged when he goes back to school."

"I bet you miss him."

"We talk on the phone and we video chat." She lifted her hands in the what-can-I-do sign.

Something started beeping in the kitchen.

"Take a seat, Andrew. I'll go check on the soup."

He did as he was told and waited for her to come back.

That beeping had sounded a lot like a microwave oven, and Andrew chuckled when a suspicious thought flitted through his mind. Bridget must've bought the meal from some restaurant and was just reheating it. Not that he minded. In fact, he was glad that she hadn't gone to all that trouble on his account.

And here I am, sitting like a schmuck instead of helping.

He started to get up. "Do you need help in there?"

"No! I've got everything under control." Bridget's panicky answer confirmed his suspicions.

As he lowered his butt to the chair, he couldn't help imagining Bridget burying restaurant containers deep under other trash to hide the evidence. Should he play along?

Yeah, he should. She would be so embarrassed if she knew he figured out her secret. But what would happen when he complimented her cooking? Which he'd have to do, or she'd think he didn't like the food.

He wondered how good of a liar she was. Not that she could ever deceive him. He was just curious to see her try. Would she avert her eyes? Blush? Fidget with her hands? There were so many telltale signs if one knew what to look for.

"Here is the soup, I hope you like it. It's cream of mushroom." She placed a steaming bowl in front of him and sat down on the other side of the table with her own.

The table was smallish in size, which was good because even across from him Bridget was still close and he liked the intimate setting. Scooping some of the thick, brown liquid together with the dried onion flakes she'd put in the center of each bowl, he brought it close to his mouth and blew on it to cool it. The soup was hot and he didn't want to risk burning his tongue.

It was important for that particular part of his anatomy to remain in good working condition because he was planning on using it expertly on her later tonight. Maybe if he gave Bridget several orgasms this way, she would be satisfied with his less than spectacular staying power. Even with the energy drinks he'd chugged, Andrew doubted he could keep up.

Damn, with the images this line of thinking was evoking, dinner was the last thing on his mind. Andrew would've gladly skipped straight to the main dish on tonight's menu, but Bridget was eyeing him from across the table, waiting to hear his opinion on her culinary skills.

"It's delicious," he said.

"I'm glad you like it. I used four different kinds of mushrooms. The texture is creamy, but there is no butter or milk in it, just the blended mushrooms."

She hadn't lied about cooking the soup.

After all the effort she'd put into this, he couldn't just tell her to forget it and drag her to bed. But he could sure as hell speed things up. It took him half a minute max to reach the bottom of the bowl, and he got up to carry it to the sink. "Are you done?" he asked and reached for hers even though it was still mostly full.

As she glanced up at him, Bridget's lips curled up in a knowing smile, and she handed him her half-eaten soup. "Impatient for the second course?" Her voice was husky.

Was he a lucky guy or what? A sharp brain and a lustful disposition were such a sexy combination. "You have no idea." He bent down and took her lips. They instantly parted in invitation. He entered. Her mouth was still hot from the soup, and the short kiss he'd intended turned into a lingering, passionate one, even though his back was painfully contorted from bending sideways while holding the two bowls up and away.

Eventually, she pulled back and smiled. "How about you put these in the dishwasher while I serve the beef Wellington with roasted fingerling potatoes." Bridget affected a British accent while describing the dish.

He moved to let her get up and followed behind her to the kitchen. "Sounds interesting, though I have no idea who that Wellington guy is, and what's his beef."

She chuckled. "It's a filet mignon and some other stuff put together and wrapped in puff pastry. I'm not exactly sure what goes in it, I didn't make it, I got it from a restaurant." She cast him an apologetic smile. "My cooking skills are limited to a few simple vegetarian recipes I can count on the fingers of one hand, none of which I thought would satisfy a manly man like you. But the soup and the salad are mine."

Well, she'd fessed up. Good girl. Not that it would've mattered to him if she hadn't, but he was glad that she had. Except, it made him even more uncomfortable realizing the extent of effort and thought she'd put into this dinner.

"That's very thoughtful of you, but you shouldn't have gone to all that trouble on my account. I'm not choosy about food. I would've eaten whatever you served."

"Think nothing of it. I do the same for Julian when he visits. He likes to eat steaks and ribs, and I can't stand to cook them." She shrugged. "Would you grab the salad bowl, please?" She lifted the tray with the fancy beef dish and carried it into the dining room.

Andrew followed, put down the salad bowl, and took his seat. "You know, I was under the impression that all of you guys stayed away from meat. Bhathian said something to that effect the other day when he invited me to share leftover lasagna with him. He said that that's all the cook serves. But then when I asked him if you had a cook he said not really. Not much for talking, that guy."

Well, that wasn't entirely accurate. The story Bhathian had told Andrew was still haunting him. He couldn't imagine carrying such a burden, not knowing whether he had a child or not. Finding closure for the guy was important to him.

He piled his plate with the beef, whatever it was called, and the tiny potatoes. Bridget had only salad.

"That's all you're going to eat?" he asked, motioning to her plate.

"Yeah, I would've eaten the potatoes if they weren't cooked together with the beef. But that's okay. I usually eat only salad for dinner. And as for the rest of the clan, some are vegan, some are vegetarian, and some are omnivorous. It's a matter of personal preference. Kian is vegan, and his butler Okidu cooks for him and sometimes for the other Guardians, but only stuff Kian eats." Bridget chuckled. "Bhathian eats everything—as long as someone else cooks it—so he really shouldn't complain."

Andrew cut a piece of the pastry-covered beef and put it in his mouth. It was so good that he closed his eyes and felt like moaning in pleasure.

"I see you like it."

"It's the best thing I've ever tasted. Well, food wise, that is." He winked.

"Oh, yeah? And what might that other thing be?" she teased.

"You'll find out after dinner."

"Oh, you're such a naughty boy."

Yes, he was.

Sebastian

Clipboard in hand, Sebastian took the stairs down to the newly completed dungeon. Inspecting each of the small rooms and their compact attached bathrooms, he imagined them populated by beautiful girls and bursting with activity.

At first, he'd planned to simplify things by furnishing all of the rooms identically, but now that his vision was taking shape, he had second thoughts. Diversification would add spice to the clients' experience.

He pulled out his phone. "Tom, contact that hotel furniture supply store and tell them to cancel the order. I want to take another look at their catalog."

"Sure thing, boss. But I want to make sure that you're aware it will cause a significant delay. You wanted the dungeon to be ready as soon as possible."

"Good point. Have them ship four sets of what I've selected before. I'll let you know about the rest."

"How about the linens and towels and other small stuff? Do you want to change that order as well?"

"No, plain white will make handling cleanup and laundry simpler to manage. But I'm considering ordering a variety of colorful bedspreads and decorative pillows, as well as framed reproductions to hang on the walls. I want the girls to be able to personalize their rooms."

"That's very nice of you, boss. You want me to take care of it? Or do you want to make the selections yourself? It's in the same catalog as the furniture—under accessories."

"I'll make the selections and forward you the links."

"Good deal."

As Sebastian returned the phone to the back pocket of his jeans, his lips curled in a sardonic smile. His decision had nothing to do with being nice. It was about good business practices. And there was no better model to emulate than the success their exalted leader Navuh had achieved with *Passion Island*. Other than fear and intimidation, a little kindness and some degree of personal choice regarding inconsequential things went a long way toward ensuring the girls' cooperation.

Besides, Sebastian's team, as well as his future business contacts, would surely appreciate the variety, not only in the selection of girls providing services, but in their rooms' decor as well. For the place to function as an effective incentive, it had to provide an atmosphere of luxury and exclusivity. Esthetics were a crucial factor in creating that effect.

With this in mind, Sebastian had dedicated a sizable section of the dungeon to a bar and cigar lounge, sacrificing some of the space that could've been used for more private rooms. He'd had one hell of a ventilation system installed to suck out the smoke so the cigar fumes wouldn't poison the whole area. Personally, he wasn't overly fond of the things, but a lot of *Passion Island's* patrons were, and he wanted to provide his future clientele with a similar experience—his own miniature replica of Navuh's success story.

Robert's heavy footsteps on the concrete stairs announced his approach. The guy stomped like a gorilla. He was tall, but not as bulky as his footsteps implied.

"The first batch of soldiers has arrived, sir. Would you like a word with them before I show them to their quarters?"

What he would've liked was for Robert to drop the honorific. Perhaps punishment would drive the lesson home. "Robert, from now on I'll impose a one-hundred-dollar fine for each *sir*."

"Yes, S...Sebastian."

Sebastian sighed. The guy was hopeless. "How many have arrived?"

"Five, s...shit..." Robert dropped his head. "Why is it so hard?" he mumbled, addressing his boots.

"Tonight, after you're done with your duties, I want you to stand in front of the mirror and practice. Your trouble is that you're programmed to say sir after a yes; try responding with words like okay, sure, and no problem. Or even I got it, or I'm on it."

"I got it." Robert sounded like he was talking with a mouth full of spaghetti.

"That's a good start." Sebastian slapped the guy's shoulder.

They climbed the stairs, and as they reached the main level, Sebastian punched the code into the electronic lock. The new, reinforced steel door he'd had installed clicked open. Originally, the door to the basement had been visible to anyone walking down the hallway to the kitchen. He needed the new door hidden, so he'd had that part of the corridor sectioned off, enclosing it with a new wall and another plain-looking door. The corridor was wide, and the new enclosure created a small vestibule that was nevertheless sufficient in size for a guard station that included a desk with a monitor and a chair.

Robert pushed open the door, and as they emerged on the other side, the five new arrivals stood up from where they were seated around the dining table and saluted.

Sebastian smiled without returning the salute. "How was your trip? Good?" He shook hands with each one. "What do you think of the place? Nice, huh?" They kept nodding and mumbling their approval. "Robert will show you where everything is. The rooms are still unfurnished, but everything you need is in the containers outside. Each of you will be rooming with another warrior, and you are free to choose who you want to room with. The good news is that each room has its own bathroom."

That last bit got them excited. The facilities at their home base were communal. It wasn't as if the men had to stand in line for the showers or minded doing so in front of other males, but toilets were another story altogether. Having a semiprivate one must've seemed like the height of luxury to them.

"Tonight, after you get settled in your rooms, you're free to roam and acquaint yourself with the grounds. Tomorrow morning, you'll report to Robert. Your first task will be to prepare the base for the rest of the men, distributing furniture to the other rooms and whatever else Robert assigns to you. You are dismissed."

"Yes, sir." The men saluted.

Robert hesitated a moment before asking, "Should I tell them not to do it?"

"No, it's fine, Robert. It's not as if I'm planning on taking anyone other than you and Tom to meetings."

Robert nodded.

Well, that was one way to circumvent the compulsion—refrain from saying anything. He clapped the man's shoulder.

As the soldiers followed Robert to their ground-floor quarters, Sebastian waited a few seconds before climbing the stairs to his third-floor residence. Out of all the guys who'd worked on it throughout the day, only the tile man remained, applying gray grout to the gleaming white marble walls in the bathroom. But other than these last finishing touches, and the furniture Sebastian was still waiting for, the place was done. In the meantime, he had furnished his spacious quarters with standard issue items from the containers outside. One double bed took a small corner of his bedroom, and in the study, he'd positioned the simple student desk to face the tall, double glass doors leading out to the balcony. There was nothing in the living room aside from the built-in bar and the granite mantel surrounding the fireplace.

Sebastian dropped his clipboard on the desk and sat down. For a moment, he got distracted watching the setting sun reflected on the bookcases that had received their last coat of deep burgundy stain this afternoon. The fresh varnish was still wet, and its strong smell permeated the study. Breathing in the fumes, Sebastian contemplated taking his laptop down to the kitchen and working from there.

Except, he didn't want to interact with the soldiers who would no doubt frequent the place. His study was peaceful, and he found the pastoral view oddly tranquil.

The wholesaler's website selection of hotel room furniture and accessories wasn't extensive, and as Sebastian flipped through the limited assortment, he was tempted to look elsewhere for what he had in mind for the girls' rooms. Trouble was, he needed to bundle all of the purchases together and present them to headquarters as expenses related to housing his men. Buying nice things from a department store or some specialty bed-and-bath place would've raised suspicion. It was one thing to make these kinds of purchases for his private consumption; it was a different thing altogether to buy large quantities of the same.

The upside of the limited selection was that it didn't take him long to finalize his new list of items. Once he was done, he forwarded it to Tom with instructions for expedited shipping.

In a week, everything would be ready for the girls. It was time to make some phone calls and arrange for a timely delivery of the most important item on his supply list—the females themselves.

Amanda

Annani's sage advice could've been condensed into one sentence—*follow your gut*—and Amanda had realized that talking with Andrew and her mother, although helpful, hadn't been all that illuminating.

It was still up to her to figure out a way to live with Dalhu, or conversely without.

If not for Annani's presence, Amanda would have done her thinking while pacing back and forth the length of her living room with short detours to replenish her drink. But doing so while her mother's wise and concerned eyes followed her every move wasn't going to work.

Soaking in a tub was the only other activity she found conducive to deep thinking. Not that it was doing her any good now. The only thing that kept going around in her head like a broken record was—*follow your heart*. No other thought managed to break through the never-ending cycle of that mantra, and the water was getting cold.

She reached for the hot water lever, but her hand landed on the drain knob instead. She twisted it open. It seemed that her subconscious had reached the same conclusion her conscious mind was beginning to form.

The time for thinking was over.

She needed to go down to that dungeon and confront Dalhu and his demons—or rather hers—head-on. Whatever came out of it would be better than this endless self-doubt and torment.

As she saw it, there were only two possible outcomes.

She would either jump his bones—and finally have the mind-blowing sex she'd been fantasizing about since the first time he'd touched her, or she'd be repulsed by him and leave—this time for good.

However, the first outcome presented a practical problem. With the unseen spectators monitoring what was going on in Dalhu's quarters, audio and visual, there was no privacy, and the bathroom's floor was definitely not part of her fantasy.

She had to figure out a way to circumvent the surveillance.

With the newfound resolution, Amanda stepped out of the tub and wrapped herself in a towel.

The idea of how to go about it came to her while applying mascara. She could render the cameras blind with black spray paint. Problem was, she had none and was too impatient to wait for Onidu to go down and get it from a building supply store. Maybe she could duct tape the lenses. Though that too was problematic. Even with her impressive height, and standing on top of a chair, she wasn't sure she could reach them. The ceilings in the dungeon were ten feet tall, if not more.

Spray paint, on the other hand, would work even from a couple of feet away. She had no choice but to send Onidu for it. If he hurried, he could be back with the stuff before she was finished dressing.

Still wrapped in the towel, she dashed out to her bedroom and pulled her phone out of her purse.

Please run down and buy me a can of black spray paint. Be back ASAP.

His reply was almost instantaneous. *Right away, mistress.*

She was so lucky to have him. Who else would've obeyed her wishes without a moment's hesitation or asking questions she didn't want to answer?

Standing inside her spacious walk-in closet, she dropped the towel and began sifting through the hanging garments, pulling out hangers and holding the outfits in front of her nude body as she examined herself in the mirror.

The outer layer determined the choice of undergarments.

No, and this one no, and that one... maybe, but no. Something super sexy...not slutty, but easy to take off... Aha!

The Diane von Furstenberg—classy and sensual.

The thing about a von Furstenberg wrap dress was that it rocked on someone tall and skinny but made everyone else look like crap. Lucky for her, she was tall, and although not rail thin, she wasn't busty either.

The dress looked fabulous on her.

The deep lapis blue complemented her eyes and the soft fabric molded beautifully to her figure. Problem was, the effect wouldn't be the same with underwear lines showing through. If Dalhu were the only one she was going to see, Amanda would've gone commando.

Just the thought of being bare under the dress—which could come undone with one tug on the loose knot holding it together—was so deliciously naughty that it was making her horny.

Regrettably, wrap dresses had a tendency of parting at the most inopportune moments, revealing more than a sexy thigh, and she still needed to get Anandur to take her to Dalhu.

With a sigh, she pulled on a black satin thong and matching bra. After putting the dress on and tying the belt in a loose knot, she did a couple of twirls in front of the mirror, enjoying the gentle caress of the fabric as it swished around her legs.

It turned her on.

Damn, evidently every little sensation was getting her all hot and bothered, and she wondered whether the culprit was her anticipated reunion with Dalhu or simply the result of going without sex for a few days.

Nah, it was Dalhu.

Fates, that male's pull was infuriating.

Her inability to resist Dalhu was so frustrating that she felt like punching him before making love to him. It wasn't a particularly noble sentiment, but perhaps the token revenge for Mark's murder would quiet her guilty conscience.

There was a gentle knock on her walk-in closet's door. "Mistress, I have the spray paint you requested," Onidu reported.

She stepped out and took the can. "Thank you, that was fast. How did you manage to get to the store and back so quickly?"

"I stopped by security to inquire about the whereabouts of the nearest paint supply store, and when I told the guard which item I was looking for, he suggested I visit the maintenance office first. Fortunately, they had the item in question." Onidu inclined his head.

"Wonderful." She gave him a quick hug before going back into the closet and closing the door behind her. A big purse was needed to hide the can from Anandur. Eventually he'd find out, but by then it would be too late for him to do anything about it.

Once she was done transferring everything from her smaller purse into the big satchel, she called Anandur.

"Good evening, Princess, how can I be of service?"

"What? No hi-how're-ya? Where have you been? Nothing?"

Anandur harrumphed. "The only reason you ever call me is because you need something. It's never just to chitchat."

Ugh, he was right. "I'm sorry. It's no excuse, but with everything that was going on, I kind of took it for granted that you'd be there for me. But that's just because you're such a great guy, and I know I can count on you." It was true, despite her not so subtle wheedling.

"Okay, you're forgiven. So, where have you been? And more importantly, what have you been doing?" By the dip in his voice, it wasn't hard to guess the activity he was implying.

"Nothing exciting, Anandur. Get your head out of the porn flick. I borrowed Alex's boat and took it out for a short cruise to Catalina."

"Sweet, I heard she's a beauty."

"The *Anna* is, but her crew leaves a lot to be desired."

"What? No hunky sailors?"

"No, Alex's crew is all female."

"And you didn't invite me? I'm wounded."

"Trust me when I say it, even you wouldn't have found them particularly appealing."

"What do you mean—even me?"

She snorted. "I know your standards. If it's female and moving, it's kosher."

"That's not true. It has to be over twenty-five as well."

"Really?" Come to think of it, she had never seen Anandur approach the younger girls.

"I prefer experienced wenches."

"Yeah, I get it, same here—not the wenches part, but the experience. The younger ones are too emotional and tend to cling."

It took a lot of meaningless encounters to develop the necessary detachment to treat sex impersonally.

"That's part of it... Okay, but how did we get from talking about your love life to talking about mine? I guess your call has something to do with a certain frog."

"I need you to take me to him."

There was a moment of silence. "Had a change of heart?"

"Yes and no. I can't decide. I figure the only way to do it is to confront Dalhu. Not so much to hear what he has to say, but to see how he makes me feel. I haven't seen him since Kian shoved reality down my throat and made me face the fact that Dalhu is responsible for Mark's murder." Saying it out loud was akin to pricking a balloon and letting the air out—not in one explosive boom, but slowly in a quiet hiss.

The result was the same, though.

Feeling deflated, she walked over to the couch and plopped down with a sigh.

"It shouldn't have come as such a big surprise," Anandur said gently.

"I know. Some people have selective hearing; I have selective thinking. I don't let upsetting or inconvenient thoughts pass through the barrier of my conscious mind. I'm dimly aware of them floating somewhere in my subconscious, but that's all."

"Not good, Princess. You're not a child, and closing your eyes and plugging your ears to avoid ugliness will not make it disappear or protect you from its consequences. Better to face the demons and fight them head on than cower in the corner, hoping they'll go away. They never do, they just wait to ambush you when your guard is down. But if you acknowledge them, at least you have a fighting chance. The other way turns you into a helpless victim. Not a position I would have liked to find myself in."

Easy for him to talk.

Anandur hadn't had to mourn his own child or anyone else who'd been dearer to him than his own life. Except, she couldn't deny that he'd lost his fair share of friends—warriors that had been like brothers to him.

However, their respective miseries aside, he could no longer accuse her of hiding her head in the sand.

"Exactly. That's why I'm here and in need of your services. So, should we meet down at the dungeon, or do you want to come here and escort me there?" she asked.

"Stay put. I'm coming up."

Kian

"I can't believe how good this is." Syssi's eyes practically rolled back with pleasure. "And the presentation, my God, each dish is like a mini work of art. How many people do you think he has, working in that kitchen?"

"I don't know. Would you like to take a peek? I'm sure Gerard wouldn't mind."

His nephew had greeted them when they'd gotten in and had spent a few minutes with Syssi, going over his menu suggestions for the wedding. But the busy restaurant required his stewardship, and he'd had to excuse himself.

Though not before Syssi had thanked him for his help about a dozen times. You'd think the guy had volunteered his services out of the goodness of his heart, and not because he was being paid through the nose.

It had been agreed that all of it would go to Gerard's private account instead of the restaurant's, which meant he'd get to keep it all without having to share profits with Kian. But whatever, Kian wasn't complaining. Gerard could've asked double what Kian had offered and would've gotten it. Because not only was he the only chef of his caliber willing to at least part-cater the wedding on such short notice, but also the best.

Not to mention Syssi's profound relief at having this major burden taken off her shoulders.

Syssi laughed. "Are you kidding me? Have you ever been inside a busy restaurant's kitchen? It's a madhouse in there."

"Oh, yeah? How would you know?"

Their date was turning out to be everything he'd hoped for and more. This was the perfect place for a romantic proposal—candlelight, soft music, and a procession of tiny but exquisite dishes. Syssi looked so happy that he wanted to kick himself for not taking her out more often. But he was intent on remedying his neglect from now on.

All dolled up, Syssi was wearing a short black dress that at first glance appeared plain but fit her like a second skin, and the earrings and necklace set Amanda had given her provided just the right sparkle to add some glamor to the simple outfit.

She was elegance and sophistication personified.

Spiky black heels added at least four inches to Syssi's petite figure, making her legs look a mile long. Kian was having a difficult time trying to banish the image of those legs, heels on, wrapped around his waist, and that clingy dress hiked all the way up.

Only his unwavering determination to make it a memorable evening for Syssi stopped him from taking her home. Hell, he wouldn't have even waited for them to get there. After all, they'd had some memorable adventures in the limo, and the elevator.

"After my second year of college, I tried waitressing during the summer break." She smiled sheepishly.

He hoped the restaurant's dim light hid his grimace as he adjusted himself as surreptitiously as possible. "And? What happened?"

Thankfully, Syssi was too wrapped up in her story to notice. "I discovered that holding several plates at once was harder than it looked. In fact, it was a tough balancing act that I had no talent for."

"Did you get fired?"

"No, it was my first day and they wanted to give me another chance. But I was too embarrassed to stay. I was already making decent money from tutoring and decided that it made more sense to stick with what I was good at. I printed a bunch of flyers and distributed them to a few local high schools. Soon, I was turning away students because I was maxed out. And I wasn't cheap." She sounded proud.

Kian leaned to take her hand. Clasping it, he rubbed his thumb over her palm. "My sweet, practical, levelheaded Syssi."

She blushed and lowered her eyes.

He chuckled. "And so demure..." He leaned to kiss the back of her hand before lifting his gaze to her smiling eyes. "But outward appearances are misleading, there is a whole other Syssi hiding under there, and I thank the merciful Fates each and every day that I'm the only one who gets to see that wildly passionate girl..." He leaned even closer. "And the one who gets to spank her gorgeous little behind," he whispered in her ear before catching her soft earlobe between his teeth.

"Oh...," she moaned involuntarily as a shiver ran through her.

He let go of her earlobe and smoothed his lips down her long neck.

Panting quietly, she closed her eyes, the flush on her face traveling down to paint her cleavage a rosy pink.

Beautiful.

To abandon that swan neck wasn't easy, and as he leaned back his words came out a little hissed. "Am I the luckiest guy on earth, or what?"

She opened her eyes and smiled. "I'm not sure about that, but I'm positive that I am the luckiest girl on the planet." She leaned toward him. "And every woman in this restaurant agrees with me. They are eating you up with their eyes and shooting murderous glares at me." She tilted her head and winked, pointing to a couple sitting across from them.

The man was a well-known businessman in his early sixties, and the young woman was his latest eye candy. Not that Kian was in any position to criticize.

Nearing his second millennial birthday, he was guilty of much worse. But at least he didn't look it.

The girl was the Barbie type. Though considering the vapid expression on her face, he would not have classified her as pretty. And as far as her Barbie-like figure, he didn't think it was attractive either. The pair of overinflated balloons that were filling her dress could've served as lifesavers in case of an emergency water landing. Vest not required.

"I have eyes only for you."

"I know."

"Good, because this kind of commitment comes with certain conditions and limitations."

"Oh, yeah? Like what?"

"You belong to me."

She waved a dismissive hand. "I know that, and you belong to me. Any other clauses?" Without even batting an eyelash she asked seriously, "Do you want a prenup?"

A prenup? I'll give you a prenup...

"In fact, I do." He smiled wickedly as he reached inside his suit jacket and pulled out two velvet-covered boxes. "First clause. I don't want to hear any arguments about these." He pushed the boxes to her side of the table.

Syssi's hand flew to her heart, and she blushed. "Is this what I think it is?"

He put his hand over the boxes. "You'll need to agree to the terms of my prenup first... if you want to open them and find out, that is."

"Okay." She reached for the ring box first, and he could tell she was holding her breath as she lifted the lid. Her eyes popped wide. "Please tell me this is a very shiny sapphire..."

Kian chuckled and took the box from her hand. "Let me do it right and put the ring on you."

Her hand was shaking as she held it up.

He slid the ring on her fourth finger. "Now it's official." He brought her ringed hand to his lips and gently kissed each digit.

"I don't want to know how much you paid for it."

"Good, because I'm not going to tell you. Now open the other one."

She smiled. "No more clauses before I open it?"

"Nope. This one is self-explanatory."

"I can just guess what's in it." She lifted the lid slowly, only halfway, and peered inside before letting it close. "You didn't..."

Kian pushed to his feet and walked over to stand behind Syssi. He opened the clasp of the necklace she was wearing and slipped it inside the inner pocket of his suit jacket. He then bent down and picked up the larger box.

The moment he lifted the lid, the choker he'd bought for Syssi reflected and refracted the candlelight, catching the attention of everyone in the vicinity. And the fact that the thing was studded with enough diamonds to render someone blind filled him with a sense of pure male satisfaction. He took it out, slipping the box into the same pocket as the other necklace.

As he gently fastened the choker around Syssi's slender neck, Kian leaned to whisper in her ear, "Just as I've promised."

Sebastian

"I'm sorry, Mr. Shar, Sebastian, but I can't."

"Mr. Ax," Sebastian hissed through clenched teeth, "I'm sure you can arrange for at least one or two girls. I'm willing to pay premium for the first delivery."

The LA supplier of females for the island, who identified himself only by the unimaginative moniker Mr. Ax, was a tough and unyielding negotiator. Even without the benefit of a face-to-face conversation, Sebastian was starting to get the impression that the guy, although unwaveringly polite, was a most unpleasant fellow.

Which wasn't all that surprising considering Mr. Ax's chosen occupation.

Sebastian didn't like having to rely on someone nameless and faceless for something this important—regardless of the man's good reputation. There was something to be said for the way things used to be done when contracts and agreements had been finalized upon a handshake.

There was nothing like observing your associate's facial expressions and body language to determine if he was trustworthy. And seeing a man's interaction with his subordinates was another piece of crucial information. Usually, a guy like this would show up with a couple of bodyguards, and one could tell a lot from how they behaved around him. Respect and loyalty were good signs; fear less so.

He wondered what the Ax stood for, but the only options he could think of were either the tool or a tribute to Axl Rose.

"No can do. I just made a delivery of six new specimens five days ago, and I'm not due for another one until two months from now. Your bosses are not my only customers, and I have other clients who are waiting for merchandise that I've promised to deliver by certain deadlines. The best I can do for you is three weeks to a month, and even then only one or two girls. For larger orders, I need the info at least six months in advance—including half of the agreed price."

Lucky for the guy, Sebastian couldn't reach through the phone and tear his heart out.

Instead, he acquiesced in the most businesslike, calm tone, "I understand. I'm sure you're going to do your best. Let me know when you have something for me." After all, he still needed the guy's cooperation, and it wasn't going to happen if he antagonized his only supplier.

For now.

"I will, Mr. Shar. Good day."

Such a polite fellow.

Sebastian clicked off the phone and set it with deliberate care on the desk. Hurling it at the wall would've been so much more satisfying—but pointless and indicative of a lack of self-control.

Who else could he call? Maybe some of the drug or arms dealers would know who to refer him to?

Nah, it was bad business.

Smuggling drugs or weapons was one thing; trafficking in human sex slaves was another.

People found ways to morally justify an illegal business activity, even if their reasoning was convoluted. Evil was subjective. A crime lord who dealt in either drugs or arms could regard the activity as perfectly honorable, but he wouldn't necessarily extend the same rationale to slavers. Suggesting to a man that he had contacts with such *lowlives* could be seen as a grave offense.

With that avenue barred and no other leads, Sebastian had no choice but to find a solution himself.

There were the seven immortal males currently residing at his base to take care of, and more warriors were scheduled to arrive over the next couple of weeks. But until he came up with a plan of how to procure girls for his basement brothel, the men would have to seek sexual satisfaction the old-fashioned way—thralling random females and having their way with them.

A risky proposition at best.

In the old days, a woman who'd found herself lost and confused—with a sore cunt and semen dripping down her inner thighs—would have kept it to herself. Nowadays, she would run as fast as her shaky legs could carry her to the police. Some rape drug would be blamed, and every male she'd come in contact with around the time of the incident would be questioned.

Too many such reports would start a big stink.

Tapping his fingers on the desk, Sebastian gazed out the window at the dark sky. He would have no choice but to prohibit the practice. The men would have to work for a piece of ass, same as the males of Annani's clan. They'd have to seduce willing women in the places where such activity was welcomed, and then thrall the incriminating parts of the memory away.

Sebastian flipped his laptop open and googled dance clubs, but a sidebar ad caught his attention. Something about online dating.

Interesting.

Ha, if the site's ad copy were to be believed, men no longer needed to go out to meet women, they could do so from the comfort of their own homes. Online dating was what everyone was doing these days, and picking up women at bars and clubs was supposedly frowned upon.

Genius.

Problem solved.

His men, handsome immortals one and all, would have no trouble scoring dates on a site like this. And apparently, the rules of just a few decades ago, which had dictated a period of dating before having sex with a man, had evaporated with the last vestiges of Western morality.

Not that Sebastian had a problem with it. This part of Navuh's propaganda was meant for the consumption of his Eastern allies and the simple rank and file.

Navuh's inner circle had no such illusions.

The ultimate goal was world domination and everything else was just fodder for the ignorant masses.

Thinking of the interesting possibilities online dating presented, Sebastian leaned back in his chair. It would be so incredibly easy to find the perfect candidates for his brothel. Mr. Ax's services would no longer be needed. And a lot of money could be saved.

Between their online profiles and their Facebook pages, he could discover everything he needed to know—from how attractive a girl was, to what her financial situation was like, and whether she had family and friends who would notice that she went missing.

Come to think of it, Dalhu might have been wrong in his assumption that Annani's clansmen searched for sex partners in clubs and bars. As part of the Western society, they must've been exposed to this new dating phenomenon and were taking advantage of it.

But if this was indeed the case, it meant that Dalhu's plan was useless.

Still, Sebastian had no choice but to implement the plan regardless of his newfound doubts as to its chances of success. The alternative was giving up the hunt before it even began and it wouldn't fly with headquarters, no matter how well he justified his decision. After spending all this money and allocating the resources to its execution, he couldn't just abandon it without at least giving it a try.

Sebastian signed up as a member of the dating site and paid the fee, then set about creating a compelling profile for himself. Something that would lure the kind of girls he was looking for—young, pretty, lonely, and desperate.

Amanda

"What's in the bag?" Not surprisingly, Anandur eyed her large tote with suspicion.

Amanda had hoped that being a guy he would dismiss it as just one of her peculiar fashion choices, but apparently he was more astute than that.

Luckily, she came prepared.

"If you really want to know, I packed an extra set of lingerie, a nightgown, a toothbrush, a hairbrush, a can of hairspray, perfume, lotions, and makeup. Want to search it in case I'm hiding a weapon there to spring Dalhu out of jail?" She opened the top and lifted it up to his face.

Unfazed by her sarcasm, he took a quick peek inside. But seeing the lacy red thong and matching bra that she'd put on top, he scrunched his nose and shoved the tote away. "How long are you planning on staying there that you're bringing all of this?"

"I don't know yet. I might leave right away. But in case I decide to stay the night, I came prepared." She wasn't lying. There was still a chance she would just walk out of there and never come back.

"Dream on, Princess, I can't babysit for so long. I can allow no more than an hour," he said as they entered the elevator.

We'll see about that. She shrugged and turned to the mirror to examine her makeup. *Perfect.*

"You look good, no need to check." Anandur's reflection was smirking at hers.

"Thank you."

"New dress?"

"No, I just haven't worn it in a while."

"Must have been a really long while...," he muttered as he eyed the outfit with a critical eye.

"Why? You don't like it?"

"Don't get me wrong, you look as stunning as always. It's just that this thing reminds of the seventies. Not a decade fondly remembered for its style." The elevator stopped and Anandur motioned for her to precede him.

With a raised eyebrow Amanda gave him a thorough up and down look over, taking in the worn-out Levis and plain green T-shirt. "I didn't know you followed fashion trends."

"I don't. But I know what I like and what I don't. The miniskirts were fine, more than fine, but everything else not so much."

"Well, this wrap dress is having a big comeback. It's the latest fashion trend."

"I'll take your word for it." He started to punch in the code, then stopped and turned to her. "I just wanted to warn you. You're in for a bit of a shock."

What the hell was he talking about? Had someone hurt Dalhu? "Why, what's wrong with him?"

The alarm in her voice prompted him to quickly qualify. "Nothing. It's a good thing." He pushed open the door and just let it swing all the way in while stepping aside to allow her an unobstructed view of the room.

"Oh, sweet Fates..." Her face was staring at her from at least a dozen portraits, if not more, covering every exposed stretch of wall in Dalhu's small living room. He'd drawn every possible expression—happy, aroused, contemplative, worried, challenging, argumentative, and there was even one of her sleeping. The simple charcoal sketches were so beautiful, so full of life, that she was tempted to get close and touch each one.

But where was the man who'd drawn them? She looked at Anandur.

"Probably in the bathroom. It's not like he can go anywhere."

The door to the bedroom was open, and as she was about to step inside, the bathroom's door banged opened and Dalhu emerged with a small towel still clutched in his wet hands.

Freezing in place, he whispered, "Amanda..." as if he saw an apparition.

Her heart felt as if it was swelling to monstrous proportions, choking her, then shattering, the broken pieces carving bloody furrows in her insides.

She was fighting for breath as desperately as she was fighting for a coherent thought. She wanted to run to Dalhu and hug him so hard that his ribs would crack, and then keep tightening her embrace until she squeezed him within an inch of his life.

Need and rage.

Love and hate.

Longing and loathing.

Compassion and cruelty.

No wonder her heart couldn't handle all of these contradicting feelings and was swelling and bursting in turns.

Why did I leave? How could I've stayed?

How could I've abandoned him when he needed me so desperately? He deserves much worse...

I love him... I detest him.

Amanda shook her head in a desperate attempt to dispel the disabling maelstrom of confusion and turned away from Dalhu. It took her a couple of seconds until she was able to breathe. She glanced at Anandur, who was still standing outside the opened door, watching her and Dalhu with an amused expression plastered on his face.

Nothing about this is funny, you moron.

Amanda grabbed the door and gave it a powerful shove with the intention of closing it in Anandur's smug face. But he blocked the door from slamming shut on him by wedging his boot against the doorjamb. She'd anticipated the move and leaned on the door.

Peering at him through the crack, she stated rather than asked, "Do you really think I need protection from this male?"

"No, but your brother doesn't share my opinion. I have my orders." He tried to push the door open again.

Anandur must've exerted a halfhearted effort because she had no problem preventing him from doing so. "Tell him I ordered you to leave. I'm sick and tired of him trying to run my life for me. I don't have to follow his orders in anything other than council business. I'm running this show from now on." She gave another shove, but the door didn't budge.

Anandur was quiet for a moment, then pushed back, just enough to make room for his big head to fit through the crack. "Good luck, Princess," he mouthed before jumping back and letting her shove the door closed.

What a pain in the ass, but a real prince of a guy nonetheless. She would thank him later.

Her hands still splayed on the closed door, she touched her forehead to the cool surface and just breathed. Getting rid of Anandur had been the easy part of her plan. Now that it was done, she was terrified by the prospect of facing the real challenge of confronting Dalhu and her warring feelings about him.

Amanda felt Dalhu rather than heard him come to stand behind her, and she turned, leaning her back against the door.

He was on her in a flash. Kissing, touching, groping. There was nothing gentle or loving about this. His mouth and his hands attacked her with bruising force. This was pure, desperate hunger.

There was no need for words—hell, there were no words to express what she was feeling, but this was a language they were both fluent in. She gave as hard as she got, pushing her hands under his T-shirt and clawing at his back with the intent of drawing blood.

He bit her then, his fangs two agonizing burning spots at the bottom of her neck. No venom came rushing into her through the entry points. Instead, he pulled back and bit her again at another spot. The pain was both excruciating and exquisite, and she snarled, digging her nails into his scalp to hold his mouth to the wound he'd inflicted. "Lick it!" she commanded.

He did, and the pain subsided immediately, as well as some of the frenzy. As she felt him reach for the loose knot holding her wrap dress together, she grabbed his hand to stop him. "Wait—"

"I can't—" He pushed his groin against her and rubbed, pulling his hand out of her grasp at the same time and going for the knot again.

She gave him a shove. "You have to stop."

He didn't move an inch, his wide chest heaving, but he forced his hand away.

"We are giving the guys in security one hell of a show," she whispered.

"I don't care."

"But I do. Now move so I can do something about it."

Reluctantly, he took a tiny step back, just an inch or so. "What now?" he hissed through his protruding fangs.

"Go to the bathroom and stay there while I handle this."

"Like hell, I will. I'm not going to make love to you on that bathroom floor, and have no doubt, this is going to happen even if I have to do it with them watching."

"Don't be an idiot, Dalhu. I have no desire for bathroom floor adventures either," she whispered. "I just want to keep you out of trouble. You need to stay out of it while I spray paint the camera lenses and order the guys to turn the audio off. I want it to be clear that you had nothing to do with it."

That shut him up, though he didn't move and was still crowding her.

As she tried to duck to the side, he stopped her with a hand on her shoulder. "Do I look like the sort of man who hides in the bathroom while his woman takes care of business?"

"Well, no, of course not. But you're in my territory, and I expect nothing more than a scolding for my actions. You, on the other hand, are a captive. And Geneva Conventions not only do not apply to you but are nonexistent here."

She might have not spoken at all as far as he was concerned. With a mulish expression on his handsome face, he extended his hand. "Give me the spray can. I'll take care of the cameras while you take care of the audio."

He was offering her a compromise.

There was no way Dalhu would do as she said, and anyway, he was taller and could probably spray the lenses without the benefit of a chair to stand on.

"Okay." Amanda reached into her tote and rummaged until she found the can all the way at the bottom. "Here, take it." She handed it to him.

"I'll start with the bedroom." Dalhu took the paint and headed for the door to the other room.

Amanda ambled to the center of the living room and glanced up at one of the camera lenses attached to the ceiling.

"Steve, I hope you're there, and if not, whoever is in charge, please listen carefully. From now on, I'll be staying down here, with Dalhu."

Up until that moment, she hadn't realized she'd already decided that she wasn't leaving. If Dalhu couldn't come live with her at her penthouse upstairs, she was going to move in with him down here.

The phone on the coffee table started ringing.

Fates, she was so stupid for not noticing it before and making a fool of herself—talking to the ceiling.

She grabbed the receiver. "Is that you, Steve?"

"Yes, ma'am."

She couldn't decide whether he sounded amused or worried. "Good, now listen and do as you're told. Surveillance of clan members' private quarters is not allowed, and as I consider this my personal residence from now on, I demand that all audio and video recording from inside this apartment be turned off. The cameras in the corridors will have to suffice as far as security goes."

Assuming an akimbo pose, she glanced at her wristwatch before narrowing her eyes at the camera. "Make no mistake, later on, I intend to make sure that you guys complied with my demand, and I will check if the recording stopped, starting five minutes from now. Noncompliance will result in severe consequences. Do you understand?"

"Yes, ma'am. I will turn everything off momentarily, but I have to notify Onegus."

There was no way to prevent him from doing so, but perhaps she could convince him to delay his report. "Listen, Steve, I know you have to, but could you wait a little? Like a couple of hours? I'll owe you big time..."

"I'll do my best."

"That's all I can ask for."

Hopefully, this would do the trick. But just to be on the safe side, painting the lenses black was a good precaution. She preferred being extra careful than later finding porn flicks of her and Dalhu circulating the keep.

Spray can in hand, Dalhu emerged from the bedroom. "That area is done."

"You can go ahead and spray these too." Amanda pointed at the three cameras near the ceiling. Maybe she was paranoid, but she couldn't help a suspicious glance at the large TV monitor. Grabbing two of Dalhu's creations from the corner they were propped against, she carried them over to the screen and attached them with the adhesive tape Dalhu had been using to hang those he couldn't fit on the walls.

Fates, there were so many of them. He must've been drawing like a madman to produce so many in such a short period of time. True, they were done in charcoal, some in simple black and white and others in full color, a medium which was not as time-consuming as oil paint or even acrylic, but still, the sheer number of them and the quality were awe-inspiring.

And humbling.

Not that she'd doubted Dalhu's love for her before, but it was more as an almost philosophical concept. She hadn't really internalized how fully he was consumed by it.

Would she ever be able to love him like this? Even if she found a way to forgive him about Mark? Was she even capable of feeling so much?

That was the problem with feelings. If she were to let go of the protective numbness and let the good ones bloom, the bad ones would inevitably emerge as well. And there was no way she could deal with those without the protection of a thick mental buffer.

She wasn't ready to discard her Teflon suit yet.

What she wondered, though, was how Dalhu had managed to shed his much thicker protective armor, one that must've grown over his nearly eight hundred years in the Brotherhood to the size of a nuclear-bomb shelter.

Evidently, he was much braver than she.

Dalhu

After the last camera had been dealt with, Dalhu tossed the can into the trash bin and turned toward Amanda.

He was so proud of her. She'd dealt with the guys in security as effectively as an attorney, and he doubted they would dare disregard her orders. After all, if what she'd said about the mandatory exclusion of private clan members' quarters from surveillance was true, her case was perfectly valid. And he had no reason to doubt that Amanda knew what she was talking about. It was obvious that she'd come well prepared to wage war.

And what a fearsome warrior she made.

A tigress.

He could still feel the sting of the deep furrows she'd left on his back.

What a wildcat.

Apparently, he'd been wrong to think that she'd succumbed to her brother's diktat and had abandoned him without a fight. Amanda had done the smart thing, taking her time to devise an effective strategy for them to be together.

"I'm so proud of you." He pulled her into his arms and kissed her forehead.

"For what?" She regarded him as if she had no idea what he was talking about.

"For this." He waved his hand at the cameras. "For fighting for us."

She shrugged. "It's no big deal. All I want is some damn privacy, that's all."

Slowly, he was becoming aware that there was something off about Amanda's demeanor. The woman he had known would have been laughing and joking about her successful stunt, or even better, ripping off his clothes. But there was something dark clouding Amanda's expressive blue eyes, some sort of weariness or worry—he couldn't decipher her odd mood.

Was she afraid of her brother's reaction? Not that it was unwarranted. The moment Kian heard about this, he would come storming down here, and all hell would break loose. Except, Dalhu had gotten the impression that other than a cold shoulder there was nothing Kian would or could do to her. At least not as long as Amanda had her mother's unwavering support.

"What's wrong?"

Amanda looked up at him as if he was missing a screw. "What's right, is a better question."

"What do you mean?"

She sighed. "Sit down, Dalhu."

Why had it sounded so ominous? As he sat on the couch, Dalhu felt his whole body coiling up with tension, and a heavy, uncomfortable sensation was settling in the pit of his stomach.

Amanda walked over to the bar and opened the doors. Inspecting the small selection, she muttered, "Figures, nothing to make a margarita with. How about gin and tonic?" she asked.

"Whiskey, straight up, in a tall glass, please." He had a feeling he was going to need it.

She poured them both a drink and came to sit next to him on the couch. "Here you go." She handed him his drink.

He was relieved that she sat beside him and not across from him.

For a while, Amanda just swished the ice cubes in her tall, clear drink, then took a small sip before setting it down on the coffee table.

She seemed nervous, which wasn't like her, and he felt a chill of foreboding rush up his spine.

"Just spit it out. Whatever it is can't be as bad as this damned suspense. You're killing me."

"Funny that you would phrase it like that."

"What's that supposed to mean?"

"My nephew, Mark, you were the one who ordered his murder."

That heavy, uncomfortable sensation in his gut had just turned into a dark, bottomless pit of dread. He'd known that at one point or another Amanda would put two and two together and come to this rather obvious conclusion, but he'd hoped that by then she would be too deep into the relationship to just get up and leave. But nothing had gone down as he'd been hoping it would.

The way things had unfolded, he should be grateful for the few moments of grace he'd been granted with Amanda.

"Is that why you left?"

"Yes."

"I thought Kian forbade you to see me."

She snorted. "He did, but he can't order me to do anything unless it has to do with safety issues. I can do pretty much as I please."

"But you came back."

"Yes."

What did she expect him to say? That he was sorry? That he'd been following orders? Or maybe try to deny his part? There was absolutely nothing that he could do or say about her nephew's murder that would make it less painful for her, or less damning for him.

Still, she was back, and it looked like she had every intention of staying, so she must've come to terms with the knowledge.

Otherwise, she wouldn't be here.

"I can say I'm sorry, and believe me, I am. But it would not change a thing. So tell me what you want to hear me say, or just scream at me, or scratch my eyes out. If it makes you feel better, I'll welcome it."

She chuckled. "You know me so well it's scary. I don't know what I want to do first, punch you in the face or screw you until we both see stars."

He raised two fingers. "I vote for the second one."

"I bet you do."

He took her hand, and she didn't object—a good sign. "I will do whatever it takes, but you need to tell me what's going on in your head."

She sighed. "A big mess, that's what's going on." She reached for her drink and took a few sips.

"Somehow, you've managed to get under my skin, to penetrate the protective shell I've built to keep emotions out. I wasn't aware of how much I grew to enjoy the intimacy we shared, and I'm not talking about the sex, although that too, until it got literally blown away by Kian and his rescue team. At first, I refused to give it up just because of my brother's conviction that Doomers are the worst filth to walk the earth. Not that I disagree with him, necessarily, but you're different, and he wasn't willing to give you a chance." Amanda paused to bring the drink to her lips and kept drinking until there was nothing but ice cubes left at the bottom of the glass.

"I'm not stupid, and the connection between you and Mark's murder wasn't something that I could've missed or not realized. But subconsciously, I must've repressed it. It shouldn't have come as a big shock when Kian shoved it in my face and forced me to acknowledge it, but it did. I had to get away. And I seriously thought that I could forget about you because there was just no way I could consort with my nephew's murderer...Trouble was, I couldn't stay away." She looked down at the melting ice cubes in her glass.

A pregnant silence stretched between them as Amanda gathered her thoughts. He gave her hand a squeeze for encouragement, and she squeezed back. "The truth is that I need you, and I hate myself for it," she whispered while avoiding his eyes.

"I'm not strong enough to sever this connection between us. And my only *smart* conclusion is that wishing for a perfect solution is futile. That real life is full of compromises. That I will have to learn to live with you and with my resentment."

She chuckled. "For a moment, I even considered asking my mother to tinker with my head and make me forget about Mark, but that would've been the ultimate betrayal, and also disrespectful to his memory."

Lifting her head, she looked up at him—her beautiful eyes gleaming with unshed tears. "As things stand now, I can't give you my heart, only my body and my company. But, perhaps, in time, my resentment will fade enough to release my heart."

She turned her head and glanced at the walls. "I know that you love me. Looking at all these pictures you drew of me, it scares me how well you've gotten to know me. Unfortunately, I can't say the same. I still have a lot to learn about you, and maybe what I'll discover will help me forgive you, but it might not. Right now it's the best I can offer you."

"I'll take it, even if you'll never return my love. To go on without you is a fate worse than death for me. I have to believe that my love for you burns strong enough to sustain us both."

Amanda smiled and wiped her eyes with the sleeve of her dress. "I knew you were going to say that. I must know you better than I thought I did."

Amanda

"That predictable, huh? Must be boring...," Dalhu teased.

She felt lighter after getting that little speech off her chest. Dalhu had actually taken it better than she'd thought he would. Instinctively, he must've realized that trying to excuse his past would do him no good. After all, she had been well aware of the cold facts, and nothing he could've said would have been news to her.

It hadn't been personal.

Dalhu hadn't known her, or even of her, or Mark. He'd been doing his ugly job for an even uglier organization—following a cause he'd no longer believed in and taking orders from superiors he'd despised.

He should've left the Brotherhood long before he'd met her. But prior to that, he'd lacked the impetus to make such a radical change. He'd known nothing else, had believed in nothing at all, and had cared about no one.

In a way, she'd given him a new lease on life, a chance for an existence that wasn't as meaningless—bleak. For now, his love for her was like a flotation device in an ocean of hostility and indifference. But in time, maybe her family would accept him, and he'd become part of the force for good. And the meaning he'd attach to his life would expand beyond his love for her to include a sense of belonging and purpose.

She winked at him. "You compensate in other departments."

He got closer, his hand resting innocently on her bare knee. "Yeah? Which ones?"

The hand traveled a little north, and the wrap dress parted farther, exposing her thighs to a little below her panties. An inch higher and they would be on full display.

She placed her palm over his large hand, halting his progress. "No more bathroom floors and no more couches. Take me to bed, big boy."

"With pleasure."

For such a large man Dalhu moved incredibly fast.

She was up and cradled in his arms before the second word left his mouth. Relaxing into his warm chest, she wrapped her arms around his solid neck as he carried her the few feet to the bedroom and kicked the door closed behind him.

With infinite care, he lowered her to the bed, then climbed on and straddled her hips with his knees.

"May I?" He reached for the knot holding her dress.

"Yes, you may."

Dalhu gave a gentle tug, and it unraveled. Slowly, he parted the dress—a look of reverence spreading over his harsh features.

Leaning back, he rested his palm on her soft belly—his large hand hot and heavy on her skin. For a moment, he didn't move, just looked at her—his eyes betraying his thoughts. The smoldering desire, the love, the unmistakable ownership his hand on her belly symbolized.

There was no question in his gaze, it was a statement—a claim he knew she wasn't ready to hear but was true nonetheless.

She wondered if he could read the truth in her eyes—that deep in her soul she'd known it from the start—from when she'd first seen him at that jewelry store. For a suspended moment in time, before her mind had taken over and the chasm of reality had opened between them, she'd reacted to him as a female would to her chosen male. And yet, she was still miles away from admitting it even to herself.

It seemed that he knew exactly what she'd been thinking. His harsh countenance softened, and the hand on her belly lightened and moved in a gentle caress—as if to say that it was okay, that there was no pressure, that he was going to wait for as long as she needed him to.

Damn, the man was reading her like an open book. She doubted even her own mother knew her so well. Amanda was just too good at putting up a show.

But for some reason, it didn't feel as intrusive or scary as she would've expected it to. Because Dalhu loved her unconditionally, and she knew that whatever he saw deep down in her heart wouldn't change it. Not a bit.

With him, she was free to be who she really was—imperfect, selfish, vengeful, hurting—and despite all the ugliness she worked so hard to hide from everyone, including herself, Dalhu would love her no less.

The silent communication between them must've lasted no more than a few seconds, but when Dalhu's hand finally reached up and his fingers snapped the fastener of her bra, it felt as if she'd been waiting a long time for him to make a move.

Her nipples stiffened in anticipation of his touch, and she couldn't help but arch her back in a long sinuous wave. He didn't reach for her breasts, though. Instead, he hooked his thumbs in her thong and pulled it down her legs. When they were off, she lifted her torso to let the bra straps slide off her shoulders, and got rid of it.

Completely bare now, she relaxed on her back with the fingers of her hands entwined behind her head.

"Your turn," she said. "And do it slowly, I want to watch the unveiling." Amanda hadn't seen Dalhu fully naked yet. She'd seen all the important parts, but not all at once, and she couldn't wait to see him in all his nude glory.

"Your wish is my command, Princess." He smiled before grabbing the bottom of his T-shirt and pulling it up in slow motion.

"You'd better believe it."

She watched him struggle with the slow pace. The poor guy wouldn't have much of a career as a stripper. He was kind of clumsy in his attempts to look sexy for her, but she didn't have the heart to tell him that. And anyway, if she hadn't insisted on him going slow, he would've been out of his clothes and pouncing on her in a heartbeat.

As it was, even his awkward moves had done nothing to detract from the sexiness of his amazing body as he bared it for her hungry eyes one piece of clothing at a time.

Dalhu kept the best for last, and her mouth watered in anticipation of the grand reveal. He hooked his thumbs in the elastic band of his shorts and shimmied out of them.

Oh, sweet Fates in heaven have mercy.

She remembered that magnificent shaft well, but that didn't stop her from drooling in appreciation as it sprung free out of his boxer shorts.

"Come here," she commanded, beckoning him to her with a crooked finger.

He came to stand by the side of the bed, and she seized him not too gently. This wasn't going to be tender lovemaking, at least not on her part. She still felt like hurting him, and if it meant that she was a vengeful bitch, so be it.

Dalhu could take whatever she'd dish out and would probably beg for more.

She pulled, and he obediently climbed on the bed, kneeling in front of her. But if Dalhu thought that she was going to take him in her mouth, he should think again. Getting up on her knees, she pushed him back until he was spread out before her.

The man was huge, his long body barely fitting the length of the bed. He must've been sleeping diagonally across it because he sure as hell couldn't have slept comfortably otherwise.

It was a heady feeling to know that this fine exemplar of manhood was willingly submitting to her mercy, or lack thereof.

She used to think that there wasn't much difference between a bully and a dominant, but now it occurred to her that the resemblance between the two was only superficial. The bully thrived on fear, deriving pleasure from terrorizing and hurting a weak or meek partner, as opposed to the dominant who derived it from the submission of a strong, willing one who chose to participate in the game for his or her own pleasure. Still, she could easily see how the distinction could sometimes be blurred, and naïveté could be taken advantage of.

For a brief moment, a disturbing image of Dalhu tied to a post with whip welts marking his back flushed through her head. It disturbed her not only because she was the one wielding the whip, but because the image was making her wet.

When did I turn into a damn dominatrix?

No, she might scratch, and she might squeeze, and she might even bite, but she could never go that far.

Closing her eyes, she lowered herself on top of Dalhu. Her lips found his, and she kissed him, her tongue gently seeking entrance into his warm mouth. She felt his hands on her back, lazily caressing up and down until the kiss grew heated and he groaned, cupping her butt cheeks—each one fitting perfectly inside a large hand.

He was so hard and hot beneath her, swiveling his hips and grinding his erection against her pubic bone. She knew he was desperate to flip her under him and drive this hot rod inside her, but he was tolerating his subdued position for as long as he possibly could, waiting for her to give him permission to take over.

Not yet.

She kissed him deeper, her tongue caressing his elongated fangs in slow circles and driving him wild. His fingers were digging into her fleshy buttocks with bruising force, and his groans were getting louder. But then he must've realized he was hurting her and eased up, only to go on exploring the valley between them all the way down to her dripping wet, hot center. He lingered there for a moment, circling her opening with the tips of three fingers, but he didn't push in. Instead, he scooped some of her moisture and brought it up to her tight sphincter, shocking her with pleasure when he repeated the same move there.

Her eyes popped open, and she looked at his smug face. "What are you doing?"

"What does it feel like I'm doing?" He nipped her chin with his blunt front teeth, and she felt his finger apply light pressure as if seeking entry.

"Don't," she breathed, though what she really wanted to say was *please do*.

It wasn't that she was ignorant. Amanda was well aware that some people found this sort of thing pleasurable, but she had never tried it and had no desire to experiment. Except, although somewhat distasteful, it was also oddly arousing, and she was reluctant to insist that he stop his explorations.

"Please... I don't...," she mumbled into his neck.

Trouble was, the odd sensation wasn't restricted to the area in question. And the shockwave of intense heat sweeping through her made her sweat worse than one of her breakneck runs on the treadmill.

Fates, what's wrong with me?

Dalhu

The fact that Amanda wasn't as experienced as she thought she was had taken Dalhu by surprise. Evidently, there still remained a thing or two he could teach her.

But this was probably not the right time.

Nevertheless, he was so damn thrilled at the prospect of being her first in yet another sexual experience.

So unexpected, yet so deeply satisfying.

Amanda's lithe body was hot and sweaty on top of his, and her breath was coming out in short, shallow puffs against his neck. Dalhu felt a wave of tenderness wash through him, and he wrapped his arms around her, hugging her to him gently.

Just for a moment, to let her regain her composure.

He had gotten a strong impression that Amanda didn't want gentle. She was too angry—with him for being who he was, and at herself for wanting him despite it—to tolerate tenderness.

It was a shame, really, because he wanted their first time to be about making love, not about angry sex. But he would take whatever she could give and would be thankful for it.

"I love you," he whispered against her damp temple.

She sighed and lifted her head to look at him. "Kiss me," she commanded.

He did, his lips just a light caress against hers before he slid his tongue into her mouth and began a lazy exploration, slowly rediscovering her, getting reacquainted.

At first, she followed his lead, her lips and tongue just as tender, but then a low growl started deep in her throat, and he knew the time for gentleness was over. She sucked his tongue into her mouth, forcefully, and when it was all the way inside she bit down.

The tangy taste was unmistakable—she'd drawn blood. But it had done nothing to cool his fervor; on the contrary, it had awakened the animal inside him. He felt an overwhelming need to flip her under him, to pin her hands over her head and ram himself inside her. But he squashed the impulse with all the force his willpower could muster. He had to allow her to be the aggressor this time, to take out all of her anger and frustration on him.

She let him withdraw his tongue from her mouth and licked his lips, smearing the few drops of blood she'd scooped up over them. "You taste good," she said with a smirk.

"So do you."

"Hmm, I wonder if the taste is the same all over." She dipped her head and bit a soft spot between his neck and shoulder, her sharp little fangs drawing blood again.

She licked the wound she'd inflicted and looked up at him, her blood-smeared lips looking cruel yet sexy as hell. "This tastes good too. Let's see if it's the same over here." She moved her lips up his neck and bit down there.

Dalhu's bonds of restraint were starting to unravel, and he was sweating with the effort of lying still and letting Amanda have her way with him. His damned fangs were throbbing with the urgent need of returning the favor.

But was he doing the right thing? Maybe she was spurring him on, on purpose, because she wanted him to overpower her? To take over so she could pretend that what was happening between them was out of her hands?

She'd bitten him two more times before he snapped and with a loud growl banded his arms around her and flipped her under him. She put up a half-hearted struggle when he caught her wrists and pinned them above her head, then held them there with one hand while the other one went behind her head and fisted her hair.

She was a strong female, but she was no match for him.

Gazing into her impossibly beautiful face, he read her expression to make sure that he'd not misunderstood her intentions, conscious or subconscious, and this was really what she'd been after. Her eyes were glowing, feral with a mixture of anger and need, and she was trying to free her head from his grasp so she could bite him again. He held on, tightening his grip on her hair and pulling back, which was no doubt causing her some pain.

And yet, she wasn't telling him to stop or let go.

Wedging a knee between her closed thighs, he forced her to spread for him and positioned his shaft at her entrance. But he refused to let himself shove inside her before ensuring she was ready—even though she was sopping wet.

"I'm going to let go of your hair, but if you bite me again, I'm going to bite back, and my fangs are longer." It wasn't much of a threat, considering the properties of what his fangs could deliver, but it worked. Apparently, Amanda didn't want to be out of it while experiencing his penetration for the first time any more than he wanted her to be.

He released her, waiting for a moment to see if she was going to behave before bringing his hand down to her wet center. He teased her a little, gently circling his finger around her engorged clit while his mouth went for one sweet nipple, and he repeated the same slow circling move with his tongue. Amanda groaned—though he wasn't sure if in pleasure or impatience.

Perhaps it wasn't such a good idea to stretch things out for too long, considering that she was already angry and frustrated.

"Ah...," she groaned and arched her back violently when he penetrated her with two fingers, then shuddered when he pressed on her clit with his thumb.

He'd managed about a minute of foreplay before his need became too great.

Amanda was more than ready for him, and there was no point in prolonging the wait for what they both so desperately wanted. Needed.

He reached for his shaft and fisted it, positioning at her entry. She closed her eyes, her lips slightly parted to allow her rapid breathing.

"Look at me," he growled. "Look at me when I take you." He pushed just an inch inside her and halted, waiting for her to obey.

"Oh, Fates," she groaned, peering at him with hooded eyes.

With a grunt, he rammed all the way inside her, eliciting an echoing sound from her.

He hadn't intended to do it like this, but going slow and penetrating her in increments had become impossible. The best he could manage was to refrain from moving until she grew accustomed to the intrusion.

Sweating, he held still on top of her, bracing his weight on one hand while his other was still shackling her wrists over her head with brutal force. He let go the moment he realized that he must be bruising her delicate skin, and probably restricting circulation to her hands as well.

Immediately, her hands went to his ass and her nails sunk into his flesh.

"Move," she hissed.

Wild…feral…stunning… his woman was beyond compare.

And he moved—like he'd never moved inside a female before for fear of breaking her. But he had no such concerns with Amanda.

She could take it.

Loving every battering ram, moaning and growling in turns, she spurred him on, her hands gripping his ass and guiding him to go deeper, faster, stronger.

Amanda

Fates, this was a ride of a lifetime.

Dalhu was an animal—a wild alpha male in the midst of frenzied rutting. And she meant no insult by it. Coming from her, it was the best of compliments.

Their prior interludes had already raised the bar on her sexual expectations, but this was so much better than she could've imagined. It wasn't only that he was bigger than any male she had ever had inside her, or that he was pounding into her with the force and stamina of a locomotive—there was something additional in play. A chemistry, a coming together of two formidable forces so powerful, so all-consuming, that nothing else would ever do.

As she was losing her tenuous grip on lucidity, Amanda had the passing thought that this might be the start of the addiction.

A point of no return.

Or maybe this was a foregone conclusion from the moment she had decided to come back.

Too late for second thoughts now.

Dalhu's thrusts were becoming even faster, and she had to relinquish her hold on his ass to grab hold of the bed's headboard and brace against it to prevent him from driving her head into it.

As she felt him swell inside her, she began orgasming, and a moment later he roared his completion and sank his fangs into her neck.

Complete and total ecstasy.

This was how she would describe it later when verbal reasoning returned. In the meantime, she was floating in a haze of pleasure and euphoria and thinking of nothing at all.

When she came to, a few minutes later—or maybe longer? Who knew?—Dalhu was slumped on top of her, crushing her with his weight, and still out of it as if he'd been the one dosed with venom.

She pushed on his chest, first gently, and when that didn't help, forcefully, managing to lift him a bit, just enough to wiggle out from under him. But that effort had drained the last of her energy, and she just lay next to Dalhu spread-eagled as much as the space he wasn't occupying allowed.

After a moment, she regained enough strength to move her head and look at him. She smiled. Lying face down, the only indication that he was still alive and breathing was the slight up and down movement of his wide back.

"Are you alive, big guy, or have I drained all of your life force?" She teased with a smirk.

He turned his head toward her, his face the most relaxed and peaceful she'd ever seen it. "If you did, then I must've died a happy man."

"So that's it? You're done?"

He reached a long arm and pulled her to him, half turning to face her. "Not even close, I'm just taking a one-minute rest. After all, I was the one doing all the work..." He kissed her lips before collapsing again—dramatically.

"Well, it's not my fault that you wanted to be the big macho male. I was perfectly happy being the one on top."

"I'll tell you what, this time you can be." He flopped to his back, pulling her with him to lie on top of him.

Bracing her elbows on Dalhu's broad chest and her chin on her hands, she taunted, "Admit it, you're too wiped out to move a muscle and just want me on top to do all the work."

He smiled, not rising to the challenge. "I'll admit that I'm a red marshmallow if it makes you happy."

"A red marshmallow?"

He shrugged. "First thing that popped into my head, not very witty I'm afraid."

"Hmm..." She frowned. "I wonder what it means..."

"It doesn't mean anything, Professor, don't psychoanalyze me— especially not while we are engaging in sexual activity. It could have, potentially, a damaging effect on my fragile ego."

This was fun, this postcoital easy banter. She had never stayed with a guy long enough for small talk after she'd had her way with him.

As soon as she was done, she would thrall her partner, and the poor thing could barely remember his own name let alone conduct a conversation. And anyway, she doubted it could have been like this with anyone but Dalhu.

"Well, if your ego is that sensitive then it probably needs a little boost. You are a force of nature, absolutely magnificent."

He smiled. "Go on—"

"You want more? Okay. You're the best I ever had."

"Of course. Please continue—"

"Without compare."

"I'm all ears."

She narrowed her eyes at him and husked, "I'm ready for more."

"Are you now?"

She felt him stir beneath her. *Good boy.*

Her kiss was gentle this time, and attuned as he was to her, he responded in kind. Their tongues danced lazily around each other, and his hands on her back caressed and kneaded in turns before moving to her front and paying homage to her breasts.

He lifted and pulled her up, bringing one nipple into his mouth and lapping at it gently. Then he moved her, so the other one was hovering above his lips and repeated the treatment.

It felt so good to let him carry her weight, knowing that he was holding her up with ease, watching his incredible biceps flexing.

Once he had his fill of suckling and licking, and her sensitive nipples could take no more, he pulled her up even higher to worship her nether lips with his tongue.

She was indeed the one on top, but he was definitely still the one in charge. It was fine with her, though. His talented tongue was doing a fantastic job of bringing her to the verge of another orgasm. Incredibly dexterous for a tongue, it was somehow pushing and twisting inside her at the same time.

"You're going to make me come like this."

"I know," he mumbled and continued his assault.

She wasn't about to argue. Letting herself go, she climaxed with a soft gasp.

They made love a few more times, unhurriedly, learning each other's bodies, and the easy, gentle pace brought its own unique kind of pleasure—an intimacy that neither had experienced with anyone else before.

Other than that first time, Dalhu refrained from biting her, and she suspected that he didn't want her dopey from the effect of the venom because he wanted her to savor the closeness just as much as he did.

Amanda sighed contentedly as he pulled out and plopped beside her on the bed. She was so exhausted, it was a struggle to keep her eyes open, and after a moment she gave up, letting herself drift into sleep.

"I can't believe I'm saying it, but I think that you successfully drained the last drop of life out of me," she heard him say.

"Mm-hmm...," she murmured, not willing to lift her eyelids.

He turned sideways and draped his arm around her middle, turning her limp body around so he could snuggle up from behind. "Isn't it the guy who's supposed to turn around and go to sleep after?"

"Mm-hmm..."

Sebastian

"Stay together and give Robert a buzz when you're done. He'll pick you up. Is everyone clear about what to do?" Sebastian eyed the small group of men he was dropping off at what was supposed to be a raunchy bar.

"I still don't understand about that Uber service. Why not use a taxicab?"

Sebastian rolled his eyes. "First of all, you might not need the service if you can take care of business in some secluded corner right here in the bar or in the alley behind it. But we don't want accidental witnesses, so in case privacy is a problem, you call up a car, using the Uber application on your phone like I showed you, and take the woman to one of the motels on your list. It's easier and cheaper than a taxicab, and the drivers do it as a part-time job and don't pay as much attention to their passengers."

The guy nodded, and the group headed for the bar's front door.

He really needed to solve the problem of females for his men, and the sooner, the better.

Sebastian eased into the sparse late-evening traffic and headed for the nearest coffee shop with Internet service. He had chosen the neighborhood carefully, searching for a lower-middle-class area that was becoming trendy, and had settled for Glendale. His research had yielded a few popular bars and clubs as well as coffee shops that were open late—a rarity in most of LA and its surrounding cities, whose residents apparently went to sleep with the birds.

As he spotted what he was looking for, Sebastian drove a little farther down the street until he found a parking spot big enough for his brand new Escalade. Tom had convinced him that it was best suited to his needs, but even though the car was pretty luxurious and surprisingly easy to drive despite its monstrous size, he would've preferred something more refined—like the Range Rover he had back home. Except, Tom's argument had been that Sebastian needed a car that could seat more passengers than the Rover and that the Escalade was in fact considered trendy. It remained to be seen. He would drive the thing for a week, and if he didn't like it, he'd fob it off on Tom and have the guy buy him something else.

The small coffee shop was almost deserted at only ten o'clock at night. He made his way down the narrow aisle separating the two rows of booths, benches that were covered in ugly burgundy Naugahyde and tables that were topped with cheap Formica, settling in the last one next to the front window. The only other customer was an older guy sitting in the booth across from him. The man was staring into space while mumbling something incoherent to his invisible companion.

A loon.

Sebastian pulled out his laptop from its leather carrying case and put it on the table. The Internet access code was printed on top of the plastic menu, and he logged in. Maybe some flies had been already caught in the dating web, and someone had responded to his ad, or profile as the dating service called it. He wondered if the other *profiles* were as fabricated as his. Probably. At least his picture wasn't fake. It was slightly altered, but not to make him look better, just to obscure his identity.

"What can I get you?" A waitress with a white apron and ratty sneakers, holding a little notepad and pencil, was giving him an appreciative look-over.

She didn't smile for him, though, or strike a pose like most girls would've done when they wanted to get noticed. Probably figured he was out of her league, and rightfully so. Too skinny, with a limp ponytail that looked like it needed shampooing. Perhaps with a little spiffing up and some meat on her bones she could've been pretty, not beautiful, but at least attractive.

He put on a charming smile and glanced at her name tag. "Tiffany, what a lovely name. How is your cappuccino? Any good?"

She shrugged. "I guess. A lot of the lunch regulars order it, so it must be good. I don't drink coffee, so I wouldn't know."

She didn't drink coffee?

Who didn't drink coffee? There must be something wrong with the girl. "I'll give it a try. How about those cakes over there?" As he tilted his head sideways to look at the pastries and cakes in the display case up front, he noticed the woman standing behind the tall counter.

Now, that was a looker.

Not as young as Tiffany, the woman was probably the proprietress. Only her face and a small part of her upper body were visible from behind the display, but unless she had a backside the size of his Escalade or crooked legs, she was definitely on the beautiful side of the scale. Except, she looked tired, with dark circles under her big brown eyes, and the expression on her face was decidedly unfriendly. In fact, she was eyeing him with almost open hostility.

It happened sometimes.

Here and there he'd encountered a woman who possessed some kind of a sixth sense about what was hiding under his charming veneer.

No big deal.

Very few females possessed this innate ability, and he had no problem ensnaring most others with his silver tongue and his charming smile.

However, it was a shame that this one was among those select few.

Even with that dour and tired expression, hair that was pulled back in a simple braid, and no trace of makeup, her face was arresting. Her features hinted at a mixed heritage, a combination of Hispanic, maybe Cuban, and Middle Eastern. Perhaps some Egyptian or even Ethiopian. It made her beauty unique.

Like a rare masterpiece.

One that he would've loved to possess.

"The cakes and pastries are to die for. I can say this with confidence because I've tasted most of them. I promise that anything you choose will be amazing—" He listened to the skinny waitress's gushing endorsement while locking gazes with the proprietress.

She didn't back down.

Gutsy bitch, he'd give her that.

"What's your favorite?" Sebastian smiled at the dark-haired beauty before turning his attention back to the waitress.

She hadn't returned his smile.

"Oh, I can't say, they're all so good." She leaned over a little as if to tell him a secret. "My boss makes them herself, and the recipes are a family secret."

"In this case, I must sample more than one. Bring me an assortment."

The waitress's face visibly brightened, probably calculating the tip she was going to get. "How many would you like?"

He glanced at the woman behind the counter and winked. "Let's start with six."

"Yes, sir!" she chirped. Tucking her small notepad inside her apron pocket, she hurried away to fill his order.

He'd definitely succeeded in winning the waitress over, but her boss's expression remained unchanged.

Oh well, he couldn't win them all. The waitress would do.

Come to think of it, with a little fattening and styling she might be good enough for his men.

Kian

"I don't know what to say." Syssi touched her fingers to the choker.

Kian leaned over her shoulder and kissed her cheek. "A simple thank-you will suffice, my love." He walked back to the other side of the table and sat down.

Syssi looked like a queen, and for the first time in his life, he was truly thankful for his wealth. He felt a purely male sense of satisfaction at being able to buy his fiancée things few other men could. Never mind that it was unwarranted. After all, it wasn't as if he had slain a dragon or bested numerous opponents in a tournament to win her hand in marriage. But dragons didn't exist and knights no longer jousted for ladies' affections. Nowadays, acts of bravery and combat skills were replaced by business acumen, and battles were waged in the financial arena. The measure of success for men, and for women, was how well they managed to distinguish themselves in either politics or the art of money making.

"Thank you." She shook her head as she lifted her hand to examine the ring. "But seriously, Kian, these two pieces of jewelry can feed a small country. Don't get me wrong, I'm flattered, but I'm also somewhat perplexed. And even though I promised not to argue about accepting these, I just have to know; what in God's name possessed you to spend a fortune on diamonds for me?"

Luckily, he'd come prepared with an argument even his practical Syssi couldn't find fault with. "It's a sound investment. Diamonds of this caliber that come with authentication certificates appreciate in value. So in case we ever find ourselves in a situation where we need to feed a small country, and all our other resources are gone, we can sell them for more than their original cost." *Checkmate.*

Syssi opened her mouth to say something, but then closed it, slumping back in her chair. For a moment, she just gazed at him with narrowed eyes.

His lips twitched with the effort of stifling a smirk.

Crossing her arms over her chest, she finally smiled. "Very clever, aren't you? You had it all carefully planned."

"Obviously, I know who I'm dealing with. I have more."

"Oh, yeah?"

"You know, it's not very romantic to argue with your fiancé when he presents you with a ring."

"Oh, that's a good one, laying a guilt trip on me. But seriously, where am I going to wear these? I'll need armed guards to accompany me if I leave the keep with this on—to protect your *investment*."

Kian leaned forward and beckoned Syssi with his finger to get closer. "Remember my original proposal?" he whispered.

She blushed, "How could I ever forget?"

"So you know exactly where and how you're going to wear these."

Syssi grinned and leaned even closer. "With nothing on besides spiky high heels."

"You got it."

"Pervert."

"What else is new?"

"I love you."

He took her hands and kissed each one. "That's not new, and neither is how much I love you and how grateful I am for you. You make my life worth living."

Syssi's eyes shone, but he suspected that it wasn't the supernatural glow of his kind. She was tearing.

He gave her hands a gentle squeeze. "I hope those are happy tears."

"Oh boy, and here I thought I was doing such a good job of holding them back. But yes, these are happy tears... mostly."

Mostly?

"Why, what's wrong?"

Just as Syssi was about to answer, his phone buzzed in his pocket—again. He'd silenced the damned thing's ringer but the vibrate was still on, and every time an e-mail or a text message came in it buzzed. Which meant that it was buzzing almost continuously. It was like having a damned vibrator in his pocket. For a moment, he eyed his Perrier glass and considered drowning the phone in it.

But it probably won't fit.

"Give me a second." He took it out and shut it down completely. If a catastrophe struck in the next two hours, they'd have to manage without him.

"Okay, I'm listening."

Syssi glanced at his phone. "Are you sure that's smart? What if something happens and they can't get a hold of you. I didn't bring mine. It didn't fit in this tiny purse." She lifted what was the size of his wallet to show him.

Why the hell had she bothered to bring it with her at all? It could barely contain a lipstick. Though he remembered that Syssi had her driver license in there because she showed it to the waiter who had taken their drink order.

As if anyone would've asked to see it in a place like this.

"It's fine. The world will manage without me for a couple of hours. Now, tell me what troubles you before I start blowing smoke out of my nostrils."

"For real?"

"No! You're driving me crazy. Talk, woman."

"It's not about us, so you can relax. It's just that I feel guilty for being so happy—with you—planning our wedding, joking, having fun, while Amanda suffers because she can't be with the one she loves."

Aha, so that is her story. Well, at least she said she is happy and having fun.

"She was the one who sobered up and left. I had nothing to do with it." *Technically.*

"So what are you saying? That if Amanda comes back and wants to be with Dalhu, you will not stand in her way?"

"That, I didn't say."

Syssi pulled her hands out of his grip and crossed her arms over her chest. "You're not doing the right thing here, Kian. I know you think it's best for Amanda to forget about Dalhu, but you can't make this kind of a decision for her. And from what I hear Dalhu is a decent guy, for a Doomer, and he is cooperating with us. If they truly love each other, you should give them a chance."

He could've strangled that damned Doomer. The guy was intruding on Kian's perfect date.

"Can we not talk about this tonight? This evening is about us, and I don't want to think about anything other than you and how soon I can get you naked."

Syssi smiled and dropped her arms. She returned her hands to the table and slipped them inside his larger ones.

"Do you ever think of anything else when you're with me?"

"Let me see... nope. And I don't think of much else when I'm not with you either. I'm just a simple guy with simple needs."

She snorted. "Yeah, right, and here is the evidence of that." She lifted her hand and twisted it around, so the big diamond was in his face.

He took her fingers and brought her hand closer for a kiss. "Did you forget already? Should I repeat my *pervy* proposal?"

Syssi threw her head back and laughed out loud. "Oh, God, you're right, this too is about getting me naked."

"Absolutely."

Sebastian

"A pretty girl like you shouldn't be walking all by herself in the middle of the night." Sebastian sidled up to the little waitress. He'd said it jokingly, the street wasn't deserted, and people were still going in and coming out of the trendy cafés and restaurants that were still open. Only the boutiques and other small shops were closed, but their window fronts remained brightly illuminated.

It hadn't required a Sherlock-Holmes-caliber deductive skill to guess that the girl was dirt poor and didn't own a car. One look at her ratty sneakers and her old, threadbare jeans—and not the fashionable kind that just looked worn out—had told him all he needed to know.

He had waited outside the coffee shop until her shift had ended and followed her from a safe distance for a couple of blocks. After all, someone might have come to pick her up, a boyfriend or maybe even her lovely boss. But no one had.

"It's not that late, and I live just around the block," she said with a thin, nervous smile.

"You're right, it is definitely too early for calling it a night. How about a drink somewhere, you and me? Or are your legs killing you after your shift?" He flashed her his best shy smile, the one he had perfected over the years to lure countless females into his trap. Stuffing his hands in his pockets, Sebastian slouched a little, not because he was tall—his height was average for a male—but because he wished to appear as nonthreatening as possible.

She hesitated for about a second and a half. "Okay, there is a bar a few minutes' walk down the other way." She turned around and pointed to a red neon sign that read McClintock's.

The place was one block away from the coffee shop she worked in. It wouldn't have been his first choice, someone might know her there, but he'd gotten the impression that she wouldn't go with him anywhere else. He could've thralled her right there on the street, but that wasn't a good idea either. He needed to find out more about the girl before deciding if she was a good candidate for abduction.

"Sounds great, lead the way," he said.

The girl relaxed visibly.

"Do you go there often?" he asked.

"No, not at all. But I heard it's a nice place."

Perfect.

It was dark inside, for a human that is, and they settled into one of the intimate booths. He ordered them drinks, a plate of nachos, and fried calamari. The girl needed some fattening.

Over the next hour, he coaxed her to tell him her story.

After graduating high school, Tiffany had packed her meager belongings and left her miserable childhood home in Alabama to pursue an acting career in Hollywood. She'd covered the distance mostly by hitchhiking and only occasionally taking a bus. She'd made it to the *promised land* two and a half months ago, and until her big break arrived, she was waitressing and sharing a two-bedroom apartment with four other girls. What she made at her part-time job paid her share of the rent with little left over for other necessities. She was dedicating most of her time to an endless parade of auditions for any part that was open to nonunion members—she couldn't afford the fees.

No wonder she was so skinny.

Poor Tiffany was in over her head. Sooner or later someone was going to take advantage of her naivety and youth. She wasn't exceptionally pretty, or smart. Girls like her weren't likely to get their big break.

By providing her with shelter and food, he'd probably be doing her a favor—and saving her a lot of heartbreak.

Kian

The blinking red light on the bedside phone was the first thing Kian saw when he cracked his eyes open the morning after his and Syssi's date.

Damn, I forgot to turn my cell phone back on.

Ignoring it, he rubbed his eyes and turned to his side. Syssi was snoring lightly beside him, nude save for the choker and the ring—a testament to last night's sexcapades. The poor thing had been too exhausted to take the jewelry off before falling asleep. He would have taken it off for her. Trouble was he'd passed out as well.

Syssi's stamina in bed had improved so dramatically since her transition that he had a nagging suspicion she was capable of outlasting him. But he'd be damned if he ever allowed this to happen. He'd keep on going until one of two things happened: either Syssi was done or he dropped dead.

Not a moment earlier.

He wrapped his arm around her and snuggled closer. Sleepily, she swept her voluminous hair to the side and over her shoulder, exposing her long neck. Kian frowned. There was a red indentation where the choker's clasp had been pressing into her skin. She shouldn't have slept with it on, must've been uncomfortable. In fact, it was probably dangerous. The thing was called a choker for a reason. He pinched the clasp open and gently removed it from Syssi's neck. The ring could stay.

"What time is it?" she rasped in her sexy morning voice.

"Seven fifteen."

Syssi bolted up and twisted to face him. "Really? We overslept?"

"Yep." He pulled her down to him and kissed her dry lips.

She covered her mouth with her hand and spoke through slightly splayed fingers. "How did it happen? And how come you're not freaking out?"

"I turned off my phone last night and forgot to turn it back on. And guess what? The keep is still standing, we are not under attack, and I feel damn good, relaxed." He kissed the fingers she was shielding her mouth with. "You're still obsessing about your morning breath? I told you it's all in your head, and even if it were bad, which it's not, I wouldn't mind. I'd rather kiss your mouth even when it's stinky, which it's not, than not kiss it at all."

She wiggled out of his arms and rolled off the bed, holding her hand in front of her mouth until she was a safe distance away. "I'm going to brush my teeth and get us something to drink. I'm thirsty." She disappeared into the bathroom.

With his excuse for not checking his messages gone, Kian picked up the receiver and punched the blinking button. There were a couple from Shai about rescheduling a meeting and one from William about some new equipment he wanted to order—as if he needed Kian's approval for that. He'd told the guy, countless times, to buy whatever he deemed necessary as long as it was within the budget allotted to him, and only to call if he ran out.

Kian suspected that William's calls were more about sharing his latest ideas than asking permission to spend money.

The last message was from Onegus.

"Eh, Kian, I know that you're out with Syssi, and I'd hate to ruin your date, that's why I'm leaving the message on your home phone instead of calling your cell phone. Steve from security called me. There is no way to sugarcoat it so, yeah, here goes. Amanda is back, and she moved in with the prisoner. She told Steve that from now on the cell apartment was going to be her residence and demanded that he cut the surveillance. He had no choice but to do as he was told because it is clearly stated in the bylaws that monitoring clan members' personal quarters is not allowed. I double-checked, and he is right, so there is nothing I can do about it either. It's up to you, tell me what you want to do."

Fuck, Amanda was one hell of a clever manipulator. But it was not going to help her with him. He would go down there and drag her out by her hair if need be. Playing house with a Doomer was not going to happen, not on his watch.

Kian was out of bed and in the bathroom before finishing his internal rant. Even Syssi's sumptuous naked butt, which was shaking enticingly as she brushed her teeth, failed to lighten his mood.

Syssi spat out the last of the toothpaste and wiped her mouth with a towel. "Why are you out of bed? I only wanted to freshen up and was coming back to you."

"Amanda is back." He grabbed his toothbrush and toothpaste. "Fuck!" He squeezed the tube too hard and a big blob landed in the sink. Struggling for control, he applied gentle pressure on his second try and got the right amount.

Syssi turned around and leaned against the counter, crossing her arms over her naked breasts. "You're not happy to have her back home?"

Kian spat out the paste. "She is down in the dungeon with that Doomer and has no intention of leaving anytime soon. She ordered security to cut surveillance to his cell."

Syssi was quiet for a moment. "Is it really so bad, Kian? Do you really believe he'll hurt her?"

"No, but that's beside the point and you know it." He wiped his face with a towel and headed for the closet to get dressed, hoping Syssi wouldn't follow. The last thing he wanted was to argue with her while he was fuming with rage.

The one who deserved his wrath was Amanda and not Syssi, but she was in the way.

Except, of course, she had to follow him. The girl had no sense whatsoever when her romantic ideas hijacked her otherwise sensible brain. In this, Syssi was the quintessential female.

"What are you going to do?" she asked.

"What do you think? I'm going to drag her out of there, lock her in her apartment, and reinstate the surveillance."

"You can't do this. She's a grown woman, and you can't behave like a caveman. What do you think is going to happen? You think you'll order her to get out and she'll meekly obey? Or are you planning on throwing her over your shoulder and carrying her up to her penthouse?"

Kian buttoned his jeans and grabbed a T-shirt off the shelf. "If she will not listen to reason, then yes, I have no problem with hauling her out of there caveman-style. I'm in charge of this keep, and everyone here answers to me, including the spoiled princess."

Syssi shook her head. "I can't believe how unreasonable you are. They are in love, Kian, let them be, for God's sake."

Slipping his feet into a pair of loafers, he turned around and pointed a finger at Syssi's chest. "Stay out of it, Syssi. I know you mean well, but I'm in no mood for silly arguments."

"Silly arguments?" She was the one fuming now. "You dare call me silly? When you're the one who is not thinking straight? What's wrong with you?"

"Nothing. This is who you're marrying, sweetheart. Deal with it." Kian was well aware that he was behaving like a monumental jerk, but he was too pissed off to control it. Why the hell was she antagonizing him? She should know him better by now.

"Maybe I shouldn't marry a man who was born in the Dark Ages and evidently has never left." Her voice quivered, and there was a sheen of tears in her eyes.

Damn! Kian gritted his teeth and summoned the last of his self-control, reaching for Syssi and pulling her into his arms. "I'm sorry, baby. Please, let's talk about it later, when I'm not so close to the edge."

Syssi's arms were still crossed over her chest, and she didn't return his hug, but her stiff shoulders relaxed a bit, and her voice was almost steady when she asked, "Don't you think it's also a good idea for you to calm down before confronting Amanda? You don't want to say or do something that you'll regret later."

"I'll try, that's all I can promise."

Syssi

The moment Kian had left, Syssi collapsed onto the wardrobe's footstool and let the tears flow freely. She felt disappointed and disillusioned. Once again, she had discovered that Kian wasn't all that she'd built him up to be.

He wasn't perfect, far from it.

The dominant alpha tendencies that she found so arousing in bed were annoying as hell outside of it. The man was a Neanderthal. Living by some outdated notion of a man's supposed authority over his family.

Question was, would she be able to live with them?

Did she have a choice?

Kian was the love of her life, warts and all. Perfect or imperfect, it didn't really matter. She loved the big arrogant jerk too much to even think of leaving.

She'd have to learn to deal with him and his heavy-handed attitude.

He'd hurt her feelings, though, big time. The dismissive manner in which he'd talked to her—as if she was some silly little girl, a pest. Where were his proclamations of appreciation for her intellect? Her common sense? Were they just empty compliments?

It certainly seemed like it. This morning, he'd showed her his real opinion of her, hadn't he?

Oh, I'm just overreacting, being melodramatic.

She needed to talk to somebody. But the only one she could confide in was Amanda, who, naturally, was otherwise engaged at the moment. True, Annani had promised to always have Syssi's back and box Kian's ears if he earned it, which he had, with interest, but running to Kian's mother every time she and Kian had a fight wasn't a good idea. Not in the slightest.

That left Andrew.

Oh, God, she needed to make more friends. Immortal female friends, so she could pour her heart out to someone other than Amanda without worrying about exposing the clan. Andrew loved her dearly, but he wouldn't understand, or worse, would get mad at Kian and initiate a fight. Who could predict how far men were willing to take their macho posturing and what idiotic things they might do?

Pulling on her soft yoga pants and a T-shirt, her comfort clothes, she plodded to the bedroom to get her phone.

She selected Andrew's name from her short list of favorites and waited patiently for him to pick up. Weird. Andrew almost always answered immediately, but this time, the phone kept ringing and ringing, and she was considering ending the call when he finally picked up.

"What's up, Syssi?"

"Nothing much, just wondered if you have a few minutes to shoot the breeze with your sister."

Andrew wasn't fooled by her casual tone. "I'm coming up. I'll be there in a minute. Start the coffee."

"What do you mean you're coming up? Are you here? In the building?" She glanced at the bedside clock. "At seven thirty in the morning?"

"I'll tell you all about it when I get there."

What the hell was Andrew doing in the keep so early? Even if Kian had called him, perhaps summoning him to help with Amanda's situation, Andrew couldn't have made it here so fast. He must've crashed at someone's apartment overnight.

But who? Had he befriended one of the Guardians?

That was the most reasonable explanation. He'd probably gone drinking with some of the guys, and they'd brought him here because he'd been too wasted to drive home. If Amanda was a typical example of an immortal's drinking capacity, then Andrew was no match for them in that department. No wonder he had gotten drunk. And that's why he wanted coffee.

Mystery solved.

Syssi went back to the closet for a pair of clogs, then headed for the kitchen.

The doorbell rang just as the machine finished brewing and began spewing little steaming jets into the two tall porcelain mugs Syssi had placed under the twin spouts.

She opened the door with a smile. "You're right on time. The coffee is ready."

"Good, I need it." Andrew followed her to the kitchen counter and pulled out a stool.

She chuckled. "I can imagine."

His brows lifted in surprise. "So you know?"

"About what?" She placed a mug in front of him and sat down.

"Me and Bridget."

"You went out drinking with Bridget?"

"Drinking? Why would you think that I went out to a bar? And with Bridget?"

"You said Bridget, not me. I thought you went out drinking with the guys and crashed in one of their apartments." She turned to him, and a small smile bloomed on her face. "Wait a minute, so if you went out with Bridget and then crashed at her place, does it mean what I think it means?"

"Yes, just minus the drinking part. Bridget invited me to dinner at her place, and I fell asleep."

Syssi snorted. "I bet the interesting part of the story happened in the interval between eating and falling asleep, you naughty boy." She slapped his shoulder. "I like Bridget, and I'm very happy for you."

"It's nothing serious, so please don't make a big fuss about it. I don't think Bridget wants to advertise our whatever it is. Anyway, I came up here to talk about you, not me. What's going on? And who do I need to beat up?"

"I had a fight with Kian."

"You want me to rough him up for you?"

"Why does everything have to end up with you beating up somebody? I just need someone to vent to, and you happen to be the only one available."

He made a sweeping motion with his hand. "Vent away, I'm all ears. But after you're done venting, my offer still stands."

"Fine." She took a few sips from her mug while Andrew finished his. "Last night, while Kian and I were out, Amanda came back."

"I know, I met her on my way to Bridget's."

"Did you know that she was planning on moving in with Dalhu in his dungeon apartment?"

"No, but good for her."

"That's what I think too, but obviously Kian doesn't. As soon as he heard about it, he wanted to storm out and head over there. I barely managed to get in a few words, trying to convince him to calm down before he went to talk to her. But I only succeeded in annoying him even more, and he told me to stay out of it, very dismissively, as if my opinion was irrelevant. And now I'm thinking that maybe I'm making a mistake marrying him. He made it very obvious that he doesn't see me as his equal. What kind of marriage will I have? The little wife who is expected to say 'yes, sir'? I can't live like that." She was getting more and more agitated as her rant went on, and, of course, the tears came as well.

Andrew laughed—out loud—and she had to fight the strong urge to take off one of her heavy wooden clogs and chuck it at his head.

"I'm sorry," he said. "It's just that you were spouting one nonsense after the other, and your face looked so pouty, it was comical." He took her hands, and she let him, even though he was infuriating.

"I'm not pouting."

"Yes, you are. Now listen, you know perfectly well that most of what you said is not true. Kian worships the ground you walk on, and his opinion of you is probably higher than what you deserve."

"Hey," she objected.

"You're a twenty-five-year-old woman, who is smart and compassionate and loving and the best person I know.

But, you cannot compare your life experience or your level of responsibility to Kian's. There will be times, probably many, that you'll have to defer to him and abide by his judgment. That being said, I'm sure there are many things that he can learn from you. In a good marriage, each partner contributes his or her strengths to the unit and trusts the other one to handle matters which he or she is more knowledgeable or is better equipped to deal with. It should be an equality of value, where one partner's contribution is deemed just as important as the other's. Both partners are equally valuable—but that doesn't mean that they have to share every responsibility equally. It doesn't make sense. It's like the CIA and the Air Force are both equally important, true? But pilots shouldn't go spying, and spies shouldn't go flying jet planes."

"In theory, you're absolutely right. But in real life, men used that same argument to excuse delegating inferior tasks to women, claiming that females were ill-suited to do this or that."

"All those mean, mean males. You girls should've gotten rid of us a long time ago," he mocked.

"Don't make fun of it, you know I'm right."

"I do. It's just that accusing Kian of misogyny is preposterous. His clan is headed by a woman."

"Yeah, I know." Syssi sighed and slumped her shoulders. "Here I am, feeling all sorry for myself when there is probably an all-out war going on down there. Maybe we should go and try to help. Amanda and Kian's relationship is already strained as it is, and I know Kian is going to make an even bigger mess of things."

"They are both big kids, and they'll figure it out. If not today, then tomorrow, or in a month, or a year from now. Putting yourself in the middle will only get you hurt."

Syssi chuckled as Andrew's argument evoked an image of Kian and Amanda as kids. Annani had been lucky to have them eons apart. Both were so hardheaded and stubborn that raising them together would've been a nightmare.

Suddenly, her vision blurred.

Oh no, here it comes.

It had been such a long time since her last premonition, but the sensation was unmistakable.

All outside stimuli receded. Vision, sound, smell, all of it was no longer there. A small swirl of intense bright color started filling the void, getting bigger and bigger until it completely filled her inner sight. Then it began to coalesce into a picture, or rather a movie—the image wasn't static.

It was a beautiful summer day in a park. Somewhere where the green was strong and vivid, the trees and the grass and everything that grew appeared healthy, like in Hawaii. Andrew and a little girl were the only ones there. He was tossing the giggling child up, or rather just pretending to throw her because his large hands never left her tiny waist, then pretending to catch her, sneaking hugs and kisses in between the tosses.

His daughter—Syssi had no doubt that the child in her vision was Andrew's—was a beautiful little girl. No more than two years old, she had long, thick dark hair that curled at the bottom, a rosebud of a mouth, and cheeks that were pink from exposure to the fresh air and from laughter. A perfect little girl. And Andrew looked so happy, the happiest she'd ever seen him.

The vision blurred, the child's laughter fading into the distance, and Syssi opened her eyes with a gasp.

"Are you okay?" Andrew was holding her shoulders with a worried look on his face.

"I'm fine. In fact, I'm better than fine." She smiled, but then her smile wilted when she reminded herself that her premonitions were mostly about impending disasters, and not about happy fathers and giggling daughters.

And yet, this time, it had been different. It had started the same as the others had, but then it had changed. And in the aftermath, she wasn't left with a dark cloud hanging over her head like with her other premonitions.

"What did you see?"

"You. And your little girl."

"My what?"

"Your daughter, Andrew. You're going to become the proud father of the most gorgeous and sweetest little girl."

Who was the mother, though? Was it Bridget? But the child had dark hair and a darker shade of skin than Bridget's white, translucent porcelain complexion. Maybe his daughter would take after Andrew, who was slightly darker than Syssi and had brown hair. Except, the girl's hair looked almost black, not brown. And even if Amanda were still a possibility for Andrew, her black hair wasn't her natural color. Amanda's real color was dark red like her mother's—and Bridget's.

A mystery.

"Are you sure? What exactly have you seen?"

"You and this little girl playing in a park."

"Maybe she was someone else's daughter? Like maybe yours?"

Not unless she ended up with a dark-haired husband instead of Kian. And that was not going to happen.

"No, she was yours."

"Damn."

Kian

At the last moment, Kian punched the button for the gym's level instead of the dungeon's. Syssi was right, he should calm down if he hoped to have a civilized talk with Amanda. Not that it was likely to happen, they'd probably end up tearing at each other's throats, but then he could at least tell Syssi that he had done his best.

The loafers weren't suited for running, but he could release steam by lifting weights almost as well as by running on a treadmill. He was not about to go back for gym shoes.

The prospect of seeing Syssi and her disapproving expression wasn't something he was ready to face.

Not yet.

Maybe later, when he could report to Syssi how civilized he had been with Amanda so she'd be proud of him again.

Fates help me. How am I going to achieve that?

Buckets of sweat, that's how. Maybe if he pushed himself to a level of exhaustion that drained all of his energy, negative and positive alike, he'd be able to pull it off.

"Kian, over here," Anandur called out.

Great, he was hoping for Yamanu as a lifting partner. Today he was in a mood that could only be satisfied on the bench, pressing some serious weight. Yamanu was perfect for that. But the guy was usually done with his routine by six in the morning, and it was almost eight now. The only two left in the gym were Anandur and Bhathian. The clown and the undertaker.

Reluctantly, Kian walked over to Anandur's lifting station. "I need someone to spot me on the bench, you volunteer?"

Anandur cast a quizzical glance at Kian's loafers. "Last minute change of heart?"

"You can say that. So? Are you going to assist or not?"

"You know I can't say no to you, *boss*." Anandur replaced the kettlebells he'd been training with on the rack and wiped his hands with a towel. "Lead the way."

Kian lay on the bench, adjusting his position until his arms were at the right angle to the bar. "I'll start with four hundred for the warm-up."

"On each side or total?"

"Total, you smart ass."

"Yes, boss."

Kian gripped the bar, tightening his hold to create more tension in his lower arms and chest, then tucked his elbows to his sides and unracked the weight. He held it for a moment before bringing it down to his chest, then drove his feet downward and reversed the movement.

"So, how did your date with Syssi go?" Anandur asked.

"Great, not that it's any of your business."

"I was just wondering why you look so pissed." He chuckled. "For a moment, I was harboring hope that Syssi had smartened up and broken off the engagement."

The bastard, taking advantage of Kian's compromised position. Joking aside, though, after this morning this wasn't such a far-fetched possibility. "You're lucky my hands are busy."

"That's what I was counting on. But seriously, what has gotten your panties in a wad?"

"As if you have to ask. I'm sure Amanda didn't get into the Doomer's cell by materializing through the door," Kian bit out.

"Aha..."

"Did you know that she intended to move in with him?"

"No, I didn't. Before kicking me out, she said she was going to stay overnight, which wasn't all that surprising, but I had no idea she was planning on playing house with the dude."

Bloody Anandur hadn't sounded bothered at all, talking about the incident as if it was just another piece of gossip. And what had he meant by *not surprising*?

"What made you think she'd want to stay the night?"

"Really? You want me to spell it out for you?"

"To scratch her itch, she could've fucked him and left. No need to stay."

Anandur sighed melodramatically. "You still refuse to face the facts. She is in love with the dude, it's not only about the sex."

"She is not in love with him. If she were, she wouldn't have left. Fates know that I wanted to do the right thing by Syssi and let her go before she transitioned, when I didn't believe that she would, but I couldn't."

"Are you done with the warm-up? Or do you want to continue with the light weight?"

"No, put another two hundred on."

"On each side or total?"

"Total, you moron."

"Hey, no need for name calling, it was a legitimate question. After a good warm-up, I press eight hundred."

Show-off.

"Good for you."

Anandur was silent for a moment, but Kian had no illusions about Anandur dropping the subject. The guy was a worse romantic sap than Syssi.

"I think Amanda is fighting it."

Yeah, Anandur was probably right. But it seemed that she was either making a half-assed effort or losing the battle.

"Not hard enough."

"It's like you couldn't resist Syssi. When it hits you, you're powerless against it, even if you know that it's not good for you or for the other person."

Damn, why is Anandur making sense?

"Well, if she is not strong enough to resist the pull, then I have to do it for her. There is no way in hell that I'll allow Amanda to shack up with a goddamned Doomer."

"If you want my honest opinion, I think you're being an ass about this."

"I don't."

Was he the only sane one in this place? Had they all lost their fucking minds? What were they expecting him to do? Welcome a murderer—a goddamned Doomer—into the family?

Amanda

Waking up next to a man in her bed felt weird, but in a good way. After more than two centuries of sleeping alone and having the bed all to herself, it was an adjustment to share the space with someone else—especially someone as big as Dalhu who was taking up most of it and hogging the blanket.

Though why he needed it was a mystery. The man was a furnace. Amanda snuggled closer to get warm.

Smooth skin over hard muscle—yum.

She ran a hand down his impressive pectoral then followed it with a kiss. Even after all their rigorous activity of last night, Dalhu's scent was still mouth-watering like that of a rich wine—distinctively his, with a hint of the simple Irish Spring soap he'd showered with the day before.

"Good morning." He wrapped an arm around her and started caressing her back, up and down, all the way to her butt.

"Is it? How can you tell time in here? There are no windows."

"Inner clock... and this." He showed her his wristwatch.

She kept caressing his chest, checking out every ridge and valley. "I must say, I'm surprised Kian didn't show up yet. I was expecting him barreling in a long time ago, breaking down the door in the middle of the night and giving me hell."

"Shh... let me enjoy this with you. We'll deal with him when the time comes."

"I don't know about you, but I'd rather be showered and dressed when he comes. One naked showdown is enough for a lifetime."

He chuckled. "You're right. Although I think you were absolutely majestic. I can't imagine any other woman, or man for that matter, who'd have the guts to confront a room full of gawking members of the opposite sex in a butt-naked, akimbo pose. You're one of a kind." He ducked his head and kissed her lips.

Well, hello... That featherlight touch was enough to ignite the hungry beast lurking inside her, and she grabbed his head, holding him in place for a proper kiss—one that involved tongues and teeth, and lasted until she ran out of breath.

"I thought you wanted to shower and dress," Dalhu hissed through fangs that were growing longer in front of her eyes.

Amanda wrapped her arms around him and pulled him on top of her. "This will only take a minute. I want you inside me—right now."

He smiled, the long, protruding fangs making him look positively evil, but his big brown eyes were soft—full of love. "Your wish is my command." He sank into her wet heat in one smooth slide.

"Ah..." She wanted to tell him *you say the nicest things,* but all that came out was a groan of pleasure.

Now, this was a fabulous way to wake up in the morning and start a day—none better—even if a quickie was all they had time for.

She clawed his ass and drew him closer—the small hurt spurring him on—and she felt him twitch inside her as he bucked between her thighs.

Soon, his thrusts were becoming frantic and his chest slick with perspiration—the sparse hair on it rubbing her aching nipples. He growled against her neck, and as she felt his hot breath on her skin, she willed him to bite her.

"Do it," she hissed.

"Not yet," he snarled and drove into her harder, faster, his powerful body a perfect male breeding-machine at peak performance.

Magnificent.

His grip on her shoulders was bruisingly rough, as he held her in place, but so were her claws on his glutes, urging him on to go deeper, harder. It didn't take long until she felt the start of an orgasm bearing down on her, building up momentum.

Her channel spasmed around Dalhu's pistoning shaft, and he swelled inside her, impossibly thick as he neared his own climax.

"Now!" she screamed, and he obeyed, his fangs sinking into her neck on a snarl.

She was pinned to the mattress by Dalhu's powerful arms, immobilized by his twin incisors burning deep in her flesh, and yet she flew, soaring on the wings of incomparable pleasure to a place where nothing but euphoria existed.

Sometime later, she felt herself being picked up, gently cradled in those powerful arms that just a few moments ago held her down with such uncompromising brutality. Only partially cognizant, she realized that Dalhu had carried her into the bathroom when he took her with him into the shower. He sat on the bench while still holding her in his arms, then, somehow, managed to manipulate the faucets with one hand while holding her with the other, and began washing her with infinite care.

So, that's how it felt to be taken care of.

Nice, real nice.

She could get used to that, like on a daily basis.

Come to think of it, from now on it would be Dalhu's job to wash her. Her personal bathing slave.

He did a great job, soaping and washing everywhere, except her hair, which she told him not to touch. Though, next time, definitely. By the time he was done, she was back to herself, but a peaceful, satisfied feeling still lingered—a side effect of the venom she was becoming pleasantly accustomed to. If Kian were hankering for a fight, he would be deeply disappointed. She'd be the epitome of clever diplomacy while he would look like a raving lunatic.

Sweet.

"Thank you, that was lovely." She kissed Dalhu's cheek.

"Just lovely? I was hoping for earth-shattering, incomparable..."

"I was talking about the shower, you nitwit." She kissed him again. "But the sex was indeed incomparable. Happy?"

"Except for being called a nitwit, yeah."

She examined his expression, but he was still smiling. "I'll stop if it bothers you. But I hope you know that I say it jokingly, right?" She shrugged and waved her hand. "It's like a term of endearment for me, I mean nothing by it."

Dalhu pulled her into his arms and kissed her forehead. "I know. And when it's just the two of us alone, I don't mind. But if you ever call me names in front of other people, I'll have no choice but to give you a spanking." He smacked her bare bottom.

"Kinky...," she purred.

He chuckled. "Do you remember the first time you accused me of being kinky?"

Amanda paused with the fresh thong she'd pulled out from her tote in hand. "No, when was that?"

"Right after I'd kidnapped you, I was afraid that you'd try to jump out of the moving vehicle, so I handcuffed you to the handle."

Frowning, she pulled her underwear on. "I remember the handcuffs, but only in the motel, when you thought securing me to the wooden bed's slatted headboard would keep me from getting away."

Dalhu buttoned his jeans and opened a drawer to pull out a fresh T-shirt. "It worked, though, didn't it?"

"Only because you drugged me."

He threaded his fingers through his short hair. "Yeah, I forgot about that. Sorry."

"Sorry that you forgot? Or sorry for doing it?"

"Both, I guess. Though I had no choice. I had no idea how strong you were, so I wasn't concerned about escape, but you would have screamed bloody murder the moment I was out of there."

"True." She shrugged and pulled out a brush and a makeup case from her tote.

As she passed him on her way to the bathroom, Dalhu glanced at her equipment. "I see that you came prepared." There was no mistaking the happy note in his tone.

"For one night. I wasn't planning on staying for good. That decision came later when I was talking to Steve." She leaned closer to the mirror to apply mascara.

Dalhu followed her inside, and she got a glimpse of him through the mirror, leaning against the doorjamb with his arms crossed over his chest.

The guy had amazing biceps.

Look away, Amanda, before you get your fresh thong wet.

She returned to her own reflection and applied a little lip stain, then ran a quick brush through her hair.

"You should bring more of your things. Unless you want to stay naked, which is fine with me, or you can borrow my T-shirts. Anandur brought me a generous supply."

"I'll have my butler bring down a few items at a time. The closet in here is tiny."

She retied the wrap dress for a snugger fit and slipped her feet into the low-heeled mules.

"By the way, what do you do for coffee? Do you have a coffeemaker here?"

"No, a short, weird-looking butler brings in my meals, each with a fresh thermos of coffee, and it usually lasts me until the next one. If I get thirsty in between, there is orange juice and Perrier in the bar fridge."

"That must be Okidu, Kian's butler. Let's go check if he left anything in the living room for us." Amanda collected her beauty supplies and put them back in their case before heading out to the other room.

"Yay, we have coffee," she enthused. "Come, sit next to me."

Dalhu joined her on the couch, and she poured them coffee from the thermos.

"How did he know to bring two cups?" Dalhu lifted the delicate porcelain cup with two thick fingers. It looked like a child's plaything in his hand. "And these are not the type of cups he gets for me. He knew that you were here."

"Of course." Amanda drank gratefully, then picked up a piece of toast from the tray.

"Did you tell him? Or was it Anandur?"

"No one has to tell Okidu anything. He figured it out the moment he opened the door and saw my purse on the coffee table. He must've gone back upstairs for what he considered appropriate for a lady."

"Aren't you bothered that he might have heard us while he was here?"

"Nope."

"Okay."

She would tell him the real story about Okidu and Onidu some other time; now she wanted to be done with breakfast before Kian showed up.

A girl had to have her priorities straight.

Sex first, shower and makeup second, food third. All the rest could wait.

Or not.

The mechanical buzz of the door's interior mechanism engaging was their only warning before Kian blew in like an angry storm descending on a cloudless, sunny day.

Anandur

"Just stay calm, okay, my man?" Anandur cautioned Kian one last time before punching the code to Dalhu's cell. Correction, Amanda and Dalhu's love nest—as the guest suite was going to be known from now on.

People in love were doing strange things for even stranger reasons. Like Kian refusing to go home and change from his sweat-saturated clothes because he was scared shitless of Syssi—a little thing who weighed maybe a hundred and twenty pounds and was as gentle as a dove.

Instead, the guy had showered at the gym and sent Anandur to get him some of Brundar's clothes—adamantly refusing to let Anandur go to his and Syssi's penthouse for his own. Again, for no good reason other than being scared of Syssi's scorn.

It was good that Kian hadn't asked for Anandur's. After donating a large portion of his wardrobe to Dalhu, he was already running low. Another trip to Walmart was unavoidable. It was either that or doing laundry.

Guess which was more likely to happen.

Kian took a deep breath, held it in, then released it in a slow stream through his mouth. "Just open the goddamned door," he barked.

So much for calming down—

Let the games begin.

As Anandur pushed open the door, he implored the Fates that he'd find the lovebirds out of bed and decently attired. Neither Kian nor Amanda would survive a repeat of what had happened in the cabin.

It was a huge relief to see the two seated on the couch—busy doing nothing naughty—enjoying a civilized breakfast.

With a quick glance at the ceiling, he mouthed a heartfelt thank-you to the heavenly Fates.

But then Amanda had to open her big mouth.

"Hello, Kian, and welcome to my new place of residence. Though, please knock next time you visit."

"As if you ever knock on my door before barging in—uninvited!"

"Duly noted, from now on I promise I will. Please take a seat, brother mine."

Oh, boy, she is pushing it. Not smart, girl. Not smart at all.

Surprisingly, Kian did as she asked and planted his butt in a chair. Anandur took the opportunity to sidle behind him and mime to Amanda to cut it out, then plonked himself in the other armchair.

"You can't stay here, Amanda." Kian served the first ball in the match.

"I don't see why not," Amanda countered.

Pity that it was too early in the morning for a drink because this was going to take a while and Anandur would have loved one. Hell, he was sure all of them could use one.

Eh, what the hell. "Drink, anyone?" He got up and opened the bar.

"I'll have whatever you're having." Apparently Kian shared his opinion.

"Dalhu? Amanda?"

"I'll have what you're having too," Dalhu said.

"Nothing for me, I'm fine with coffee," said the one with the biggest set of balls in the room.

Anandur poured three shots of whiskey, and after handing the guys their drinks returned to his chair.

Kian took a small sip and grimaced. "It's really too early for that." He lowered the glass to the table. "I hate beating around the bush, so I'm going to be blunt. There is no way in hell I'm going to allow you to stay here with the Doomer. Is that clear?"

"And there is no way I'm leaving. Is *that* clear?"

A strained moment of silence stretched between the siblings as they locked eyes, each trying to stare the other down.

Damn, this could take a very long time.

Neither was going to relent.

Luckily, a soft knock on the door saved the day. Expecting Okidu and a tray loaded with an assortment of munchies, Anandur got up and opened the door. But instead of the butler, he found Syssi and Andrew, and what was worse, no food.

"I thought we should be here," Syssi said.

"I'm with her." Andrew pointed to his sister.

Well, this was going to get even more interesting...

Because there wasn't enough drama to begin with...

Anandur let the door swing all the way for the newcomers to come in.

Syssi's hand flew to her chest. "Oh my God! This is amazing. You're so talented, Dalhu." She walked around the room touching the various portraits of Amanda, before settling next to her on the couch.

"Thank you."

"Impressive," Andrew mumbled as he drew out one of the dinette chairs and swung it around so it faced the couch.

After that, no one said a thing. Andrew cleared his throat a couple of times, and Syssi kept glancing at the pictures and shaking her head in wonder.

Kian was the first to break the silence, training his eyes first on Syssi and then on Andrew. "I don't know what you were hoping to achieve by coming down here, but if you thought you'd be able to pressure me into changing my mind, you should think again."

Andrew raised his hands, palms out. "I'm just an impartial observer. I came to prevent unnecessary bloodshed and provide my lie detector services—if needed."

"And I want to ensure that you guys are civil to each other, and maybe help negotiate a compromise," Syssi said so quietly it was almost a whisper.

Brave girl. It took guts, putting herself in the middle of a showdown between the warring siblings. And the only reason someone as gentle as her would volunteer to referee between the snarling beasts was her love for both Kian and Amanda.

Amanda wrapped her arm around Syssi's shoulder and gave it a light squeeze. "Thank you, but I can manage Kian on my own."

"No one is managing me. My word is final."

"Oh, yeah? You're not the boss of me." The professor threw out her preschool challenge.

"The last time I checked, I'm still the regent of this keep, and it is my job to ensure everyone's safety, including my spoiled, bratty sister." Kian was making a valiant effort to keep his tone in the human range, and not to snarl like a beast, probably on account of Syssi. But with the way his eyes were glowing and his words slurring he was fooling no one.

"I'm perfectly safe with Dalhu." Amanda crossed her arms over her chest and slumped back into the couch.

Kian opened his mouth to answer when Syssi stopped him by raising her hand.

"This back and forth hurling of meaningless statements and insults is going to achieve nothing other than widening the rift between you." She leveled her eyes first on Kian, then on Amanda, and then back on Kian. "I suggest that you state your case, one at a time and without interjections from the other. Amanda, you go first. Only when she's done, you'll have your turn, Kian. Agreed?" Syssi looked at Kian until he gave her a tight-lipped nod.

"Thank you," Amanda said.

"Just try to be less antagonistic, deal?" Syssi rested her hand on Amanda's thigh.

"I'll do my best." Amanda plastered a pleasant expression on her gorgeous face.

What a pity that Kian was immune to his sister's looks as well as her antics.

"I wish Dalhu's past was different, but it is what it is." Her face turned somber, and her tone lost its playful shade. "It wasn't easy for me to come to terms with it. His part in Mark's assassination, in particular, was a hard nugget to swallow. It has taken a lot of thinking and soul-searching for me to realize what my gut has known all along."

Her voice was almost a whisper. "Dalhu and I share a connection, a strong one." She glanced at the guy before returning her focus to Kian. "I don't know what it means yet, but I need to find out. If I don't, I'll spend the rest of my life wondering what if."

She chuckled. "Who am I kidding, other than a lock and key, there is no way I can stay away, even if I wanted to. The pull is too strong. I don't know if it has been decreed by the Fates or if it's nothing more than powerful immortal pheromones, but the fact remains that I need to be with Dalhu." She leaned forward and picked up her coffee mug, taking a few sips before returning it to the table.

To Kian's credit, he waited to see if she was done.

But she wasn't. "It's not only a compulsion, though. During the short time I've known Dalhu, he's shown me a side of himself that he's never shown anyone—not since his transition. He's been sheltering that vulnerable part of himself behind heavy armor, one he's been forced to erect in order to survive in the Doomers' camp. But the fact that he managed to keep the spark alive, and not let the darkness infiltrate and consume this last shred of his soul, proves, to me at least, that he is worthy, and that he should be given a chance to prove himself. After all, since

Dalhu has sworn allegiance to me, to us, he has demonstrated his commitment in every possible way."

Amanda took a deep breath and reached for Dalhu's hand. "Moving down here is the only solution I can think of. I know beyond a shadow of a doubt that Dalhu would never harm me or do anything to endanger the clan or me. But I understand that the rest of you are still wary of him, and I don't blame you. Therefore, even though I would've preferred for Dalhu to move into my comfortable penthouse, I'm willing to move down here and share with him this excruciatingly humble abode. I already asked Onidu to pack some of my things and bring them here. With the nonexistent closet space in this tiny apartment, my poor butler will have to schlep up and down every day." She harrumphed as if to emphasize the great sacrifice she was making.

In truth, though, for the princess to come slumming it in the dungeon it was probably a big one.

When no one said a thing, she announced, "That's it, I'm done."

"I kind of like the idea of a lock and key. I'd throw you in solitary confinement and wait for you to shake off the addiction. Tough love and all that, for your own good," Kian deadpanned.

If looks could kill, the dude would've been annihilated by the fury in Syssi's eyes.

Amanda emitted a deep throaty growl, something that sounded like a lioness readying for the kill.

Andrew shifted in his chair, probably getting ready to jump and defend Kian in case Amanda went for her brother's eyes.

The air in the room felt so dense that it could've been chopped into a salad, dressed with the bitter juices of resentment and garnished with a sprinkle of shredded nerves.

The knock on the door couldn't have been better timed.

Thank the merciful Fates for Okidu.

The snacks would provide a much-needed time out. And maybe chewing would help bring down the hostility.

Dalhu

Hanging by a thread, Dalhu barely managed to contain the rage from bubbling up to the surface. It was so fucking damn hard to refrain from punching something or at least clenching his fists.

But he couldn't afford even the slightest show of anger.

Regrettably, as much as he craved to get his hands on Kian and throttle the asshole, it wouldn't be in his best interest—rather counterproductive. The whole thing was resting on Amanda's ability to prove that he was harmless.

A wolf turned sheep.

And for her he was even willing to go "baa."

Her heartfelt speech had helped convince Syssi and Andrew, but it had done nothing to Kian. The jerk just wasn't willing to listen. Dalhu must've been deluding himself thinking that Kian's attitude toward him had improved.

That last nasty remark proved that nothing would ever change the guy's opinion. For Kian, a Doomer was a hell-spawned creature that could never rise above his origins.

A creature he would never allow his sister to be with.

Amanda wouldn't go down without a fight, though, and right now she seemed on the verge of losing it and attacking her brother, which would only serve to escalate the situation from bad to catastrophic.

Should he wrap his arm around her?

Prevent her from lunging at Kian?

A gentle knock saved him the trouble, providing a much-needed distraction. Anandur got up to admit whoever it was, and everyone's eyes followed him to the door.

"Clan mother…"

"I was wondering where all of you were," Annani said as she glided into the room.

Kian stood up and offered her his chair.

The Goddess glanced at the walls, and a smile spread across her face. "Such beautiful portraits of my daughter. I feel the love practically radiating from the drawings. Could I have one, Dalhu?"

"Of course, as many as you want. I can always make more."

"That would be wonderful. Maybe I should have you draw mine as well." She sat down in the chair Kian had vacated. "Thank you, dear."

"I'd be honored." Dalhu finally regained control of his voice.

Was he worthy of such honor? Not really, he wasn't that good, but he would do his best.

"I tried to phone you, Kian, as well as you, Amanda, but instead got only that annoying voice mail thing. Is there a reception problem down here in the lower levels?" she asked, then continued without waiting for an answer. "I had to contact security, and this nice young man, Steven I believe is his name, told me I could find you here, and that Andrew and Syssi were with you as well."

Kian grimaced, looking guilty as if his mother was accusing him of deliberately ignoring her phone calls.

Amanda's brows drew tightly together. "How could Steven have known that Syssi and Andrew were here? I told him to turn off the surveillance."

"And I told him to turn it back on as soon as I was informed of your shenanigans," Kian said.

Amanda jumped to her feet and pointed a finger at Kian's face. "So you think you are above the law? That it doesn't apply to you because you are the almighty regent? I declared this as my new residence, and last I checked, no surveillance is allowed inside clan members' private lodging. You can call Edna and verify this if your memory is faulty." Her voice had been getting louder and louder until she was practically shouting.

But Kian wasn't impressed. "My memory functions perfectly, sister mine, and if you had done your legal research thoroughly, you would've realized that when a clan member's safety is in jeopardy, issues of privacy can be overridden."

The smug look on Kian's face was begging for Dalhu's fist.

Amanda placed her hands on her hips and leaned forward so her face was inches away from her brother's. "Oh yeah? And who decides which situation qualifies as jeopardy? You?"

"Yes."

Exasperated, Amanda threw her hands in the air and turned to Annani. "That's just great. Our code of law needs a serious rewrite, Mother. We preach the virtues of democracy while practicing a convoluted form of constitutional triarchy, for lack of better definition."

Annani regarded her daughter coolly. "Sit down, Amanda." She waited until her command was obeyed and turned to Kian. "Do not look so self-satisfied, Kian, I have had it with your pigheaded attitude as well."

The Goddess waved her hand, and Dalhu felt a containment field snap into place. Smart move. There was no need for the guys in security to witness Annani admonishing her children.

The Goddess's intense gaze returned to Amanda. "Our code of law might need some small adjustments, but there is nothing fundamentally wrong with it or with the way we govern ourselves. We are not a country. We are a large family that is organized as a corporation because we also own a huge business conglomerate. Our clan members are treated as preferred stockholders who are entitled to a share of the profits but have no voting power. The main difference between us and other businesses is that we also hire our own shareholders for the higher up positions. Still, we do it based on their capabilities, not their popularity."

Amanda scoffed, "Do other corporations also police their shareholders?"

"I am sure they do so to enforce nondisclosure agreements and such. And, naturally, our unique situation dictates a deviation from the norm."

It seemed Amanda had exhausted her rebuttals. She slumped back, leaning slightly on Dalhu as if seeking comfort from his closeness. With a move that was guaranteed to infuriate Kian, Dalhu wrapped his arm around her shoulders and pulled her closer.

Let's see if the dickhead dares to say something derogatory in his mother's presence.

Annani waited for a moment, but when no one voiced an objection, she smiled magnanimously and continued. "Now that the legalities are cleared up, could you please tell me what the big fuss is all about, Amanda?"

Amanda perked up. "I want to be with Dalhu. I would like for him to move in with me, but if it's not possible"—she slanted a glare at Kian—"because some people are ultra paranoid, I would like to stay down here with him, and, naturally, I want the surveillance removed. There are enough cameras in the corridor outside this cell to assuage the fears of those who can see only the worst in people."

Brave behind her mother's protective shield, Amanda was once again goading her brother. Evidently, the smart professor wasn't a wise negotiator.

"I think this is a reasonable request. Kian? And please, try to be reasonable as well." Annani arched a brow in warning.

It was clear that the Goddess, bless her soul, was putting her little foot down, and Kian would be forced to accept the fact that Amanda was staying. But mindful of her son's position, Annani had left the door open for some negotiation.

Kian was a jerk and a hothead, but he was definitely not stupid. His mother's message wasn't lost on him.

"Fine, she can stay. But so does the surveillance."

"What?" Amanda blurted.

"Wait, I'm not finished. It's just a precaution. The recording will go straight to a dedicated server without anyone listening or watching—not unless there is a reason for alarm or something happens to you." Kian slanted a baleful look at Dalhu.

Annani beamed. "That sounds like a good compromise. You see? Amanda? Kian is being reasonable."

But Amanda didn't look happy. "Hold on. If you are insisting on cameras, then I see no reason why Dalhu can't come live with me in my penthouse. You can rig the whole place up to your heart's content, and we can live in the comfort of my apartment."

"That's a no, like a no way in hell."

"Why not? You can even have William put a cuff on Dalhu so you'll know where he is at all times."

"Not good enough. He'll still be able to communicate our location to his brethren. And even if you manage to convince me that the probability of him doing so is one in a million, I would still refuse to accept the risk. Too much is at stake."

"How about Edna giving Dalhu the probe? Like she did with me, see what's deep in his soul?" Syssi offered.

"And I can provide my humble services as a lie detector."

This was the second time Andrew had mentioned this. Was he a truth seeker? Dalhu had heard that one of Navuh's sons had the gift, but he thought it was just another piece of propaganda. Evidently, not this time.

"Please, Kian, just think about it. I'll be as much a prisoner in here as Dalhu. I'll have to get someone to open the door for me every time I want in or out."

"You'll survive. You should be grateful you're getting to stay at all."

"I know, and I am. But please, could you at least give it some thought? This is just a temporary solution—we can't stay here forever—you must realize that."

It broke Dalhu's heart to hear Amanda pleading, even though it was proving to be a better strategy when dealing with Kian than her previous attacks. The guy was guarded and hard to read, but Dalhu caught a slight whiff of guilt coming off him.

Maybe it was about time that he said something too. "What can I do to prove my loyalty? I'll do anything. Just tell me and I'll do it."

"Finish those goddamned profiles instead of wasting all your time on that"—he pointed to the walls—"and we'll pick it up from there."

"Consider it done."

Sebastian

Sebastian woke up a couple of minutes before his alarm went off—concerned about his little waitress. She was sleeping a heavily thralled slumber in the basement room he had locked her in last night, and he needed to go check on her. If he didn't wake her, she would keep on sleeping and might get dehydrated.

He needed to feed her too.

Last night, she'd attacked the nachos and calamari like she hadn't seen food in a week. Though why she would go hungry when working in a pastry shop was beyond him. Hadn't that lovely boss of hers realized that Tiffany wasn't eating enough? Had the girl been too embarrassed to ask for a pastry or a sandwich?

Ironic, that a sadist like him had noticed and cared about a girl going hungry while the righteous American citizen had turned a blind eye to what had been glaringly obvious and could've been easily fixed.

Sebastian chuckled. Yeah, he was such a benevolent soul. He would beat her mercilessly but make sure she was fed.

Well, not Tiffany necessarily, she wasn't his type, but some other hypothetical hungry girl. He'd give Tiffany to his men. But first, some elaborate thralling and major beautifying was in order. The guys would not appreciate a reluctant girl—except for the few who enjoyed rape—and none would be thrilled about a mousy thing like her.

First, he'd thrall her to believe that she'd been doing this for a while and was very happy with her job. Good pay or something to that effect. Then, when she was agreeable and cooperative, he would take her to a beauty salon and buy her some clothes. Come to think of it, she'd need makeup and hairbrushes and a lot of other things big and small.

Maybe his next victim should be a beautician; it would be great to have one in-house.

He was so smart. Two birds with one stone. He'd take Tiffany to a hair salon and come out with another girl for his basement.

Today and tomorrow, more men were scheduled to arrive, and he needed to fill those underground rooms as soon as possible. Regrettably, the online thing was not going to work. He'd gotten plenty of fish on his digital hook, but for some reason they were either successful career women or college students and none had fit the profile of a destitute, lonely girl. He would have to do it the old-fashioned way—one at a time.

The good news was that it was more fun; the bad news was that it was more time-consuming.

Hopefully, he would stumble upon one or two he could keep for himself. Better make it three, or even four. If he wanted to keep his stock healthy and enthusiastic, he needed to limit the wear and tear. Thralling and venom were great, but he knew from experience that they only went so far. Human females were too fragile, and eventually, not even the healing properties of venom could counteract the damage of repeated injuries.

A human girl could handle no more than two of his men in a twenty-four-hour period, and him no more than once a week, two at the most, and only if she was very resilient.

As he waited for the coffee to brew in the small kitchenette he had installed in his suite, Sebastian's thoughts wandered to the attorney. Now, that was a human he would've loved to have for himself. She was special, despite being neither young nor particularly attractive. But what she lacked in looks she made up in wit and stamina.

He wanted to play with her again.

Having her for himself was out of the question, but from time to time he could still schedule club assignations with her.

In between, he would have to settle for the peasants.

Kian

Kian's day had started shitty and had gone downhill from there.

First, the *lovely* message about Amanda, then, the blow up with Syssi, and lastly, his mother's intervention that forced his hand into allowing Amanda to shack up with the Doomer.

But wait, the day wasn't over yet. So it might not end at that.

Kian raked his fingers through his hair. He should go home and apologize to Syssi, but Bhathian and Onegus were keeping him in his office with reports he couldn't care less about.

"You should come to one of the self-defense classes," Onegus added at the end of his report. They were now running four of them a week, and soon they would need to double up because more and more people were joining every day.

All of a sudden everybody wanted to be a fucking warrior.

"I will, at some point, but don't expect it until after the wedding."

"Why? It's not as if the ladies need or want your help."

"I'm not sure about it. Syssi is going crazy, Amanda is no help at all because she is busy playing house with the Doomer, and we all know that my mother's idea of helping is giving advice and ordering everybody around."

He got a sympathetic look from Onegus. "So, go and help your girl instead of moping around."

"I will, right after I'm done here, as soon as you guys are done with the rest of your reports."

Bhathian rewarded him with a frown. "The sex-ed class went fine. From now on these boys are going to behave like perfect gentlemen."

"You threatened them with the whip."

"Naturally, after I explained everything that might be considered a sexual offense, of course, so there will be no misunderstandings." He crossed his arms over his chest.

"Good. What else?"

"That's it."

Thank the merciful Fates.

Shai took a look at Kian's face and expelled a defeated breath. "I know, take care of it or reschedule it. I already resort to pretending to be you when dealing with humans, but I can't pull it off with our people. And anyway, I'm supposed to be your assistant, not your CEO. I don't have the qualifications."

"Bullshit and you know it. You've been working with me for the past fifty years, and you have an eidetic memory. You can do my job no problem."

"No, I can't, and I don't want to. Too much responsibility and too much stress."

"You're telling me..."

Yeah, Kian didn't want the job either but was stuck with it. He got up and patted Shai's bony shoulder. Unlike the muscular Guardians, Shai was lanky, and his lifting routine was limited to hefty stacks of papers. "Did you join one of the self-defense classes?"

"No, you know I hate sweating."

"You should. In fact, I insist."

Shai grimaced as if Kian had ordered him to shovel manure. "With all the crap I have to do because you're busy with other things, I don't have the time or the energy."

"Fine, but after things return to normal, you're going."

"As if that's going to happen anytime soon."

Syssi

I hate it. I absolutely hate it.

Syssi looked at the sample centerpiece the florist had delivered, but she wasn't addressing the flower arrangement. It was beautiful. After almost despairing of finding a flower shop that would take on the project, she was thrilled when this one called that they had a cancellation. She hadn't even checked which one it was. As long as they delivered on time and the flowers were not completely wilted she was good.

She hated the tension between Kian and her.

It was killing her. She was of a mind to take a page from Amanda's book and just throw it all to hell and go away somewhere.

Let Kian plan his precious wedding by himself.

After the meeting in the dungeon, he'd stormed out and disappeared into his office.

No I'm-sorry-I-was-rude, no please-forgive-me, nothing. And the worst part was that she was already making excuses for him in her head. He was under a lot of stress. Amanda was driving him crazy. He hated Doomers... yada, yada, yada.

But the truth was that there was no excuse for the way he'd talked to her. And the only reason he'd allowed himself to act this way was because he'd known that she was a pushover and wouldn't retaliate.

God, was this whole wedding thing a mistake? With him acting like a jerk now, when theoretically she could still walk away, what would he be like after they were married? She let the tears flow freely and even allowed herself a couple of sobs before wiping her face with a kitchen paper towel.

Oh, please, stop being so dramatic. Kian wasn't a charmer before, he isn't now, and he isn't going to become one just because he loves me. But I know he loves me, and that's all that matters...

Still, for her own sense of worth, she had to make him pay for his behavior. Even if in the long run it achieved nothing—because come on, as if she had a chance in hell to change a guy that was nearly two thousand years old.

Question was, how?

Amanda would know the perfect payback.

I wonder if there really is a reception problem in the lower levels.

With William in charge, not likely, but on the other hand, she doubted that Kian and Amanda would have dared to ignore their mother's calls. Well, one way to find out. She selected Amanda's contact from the Favorites menu.

"I was just about to call you. Did you have one of your premonitions?" Amanda sounded like her old upbeat self again.

"In fact, I did, but not about you."

"Do tell..."

"Come up here and I will. If you can bear to part with your guy for a little bit."

Amanda chuckled. "I think I'll manage. Dalhu is busy with the profiles he promised Kian, and I feel guilty for abandoning you when you needed me most. I'll be there as soon as I get someone to open the door for me."

"I'll start the coffee."

Having Amanda back was such a tremendous relief, Syssi felt as if the boulder she had been carrying on her shoulders since the wedding plans had begun had lost at least half of its weight. Even her posture was markedly straighter and her step lighter as she headed toward the kitchen.

Amanda kept her promise to Kian and knocked on the door, except, she didn't wait to be admitted. Still, progress was progress.

"I owe you a big hug," she said, pulling Syssi into a bone-crushing embrace.

"It's good I don't break as easily now, or you would have cracked some ribs."

Amanda smiled as she drew out a stool and sat down, arranging her wrap dress so it didn't part. "I know. I was careful with you before, but it's no longer necessary."

"I love your dress."

"I'm glad you do. Anandur was giving me grief about it. He said it looked outdated."

"What does he know?"

"Exactly."

Syssi poured them both coffees. "I need you to use your devious mind for something." She took out the cream from the fridge and put it on the counter next to the sugar bowl.

"Oh, yeah? I'm all ears." Amanda perked up.

"Kian and I had a fight this morning, and he was really rude and dismissive toward me. I want to make him pay. Nothing big, just so he knows I don't forget and forgive that easily."

Stirring in a teaspoon of sugar, Amanda shrugged. "Easy, just don't have sex with him."

"And what? Punish myself? I was hoping for something clever, something original." Syssi made another trip to the fridge and pulled out a wedge of brie. "Cheese?"

"Sure. What have you been fighting about?"

It was a little awkward to admit that they had been fighting about her and Dalhu. But what the heck, there was no point trying to dance around it either.

"I tried to tell him to be reasonable and calm down, and he told me to mind my own business." The small plate with cut pieces of cheese clunked on the counter as Syssi let go of it instead of putting it down gently.

"Ouch... I think he deserves to sleep in the doghouse. I can send Onidu to get one, something big like for a Labrador, and we'll put it in your bedroom. After you have your way with him, just tell him to get in there."

Syssi snorted. "Yeah, like he would do as I say. Come on, Amanda, think of something devious, something he'll be forced to endure."

Amanda's eyes sparkled. "Oh, I have something. The word *endure* gave me a fabulous idea. Kian hates poetry, and he can't stand rap music. Download a playlist of this young kid, George Watsky. I saw him once on *Ellen*. He is a slam poet that raps. Just blast his stuff nonstop. If Kian complains, tell him it relaxes you when you're upset. That way he'll know he'll have to endure slam poetry every time he behaves like a jerk."

Spoken like a true master.

Syssi bowed her head in mock reverence. Well, not mock, this was brilliant. "I'm humbled by your genius, Sensei."

"I'm good, aren't I?"

"The best. And I happen to like slam poetry."

"Perfect. Now that this is settled, tell me about your vision. I'm dying to find out who it was about."

Syssi hesitated for a moment. Was it okay for her to share this with Amanda? Would Andrew mind? But now that she'd blurted it out, there was no way Amanda would let it go.

"It was about Andrew."

"Go on..." Amanda waved her hand in a circular motion.

"I saw him playing with a little girl in a park, tossing her up and catching her, then kissing and hugging her to him before tossing her up again. I knew without a shadow of a doubt that I was seeing him with his daughter."

"Was the girl a redhead?"

"So, you know about him and Bridget?"

"Yeah, he was on his way to her place when I came back yesterday, and he told me. So, was she?"

"No, she had dark brown hair, almost black. It was long and the strands curled at the bottom—very thick and lustrous for a small child. She was such a beautiful little girl, all giggles and smiling large eyes. They looked so happy together, I really hope this was a true vision." She sighed.

"I wonder who the mother is, or will be. Do you have a clue?"

Syssi took a sip of her coffee and concentrated for a moment, hoping her precognition would fire a clue. But no. "No idea."

"There is a pattern going on here. Everybody is hooking up. You with Kian, me with Dalhu, Kri with Michael, and now Andrew with some mystery woman that is probably not Bridget. By the way, what's going on with Michael and Kri, any new developments I should be aware of?"

"Michael is training with the Guardians, but Kri is pressuring him to go back to school. Oh, and they moved in together."

Amanda clapped her hands. "That's wonderful!" She grabbed her purse and pulled out her phone. "I'm going to call Kri and tell her to hop over, if she isn't busy with some Guardian business, that is." Her finger hovered over the phone's display. "How rude of me, I didn't ask if it's okay with you."

"Of course it is, anytime."

Amanda finished her text and put her phone down on the counter. "I'm going back to work on Monday. I guess I shouldn't expect you until after the wedding?"

"You guess right. And even after, I need to see what Kian wants to do. There was some talk about me helping him in the office. So we'll see."

Amanda scoffed. "Nonsense, he can get plenty of people with office skills to help him, but I have only one seer. You're coming back to work with me."

"Please, I don't want to discuss it now, I have enough on my plate as it is. We'll talk after the wedding. I still have to call my parents and need to preserve all of my cognitive power for the talk with my mother." Syssi grimaced.

"I'm glad you decided to invite them."

"Yeah, I don't know what I've been thinking. Evidently, stress makes me stupid. Of course I have to invite them, they would've never forgiven me if I got married without them. Though I'm sure my mom will refuse to believe that I'm rushing to the altar for any reason other than pregnancy. I even dreamt that she dragged me straight from the wedding, in my big white dress, to see a gynecologist, and I'm sitting in the waiting room with everybody staring at me, ugh." She shivered.

"That reminds me, Joanne said the dress designs are ready, and we should hurry up and pick one. I was thinking, though, that we should order all of them and do a fitting to see which one looks best on you. There is only so much you can discern from a drawing."

Nice try, Amanda.

"Forget it, I'm going to get my laptop and we are going to choose one."

"Party pooper."

Andrew

Andrew was the first to arrive at Barney's, despite the fact that he and Tim had left the office at the same time. He secured a quiet table at the very back, under a good light fixture, so Tim would have enough illumination for his sketching.

Not that the guy had to have good light to do what he did. Drawing from verbal descriptions, Tim could probably do it blindfolded.

The table wasn't next to a window, which was a disadvantage, but at least he had an unobstructed view of the front door.

At quarter to seven, Barney's lunch crowd had already come and gone, while the late-evening customers were only starting to trickle in. A couple in their early thirties sat at a table near the front, each with a phone in hand, communicating with someone unseen while ignoring each other. Sad, but at least they were quiet.

The same could not have been said about the two guys sitting at the bar. The idiots were watching a rerun of a football game and hollering their encouragements at the screen. The thing was mounted above the display cabinet, and the colorful drink bottles seemed to rattle in response. They were obnoxiously loud, especially the one with the red baseball cap.

Ignoring the raucous cries, the bartender was busy eyeing the red cap's tats, which were prominently displayed on his biceps. The thing was, Andrew wasn't sure what she was more fascinated by—the guy's muscles or the tattoos.

Probably the tats.

The girl had one on her neck that went down to her shoulders and around her arms, disappearing behind the skimpy little shirt covering her back.

Andrew grimaced. As a soldier, it was almost a requirement to have a tattoo, and he wasn't an exception. He had a small one of a white phoenix on his upper arm—his old unit's emblem.

It wasn't showy, and those who examined it closely thought that it wasn't finished—because while most of the bird's feathers were solid, two were only outlined.

He never bothered to explain. It was nobody's business that he prayed every day that he never had to fill those—because it meant that the two remaining men from his unit were still alive.

He didn't want or need the pitying looks.

This wasn't about making a statement—this was about carrying his private memorial on his person.

Andrew glanced again at the bartender and her wallpaper designs. What a shame that a pretty girl like her had tarnished her young healthy skin with gaudy drawings. She must've believed they were attractive. Maybe to the baseball-cap guy they were, but Andrew didn't like them on a woman, at least not that extensive. Something small and inconspicuous was okay, even sexy—something only a lover would see—but not this.

And if it meant that he was a chauvinist, so be it. If he ever had a daughter, he would never allow her to do such a thing. Heck, he wouldn't allow a son to look like a walking cartoon either.

If he had a daughter...

According to Syssi he was going to. Surprisingly, the thought wasn't as scary as he would've expected it to be. He was more apprehensive about the prospect of a wife.

Could it be Bridget?

The girl in Syssi's vision had dark hair, but then red hair was a recessive gene.

Problem was, he didn't feel it.

Bridget was an amazing woman—smart, beautiful, funny, sexy, not to mention a hellcat in bed. He liked her, a lot, but the feeling was too damned similar to what he'd felt for Susanna—just a friend with benefits.

Perhaps it wasn't in him to love passionately—the way Kian and Syssi loved each other, or even Amanda and Dalhu. He wished he knew that for a fact, because if he accepted that there was no one special in his future, he would've proposed to Bridget in a heartbeat. She was as good as it was going to get, and he could envision himself spending his life with her.

It could be nice, comfortable.

It should've been enough. In fact, it was probably more than most folks got out of a marriage, but his gut wasn't in agreement. It rebelled against the idea. And frankly, Bridget would've probably said thank you, but no, because she didn't feel it either.

For both of them it was just a temporary thing—a pleasant pastime—just until the right one appeared in a glowing beam of celestial light with angels singing in heavenly harmony to announce the arrival.

Andrew chuckled. Hell, if he was going for a fantasy then why not go all the way? True?

He took a swig from his beer, then ate a few peanuts, and glanced at his watch. It was seven on the dot. He waved the waiter over and ordered a pizza.

Bhathian walked in a few minutes later.

"I'm not late, am I?" The guy frowned and glanced at the phone he was holding in his hand.

"No, you're not. My office is a short drive away, and I didn't have to battle traffic to get here. Beer?"

"Sure." Bhathian planted his butt in the chair, his bulk dwarfing the thing.

Andrew signaled the waiter and ordered two beers.

"Pizza is on the way, you want something else?"

"No." Bhathian eyed the almost empty bowl of peanuts. "Maybe more of those." He pointed.

They waited until the waiter brought the beers, then waited some more.

"Tim will be here shortly. If not, I'm going to break his fingers."

"Yeah," Bhathian concurred without a smile.

Had he taken Andrew seriously? It was hard to know what he was thinking or feeling. By now, Andrew had noticed that there were slight nuances to the guy's perpetual frown, but he still couldn't decipher their meanings.

Waiting, they took turns with the beers and the nuts until Tim finally showed up—a sketchpad under one arm and various pencils sticking out from his dirty shirt pocket.

"Tim." He offered his hand to Bhathian but then withdrew it quickly when the guy's huge paw made an appearance. "Sorry, my man, but I need these beauties in good working shape." He wiggled his slender fingers. "I don't let them anywhere near dangerous equipment, and that hand of yours should be classified as such." Tim sat down across from Andrew.

"That's okay." Bhathian managed something resembling a smile—more like a grimace—in a weak attempt to put Tim at ease.

The thing with Tim was, though, that the guy only looked small and harmless but was a real bastard who didn't know the meaning of fear. He carried a nine millimeter and was incredibly fast with it. Rumor was that he'd been a sniper in the army before retiring and changing careers.

Tim flipped through his drawing pad to an empty page and pulled out one of the pencils from his pocket. "When is the pizza coming?"

"Should be ready any minute now."

"Good, I'm hungry. And get me a beer, will you?"

Andrew gritted his teeth and waved the waiter over. "Beer for my friend, *please*." Putting an emphasis on the please, he cast Tim a hard glance.

"Yeah, you can shove it." Tim flipped him off and turned toward Bhathian. "We'll start with the eyes."

An hour later Tim was done...with the pizza and the nachos and the third bottle of beer but not with the sketch. Bhathian kept shaking his head and trying to put into words what he saw in his head.

"Look, dude, I'm not a mind reader. I can't draw it if you can't verbalize it." Tim wasn't shy about expressing his impatience.

"The nose, it's too wide, and the lips, the bottom one should be a little plumper than the top one..."

Before, it was that the nose was too narrow and the lips too full. Andrew had a feeling that Bhathian didn't remember the woman as well as he thought he did. Or maybe he just had a tough time with descriptions.

In any case, he decided they could manage without him, at least for a little while, and excused himself to call Syssi.

"Hey, how are you holding up?" he asked.

"I'm good, what's up?"

"Nothing, you were upset this morning, and I wanted to see if you sweethearts kissed and made up."

"Not yet, but I talked to Mom." She said it as if it was a monumental achievement. "I invited them to the wedding. At first, she thought I was pranking her, as if I would ever, then she asked if I'm pregnant. But they are coming. I think that she agreed so readily to drop everything and come was because she was hoping to stop me from making a mistake. When I explained the travel arrangements, Mom realized that Kian isn't some schmuck that I just met, but someone with impressive resources, so she was somewhat mollified. But I still expect her to give me grief about it."

"Don't worry, I'll keep them occupied. What are you going to tell them when they start noticing the abnormalities?"

"I'm going to tell them the truth, and have Kian thrall that portion of their memory before they go home. I'll tell them, of course, that we are going to do it. "

Syssi was deluding herself if she thought their mother would agree to someone messing with her head. Their father was chill and would have no problem with it. Hell, he'd probably ask Kian to erase some of the things he didn't want to remember.

"It's not going to be easy."

"Tell me about it, but what other choice do I have?"

Amanda

"Can you take a break? You've been working on these profiles since morning. I'm bored." Amanda eyed Dalhu's sketchpad. Done with the written profiles, he was now working on the portraits.

"I'll just finish this one." The furious scratching of pencil on paper intensified.

Amanda sighed. "Would you like something to drink? Eat?"

He lifted his head from the pad and glanced at his untouched dinner plate. It had gone cold more than an hour ago. "A drink would be nice, thank you." The scratching resumed.

Men. What was it about testosterone and disregarding basic needs—like nourishment and sex—for the sake of completing a task? It wasn't as if she had no work to finish, but whatever wasn't done by dinnertime could wait for tomorrow.

Amanda made herself a margarita and poured Lagavulin for Dalhu.

He reached for the drink without looking, took a gulp, and put it down on the coffee table.

"You know, for someone who was supposedly so desperate for my company, you're very neglectful."

That got his attention, his head snapped up, and he wiped his forehead with a dirty hand. "I'm sorry, but you heard Kian. I need to finish this thing for him."

Poor guy, once a soldier always a soldier. Dalhu hadn't realized yet that military rules no longer applied to him, and Kian's request didn't have to be obeyed to the letter, at least as far as the time frame for completion.

"Darling, Kian is not expecting you to deliver everything by tomorrow morning. There is no real urgency. It's not like he is planning an offensive. It's just information for the sake of information. For future use."

Dalhu still didn't look convinced, but he glanced at the plate again.

"Go wash your hands. I'll warm it up for you."

"Okay." He lowered the drawing pad to the floor, leaning it against the couch's side before heading to the bathroom.

She called after him, "And wash your face too, you have charcoal smeared all over your forehead."

While Dalhu had been busy, Amanda had not only gone over her lectures for the coming week but had also arranged for some necessary improvements to their apartment and had ordered crucial supplies—like a margarita mix.

The bar's counter now sported two new appliances—a microwave oven and a Nespresso coffeemaker.

If she was going to play house with Dalhu, she needed things that were easy to operate. Both appliances required no more skill than sticking something inside them and pressing a button—perfect for someone with a severe domestic disability.

A minute and a half later, the microwave beeped, and Dalhu came back, clean and smelling of cologne. She put the plate down on the round dining table and refilled his drink.

"Thank you." He pulled out a chair and sat down.

Watching him eat, she was reminded of their time in the cabin. He was a quick and messy eater, but she found it sexy rather than offensive.

"Do you always attack your food like this? Or only when you're hungry?"

Dalhu paused with the fork a few inches from his mouth and looked down at the mess he'd made. "I'm sorry. I'll clean it up." He put his fork down and started brushing crumbs off the table and into his cupped hand.

"Leave it, my intention wasn't to comment on your table manners. I was just curious."

"No, I need to learn to slow down." He cleaned the last of the crumbs, but instead of throwing them in the trash, he put them in his mouth.

When she arched a brow, he mumbled, "What? The table is clean."

"Do you remember how you told me to be myself and not censor what I say in front of you?"

He nodded.

"I want the same from you. Just be yourself. And if you want to change something, do it because you want to, not because you think I expect you to."

He grinned. "Do you know that I love you?"

"Yeah, I do." Avoiding Dalhu's eyes, Amanda lifted the margarita glass to her lips. She wasn't ready to say it back, not yet.

"What will it take? I'm willing to do anything, just tell me."

There was no point in pretending that she didn't know what he was talking about. "I don't know. Let's just take it one day at a time and see how it goes. I can't promise you anything more."

"How about a deadly challenge? Would that help? A chance for redemption, like in the old days—when fighting lions bare-handed or competing in an arena could atone for a crime and wipe the slate clean."

"That's barbaric." So why did some vengeful and bloodthirsty part of her quicken to the idea?

You're so bad, Amanda.

"It is, but it's better than this eternal damnation. I'd much rather rise to the challenge and get it over with than endlessly squirm like a maggot."

"You're such a male, and I don't mean it as a compliment. You guys are all morons. You think that everything can be solved with either violence or sex."

Dalhu smirked. "That's right, we prefer the simple, quick, and efficient, over the complicated and drawn out."

"I'll never understand the way men think. Take Alex for example—"

"Who's Alex?" Dalhu tensed, probably thinking she was talking about an ex-lover.

She waved a dismissive hand. "He's family. Anyway, he runs a successful nightclub, and he just bought this super expensive boat. But whom did he hire to run it? A bunch of unpleasant, ex-mud-wrestling Russian females. It makes no sense to spend so much money on a yacht and then try to save on wages. They are so unfriendly that he never even invites anybody onboard to show it off. I just don't get it."

Dalhu shrugged. "It's obvious. He's not using the boat for pleasure. He's smuggling something."

"That's what I thought. When I left here"—she cast him an apologetic look—"I needed some place quiet to think, and I asked Alex if I could borrow his boat. He wasn't too ecstatic about it, but he didn't protest too much either. He lent me the use of the yacht and her strange crew. Things didn't add up, so I went snooping around, but I could find no evidence of any illegal activity."

Except for the closet.

Amanda frowned. "There was just this weird thing in the master cabin's walk-in closet. It had a false wall, and behind it were very deep shelves." She spread her arms to show the size. "I sniffed for drug residue—because that's the first thing that came to mind as a potentially illegal activity—but all I could detect were very faint traces of female products. You know, shampoos and perfumes. But there was no trace of emotions. I assume that the shelves were used for storing female clothing—which makes sense—considering that it's a closet. But then, why section it off? And why install a fake partition?"

Dalhu grimaced. "I'm sorry to break it to you, but your relative is smuggling females."

"Look, I know my sense of smell is not as good as yours, but I gave it several good sniffs and detected no residual scents of emotions. If at any point in time people were hiding there, I would have found traces of fear, or anticipation, or even boredom, but there was nothing."

"There would be nothing if he thralled them into a deep sleep before stashing them in there."

The implications of what Dalhu was saying were starting to sink in, but they were too horrible to accept. "Maybe he is smuggling illegal immigrants?"

"Get real. He is trafficking sex slaves. I've seen enough young women arrive at the island in a thralled stupor. Think about it, it's so much easier to transport them like this."

"Shit, how could I have been so stupid? It's so damn obvious."

Dalhu shrugged. "You've led a sheltered life. You hear about things like this but think they happen in some faraway place to some backward people and have nothing to do with you. The last thing you want to acknowledge is that it's not only happening in your backyard, but that someone you know is doing it. People are very good at putting on blinders."

Like she had done with him. In the back of her mind, she'd been well aware of the connection between Dalhu and Mark's murder, but she'd refused to acknowledge it.

Shit, she had done the same thing with Alex.

"I need to tell Kian."

Kian

Stretching like a satisfied cat, Syssi purred, "Make-up sex is the best."

It had taken Kian a good amount of groveling and artful seducing before she had agreed to forgive him, but it was worth it. The sex had been indeed mind-blowing. But more importantly, the uncomfortable gnawing sensation he'd had in his stomach since morning was gone, replaced by the glorious state of peacefulness that holding Syssi in his arms brought about.

He snuggled close behind her and closed his eyes. "I love you, kitten."

"Is this my new nickname?"

"Yes."

"I like it. I love you too, tiger."

Kian chuckled. "Tiger, I can live with that."

His phone buzzed. "What now?"

Syssi was closer to the damned thing, and she stretched to retrieve it. "Here you go." She handed it to him.

"Amanda? What the hell does she want?"

"Be nice." Syssi slapped his arm.

He touched the screen and brought the phone to his ear. "I'm in bed, is this important?" He managed a civil tone.

"Yeah, I think it is. Would you mind coming down here?"

Amanda didn't sound like herself, she sounded troubled, even distraught. Which, considering the fact that even their recent battles hadn't managed to rattle her, was cause for alarm.

"What happened? Are you okay?" Funny how all his animosity toward her evaporated the moment worry settled in. Behind him, Syssi sat up in bed and leaned against his back to listen in.

"I'm fine. It's not about me. But I think you were right about Alex. Though if my suspicions are correct, you've underestimated the severity of his crimes."

Hallelujah, how long had he been telling her that Alex was a scumbag? "I'm getting dressed. I'll be there in a few minutes."

"Can I come?" Syssi asked.

"Of course, what kind of a question is that?"

"Well, I don't want to be told that it's none of my business."

"You're not going to let me forget it, are you?" And here he thought that he'd been forgiven.

"Nope." She followed him into the shower.

He turned on the spray heads, the overhead one for himself and the handheld for Syssi. "How long are you going to lay the guilt trip on me?"

"You should be thankful that I decided against Amanda's idea." Syssi adjusted the setting of the spray and grabbed the soap.

"Oh, yeah? And what was her sage advice?"

"To blast slam poetry rap and annoy the hell out of you."

"That woman is evil and has a twisted sense of humor. So what happened, couldn't find any?"

Syssi chuckled. "I found it all right, but Amanda forgot to mention the amount of cussing in the guy's lyrics. I couldn't stand it myself."

"Thank the merciful Fates."

Dalhu

"Unbelievable." Syssi shuddered.

Listening as Amanda recounted the last part of her story, the girl must've grown dizzy from shaking her head so much.

Before, while Amanda had entertained them with tales of her escapades with the Russian crew of former mud-wrestlers, Kian had chuckled a couple of times, but now he looked ready to commit murder.

Not that Dalhu disapproved. For a change, he was in full agreement with the guy.

There was no worse scum on earth than slavers, especially those who trafficked in girls and women—kidnapping and selling them into sexual slavery.

"If we can prove it, I'm going to have the large assembly vote on a sentence of entombment," Kian growled.

"That's too mild for a maggot like that. He needs killing," Dalhu blurted before considering that his opinion wasn't welcomed.

Kian's answer was surprisingly amiable. "I wish I could, but my hands are tied. Our law doesn't allow it." Evidently, at the moment all of his hostility was directed toward his own clansman, while Dalhu's status had been downgraded to the role of a lesser evil.

And rightfully so.

Compared to this Alex, Dalhu was a good guy, or at least tolerable as far as Kian was concerned.

Encouraged, he took it further. "I'll gladly do the dirty work for you—you don't have to soil your hands."

Kian shook his head. "Suspicions are one thing and proof another. First, we need evidence, and then he'll stand trial."

"What if you can't prove it?" Dalhu pushed.

"Then the bastard lives."

The clan and its lofty, but misguided, ideas of due process. Protecting the rights of murderers, rapists, and slavers came at a price—which was paid out from their victims' hides.

The thing was, once identified, filth like that should be cleansed in a timely fashion—before it had a chance to cause even more damage. Dalhu would rather have taken care of business right away, trading, in a heartbeat, the occasional mistakenly accused for the lives saved.

Unfortunately, now and for the foreseeable future, he was relegated to the peanut gallery.

"You could have the yacht watched," Syssi offered.

Amanda shook her head. "I still think our best bet is to get the Russians to talk. I suspect that at least one of them is troubled by what's going on and might be persuaded to talk. Let's face it, even if Alex brings a bunch of girls onboard, it doesn't mean that he plans to kidnap them. It proves nothing. If he makes the delivery out at sea, how are we going to catch him in the act?"

"But if he returns without them, isn't it proof enough?"

"He can always claim that he'd dropped them off somewhere." Kian took Syssi's hand and patted it.

"Why go to all this trouble and let the maggot get away with more trade while you're playing by the rules? My offer to off him still stands. It will be my pleasure, and it will give me something to do." Dalhu could feel his hands twitch with the need to kill.

Damn, he'd thought that he was better than that—that the killings he'd done were just part of a despised job. So why was he suddenly craving it like a goddamned addict?

Kian got up and walked up to a wall, his nose almost touching one of Amanda's portraits. "What's the matter, Doomer? Drawing not satisfying enough?" The sarcasm in his tone indicated that he knew exactly what was going on in Dalhu's head.

He needed to think about his answer carefully. "I like drawing, but it's only a hobby, something to pass the time while I'm locked down here. But I'm a warrior, not a fairy. I prefer doing a man's job."

Amanda cringed and shifted away from him.

Fuck, he was such an idiot.

The programmer had been gay.

"I'm sorry, I really should get whipped bloody, if not for my crimes then for my idiocy."

Kian perked up.

Syssi cringed.

Amanda snorted. "Only if I get to do the whipping in a dominatrix outfit. Thigh-high boots, leather bustier—the works."

She is joking, right? And if she is, does it mean that she's softening up?

He inclined his head in mock submission. "It would be my pleasure to humbly submit to your whip, mistress."

"Oh, you say the nicest things."

Amanda

"What did you think about Kian's idea with the drone?" Amanda asked after Kian and Syssi had left.

Dalhu shrugged. "I don't know. I'm not a techie. In theory, it sounds good. The military uses them to spy on whatever and whoever, so if Kian gets his hands on a long range one, he can have it follow that boat out to sea."

Amanda sighed. "I wish I were wrong about this whole thing and Alex would be proven innocent. Well, at least of this offense. I almost hope we'll catch him selling drugs. As morally wrong as that is, it's not as bad as selling women."

"How about we change the subject? I can think of a much more pleasant use of our time." His smirk had sex written all over it.

"Oh, yeah? Like what?"

"I'll show you." He pulled her hand and placed it over his shaft. "I've been this hard ever since you mentioned that dominatrix outfit. I couldn't stop thinking about you in it."

Kinky Dalhu. "Should I look for a whip?"

His shaft twitched. "Do you want to?"

Did she? No.

Playing a dominatrix was one thing, but inflicting real pain was another. "No, but we can play." She leaned to nuzzle his neck, closing her eyes as his masculine scent filled her nostrils. "I can dress the part, tie you up, and torture you without damaging the goods."

"Your wish is my command."

Every time he said these words, her heart gave a little flutter. *My own as-you-wish guy.*

"Give me a minute, then go to the bedroom, remove your clothes, and wait for me in bed."

"Yes, mistress."

Grabbing the few items she needed from the closet, she ducked into the bathroom.

Once she was done, Amanda admired the results in the mirrored wall. *Damn, I look so hot I'm turning myself on.*

Dalhu was going to climax as soon as he saw her.

Thigh-high black stockings were held in place by a tiny, lacy garter. And the sheer, even tinier black thong was more of a decoration than an attempt to cover anything. The bra was an ingenious contraption that provided a little boost to her smallish breasts but left her nipples exposed. She'd painted a thick black line around her eyes and a blood-red rouge on her lips. With no boots to complete her outfit, she settled for a pair of black, four-inch stilettos that worked just as well if not better to make her legs look fabulous.

As Amanda opened the door and sauntered into the bedroom, Dalhu's indrawn breath was followed by an outpour of male pheromones enough to saturate a stadium let alone the small room, and a flagpole of an Olympian standard.

"Fuck, Amanda, it's good that I'm immortal or my heart would've stopped from lack of blood supply. It's all down in my cock."

So sweet, the man had a way with words.

But right now he needed to shut up. "Did I give you permission to speak?" She did her best to sound stern, stifling up the giggles that were threatening to ruin the game.

"No, mistress, my apologies." Dalhu's lips twitched, but he managed to keep a straight face.

As she turned to the dresser to get some nylon stockings to use as bonds, flashing Dalhu her bare derrière, she heard him take another hissed breath. Poor guy, at this rate he was going to asphyxiate.

"Spread your arms and your legs," she commanded.

He did, and she tied each appendage to a bedpost. The stockings were perfect bondage material, strong but flexible enough not to restrict circulation. Not that Dalhu would have any trouble getting free. Even if she were to secure him to the bed with titanium-reinforced handcuffs, he would have no trouble just yanking the posts out of the frame. Except, the last thing Dalhu seemed to want right now was to be released.

Okay, what to do now?

If she had known ahead of time that they would be playing this game, she would've made a quick Internet search to get ideas. Now she had to use her *devious* mind to come up with a plan.

Hm...

A quick sashay to the bathroom provided her first torture implement in the form of a makeup brush. Dalhu raised a brow but was smart enough not to open his mouth without permission.

With a wicked smile, Amanda sat at the foot of the bed and began to feather the wispy brush in an upward motion over Dalhu's inner thighs, stopping a hair short of his sensitive parts.

It didn't take long for him to start squirming and bucking. He was doing his best to remain quiet, but here and there a muffled groan or a growl escaped his throat.

What a shame that this game was not doing it for her.

Dalhu was turned on all right, but it might have been the effect of her sexy outfit and not necessarily what she was doing to him. She dropped the brush and slithered on top of him.

Now, this was definitely better. The feel of his big, strong body, his warmth. She craved his arms around her; she craved him on top of her. He must've read her mind because before she had a chance to notice that he'd gotten free, his large hands were on her back, her ass, stroking, cupping.

With a groan, she dipped her head and took his mouth in a hungry kiss.

"I hope you don't mind," he whispered in her ear before flipping her under him.

"Not at all." His weight was just perfect, heavy but not crushing. And those powerful arms of his, wrapped around her and holding her like he would never let go, well, that was a real turn on.

He lifted his head and bent his neck to admire her jutting nipples. "I wanted these in my mouth since the second I saw you coming out of the bathroom. This weird bra is sexy as hell." Sliding down, he did exactly that, licking, nipping, and blowing hot air on her little buds until she was squirming worse than he had a few moments ago.

Was he exacting revenge? Or just having fun?

She'd bet it was the former.

Except, it seemed that Dalhu didn't enjoy torturing her any more than she had enjoyed tormenting him. With a tender kiss goodbye to each pebbled nipple, he slid farther down her body and got busy eating her panties.

He had them shredded and off her in no time. "Spread your legs for me, my beauty," he commanded, then nipped at her inner thigh, his sharp fangs almost nicking her flesh.

She parted her legs wider, and he rewarded her with a lash of his tongue, painting a trail of scorching heat down to her slit. *So good*. He flicked her swollen clit, and her back arched on a throaty moan.

"You like?" He growled against her flesh, then thrust a finger deep inside her.

"Oh, oh, yes!" she cried when his lips closed around her swollen clit and he pushed back with two fingers. She was coming undone under the steady, gentle onslaught of his tongue and his lips and his fingers—the orgasm building up momentum like a tsunami.

He was playing her body like a master musician with his prized violin, with skill, love, and reverence.

On a scream, the tsunami crested and crashed toward shore. In a heartbeat, Dalhu pushed inside her with one powerful thrust, his fangs sinking into her neck at the same time.

Bliss.

Amanda

"Where are you going?" Dalhu asked.

Damn, she thought he was sleeping. Bending at the waist, she kissed his bruised lips. That last ride had been a little wild. Surprising, considering that it had been their fourth, or perhaps fifth? She wasn't sure.

It hadn't been gentle.

The sex, the wonderful closeness and Dalhu's skillful and reverent touch had brought about feelings she wasn't ready for. And looking into his big, warm, chocolate-colored eyes, so adoring, so devoted, she'd felt herself falling for him big time. But while her heart had been swelling with love, her gut had been churning with guilt, and the two mixed together had produced a combustible attitude.

She'd hurt him, just a little, and he'd taken everything she'd dished out with relish.

What an amazing male—

"I'm going to see Edna, our legal expert."

"Why? Can't it wait till morning? Come back to bed."

"No, I need to ask her something."

He sat up and leaned his back against the headboard. "What's so urgent that you're going to bother her at this hour?" He glanced at his wristwatch. "It's after ten."

She didn't want to tell him her idea before running it by Edna. But since this was about him, he deserved to know.

Sitting on the bed beside Dalhu, Amanda clasped his hand. "Edna has a unique ability. We call her the Alien Probe because she can see and judge what's in a person's heart. Combined with Andrew's ability to discern truth from lie, she might be able to finally convince Kian that you're not harboring some secret evil intentions and are completely loyal to us. He trusts her judgment implicitly."

"Okay." He pulled her to him for a kiss and held her for a long moment flush against his warm chest. "I love you," he whispered.

"I know." It was hard to deny him the words he so desperately needed, even cruel, but she just couldn't.

He let her go and slipped back under the covers. "I'll be awaiting your return, mistress," he teased.

They were not playing that game again. Well, except for the dress up, that part had been fun.

With a sigh, she left him and ducked into the tiny closet. The thing was no more than five by five, not nearly adequate even for a modest selection.

Before getting dressed, she checked with Edna, and her text message received an immediate and concise reply. *Of course.*

The next text went to Okidu. He was on his way to let her out, which precluded lengthy preparations. Yoga pants, T-shirt, and a pair of flip-flops would have to do.

On her way up to Edna's, at the councilwoman's new secure apartment assigned to her after Mark's murder, Amanda wondered what she looked like when not dressed for her official duties. She'd always seen the woman in either a loose-fitting pantsuit or her ceremonial robe, her hair brushed back and secured in a severe bun.

As she knocked on Edna's door, Amanda was actually excited about getting a glimpse of the formidable judge in her off time.

The improvement turned out to be minimal. Instead of a bun, Edna had pulled her hair into a ponytail, and instead of a pantsuit, she had on a dark blue jumpsuit that might have been fashionable in the late eighties but now belonged only in a Goodwill store.

Oh, well.

It seemed that Edna's appearance had nothing to do with looking professional for her job and everything to do with a complete lack of style.

Should she offer to help?

"Good evening, Amanda, please come in."

"Thank you so much for agreeing to see me so late." Amanda followed the judge into a living room that looked surprisingly well put together.

Oh, wait, that's Ingrid's doing.

"Not a problem at all, I'm always glad to help. Please, take a seat." She motioned to the couch and waited for Amanda to sit down before joining her.

"I'm sure the rumor machine has churned enough gossip to reach even your ears. You know about Dalhu and me?"

"The Doomer and you? Yes."

Edna's face didn't betray her opinion on the subject.

Amanda continued. "Ex-Doomer. Anyway, Dalhu left the Brotherhood and has sworn loyalty to us, but Kian is suspicious. We have Andrew, Syssi's brother, who is a human lie detector, or rather a Dormant lie detector, and he confirmed the veracity of everything Dalhu told Kian. But Kian remains unconvinced. I thought that since Kian trusts your judgment, and you have the ability to reach into Dalhu's soul and ascertain what's in his heart, your testimony might tip the scale in Dalhu's favor."

Again, there was no smile or frown or even inflection in her tone to hint at what she was thinking. "I don't see why not. I'll arrange with Kian to go see the Doomer, I'm sorry, Dalhu," Edna corrected.

Well, at last, a slight indication of her opinion, but it wasn't a good one. Edna thought of Dalhu first and foremost as a Doomer. She wouldn't be positively disposed toward him, and her probe would be intrusive and thorough. Which, on second thought, was better. If after such an invasive probe, Edna found no evidence of ill intentions on his part and saw that Dalhu was indeed loyal to the clan, her conclusions would carry more weight with Kian.

"Thank you, I appreciate it."

There was one more issue Amanda wanted Edna's opinion on, but wasn't sure how to approach it.

Thankfully, the Alien Probe was very good at guessing. "You want to ask me if there is a way for Dalhu to atone for his crimes. Correct?"

Amanda exhaled a relieved breath. "Yes, one crime in particular that I find extremely difficult to forgive. Dalhu was in charge of the unit that assassinated Mark. I'm aware of all the mitigating factors—that he didn't know me then or even that Mark was one of us; that he was just doing his accursed job. But still, I can't put it behind me. It's like a big ugly sore on our relationship. You know what I mean?"

Edna nodded. "Do you believe that by enduring some horrible punishment or trial he will gain your forgiveness?"

"I'm not sure. I've been thinking and rethinking this for days to no avail. I was hoping you could provide the insight I'm lacking."

"Let's start with a few questions, shall we?"

"Sure."

"Whose forgiveness do you think Dalhu should seek?"

Smart woman. When put this way, it was pretty obvious that it wasn't Amanda's place—kind of obnoxious of her to think that she should be the one granting it.

"Mark's immediate family to start with, then the rest of the clan—Mark's extended family."

"Okay. Who do you think should decide if Dalhu deserves to be offered the option of redemption by trial?"

"I guess Micah, Mark's mother."

"Exactly." Edna looked satisfied as if Amanda had just passed a test.

"Let's assume for a moment that Micah is willing to offer Dalhu a chance to redeem himself by some incredible feat of courage or endurance. Two questions need to be asked. First, would Dalhu accept the verdict and submit to whatever Micah might demand? And second, if he accepts and goes through it, would it be enough for you?"

"Yes, and yes. Dalhu is willing to do whatever it takes, and if Micah's demands are met, then I'll consider it done."

Edna nodded. "There might be a legal precedent. It's an old one, from the time of the gods, and it doesn't fit

Dalhu's situation precisely. But I think we can use it as a base.

"If a servant killed another servant, the head of the victim's household could ask for retribution to compensate the family, either monetary or physical. If it was monetary, the other head of household would pay, but the perpetrator would lose his freedom and spend his life as a slave to repay the debt. His boss could either keep him to repay over time or sell him to collect the debt right away. The system was put in place to prevent blood feuds between the victim and perpetrator's families, and at the same time provide support for those who lost their wage earners."

"I hope you're not suggesting slavery for Dalhu."

"Of course not. When the killing was accidental, whether because the men were fighting or because of negligence on the part of the accused, and it was clear that it wasn't a premeditated murder, the killer was given the option to choose physical retribution."

Amanda arched a brow. "And that was considered a lesser punishment than keeping the same job and just working without wages?"

"Certainly. Being a slave was shameful. Only the worst of criminals were sentenced to a life of slavery, and they were marked by a notch in the left ear to identify them as such. Additionally, the killer's wages most likely supported his family, and their loss would've reduced them to beggars."

"I see. Tough choice."

"Yes. Those who weren't young or healthy most often opted for slavery—fearing that they wouldn't survive the punishment. Others took the challenge."

"I assume that the victim's family determined the punishment."

"It was the only way to prevent blood feuds that would've claimed numerous lives."

Edna deserved her reputation. The woman was brilliant. There were enough mitigating factors in Dalhu's involvement in Mark's death to qualify him for the physical option. The question was, whether Micah would agree to see it this way.

To draw equivalents between that old custom and Dalhu's case—Mark would be considered a clan employee and Dalhu, Navuh's. Kian, as head of the American arm of the clan, could demand retribution, and Micah, as the victim's mother, would have the right to decide what form it would take.

"After the physical punishment was delivered, what did the victim's family do? Did they sign a release form?"

"Something to that effect. They would witness the punishment, and once it was done, the head of their household would ask if their vengeance was satisfied. They were honor bound to say yes. Besides, one-third of the killer's wages went to the victim's family. A strong incentive."

"And that was it? Case closed?"

"In theory."

Yeah, Amanda found it hard to believe that the victim's mother or wife had been able to forgive. But then, those garnished wages must've been the only way to put food on the table.

In Micah's case, however, she had no need for Dalhu's money—even if he happened to have any.

Dalhu

Last night, when Amanda had returned and crawled under the covers, snuggling up to him, Dalhu hadn't asked her about her talk with the legal expert. He'd pretended to sleep.

Holding her close had felt too good to spoil by discussing unpleasant things.

It still did. Just watching her sleep in the bed they now shared suffused him with joy—a feeling he'd forgotten existed and was so foreign to him that it had taken Dalhu a while to recognize it for what it was.

She looked so beautiful sleeping—curled on her side with one hand under her cheek—that he just had to draw her like that.

One more pose for his collection.

He got out of bed, washed and dressed in a hurry, then grabbed his supplies. Leaning against the dresser, he captured her outline with a few fast charcoal strokes. This way, if she woke or flipped to her other side, he'd have the base and draw the rest from memory.

The scraping sound of charcoal on paper must've woken her, and she flipped onto her back. "Why are you drawing me? I don't want a picture with no makeup and hair that looks like a bird's nest."

Dalhu put the pad aside and sat beside her on the bed. "Good morning, my beauty." He leaned and planted a quick kiss on her pouty lips.

Amanda smiled and wrapped her arms around his neck, pulling him down to her. "Good morning to you too." She kissed him long and hard. "Why don't you get out of those clothes and come back to bed?"

She didn't have to ask twice.

Their lovemaking was lazy and unhurried, like that of lovers who were comfortable with each other. But although the sex was as gentle as a breeze on a sunny shore, the intimacy was intense. Overwhelming.

Dalhu wanted to tell Amanda how much he loved her, over and over again, but he didn't. It made her uncomfortable. She couldn't say it back.

When they reached completion, he didn't even bite her.

Last night, he'd sunk his fangs into her so many times, sampling different spots on her body, that apparently his venom glands were spent. It was good, though, that his balls hadn't suffered similar fate. It would've been embarrassing. Even worse, Amanda would've been disappointed.

His woman was insatiable.

He was the luckiest bastard on earth.

"Dalhu, sweetheart, could you brew us some coffee?" she asked as they stepped out of their shared shower.

"Your wish is my command."

The radiant smile he got in return was priceless.

Ten minutes later, he had Amanda's cappuccino ready as she emerged from the bedroom, looking as perfect as ever in a pair of tight jeans and a blue blouse, her black hair sleeked back and her makeup done. Though why such a beautiful woman bothered with painting her face baffled him.

Females were such strange creatures.

"My lady?" He pulled out a chair for her at the dining table, not that it qualified as such with a diameter of just a little more than three feet. Still, it was the perfect size for two.

Breakfast had been already on the table when he'd stepped out of the bedroom to make coffee—Okidu must've delivered it while they'd showered. Amanda reached for a slice of toasted bread and spread a generous dollop of almond butter on top.

"You haven't tasted the cappuccino yet." It had been his first attempt at making one.

She took a small sip, following with a bite of toast.

"Did I do it right?"

"Perfect."

"Good, I'm glad." He ran a nervous hand over the back of his neck. "So, what did the legal expert say? Is she willing to test me?"

Amanda finished chewing and put the rest of her toast down. "Yes, she is. She said she is going to talk to Kian, though I don't know if she means to clear it with him first or coordinate a time that works with both their schedules. I hope it will be today, and that they'll let us know ahead of time. Not that any preparations are required, she just does her thing, it feels weird for a couple of minutes and that's it. Piece of cake if you have nothing to hide and let her in without a struggle." Amanda lifted what was left of her bread and took a big bite.

"Did she do it to you?"

"Uh-huh."

"Why?"

Amanda shrugged. "I was very young, maybe fifteen, and I'd done something stupid. I don't even remember what it was. I think I sneaked out to see a boy. Anyway, I tried to wiggle out of getting punished by inventing some cockamamie story and stubbornly clinging to it. My mother brought me to Edna."

"And..." He motioned for her to finish the story.

"I got grounded for a month. But that was nothing. What killed me was that I managed to really disappoint my mother for the first time. It was a big deal because her approval meant a lot to me. Still does."

"I bet."

Amanda lifted her mug and cupped it in her hands, her expressive face showing an inner struggle. A couple of times it looked like she was about to say something, but then she frowned and shook her head.

Just spit it out, he wanted to say to her, *don't you know that you can tell me anything?*

"Remember how you said that you should get whipped for your crimes?" she finally asked.

"Yes, what about it?"

"Did you mean it?"

"For a chance of redemption? I'd submit to any kind of torture in a heartbeat. Right now, I'm in no man's land. I'm no longer part of the Brotherhood, but I don't belong here either, or anywhere else for that matter. I'm an unwanted interloper at best—a despised enemy in the eyes of most of your relatives. I want to have a life with you, Amanda, and I'm willing to do whatever it takes to become part of your world—if not accepted, then at least tolerated."

She nodded as if he'd affirmed what she'd already known. "I had to be sure before telling you Edna's idea."

A spark of hope ignited in Dalhu's chest. "What is it?"

"There is this ancient custom, from the time of the gods, that was originally put in place to prevent never-ending blood vendettas between human families. There were no jails, so punishments were either monetary or physical. If the perpetrator didn't have the money to pay, his boss would pay it for him. As compensation, the boss had the right to either enslave him entirely or only garnish a part of his wages until his debt was repaid. The length of the enslavement depended on the severity of the crime and the amount of money owed. For a killing, it was slavery for life. Except, when it wasn't a premeditated murder—then it was up to the head of the offender's household to offer him a choice of physical punishment combined with garnishment of wages. The victim's family had the right to choose a trial that would satisfy their vendetta. After it was done, and if the offender lasted through it, they were asked if they were satisfied. Custom demanded that they say yes."

"I no longer have a boss or wages, so I don't see how this applies to me."

"I need to talk it through with Kian, but I think that this is the only way for you to earn redemption. If Mark's mother agrees to put you through a trial of her choosing and then declare that her vengeance was satisfied, then the rest of the clan would have to accept it as a done deal."

The logic was solid, except for the part of the grieving mother giving her son's killer a chance of redemption.

"Do you think she'll agree?"

"Maybe. It's worth a try. As I see it, this will give Micah something she can't have any other way. She can't retaliate against the Doom Brotherhood, and the guy who committed the killing is already entombed in our crypt. This is the only chance for retribution she can sink her teeth into, so to speak."

"Okay, let's assume she agrees. What makes you think that this will change the clan's attitude toward me?"

Amanda didn't reply right away, and a slight whiff of shame tickled his nose. What was she ashamed of?

"Look, Dalhu, this is about altering perception, and it requires a measure of showmanship. We'll need to make a production out of it, have it witnessed by a good number of clan members. They'll see you submit willingly and they'll have to acknowledge your bravery and your sacrifice. And once Micah declares you redeemed, they'll have no choice but to follow suit. You should prepare a short speech. I'll help."

"A circus performance."

"Yes. I know it sounds awful, and Fates only know what torture Micah will demand, but I don't see any other way. I won't blame you if you don't want to go through with it." Avoiding his eyes, she looked down at her plate.

He leaned toward her and engulfed her hands—together with the coffee mug they were still wrapped around. "Didn't I tell you? I will do anything and everything in my power to make a life with you. And if I die trying, at least I'll know that I gave it all I have."

Amanda

If there ever was a man who deserved to hear her say *I love you*, it was the one sitting across from her. Tears stinging the backs of her eyes, she dipped her head and kissed his hands.

She felt like such a bitch for denying him this, and still the words could not leave her throat. Because to say them out loud was like spitting on Mark's sarcophagus and stomping on Micah's grief.

Still, there was no way she could admit to him that she needed his sacrifice almost as much as she imagined Micah did. On the other hand, if Dalhu was brave enough to go through hell for her, she should be brave enough to at least tell him the truth.

"Thank you, for doing this for me," she croaked, tears running freely down her cheeks.

"Anything, you know it." He got up and lifted her, then sat down in her chair, cradling her in his arms. "You're priceless to me," he whispered.

She chuckled. "I bet you'll change your mind once I tell you this..." She wiped her eyes with his T-shirt.

"Nothing you can say will affect how I feel about you."

This made her tear up again. "How about the fact that I need your sacrifice for myself? So I can finally tell you I love you without feeling like I'm desecrating Mark's memory?"

Dalhu grinned, his whole face lighting up as if she had just given him the best of news. "I've known all along that you'll need something to help you cross that bridge. I just didn't know what that something was, which was worse than any kind of torture Micah could ever invent. And to hear you say you love me? I'll crawl to hell and back for it."

"You just might. A grieving mother's pain is so excruciating, so all consuming, that I fear Micah has no compassion left in her. She might be extremely cruel in her demands."

Amanda could testify from personal experience.

When her son had died, Amanda would've destroyed the earth and everyone on it—if she'd had the power to do so. She'd gone insane with grief, and it had taken her years to claw her way out of the bleak place she had spiraled down into.

"I had a son, once, a long time ago," she whispered into Dalhu's chest.

He tensed, his arms wrapping more securely around her. "What happened?"

"One moment he was alive and joyful, and the next he was lying dead on the ground. A six-year-old boy riding his first horse. The animal got spooked by a snake and reared up. My boy fell and broke his beautiful little neck. That's the whole story. One horrible moment in time that changed everything."

She'd been repressing her sorrow for so long that once released it erupted like the faulty lid of a pressure cooker —it hit the ceiling with a bang and whatever was cooking inside the pot followed—her guts, her blood, splattered, slowly dripping back down.

Dalhu held her while she cried, rocking her as she sobbed and screamed, "Why?"

"Why him?"

"Why me?"

It had taken a while until the sobs subsided. Dalhu had said nothing throughout her outburst, just waiting it out, caressing, rocking.

Smart man. There was nothing he could've said anyway.

"Thank you." She hiccupped, and he offered her a napkin to blow her nose into. "You're a good listener."

"Is there anything I can do?" he said hesitantly.

"No, you've been perfect. I had a good cry and now I'm better." She managed a small smile. "I could use a margarita, but I don't want to leave the shelter of your arms. I've never felt safer than I do when you hold me."

Dalhu kissed the top of her head, then lifted her up and sat her down on the tiny stretch of bar counter that wasn't occupied by appliances. "You hold on to me, and I'll pour you a drink. I don't think I can manage a margarita, though."

She did, holding on tight and pressing her cheek to his solid chest. When he was done, he handed her the drink and carried her to the couch. Sitting down with her cradled in his lap, he held her gently while she sipped on the gin and tonic he'd made her.

"Better?" he asked.

"Much. But could you hold me for a little longer?"

"I would gladly hold you for the rest of my life."

Kian

The oppressive silence in the Lexus was like a déjà vu of Kian's previous visit to Micah.

Fuck, why the hell had he agreed to Amanda's idea? This was cruel. They would be reopening Micah's wounds. Hell, those had probably never healed and were still bleeding.

Their visit would bring on a hemorrhage.

So why was he sitting in his car and driving to Micah's house?

Because he loved his sister.

He was one hell of a stubborn ox, so it had taken him longer than the others to realize the inconvenient truth. Fate had saddled Amanda with a despicable mate—not of her choosing—and she was powerless against the metaphysical forces conspiring against her.

Damn, I can't believe I'm buying into all this supernatural crap.

He'd considered severing the connection forcefully, but to do so to one's own sister was even more detestable than Amanda's Doomer. If Dalhu were indeed her fated mate, and it seemed he was, then getting rid of him would take away Amanda's one and only opportunity of a true love match.

It was rare to find your fated mate once; to find another was unheard of.

And besides, Kian had to admit that Dalhu had succeeded in chipping away at his hatred one tiny shard at a time. The profiles the guy had compiled were as thorough and complete as he could make them, including the sketched portraits. And his love for Amanda was so glaringly obvious that even a stubborn skeptic like Kian was forced to acknowledge it.

But what really tipped the scales heavily in Dalhu's favor was his willingness to submit to whatever punishment imaginable for a chance of redemption. Grudgingly, Kian admired the guy's courage and determination.

He deserved a chance, if only for Amanda's sake.

Kian cast a sidelong glance at his sister. Sitting in the passenger seat, Amanda hadn't uttered a word since they'd left the keep, but the scents of guilt and fear were doing the talking for her. He laid a hand on her shoulder and gave it a gentle squeeze.

"It's going to be tough, I'm not going to sugarcoat it, but we'll get through it together."

She turned to him, a small pitiful smile tugging at her lips. "Thank you. You don't know how much I appreciate that you're doing this for me."

"You're welcome."

From the back seat, Anandur sniffled audibly. "I'm so happy that you guys are no longer at each other's throats. Albeit entertaining, it was breaking my poor heart."

Brundar grunted, expressing his opinion that the comment didn't deserve a response.

A few minutes later they arrived at Micah's modest suburban house, and Kian eased the SUV into a spot a little farther down the street.

Leaving the three of them down on the walkway, Amanda climbed the two steps leading to the front door and knocked.

Otto, Micah's brother, opened the door. "Come in." He motioned for them to go ahead.

Mark's mother was sitting on a couch with an expression as hard as stone. Damn, this was going to be even more difficult than Kian had anticipated.

"Thank you for agreeing to see us." Amanda walked over and gave Micah a quick hug.

Micah didn't return it. "Please, sit down," she offered in a dead voice.

Fuck, this isn't going to work.

"Thank you," he said and took a seat in one of the armchairs. Brundar and Anandur joined Otto at the dining table.

Amanda sat next to Micah, her knees and torso turned sideways so she was looking straight at the woman.

Brave move.

"I know Kian already explained over the phone the purpose of our visit, but I would like to elaborate."

"Be my guest," Micah said, in a tone that suggested that her mind had already been made up, and her decision wasn't the one they were hoping for.

"I know that you don't want to hear what I came here to say, and that nothing could ever make up for your loss, but I beg of you to hear me out."

Micah seemed to soften a little, her rigid pose loosening. She slumped back into the couch. "Go ahead."

For a split second, Amanda's eyes fluttered closed in relief. "Thank you." She took Micah's hand.

"First, I need to tell you why this is so important to me. I'm not an impartial observer, and I didn't come here as a council member or in any other official capacity. I'm here as a woman seeking a chance of redemption for her mate."

Micah's gasp meant that the rumors hadn't reached her yet. "How can a Doomer be your mate?"

"I know, hard to believe. It took me a long while to accept it." Amanda smiled a sad smile. "The Fates work in mysterious ways. We can huff, and we can puff, but in the end we have no choice but to accept whatever they decree for us."

Micah sighed. "I guess you're right, and I feel sorry for you, but I won't pretend that I don't want that Doomer dead—because I do."

Amanda crossed her legs and licked her lips.

A long speech was coming.

"Let me lay out the facts. We don't execute prisoners. The worst punishment we have is entombment, and it is reserved for premeditated murder, which isn't the case here. Mark's actual killer is already entombed in our crypt as a result of a skirmish between his unit and the Guardians. Therefore, you were denied the satisfaction of witnessing his punishment—unless, you want us to revive him only to have him entombed again, which I doubt Annani would allow."

Micah harrumphed. "I'm not that bloodthirsty."

"I know, I was just stating the obvious. What I'm trying to say is that Dalhu's involvement was not direct. When he gave the order, he had no idea that Mark was one of us. Though I can't say that it would've made a difference. But in any case, I'm not suggesting that he is not to blame. He was a member of the Brotherhood and was expected to deliver their loathsome vengeance. Everything changed for him when he met me. He has forsaken the

Brotherhood, sworn allegiance to the clan, and is providing us with invaluable information about Navuh's operation. And for better or worse, he is my mate."

Micah's gaze cut to Kian, and he nodded, affirming Amanda's statements.

"He wants to become one of us, but he will never be accepted unless he is redeemed in the eyes of the clan."

Micah shrugged as if to say—what do I care.

"Please understand, I know that no matter what punishment he'll endure, his pain will never match yours. Nothing ever will." Amanda choked up a little, and this time, it was Micah who squeezed her hand to provide comfort.

"But at least you'll get the satisfaction that you've exacted some measure of vengeance. When I lost my son, I felt like my rage was powerful enough to destroy the world, but I had no one to blame, no one to punish, so I turned on myself. You have a chance to do something—to see someone punished and in the process give him the gift of redemption."

This must've been the most difficult speech Amanda had ever delivered. For her to talk about her son was like plunging a knife into her own heart and twisting.

Silence stretched across the room as Micah pondered Amanda's words, the seconds ticking off one by one like on a game show.

"I want him entombed."

Amanda's shoulders sagged in resignation. Even Kian felt an unexpected twinge of disappointment.

But Micah wasn't done. "For a week, and then you can revive him. I want him to experience dying. But before that, I want him flogged, and I want Otto to be the one wielding the whip." She crossed her arms over her chest. "Don't look at me with those accusing eyes. Because he'll be injured, I'll allow for a venom-induced stasis instead of the agonizingly slow loss of consciousness in the tomb. That's the best I can offer, and I'm doing it mainly for you. It's obvious that you feel for that male, and I know you well enough to realize that if you believe him worthy of redemption, then he must be. But I want him to earn it with a meaningful sacrifice and not a token one."

"Thank you." Amanda pulled Micah into a hug and held on. "You're doing the right thing." She managed only a whisper.

Amanda

What have I done?

That sentence had been going on a loop in Amanda's head all the way home. She might have signed Dalhu's death warrant. Entombment was horrible, but it was pretty safe. Venom-induced stasis wasn't. It had to be done with extreme precision. If not halted at the right moment, Dalhu's heart would be stopped for good.

She turned around to face Anandur. "I want you to do it." He was the most friendly with Dalhu—seemingly the only Guardian who didn't harbor ill feelings toward him.

"No problem, Princess, your frog is safe with me." He chuckled. "And when he awakens seven days later, you'll kiss him, and he'll turn into a prince. Here, I just invented a new fairy tale."

Leave it to Anandur to make fun of the most grievous of situations. "It's not funny."

"Don't worry. Dalhu is a resilient fellow, and he'll not only make it but come out stronger on the other side. Micah's trial is perfect for what he needs. Not too severe, but not too easy either. He'll gain respect by submitting to it and enduring it honorably." Looking satisfied, Anandur crossed his massive arms over his chest.

Men had such a different outlook on things. She still remembered the games boys used to play when she was a teenager—like who could withstand the most punches to the stomach, or to the shoulder. Or wrestling in the dirt, beating the crap out of each other, and calling it fun.

Idiots.

But when she'd told Dalhu the news, it turned out that Anandur had been right on the money.

"That's great!" was his response.

Really?

The guy was happy about a whipping and an entombment and called it freaking great?

Fates, she felt like shaking Dalhu. What was wrong with him?

Not that it would've made a difference if he didn't like the result of her ill-advised meeting with Micah. The verdict was irreversible. Once decreed, Micah's decision was obligatory.

"Why the angry face?"

"This was a mistake, my mistake. Nothing is worth even the slim chance of you dying."

He took her into his arms. "Of course, it is, my beauty. This is exactly what I've been hoping for, and I have no intention of dying. I'm going to be fine."

"How can you say it? Venom-induced stasis is extremely dangerous. The tiniest of miscalculations and your heart might stop beating for good. I will never forgive myself if that happens. Oh, sweet Fates, how could I have painted us into this corner?" Her mascara-tinted tears were making a mess of his shirt.

"Sweetheart, you're just overreacting."

No, he didn't just say it. Overreacting? The condescending, chauvinistic male.

She pushed, and he let her leave the shelter of his embrace.

Pointing a finger at his chest, she lashed out at him, "Just because I'm a female, you automatically assume that I'm overreacting? That I'm hysterical? Does your life mean nothing to you?"

With a tilt of his head and an expression of a dog that didn't understand why his owner was shouting at him, Dalhu reached for her again, but she swatted his hand away. He dipped his head and wiped the back of his neck with his hand.

After a moment, he lifted his head, his big soulful eyes bathing her with so much love that she almost staggered.

"Did it ever happen? Do you know of a precedent—an incident of a Guardian miscalculating and killing someone he was supposed to put into stasis?"

Did she?

Amanda shrugged. "Well, no. But I don't think the Guardians would've advertised it."

"Why don't you call and ask?"

She was ready to argue when it occurred to her that he was right. "That's actually not a bad idea," she mumbled.

Dalhu released a relieved breath and crossed the living room to the bar. The entire two steps. "Would you like a drink?"

"Yeah, the one you made me this morning was good," she said while her fingers flew over the phone's screen, composing a text to Anandur. On second thought, she copied it and sent it to Kian as well. Anandur was a great guy, but he might be inclined to twist the truth for her sake. Her brother would tell it exactly as it was.

Anandur's reply was—*No, stop obsessing!*

Kian's was—*Not recently.*

Not great, but better than she'd expected.

"The good news is that no one died of it recently. The bad news is that it happened in the past."

Dalhu handed her the drink. "When is it going to take place? And where?"

Amanda plopped down on the couch and took a few sips. "Three days from now, in the evening. I don't know exactly where, but probably somewhere in the basement, maybe the gym or perhaps the catacombs."

"Why wait?" Dalhu frowned and sat next to her, holding a tall tumbler that was filled to the brim with whiskey. "I would rather have it over and done with as soon as possible."

"That's what I said. But Anandur said it is customary to wait three days to allow for the announcement to reach whoever wants to witness it."

Dalhu nodded. "That makes sense."

"It does, right? But he later confessed to me that he pulled it out of his ass. He plans a surprise bachelor party for Kian and wants you to be there—since you're going to miss the wedding."

Dalhu snorted. "As if Kian would've invited me to his wedding."

"If we had more time, or if Micah hadn't demanded seven days, he would've. After you're considered redeemed, you will become part of the clan, maybe not a fully trusted member—yet—but certainly one who is invited to a clan-wide celebration like this."

"Then I'm double glad for Micah's demands. Attending a wedding with your entire clan present would've been a nightmare for me."

"You're being silly. Typical macho male—enthusiastic about enduring torture and proving his machismo but terrified of social interactions."

Dalhu laughed, a deep belly laugh that didn't really belong in the context of their conversation. Was it his way of dealing with fear?

"You got me there. I don't know if it has anything to do with being a male, though. I think it has more to do with what is familiar and what is not. Torture and excruciating tests of courage, those I'm well acquainted with. I know I can handle anything anyone throws at me. Celebrations? Acting all polite and pretending that I'm smart? Worldly? I have no clue how to pull it off, and it scares the crap out of me."

Amanda had never considered that Dalhu might be insecure about his lack of education, or his somewhat crude manners. She had no problem with either. In addition to loving her with everything he had, Dalhu was smart and treated her with respect. Everything else was inconsequential. Evidently, though, not for him.

"Make room." She motioned to his lap and then promptly positioned herself in the space he'd made. Wrapping her arms around his neck, she gazed into his lovely chocolate eyes. "You are smart, and worldly, never doubt this. However, I understand where you're coming from, and I'm going to help you. You've got yourself a very accomplished professor here, one who will have you sounding like a scholar in no time." She kissed his smiling lips.

"How about we start with you schooling me in the erotic arts?"

She smiled. "Your enthusiasm for furthering your education is admirable. Take me to bed, big boy."

Syssi

"You sure you don't want me to come with you?" Kian asked again. He'd looked a little hurt when she'd told him that only Andrew would be coming with her to pick up her parents from the clan's private airstrip.

The reason wasn't that she didn't want Kian to be there, but because she didn't want to show up with his bodyguards in tow. Better introduce her parents to this strange world in stages, and certainly not right upon their arrival.

"If you can ditch Anandur and Brundar, you're welcome to accompany me."

"I can't."

"How about just one? We could take the limo, and Anandur could pretend to be the driver."

"I think I can get away with it. Let me call him."

Syssi danced a little victory dance. She hadn't really expected him to cooperate.

Kian arched a brow. "You look so cute, dancing in your underwear."

"Are we back to cute?" She pretended offense.

"Sexy cute."

"That's better." She stretched up on her toes, but he was so tall that she had to drag him down to reach his lips. "I need a stepping stool just to kiss you, you big lug."

"All I hear are complaints," he joked, lifting her up and holding her pressed against him as they kissed.

Half an hour later, as Anandur stopped the limo in front of Andrew's house, her brother was already waiting for them out on the street.

"Nice hat," he said, getting into the passenger seat next to Anandur.

"I'm playing a chauffeur. Your sister doesn't want to spook your parents by showing up with a bodyguard. But why a driver and not a beloved cousin? Huh?" He turned his head to cast her an accusing glare.

He had a point. Who was she going to introduce him as? Kian's driver? And then a cousin, only later to change it to a nephew?

"You're right, ditch the hat. I'm going to tell them that you're Kian's cousin."

"Who drives a limo? We should've taken the SUV."

"The limo is more comfortable. Just give me a break, okay? I'm nervous enough as it is."

Andrew turned around in his seat and stretched his neck to peer at Kian over the partition that separated the front of the limo from the back. It was lowered, but it didn't go all the way down. "Why are we driving all the way out to the boonies instead of using the helicopter to bring them straight to your rooftop?"

"It's being serviced."

"You have only one?"

"No, but the other two are simple cargo birds."

"Got it." Satisfied with Kian's answer, Andrew turned back around. This line of questioning wasn't like him. He must also be nervous about seeing their parents.

Would they look older? What would they think of Kian? How would they react to all the weirdness?

God, two days to the wedding.

Less, it was already afternoon. Thank God that everything was good to go. And if something didn't turn out as well as planned, tough. The important thing, as Amanda had said over and over again, was that Syssi's dress was stunning and she looked fantastic in it. The fifteen thousand dollar price tag had been a shocker, but Amanda had reassured her that it was a bargain price considering that it was made by a semifamous designer and was a rush order. Apparently, Joanne had pulled some strings to have it done quickly and at a *reasonable* price.

The clan's private airstrip was about an hour's drive out of the city. It wasn't much, just one long runway and a huge hangar. Parked inside, there was a small jet that looked almost like a toy in the cavernous space. The hangar had room enough for at least five more. An office, built on a raised ramp, was accessible by a simple metal staircase. Considering the industrial look of everything else, it was surprisingly elegant, with a sitting area, a counter that held a coffeemaker and two baskets with an assortment of refreshments. Several magazines were stacked on top of a rectangular wooden table.

She picked one and was almost done flipping through it when Anandur announced that the plane was landing.

Butterflies in her belly, Syssi got up and watched the approaching aircraft through the window. Once it landed, the plane continued down the runway until it stopped in front of the hangar, waiting like a car for Anandur and the guy manning it to open the doors, then eased inside.

Syssi took the stairs down, Andrew and Kian following close behind her. It took a couple of minutes for the double engines to power down and for the door with the built-in staircase to open. The woman standing at the opening was either the pilot or the flight attendant, it was hard to tell—she wasn't wearing a uniform.

Her father was the first to emerge, and his face lit up with a big grin as he saw them standing below. Carry-on in hand, he quickly took the short flight of stairs, dropped the luggage and opened his arms.

"Come here, baby girl."

She ran into his welcoming embrace and squeezed, his groan reminding her too late that she was so much stronger than before.

She let go of him quickly. "Sorry, Daddy."

"You've been exercising, yeah? Good for you." He turned to Andrew, who was patiently waiting his turn, and the two did the manly hug with the mutual back slapping. "It's good to see you both. We've missed you so much."

Her mother came down next, and this time, Syssi was careful, hugging Anita gently. "I've missed you, Mom."

"I've missed you too, sweetie, and you, Andrew, come here and give your mother a hug."

Once the hugs and kisses were done, Kian introduced himself, extending a hand to her father. "Welcome, I'm Kian."

"Adam Spivak." Her father repeated the hug and clap ritual with his future son-in-law. "Pleased to meet you. And this is my better half, Anita."

Her mother was somewhat more reserved in her hug, but Syssi could tell that she was impressed.

Though, duh, what did she expect? Kian was one hell of an impressive guy.

"Mom, Dad, I want you to meet Anandur, Kian's cousin."

The three of them shook hands, and the introductions were done.

"Tall family," Anita remarked with an admiring up and down glance first at Kian and then Anandur. "Handsome too."

"Let me help you with that." Anandur grabbed the two pieces of luggage and carried them to the limo, holding them up as if they weighed no more than a cheerleader's pompoms.

Her mom arched a brow.

"He's a bodybuilder," Syssi muttered.

"That explains it. Is your Kian into the body building sport as well?" Anita wrapped her arm around Syssi's shoulders as they followed Anandur to the car.

"He works out, but just to stay in shape."

"And a great shape it is," Anita whispered in her ear.

Syssi blushed, slanting a quick glance at Kian, who was grinning like a satisfied cat. "Mom..."

"What? He can't hear me."

"You'd be surprised."

The drive back to the keep went by quickly, with Adam entertaining them with one outlandish story after the other. It seemed that her parents were having a great time in Africa, despite the harsh conditions and the lack of modern amenities. Both looked fit and tanned.

Back at the keep, the group took the elevator up to the eighteenth floor, where an apartment had been prepared for her parents.

"Oh, wow, this is really nice," her mother said. "Is this your place, Kian?"

"No, we are in the penthouse. This is just for you."

"Thank you," Adam said, sounding relieved.

Syssi chuckled. What was it about fathers having trouble with their little girls growing up and having a man in their lives? Mothers had no such qualms.

"I'll leave you here to freshen up and come back in an hour. Hopefully, you'll still be awake. How is the jet lag?"

"Not too bad, I think I have another couple of hours in me. How about you, Adam?"

"After a shower, I'll be as good as new."

Syssi glanced at her watch. "Okay then, I'll be back at seven."

Andrew

Syssi was fidgeting, wrapping one long strand of hair after the other on her finger and generally looking like she was about to have a nervous breakdown. Not that he could blame her; their parents were about to meet the Goddess.

"I'll go get them," Andrew volunteered.

"No, that's okay, I'll go. I promised them."

"You sure? They wouldn't mind. I can drop a few hints on the way to prepare them for the shock."

"God, I can only imagine their reaction to Annani."

"You worry too much. They'll get over it, same way you and I did."

"You're probably right. Okay, you go and get Mom and Dad while I check on dinner." She snorted. "Not that Okidu would even allow me in the kitchen, but I want to have a peek at the dining room and see if anything needs rearranging."

"You do that." He patted her arm.

It was exactly two minutes before seven when Andrew knocked. His father opened the door, looking distinguished in a dark blue suit.

"We are ready, just let me call your mom." He turned around and called. "Anita, Andrew is here."

His mom emerged from the bedroom wearing a narrow black skirt, a beige blouse, and a string of pearls around her neck. The last time he'd seen her wearing anything other than pants was at his grandmother's funeral. It seemed that Anita was making an effort to impress Kian's mother.

"You look nice," he said.

"Thank you."

"Shouldn't we lock the door?" his father asked as they headed for the elevators.

"No need. This is a secure building, and there are cameras in the corridors. See?" He pointed up.

"So, what's the deal here, Andrew? Syssi didn't say much, but it's obvious just from the travel arrangements that her guy is loaded. However, the important question is whether Kian is a good man?"

"The best. I approve of him wholeheartedly."

"Really?" Anita looked surprised. "How well do you know him?" The elevator doors opened, and they stepped inside.

"Well enough. But listen, before we get there and before you meet Kian's mother, I wanted to warn you. Be prepared for surprises and keep an open mind. This evening will probably be the weirdest you've ever experienced."

Anita frowned. "What is that supposed to mean?"

"It's all good, nothing to worry about. Just keep an open mind, that's all I'm asking."

Exiting, she shrugged. "Fine."

His father's posture stiffened, but he said nothing until Andrew opened the door to Kian and Syssi's penthouse apartment. "Impressive," he muttered, glancing at the wall of glass overlooking the city.

Syssi gave each a quick hug. "You guys look so great. Africa is good to you."

"Welcome to our home." Kian had a big friendly smile plastered on his face as he motioned for them to proceed to the sitting area. "Would you care for a drink?"

"No, thank you." Anita walked over to the glass doors and peered outside. Kian had turned on all of the lights on the terrace, including those inside the pool. Evidently, he wasn't immune to wanting to impress the in-laws either.

"What do you have?" Adam followed Kian to the bar and looked over the display of expensive bottles.

Andrew joined them. "I'll have the Jack Daniel's." He pointed at the opened bottle.

"Me too," Adam said. His father would've probably preferred to try one of the fancier ones, but he wasn't comfortable enough to ask.

Drinks in hand, they headed to the sitting area.

"My mother will be here shortly."

"I can't wait to meet her." Anita joined Adam and Syssi on the couch.

"So, what do you do, Kian?" Adam began the interrogation—the one that every groom, since the beginning of time, had been subjected to by his future father-in-law.

This should be interesting, considering what and who Kian was. Andrew got comfortable to watch the show.

"I manage the family business."

Now, that must've been the understatement of the century.

Adam made a point of looking around the luxurious living room before returning his stare to Kian. "Must be one hell of a business."

"I can't complain."

There was a gentle knock on the door, and Kian jumped up to open the way for his mother. She was accompanied by one of her butlers, whatever his name was. They all looked the same.

Andrew leaned to get closer to his parents. "Remember what I said before," he whispered.

"Anita, Adam, my mother, Annani."

The Goddess glided into the room, her long purple dress swaying gently with each small step, her skin glowing with her natural luminescence.

"It's a pleasure to meet you," the Goddess chimed.

With a gasp, Anita's hand flew to her chest. Adam gaped.

With a graceful, fluid motion, Annani lowered herself into an armchair facing the couch and smiled.

Anita was the first to recover. "What's going on, Syssi?"

"Mom, Dad, Kian's mother, Annani, is the last surviving member of a race of gods. The people who brought knowledge and civilization to humanity and were the source of most ancient mythologies."

"Perhaps it would be better if I told the story," Annani offered.

Adam cleared his throat. "Yes, please do."

"Since we are all hungry, and I do not wish to hold up dinner, I am going to tell you only a very abbreviated version. Later, Syssi can fill in the details."

Anita nodded. "First, if you don't mind, could you please clarify the meaning of the term gods?"

Annani laughed, and if his parents had any doubts before that they were in the presence of a goddess, the heavenly sound of that laugh should've been enough to convince them.

"Not the creator, or creators of the universe, of course, just a different race of beings—a small group of either survivors from an earlier civilization or refugees from somewhere else in the universe. I was not privy to that information. You should be familiar with the general gist of the story from what you have learned reading the Hebrew Bible and the mythologies of the Sumerians, the Egyptians, the Greeks, the Romans, and so on."

Annani continued to tell them about the gods taking human mates and the immortal children that had been born from those unions. She told them about the Dormants and how her people had figured a way to activate them, about Mortdh and the cataclysm that had destroyed her people along with most of their immortal progeny. And lastly, she told them about Syssi's transition.

"You're immortal," Anita stated more than asked.

"Yes."

"I'll be damned." Adam loosened his tie.

Syssi sighed and took Anita's hands. "No one is supposed to know immortals exist, but I figured it would be impossible to explain about Annani without resorting to measures that would've made everyone uncomfortable. So, for the duration of your stay, you'll be privy to the secret, but we will have to thrall you to forget this before you go home."

"Why? Don't you trust us? Do you think we'll betray our own children?" Anita looked not only hurt but furious.

"Of course, I trust you. It's just that no one outside the clan is allowed to know. Right, Kian?" Syssi's tone was pleading for him to take over.

"I'm sorry, but this is how it must be done. The safety of my family depends on secrecy. I'm not suggesting that you would deliberately disclose information you shouldn't, but you can blurt out something accidentally, or if our enemies suspect your connection to us, the information could be tortured out of you. It's better for everyone if I suppress and muddle your memories. Don't worry, you'll still remember the wedding, just not the other stuff."

Adam seemed placated, but not Anita. "Are you sure there is no other way?"

Suddenly, Andrew remembered something that Dalhu had told them. "There might be. How about a strong compulsion thrall like the one Navuh uses on his human pilots? They have the knowledge but are unable to reveal any of it without their brains short-circuiting."

Kian shook his head. "First, I'm not sure I know how to do it. Second, highly intelligent people like Adam and Anita might be able to shake it off."

"I will perform the thrall," Annani offered. "If it is acceptable to you." She trained her glowing eyes on Anita, then Adam.

"Sure, that's better than forgetting all of this, right, Anita?"

"Definitely."

Annani clapped her hands. "It is settled then. Let us adjourn to the dining room. I am famished."

Anandur

"What? No strippers?" Michael complained.

Anandur winked and leaned to whisper in the kid's ear, "Who said there won't be?"

Not that there were going to be any. Holding the party in a prison cell precluded inviting pros. And anyway, Syssi would have disapproved, and he had no intentions of antagonizing the new First Lady. The thing with the quiet, supposedly demure types was that their vengeance was often cunning and more vicious than that of the loudmouths.

Andrew chuckled. "I'll believe it when I see it."

"Blow me."

"You're not my type."

"I know that I'm irresistible, but instead of hitting on me, go open the door. I left it unlocked." Andrew's human hearing failed to register the faint knock. It was probably Okidu with the food because none of the guys would've been so discreet. There was no need—it wasn't as if a knock would've alerted Kian all the way up in his penthouse and spoiled the surprise—but apparently the word *secret* had this effect on Okidu's logic circuitry.

Andrew flipped him off and went to open the door, letting in Okidu and the stack of trays he was carrying.

There wasn't enough space on the table, and some of the platters had to go on top of the dresser in the bedroom.

Anandur had only invited the Guardians, the two male council members, and Michael to Kian's bachelor party, so all together Dalhu's small apartment would have to accommodate ten super-sized guys. Not an easy feat, but this was the only way to include the dude in the celebration.

It was the least he could do for Dalhu. The guy was facing a whipping and subsequent entombment the following evening.

He'd make it work somehow. There was enough booze to drown a platoon, and the playlist on his iPod had the best of rock 'n' roll's oldies—none of the whiny crap today's bands were barfing out, or rap, which, with the exception of Eminem, Anandur didn't consider music.

A bottle of Snake Venom beer in hand, Bhathian made a thorough inspection of the many portraits of Amanda that Dalhu had taped to his living room walls. "We should take these down for the party. I don't think Kian would enjoy himself with his sister staring at him from every fucking wall."

He had a point.

Dalhu grimaced but nodded. "Just be careful not to damage them when you pull them off."

"Where do you want to stash them?" Bhathian asked.

"Under the bed."

Dalhu and Bhathian made quick work of liberating the walls and took the stack to the bedroom.

"And what do we have here?" Bhathian pulled out a nude of Amanda from under the bed and held it up for everyone to see.

It happened in a blink of an eye.

Dalhu's hands closed around Bhathian's neck in a deadly chokehold, and the large rectangular sheet of white paper fluttered to the floor like a discarded peace offering.

Even Bhathian's powerful arms were no match for Dalhu's fury— his face turning red as he grabbed Dalhu's thick wrists, trying to pull the grip free with all his formidable strength. But it was getting him nowhere.

His eyes blazing, the Doomer snarled, baring fangs that were already at their extended full length.

In one swift move, Anandur attacked, grabbing Dalhu from behind in a rear naked choke. "Let him go before I break your neck." He was already applying force that would've felled most guys on the spot, but Dalhu was not only still standing, but his grip wasn't slackening in the slightest.

"You fucking idiot," Anandur hissed in Dalhu's ear, "Amanda is like a sister to us. She could've been parading naked in here, and no one would've even gotten a rise out of it."

It was true.

Regarding all clan females as mothers or sisters had been drilled into them since infancy, and the only thing her nudity would've evoked were some snide remarks.

Something must've penetrated the lunatic's malfunctioning brain, and he let go. "I'm sorry," he said, sinking down to a sitting position on the bed.

Bhathian rubbed at his thick neck. "You're a strong motherfucker," he said in a tone that suggested respect rather than animosity. "If I didn't get what got you so pissed off, I would've killed you." Again, the guy didn't sound angry. It had been more of a statement than a threat.

"Come on, girls. Time to party." Anandur motioned for them to get back into the living room.

Dalhu followed, sidling up to Anandur. "Thanks, man, I owe you. But just to be clear, the sisterly attitude doesn't extend to him." He tilted his head toward Andrew.

True. Up until a few days ago, the dude had been pining for Amanda, but being the smart operative that he was, Andrew had realized that it was a losing proposition and had hooked up with the good doctor. Not that it was supposed to be common knowledge, but there was little that escaped Anandur's notice.

"Relax, and go get yourself a beer. These beauties cost me eighty bucks a pop, so enjoy while Scotland's finest lasts." At just over 65 percent alcohol by volume, Brewmeister's Snake Venom was the strongest beer available commercially and was priced accordingly.

His plan was to get the guys drunk, fast, especially Kian who needed it most. Problem was, immortals had a high tolerance for alcohol; add to that his clansmen's Scottish roots, and a barrel of regular beer each would have achieved nothing other than filling the guys' bladders.

When all was ready and the rest of the guys had arrived, Anandur texted Kian. *Could you stop by Dalhu's cell for a moment? There is something he needs to show you. It's important.*

I'll be there in five.

"Get in the bedroom and close the door," Anandur instructed the men. "And take the table with you. I don't want him to see the food."

Brundar and Arwel lifted the thing and carried it to the other room. Dalhu closed the doors to the cabinet housing the bar, and that was it. All traces of party were gone.

A few moments later the door opened, and Kian strode inside.

"I'm here, so talk. I don't have much time."

"I need to show you something." Anandur put on a grave face. "Follow me." He stepped up to the bedroom's door. "Go ahead, take a look." He tilted his head toward the door.

Kian arched a brow, pushing the thing and letting it swing in.

Immediately, the party horns began blasting, and he was pelted with several pounds of hard candy.

"What the hell?"

"Party time!" Anandur clapped his back.

"What's the occasion?"

Sometimes the dude was dense.

"You—getting married."

"A fucking bachelor party?"

"What else?"

"The tailor is bringing my tux. I have to be there in ten minutes."

"No, you don't. Syssi rescheduled it for tomorrow morning."

"So, all of you are in cahoots." He finally smiled.

"Yep. Go get yourself a beer. I brought Snake Venom."

"Went all out, I see."

"Only the best of the best for my best buddy."

"I'm touched." Kian put a hand over his heart.

The rest of the guys spilled out from the other room, William and Yamanu carrying back the dining table. Once they put it back in place, William stayed nearby to sample the goodies. Yamanu grabbed a beer and parked his ass on the couch next to Brandon.

"Okay, so where is the stripper you promised?" Michael asked, his speech already slurred after only one beer.

Lightweight.

Anandur pretended to check the time on his watch. "Fifteen minutes."

A big grin on his puss, Michael saluted him with the bottle.

Ten minutes later, Anandur ducked into the bedroom and closed the door, locking it behind him.

Hopefully, Amanda had some sexy lingerie in there. Sifting through the contents of five out of the six dresser drawers that she had appropriated for herself, he found a pair of fishnets that seemed stretchy enough, a lacy bra, a thong, and several silk scarves.

If he wanted to pull this off, he needed to think creatively.

There was no way the thong would fit him, and the bra had to be extended by tying a scarf to each end. He tied another scarf around his hips to cover his briefs. The fishnets barely made it past his knees, and after all the tugging and pulling there were a few extra holes in them—with his red curly leg hair poking through.

Fuck, he'd have to buy Amanda new ones.

Anandur didn't even bother to look for Amanda's shoes. Obviously too small. Which was a shame because high heels would've worked better with the torn fishnets than his scuffed combat boots.

He found Amanda's makeup case in the vanity drawer and pulled out a red lipstick and a black eyeliner pencil. The thick line he'd painted around his eyes made him look like a raccoon, and he got some of the lipstick on his bushy mustache. He left the eyeliner alone but wiped the smeared lipstick off with a wet washcloth.

Damn, I look good. He blew a kiss at his reflection before heading out.

A firm shove had the door to the living room fly open with a bang that caught everyone's attention.

Andrew choked, then sprayed beer all over Onegus, who was unlucky enough to stand next to him.

"Hello, boys." Anandur sauntered into the room and grabbed his iPod, switching playlists to something slow and sexy.

"Are you ready?"

"No, go away, you ugly mutt!" Arwel shouted.

Anandur ignored him and began his version of a belly dance.

Between bursts of hoots and hollers, the guys were laughing their asses off. Kian included.

Anandur smirked and untied the knot holding the bra in place, making a production of slowly sliding the straps off his shoulders.

"No! Please! Stop! I'm too young to witness such horror!" Michael crouched down and grabbed a fistful of candy from the floor, then chucked it at Anandur. Soon, everyone joined the offensive, forcing Anandur to flee into the bedroom.

Their laughter continued long after he was gone.

Mission accomplished.

Dalhu

"I can't. I just can't let you go through with it," Amanda said for the umpteenth time while pacing like a caged tigress in the confined space of their living room.

There were tears in her eyes, and the pungent scent of guilt emanating from her body permeated the small space, overpowering what had remained of their recent lovemaking. Which was saying a lot, since they had been at it for hours. The smells of sweat and sex had been so strong that he was sure they had percolated out to the corridor and adjoining cells. It was good that, as far as he knew, they were the only occupants of this basement floor.

"For the love of Mortdh, fuck!"—Dalhu shook his head—"I can't believe I invoked that name," he murmured. "Just give it a rest, will you?"

Amanda strode up to him. Tilting her head and sticking her chin out, she poked a finger at his chest. "How the hell am I supposed to do that? It's entirely my fault, my stupidity that underestimated Micah's thirst for vengeance. I never expected her to be this cruel." She let her head fall upon his chest.

Wrapping her in his arms, he kissed her forehead. "Anything less would not have been enough, and you know it."

"Enough for who?" she whispered.

"For the clan, for you..."

"I don't need it."

"Yes, you do. And I want it over and done with. I want nothing to cast shadows over our relationship. I want to be free of the accusing eyes and the hate-filled hearts, and I'm willing to pay any price for it. I will not get what I want by submitting to a punishment that is deemed insufficient by you or any other member of your clan. If I could've conceived of something harsher, I would've gladly paid an even greater price. Do you understand?"

She nodded, tears running in rivulets down her cheeks and onto his shirt.

"You don't have to watch."

"Yes I do, it's the least I can do."

He sighed, caressing her back in small circles. "It will go easier if I don't have to worry about your reactions. I'd rather spare you the anguish," he whispered, hooking a finger under her chin to tilt her head up. "Can you do this for me?" He gazed into her moist eyes.

After what seemed like long minutes, she nodded.

Dalhu released a breath he hadn't been aware of holding. "Thank you." He took her lips in a tender kiss.

"Can I at least accompany you there and then leave before it begins? Though if it makes things harder for you, I'll stay here."

"I would love for you to be with me at the start of the ceremony—just looking at you will lend me strength."

She reached for him, and her desperate kiss and crushing embrace were a mute declaration of love—nearly as good as a spoken one.

He was almost there. One whipping and seven days of entombment would get him this most coveted prize. The woman he loved more than anything, more than life itself, would tell him that she loved him back.

To finally hear her say the words, he would've endured this trial ten times over.

Later, when Kian and Anandur arrived to escort him to the catacombs, he was ready and anxious to get it over with.

"Shall we?" Kian asked.

"Lead the way."

Dalhu was wearing the attire he'd been given for the ceremony—a short, black robe and loose black pants resembling a judo uniform, but made from some thin silky material, and no shoes.

He wasn't the only one who was dressed up for the occasion. Fancy, long robes covered Amanda, Kian, and Anandur from head to toe, and he noticed that Anandur had exchanged his scuffed combat boots for a pair of shiny black dress shoes.

As they made their way in silence, the clicking of Amanda's heels on the concrete floor was the only sound echoing from the walls of the long, winding corridor. The large chamber they arrived at was surrounded on three sides by recessed niches that had been carved into the stone walls. They were empty, waiting like silent gaping mouths to swallow their future residents.

Dalhu glanced at the small group of people assembled to witness his trial and, hopefully, subsequent redemption. He recognized some as Guardians by the robes they were wearing, including a tall, muscular woman who must've been the Guardian friend Amanda had mentioned. There were two other females present. The one with the smart, sad eyes, wearing a robe in different colors than those of the Guardians, was most likely the legal expert. The one in civilian clothes—who was also the only one seated— was no doubt the bereaved mother, Micah.

He bowed his head to her, for the simple reason that he had no idea what else to do or say. Dalhu prayed that Kian would do the talking and get the ball rolling. Though he had no idea what to expect as far as procedure.

There were no chains in sight, no podium, not even chairs, and everyone aside from Micah was standing.

How were they going to whip him?

He was relieved when Kian clapped his back and pointed to the spot he wanted him to stand on. But then he realized he would be directly in front of Micah.

The man standing behind her with his hands on her shoulders looked just as grief-stricken—the pained expression and family resemblance identifying him as either a brother or another son.

Unable to look them in the eyes, Dalhu felt like the worst of cowards. But Amanda's presence and, surprisingly, Kian's gave him strength.

And there were others.

He was not alone.

At least two people in this crowd were rooting for him, Amanda and Anandur. And there was Andrew, who at least believed him to be forthright. Even Kian, who finally seemed resigned to give Dalhu a chance.

Could've been worse.

Kian raised a hand to get everyone's attention. "Before we begin Dalhu's trial, I would like Edna to come forward and search his soul. If she finds that he is harboring nefarious intentions toward us, we will not proceed with this ceremony, and he'll suffer the same fate as his fellow Doomers—a permanent resting place in our catacombs. If, however, Edna declares his intentions pure, Micah will extend him the offer of redemption through a trial of her choosing. If he accepts her challenge with gratitude and endures it with courage, Dalhu will earn redemption.

"He will then be granted conditional acceptance into our clan for a period of three years. During that time, he will be watched and tested. If he proves to be loyal and worthy by the end of this trial period, I'll personally welcome him as a full member of our family."

Edna wasn't a tall woman, and as she came closer and cranked her neck way up to look into his eyes, Dalhu dropped down on his knees, making it easier for her.

A small smile made a brief appearance on her austere face. "Thank you, that's very considerate."

He took her small, cold hand and placed it over his heart. "My life is in your hands. I wasn't a good man, and my past is dark, but I have nothing to hide. I'm an open book. My soul may not be worth much, but whatever there's left of it belongs to Amanda. I pledge my life and my loyalty to her and to you—her people."

Edna touched the fingers of her other hand to his cheek. "Don't resist, and it will go easier. The more you fight it, the more discomfort you'll feel."

"As I said, I'm an open book. I welcome your inquiry."

"Good, that's very good."

Her pale blue stare didn't faze him. On the contrary, he felt warmth and comfort as her ghostly fingers gently sifted through his memories, his feelings, going deeper and deeper until they reached the very essence of him.

The place where Dalhu the warrior didn't exist—the small sheltered enclave where Dalhu the boy could still be found, a boy who'd been loved and cherished by his mother.

Time and space lost meaning as Edna's tender tendrils wove through the story of his life, and when she withdrew, he was startled to find himself back in the stone chamber.

She palmed his feverish cheeks with her chilly hands and kissed his forehead before turning to face the small crowd.

"The love in this man's heart burns brightly enough to purify his sins, and perhaps even restore his soul to the beautiful sapling it once was—before Navuh's tutelage shriveled it. He regrets his past deeds and wholeheartedly seeks redemption by paying any price Micah would demand of him. In light of his good intentions, I would have asked for mercy on his behalf, but he would not have welcomed it. Dalhu wishes the price he pays to be worthy of forgiveness and acceptance even by his most vehement detractors' standards."

There were tears in Amanda's eyes as Edna finished her unequivocal endorsement, and Anandur, who was standing behind the small group, smiled and lifted both hands with his thumbs up.

Andrew nodded to no one in particular.

The speech Amanda had helped Dalhu prepare was no longer needed. Edna had done a much better job of pleading his case than he and Amanda could have ever done.

Kian moved closer to Dalhu and pulled out a scroll made of parchment from inside his robe, unrolled it, and held it in front of Dalhu as if to show him what was written on it. Not that it did him any good—the writing was in some ancient script that looked like a strange hybrid of hieroglyphs, Hindu, and old Hebrew.

"Edna composed it in the old language. I'm going to translate," Kian clarified.

"On the fifth day in the month of Kislimu, in the year 3942 after the cataclysm, Micah mother of Mark is graciously extending to Dalhu, formerly of the Brotherhood of the Devout Order Of Mortdh, a chance to atone for his part in the crime perpetrated against her beloved son Mark. He is to be flogged by her brother Otto, until she says enough, then put into stasis and entombed for a period of seven days. If at any time during his atonement, Dalhu is unable to endure, and he asks for the punishment to stop or impedes it in any way, it will cease immediately, and the offer of redemption will forever be revoked. However, if he prevails, Micah will deem Dalhu redeemed and would seek no further vengeance against him."

Kian produced a pen from a pocket inside his robe and handed it to Dalhu. "By signing this document, you accept these terms."

Without a shred of hesitation, Dalhu scribbled his name on the line Kian had pointed to.

Kian took the pen and parchment back, walked over to Micah, and handed her both. "By signing this document you accept these terms," he repeated.

As she held the pen, Micah's hand hovered over the parchment, her tormented expression revealing her inner struggle.

Please sign, please sign, please sign, Dalhu kept chanting.

The complete silence in the chamber was suffocating. It seemed as if no one dared to move, and all of them were holding their breath with him. Except, it was only his heart that was racing and only his palms that were sweating worse than if he were facing his own execution —and not the temporary one of entombment.

After what felt like an eternity, Micah's brother gave her shoulders an encouraging squeeze, and she released a breath, lowered her hand to the parchment, and signed her name on the dotted line.

As if someone had pressed play on a paused scene, a communal release of breath and the swishing of robes shattered the silence.

Kian took the parchment and lifted it for everyone to see. "The contract was signed and witnessed." He held it up for a few moments, moving it from side to side so everyone had a chance to see, then rerolled it and stashed it back inside his robe.

Turning to Dalhu, he asked, "Are you ready?"

"Yeah, I am. How do you want to do this?" He took another glance around to see if a whipping post had magically appeared.

"Nothing will hold you, it's part of the test. You're going to lean against that wall"—Kian pointed at a narrow stretch of wall that was free of niches and nearly smooth—"without a thing to grab onto—the only thing holding you up is going to be the power of your will."

This was going to be a lot tougher than he'd anticipated. To endure the pain while immobilized and restrained was one thing, to maintain position voluntarily was another.

"I can do it. I will do it."

"I know."

Kian

On his way to Amanda's penthouse, Kian deliberated how much to tell her. On the one hand, he'd promised to give her a full account, on the other, he didn't think she could handle the uncensored, blow-by-blow report.

Damn, it had been hard to watch.

But he had to admit; Dalhu had gained his respect and then some. Kian couldn't think of a single man, himself included, who could've taken the whipping Dalhu had, without moving an inch, without crying out even once, and without collapsing from the massive blood loss and exhaustion.

To say that the guy had an iron will was an understatement—a will hard as a diamond was more like it.

Micah had chosen a vicious implement, a three-stranded whip with metal tips for added injury.

At first, Otto had seemed to relish wielding the thing, but after only a few blows he was looking at Micah before delivering the next one, hoping she'd give the signal to end it.

Dalhu's blood had formed a pool at his feet, and speckles of it as well as pieces of his flesh had landed on Otto's clothes and even as far as the line of spectators.

When she had finally raised her hand and given the signal, Otto had thrown the whip to the ground. "I want this evil thing destroyed—" had been his parting words before he'd stormed out, leaving his sister behind.

Anandur hadn't wasted any time before going over to Dalhu and taking him in his arms with infinite care for his injured back, then sinking his fangs into the guy's neck and ending his misery.

The one good thing about the brutal whipping was that the fangs of all immortal males present had been ready for action with no additional aggression required.

Dalhu had proven to be one of the strongest males Kian had ever encountered. But there was no way he could've offered even a token fight after the beating he'd taken.

As he reached Amanda's door and knocked, Kian pondered the peculiar feeling that had been on the edge of his awareness since Dalhu's trial had ended. He felt at ease for some reason, like there was one less thing he had to worry about. At first, he'd thought that he was simply relieved that Dalhu had prevailed and that he wouldn't have to deliver bad news to Amanda. But now, standing in front of her door, he realized that there was more to it.

The truth was that there was no stronger protector for Amanda than Dalhu. The guy would not only give his life for her without a moment's hesitation, but more to the point, he could single-handedly take down an army to save her.

The Fates hadn't been cruel to Amanda when they'd paired her with Dalhu. They'd given her exactly the kind of male she needed.

The door opened, and the woman standing before him looked like a wreck, emotionally and physically. Amanda's eyes were so red and puffy that he suspected that she'd been crying the entire time since leaving the chamber.

"It is done, and Dalhu passed with flying colors."

She stepped aside to let him in. "Is he okay?"

"He is in stasis."

"Thank you, merciful Fates." Amanda collapsed into a chair. There was a pile of used tissues on the floor next to it. "I want you to tell me everything."

Kian glanced at his mother who had the I-knew-he-would-be-fine expression on her face and was probably itching to say, "I told you so."

"Let's just say that you should be proud of your man. I don't know of anyone who would've taken Micah's punishment as well as he did."

His choice of words hadn't escaped Amanda's notice, and her eyes widened. "You called Dalhu *my man*."

"Yes, and I also said that you should be proud of him."

"So you have no more reservation about him and me? You accept Dalhu a hundred percent?"

"How about ninety-nine?"

"I can live with that."

Amanda

The good thing about clan celebrations was that no one had partners. Otherwise, Amanda would've felt even worse than she did.

It didn't seem right to stand there in a designer evening gown and diamond jewelry, surrounded by her family's smiling faces, while her man was all alone in a dark, cold tomb. But there was no way she could've missed Kian and Syssi's wedding. After all, she was the matchmaker who had made it happen. Not to mention that her only brother was marrying her best friend and the whole clan was celebrating for the first time since its inception.

Her sisters, Sari and Alena, had arrived this morning and the three of them had a nice, tearful reunion. Kian had stopped by her apartment a little later, but hadn't stayed for long, so he'd escaped the guilt trip her sisters had laid on her.

There was really no good excuse for why she hadn't visited them more often. Sari had her hands full running the Scottish arm of their clan, and it had taken some juggling for her to get away for a couple of days to attend the wedding. And Alena was busy managing Annani, which the three of them agreed was a much more challenging job than Sari's.

Searching for her sisters, she stretched her neck, which was all she needed to do to peer over the crowd. The four-inch heels she had on made her just as tall as most of the Guardians. She spotted Sari chatting up a storm with Brandon, while Alena was standing amidst a large group of females. Someone must've told her a joke because she was doubling over with laughter.

It was good to see them having fun, and Amanda felt the vise squeezing her heart loosen a notch, allowing her at least to fall back on her well-practiced routine.

Plastering a confident smile on her face, she sauntered over to where Syssi's parents and Annani were greeting the guests. She got there just in time to see Anandur and Brundar enter.

"I thought the day would never come. You? In a tux? And Brundar too? You guys look amazing."

Brundar's long blond hair was tied at his nape with a black leather cord, his fallen-angel face looking as austere as ever. Anandur must've spent time at the barber's because his wild, curly red hair was sleeked back away from his face with the help of plenty of hair product, and his beard and mustache were trimmed a lot shorter than usual. The brute looked almost civilized.

"Syssi made me do it," Anandur complained. "I can't even move my shoulders in this damned penguin suit." He demonstrated, the seams on the tux straining from the pressure of his muscles flexing beneath them.

Amanda slapped his shoulder. "Stop it, you big oaf. The tux was custom made for you and it fits perfectly. You are not supposed to play football in it, just stand next to Kian during the ceremony and look handsome."

"I'll play my part because Syssi asked me to, but I still think bridesmaids and groomsmen do not belong in this ceremony. It is not part of our tradition."

"What tradition? We have none. This is the first wedding we ever had. We are creating tradition tonight."

"Exactly. And from now on we'll be stuck with this stupid human custom." Anandur bunched his shoulders again.

Amanda rolled her eyes. "You'll get used to it. I don't see Brundar complaining."

Brundar shrugged.

The range of the guy's emotions spanned between indifferent and stoic, oscillating at the rate of once a month.

Someone tapped her bare shoulder. "Good evening, gorgeous." Drink in hand, Andrew, the third groomsman, looked much more comfortable in his fancy suit than the brothers. He kissed her cheek. "I'm taking advantage of the opportunity that your guy is not around."

She kissed him back. "Don't be silly, Andrew, you can kiss my cheek whenever you like. Dalhu is not the jealous type."

Andrew's quick reflexes saved her gown—he spun around before spewing his drink on the floor. His shoes, however, hadn't escaped the splatter. Anandur's deep belly laugh almost popped the buttons on his tux jacket. He fished out a folded kerchief from a back pocket and handed it to Andrew. "Here, buddy, for your shoes."

"Thanks." Andrew wiped his face before attending to his footwear.

"What's so funny?" What did they all know that she didn't?

"You are one clueless princess."

"Okay, just tell me. I can see that you're dying to."

"Your guy almost choked the life out of Bhathian at Kian's bachelor party. Dalhu had a nude picture of you stashed underneath his bed, and when Bhathian found it and showed it to everyone, he attacked him so viciously that even I couldn't pry him away—not until I explained to the idiot that your nudity has no effect on the males of your own family."

Oh, wow. Her guy was jealous.

Sweet. Amanda likes.

Syssi could cling to her opinions and regard ungrounded jealousy as offensive, but Amanda was flattered. Heck, if Dalhu were near she would've grabbed him and kissed him long and hard to show him that she was all his, and that he had nothing to be jealous about.

Regrettably, Dalhu wasn't there, and she couldn't show him or tell him anything. She would, though, in four days, eighteen hours, and fifty-three minutes.

Syssi

"Are you ready, my love?" Kian smiled and offered Syssi his arm.

Taking a deep breath, she nodded.

It was time for their big entry.

She and Amanda had planned the ceremony, incorporating traditions they both liked and replacing the ones they didn't. After all, they were in charge of creating a new script that would provide the foundation for future clan weddings.

They had agreed that bridesmaids and groomsmen were nice to have, but there was no need for more than three each and the girls should choose their own gowns. Amanda had been adamant about that.

Kian had chosen Andrew, Anandur, and Brundar, and Syssi had chosen Amanda, Kri, and Bridget.

The walk down the aisle with a father giving away the bride had been thrown out the window. The obvious reason was that aside from Syssi, other clan females had no fathers to call on. Besides, it was an outdated custom that should've ended along with everything else that still stunk of patriarchy—like taking on the husband's last name.

Amanda had insisted, however, that a grand entry was necessary and that Syssi should walk down the aisle by herself.

Syssi had refused.

To make the walk alone while everyone was watching?

No way.

Not her style.

It was her wedding, and she was the one making the rules.

She would walk down the aisle with Kian by her side.

"You look stunning." Kian kissed her cheek, gently, careful not to mess up her makeup—per Amanda's instructions. She had warned him, threatening to unman him if he dared.

Syssi had to admit that this was the most beautiful she had ever looked. Her dress was long-sleeved and had a simple cut, the bodice following her contours without being too clingy, and a long train that she was certain would get stepped on—a lot. The décolletage was wide and low, leaving the tops of her shoulders bare but stopping short of her cleavage. Her concession to tradition was that the dress was white and long, but she refused a veil—another outdated custom that should've been tossed out a long time ago.

Kian had requested that she leave her hair down, and Armando, who had shown up with two assistants each carrying two cases filled to the brim with tools of his trade, had been so proud of the job he'd done with her hair and makeup that he'd cried. Not a few pretend teardrops for drama, but for real, claiming that this was his masterpiece and he would never achieve such perfection again. So he should quit and retire while at his peak.

The guy was no more than thirty.

And yet, after all the effort everyone had invested so she'd look her best, gazing at Kian, she doubted anyone would be looking at her while this Greek god in a tux walked beside her. There was no way she could compete with his perfection.

"Not to add to your already overinflated ego, but you must be the most good-looking man ever to exist." She took his hand.

Kian dipped his head in a slight bow. "Thank you, my lady. But I assure you that no one else shares your opinion. Beauty is in the eyes of the beholder."

Yeah, right.

There was a moment of quiet as the soft music that had been playing in the large assembly hall stopped.

A new, familiar tune began.

Ooga-Chaka Ooga-Ooga

Ooga-Chaka Ooga-Ooga

Kian grinned from ear to ear. "This is our cue."

Syssi laughed. "That's the song you've chosen? "Hooked on a Feeling?"

"Isn't it perfect?"

"It is."

"Then let's go." He pushed through the double doors, and they danced their way up to the podium to the beat of Blue Swede's *Hooked on a feeling* while their guests clapped, cheered, and sang along.

I can't stop this feeling deep inside of me.

Andrew

It was after seven, and even the most diligent of his fellow agents had left—some to go home, others down to Barney's.

Like in the old days, before he'd gotten involved with the clan and had taken on an after-hours part-time job, Andrew was the last one in the office and wasn't expecting to be done anytime soon.

Tim's sketch had been sitting inside a large shopping bag next to Andrew's desk, calling to him throughout the entire day.

He couldn't wait to sink his teeth into the investigation.

Now that he was no longer on the clock, he could finally pull it out and start digging.

There was something very compelling about the woman in the picture. It wasn't her beauty, though she was a looker. It was something about her eyes—a mystery begging to be solved. Andrew had the odd feeling that she was staring at him from the paper and imploring him to find her.

Doubtless, it was all in his head. The expressive eyes were nothing more than testament to Tim's talent, and his interpretation of Bhathian's longing for a lover the guy had lost more than thirty years ago.

I'll do my best, he promised her anyway.

Trouble was, Patricia would be seventy-five years old. If she was still alive, that is. She could've died from natural causes by now, and there was always a possibility that someone other than herself had arranged her disappearance.

People disappeared all of the time—some voluntarily, some not.

Sadly, in the case of beautiful women, it was more often than not the latter.

Fuck, he hoped Patricia hadn't been the victim of some scumbag like Alex.

True, they had no proof yet that Amanda's cousin was engaged in the business of kidnapping and trafficking women for sexual slavery, but the circumstantial evidence Amanda had gathered during her trip aboard Alex's yacht, together with Dalhu's observation, suggested that he was.

This was going to be Andrew's next pet project.

He just needed to figure out the logistics first. There had been talk of using the clan's private satellite to spy on the boat, but William had shot it down. Their communication satellite wasn't designed for that purpose. However, the clan had the resources to build one, and it had been decided to hire a team to start working on it.

Obviously, the thing wouldn't be ready anytime soon.

He'd have to resort to more mundane means—like finding the weak link in the Russian crew and manipulating her, one way or the other, to cooperate with them.

Later.

Now, he needed to focus on finding Patricia.

There were several databases to go through. But first, he decided to run the social security number, even though he was certain it was fake. Government agencies issued them for various purposes, and if this were the case, then he would strike gold. They typically made use of a real, recently deceased person's social security number instead of producing an entirely fake one—which was the method most amateurs and small-time criminals used.

A minute later he found it. The number belonged indeed to a Patricia Evans, born September 1951 and deceased November 1987. For a moment, his heart sank. Patricia had died about a year after meeting Bhathian. But then he glanced at the year of birth again. The math didn't add up. Patricia had claimed to have been forty-five at the time, which would've put her birth year at somewhere around 1940, not 1951.

Was it possible that she'd lied about her age? Claiming to be a decade older than she actually was? Not likely.

And the fact that the year of death was not before, but after she had met Bhathian? A death certificate could've been falsified. The elaborate setup, however, was more appropriate for an undercover operative than someone in the witness protection or relocation service.

The year of birth didn't match Pat's real age, but it matched the way she'd looked at the time Bhathian had met her. The guy had thought she was in her late twenties. If Pat had been working undercover at the time, her assumed social security number wouldn't have raised suspicion. If anyone had bothered to check, they would've found a Patricia Evans who matched the agent's perceived age—and who wasn't dead. The death certificate hadn't been entered into the system.

Andrew stretched his arms over his head before diving back in. This was going to make his job so much easier. Fewer databases to check.

Bingo! Pat was, or rather had been, a drug enforcement agent. Her real name was Eva Paterson. Funny, the guys in charge of producing the fake social security numbers must've liked that one. The real Patricia Evans, a name that would've been very easy for Eva Paterson to remember, had conveniently passed away at the right time.

A little more digging produced Eva Paterson's file and the rest of the pieces fell into place.

As a drug enforcement agent, she'd been working undercover as a flight attendant, investigating the involvement of airline personnel in drug smuggling. The setup had been long, and that particular stint had lasted more than three years. She had retired from the agency shortly after meeting Bhathian—for health related reasons. The government was still depositing monthly pension checks into her account.

Eva was still alive.

Okay, next step was to find out what she'd been up to.

Andrew switched to the IRS database. Other than Facebook, there was no better source of information about people's lives than their tax returns, which he had unrestricted access to.

Interesting.

A month after leaving the agency, Eva had married a guy named Fernando Vega, a Cuban immigrant, and seven months later the couple had a daughter, Nathalie. Five years after Nathalie was born, they'd moved from Florida to Los Angeles and had opened a bakery in Studio City.

Judging by the couple's tax returns, their small-business income combined with Eva's retirement checks had been just enough to provide their family of three with a comfortable middle-class living.

Nathalie had remained their only child.

Thirteen years ago, Eva had filed for a divorce.

Andrew had to look up both spouses' tax returns to continue.

Fernando kept filing as a single man, but three years later he'd apparently been declared mentally incompetent, and the daughter had been the one filing the returns since.

Eva's last tax return had been filed seven years ago.

Damn, what happened?

He ran her name again through a couple of other databases, and what he found wasn't good.

The daughter had filed a missing person's report with the police six years ago. With no evidence of foul play, the case had been closed even though Eva hadn't been found.

Fuck.

Andrew felt like punching the computer screen. He'd been so close to finding the woman, and she had to go and disappear. Again.

With a sigh, he pulled up the police report.

Damn! Eva must've had extensive plastic surgery done because the woman in the photograph looked exactly the same as the woman in Tim's forensic sketch. She hadn't aged at all...

It could've been the result of a skillful surgical knife, or... immortality...

But Bhathian had claimed that he hadn't bitten her.

Had any Dormant ever turned without the help of venom?

Searching his memory, Andrew sifted through everything he'd been told about a Dormant's turning, dimly recalling something about the little girls' turning facilitated by Annani's presence alone.

Under no circumstances, though, could Eva have been exposed to the Goddess as a child. He doubted the clan would've surrendered any of its precious children for adoption in case something had happened to the child's mother.

But just in case, he would check if they had lost track of any of their females. Maybe someone who had moved far away and hadn't kept in touch with her family had been abducted or killed, and her young child had been adopted by unsuspecting humans.

There was a more expedient way to find out, though; he could check Eva's birth record.

Thank God for Uncle Sam and the access to information Andrew had been granted. Adoption records and the birth certificates of adopted children were guarded better than the government's strategic secrets.

Eva's birth record, however, was easy to find and as fascinating as yesterday's porridge. She was born at Tampa General Hospital, previously known as Municipal Hospital Davis Islands, to Alfonso and Fawn Paterson.

Nevertheless, it wouldn't hurt to ask Kian if he was aware of a long lost female clan member.

Damn, Bhathian would be disappointed that Andrew hadn't found Eva. But at least he could deliver the news about the daughter.

Okay, Nathalie, let's see what we can tell Daddy about you.

Husband—none. Children—none.

Her father was the only dependent listed on her tax return.

She'd closed the Studio City coffee shop less than a year after her father had been declared mentally incompetent, and opened a new one in Glendale. Most years the profits hadn't been great. Nathalie was barely scraping by.

He wondered why she hadn't closed the place a long time ago. She could've been making more as an employee somewhere. Perhaps she was the type who valued being her own boss above everything else. Or maybe it had something to do with the father and preserving his business for sentimental reasons.

A closer look at her tax returns provided the answer. Her residence address was the same as her business, save for the suite number. Nathalie had moved the shop to an area that allowed mixed-use housing—business and living quarters combined. A perfect solution for someone who needed to work and at the same time keep an eye on a parent who had suffered a severe mental decline. Apparently, Nathalie was a very devoted daughter.

Did she know that Fernando wasn't her real father?

How would she react if she ever discovered who her biological father was?

Andrew pulled out his cell phone and selected Bhathian's number.

"You found something?" There was no mistaking the excitement in the guy's voice.

Andrew delivered the good news without preamble. "You have a daughter. Her name is Nathalie, and she lives right around the corner from you, in Glendale."

"Thank the merciful Fates," Bhathian breathed in a shaky voice. "And Patricia? Is she"—the guy swallowed—"you know…"

"As far as I know."

"What do you mean?"

"Patricia's real name is Eva Paterson, and she went missing six years ago. Nathalie filed a missing person's report, but the case was closed."

"What the hell? She disappeared again?"

"Meet me at Barney's in half an hour, and I'll tell you everything I was able to find."

"I'm leaving right now. I can be there in fifteen minutes."

"Good deal, see you there."

Eva's missing person's file was still opened on his screen, and he printed an enlarged version of the photograph Nathalie had given the police.

While his terminal was powering down, Andrew stashed both the forensic sketch and the printout in the shopping bag. Keys and wallet went into his jacket's inside pocket, and he switched off the lights on his way out.

The drive to Barney's took less than ten minutes, and as he entered the bar, Andrew felt an irrational rush of satisfaction that he'd made it there before Bhathian.

Selecting a quiet booth at the back, he ordered two beers and a platter of nachos.

It took Bhathian another fifteen minutes to storm into the bar, and people scurried to clear the path for the hulking guy with a murderous expression on his face.

"Goddamned LA traffic." He pulled out a chair, grabbing a beer as his butt landed in the seat.

"It's a bitch," Andrew agreed.

Bhathian sucked half the bottle on a oner, then pinned Andrew with a hard stare. "Lay it on me."

Andrew moved the nacho platter over to the edge of the table before leaning sideways and lifting the shopping bag. He pulled out the large forensic sketch and the letter-size printout, laying both side by side so they were facing Bhathian. He pointed to the photograph. "This is the picture Nathalie gave the police when she filed the report six years ago. I don't think she would've given them an old one."

Bhathian picked up the photocopy, his gloomy features softening as he caressed it with his finger. "She looks exactly as I remember her," he said quietly.

It seemed that the guy was so used to being around people who didn't age that the significance of what he was seeing escaped him.

"Does it not strike you as odd? Eva, your Patricia—a human—not aging in the slightest?"

Bhathian lifted his head, the momentary softening of his features giving way to a frown that was impressive even for him. "What are you implying?"

"Look"—Andrew pointed to the picture—"the woman hasn't aged in thirty years. So she is either an immortal or has undergone extensive plastic surgery. Frankly, though, I don't think any surgeon is that good."

"I didn't bite her."

"I know, I'm not saying that you did, there must be some other explanation."

"Like what?"

"Maybe she was already immortal when you met her? You said she looked a lot younger than what she claimed to be, and looking at this picture I agree. This woman looks like she's in her late twenties, not midforties."

Bhathian rubbed his neck. "Immortal females are supposed to smell different than humans when aroused."

"And she didn't?"

The guy shrugged. "All I can remember is that everything about her was amazing. My head was all into the sex and wanting to bite her. Then when I realized she wasn't responding to the thrall, all I could think of was how to refrain from sinking my fangs into her neck. It took all I had just to hide what I am from her."

"So there is a chance she was an immortal."

Bhathian shook his head. "There are no immortal females other than ours. Maybe the Doomers have some, but even if they do, there is no chance in hell even one managed to get away."

"Are all the clan females accounted for? Is it possible that you guys lost touch with one who had a young daughter? A child who was already turned and somehow ended up being adopted by humans?"

Bhathian kept shaking his head from side to side. "We know where every clan member is at all times."

"You sure? How can you keep tabs on everyone, every moment?"

"I didn't say every moment. But everyone who lives outside the keeps or travels for extended periods of time calls in once a week."

"What about before there were phones?"

"Back then hardly anyone lived outside the community and the few who did, lived nearby."

"Travelers?"

Bhathian shook his head. "Never alone, always in groups."

"Okay, I'm stumped. I can think of no other explanation."

Bhathian's neck rubbing intensified, the furrow in between his brows so deep that the bushy things became a unibrow. "There is one more possibility. But it's a one in a billion chance. She might have had sex with another immortal before me, and he turned her without him or her realizing it. Otherwise, he would've never let her go."

"Yeah, it does sound extremely far-fetched. There must be a simpler explanation. Like your daughter, for some reason, using an old picture. Maybe Eva was...is...one of those women who hate being photographed and this was the only picture Nathalie had of her."

"Yeah, that's sounds more likely." Bhathian sighed. "I would like to meet he... my daughter." There was wonder in his tone.

Andrew grimaced. "That's a really bad idea. Eva married a guy named Fernando Vega shortly after you'd last seen her, and Nathalie was born seven months later. She might not know that Fernando is not her real father. And anyway, you look too young."

Bhathian stared at Andrew. "So, there is a chance she isn't mine. Premature babies are not uncommon."

"Nah, she's yours. Too much of a coincidence."

"Do you have her picture?"

"No. What I know about her, I got mostly from her tax returns—she's not married, doesn't have children, owns a coffee shop, and takes care of her father—adoptive father that is—who suffers from mental decline. I didn't have time to dig any deeper. I can, if you want."

Bhathian's frown eased a fraction, relaxing the pissed-off expression he normally wore. "Can we go see her? You know, at her coffee place, like random customers. I just want to get a look, hear her voice."

"Sure, but you don't need me. I'll give you the address."

Bhathian swallowed a couple of times before spitting it out. "I don't want to go by myself."

The big guy was asking for moral support, and Andrew could think of no good reason to deny him. In fact, it would be better if he went with Bhathian. After all, a man who looked like that, sitting alone and staring at the woman for God knows how long, would scare the shit out of her. Andrew could provide a cover and soften the impact.

"No problem, when do you want to do it?"

"How late do you think her place is open?"

"Let me check."

Amanda

The crypt was awfully quiet as Amanda waited for Anandur and Brundar to arrive and revive Dalhu.

Since she'd gotten there more than an hour early, she'd been breathing shallowly and barely moving, afraid of making any noise lest it disturbed the dead. Their ghosts might rise to haunt her.

Or rather one ghost—Mark's.

Please, dear Fates, let Mark be satisfied with Dalhu's sacrifice.

She wished Mark would give her a sign, let her know somehow that he was okay on the other side and that he had forgiven her.

This entire week, ever since Dalhu's atonement, she'd been going to bed early, hoping that Mark would visit her in her dreams. But, of course, he hadn't.

It was stupid. Just wishful thinking.

Fates, she was lonely.

Her mother and sisters had gone home the day after the wedding, as had Syssi's parents, while Syssi and Kian had left for their honeymoon in boring Dana Point. She had tried to convince them to pick Hawaii, but Kian had refused to go any farther—claiming that he needed to remain close by in case he was needed urgently.

Like the keep couldn't function without him for one measly week.

At least he'd been nice about leaving Anandur and Brundar behind, taking Onegus and Arwel as his bodyguards instead.

She didn't trust anyone other than Anandur to revive Dalhu.

Her man had already suffered so much.

He'd paid with his flesh and blood. And in a way—his life. Experiencing entombment came too damn close to dying.

And yet, there was a sense of poetic beauty to it—death and rebirth.

Dalhu would be reborn as a new man.

Both Andrew and Edna had vouched for him, and he'd provided the clan with loads of vital information about the Doomer organization that couldn't have been obtained in any other way.

Feeling like an idiot, she murmured, "Come on, Mark, this must be good enough, give me a sign that you've forgiven me."

Not that she was really expecting a response, but she couldn't help the pang of disappointment when the crypt remained silent. She wondered if Mark could hear her, wherever he was. Probably not, because otherwise he would've answered. Mark had been such a nice guy—he would not have let her suffer like this even if he was still angry with her. Come to think of it, she was pretty sure he would've forgiven her even without Dalhu's sacrifice.

The one who had been seeking retribution was she, not Mark.

Mark had been a good person, she wasn't.

Maybe that was why she was carrying around such tremendous guilt.

Her mind couldn't focus on anything, and even though she had gone back to work the day after Dalhu's trial, she had done nothing more than going through the motions—lecturing and supervising the standard university research. Using the convenient excuse of Syssi's absence, she hadn't conducted a single paranormal test—as if she hadn't done it for years before hiring Syssi.

She just hadn't been in the mood.

It was hard to concentrate while counting the seconds until Dalhu's *rebirth*.

She heard the brothers coming down the corridor even though they were making very little noise. The crypt magnified the slightest sound—she could hear the swish of their robes.

"Hi, guys," she greeted them as they entered the chamber. "Why the formality? Is there a ceremony involved that I wasn't aware of?" She was wearing jeans and a T-shirt.

Anandur shrugged. "I guess not, but I kind of like these." He waved a hand between his and Brundar's robes.

Brundar arched a brow as if to say, *really?*

Amanda sighed. "Okay, you had me scared for a moment there. I don't want to waste one more minute of Dalhu's life, and I would've hated to have to wait for Onidu to bring my robe."

"Well, then let's get down to business. Follow me."

Anandur led them down another corridor and into a smaller chamber, where a simple, unadorned sarcophagus was resting on top of a stone platform.

"Amanda, you stand over there." He pointed to the wall. "Brundar, you grab the lid from the other side, and we lift on a count of two."

He waited till his brother had a good grip on the stone lid.

"How heavy is that thing?" she blurted before thinking. "Sorry..."

Anandur gave her an exasperated look. "It's heavy. Not to say that I wouldn't have been able to lift it by myself, but you don't want that thing to accidentally fall and smash your frog. Broken bones take much longer to heal than broken skin."

"I'm sorry. I'm going to keep my mouth shut from now on."

Anandur's smirk implied that he doubted she could keep her promise.

"Okay, Brundar, on the count of two. One, two…" They lifted the lid simultaneously, then laid it carefully on the stone floor.

Anandur reached inside his robes and pulled out two large glass containers the size of a two-liter soft drink bottle each, filled with some clear liquid. Brundar produced a large box of saltine crackers.

"What's in the containers?"

"Holy water." Anandur winked.

"Really?" What the hell was he talking about? What holy water?

"Just plain water, Princess. Clear, uncontaminated, chemical free, spring water."

"Oh…can I come closer?"

"No," both brothers said at once.

"Wait over there." Anandur pointed a finger at where she was standing.

"Okay," she whispered. Dalhu must look awful if even Brundar didn't want her to see him.

Anandur lifted one of the containers over the sarcophagus and began pouring water over Dalhu's body in a thin steady stream, careful to wet him all over. She watched, expecting him to grab the second container once the first was emptied, but he didn't. Instead, he pulled out a piece of cloth from the inside of his robe and began rubbing Dalhu's body in circular motion.

"He's dehydrated, like a freeze-dried piece of fruit. Once his skin absorbs the water, his systems will gradually come online until he's able to drink on his own. I guess we could've used intravenous rehydration, but this is the way it has always been done."

"What the hell? Why didn't you?"

"Don't get your panties in a wad, he'll be fine. In fact, his pulse is already getting stronger."

Amanda could've punched him. Why stick to some old and outdated custom when modern medicine provided a safer, easier way?

Men were such idiots.

"Brundar, check if he can drink," Anandur instructed.

Brundar bent to reach into the sarcophagus, lifted Dalhu's head, and brought the container to his lips. Not that she was able to see what was going on inside the box, but it was easy to guess from Brundar's movements. What surprised her, though, was the gentleness with which the guy performed his task. She would've never suspected that the brutal weapons master had it in him.

"Good, keep giving him a little at a time." Anandur kept rubbing.

Thank you, merciful Fates, Dalhu was drinking on his own.

To say she felt relieved was an understatement. A massive weight had lifted off her chest.

He was okay.

A moment later his hands shot out and grabbed the container Brundar was holding. Brundar held his head up as he gulped loudly.

"Easy there, slow down, you don't want to choke or vomit." Anandur put pressure on the container's other end, reducing the tilt. "That's it, slow and steady," he encouraged in a soft voice.

Dalhu kept drinking for what seemed like forever—until all the water was gone.

"Good job. Brundar will help you sit up, slowly, we want all of that life-giving water to stay inside, okay?" He was talking slowly and quietly, as if to not frighten a child or spook an animal.

Amanda held her breath as she waited to get her first glimpse of Dalhu's face. When she finally did, a gasp escaped her throat. His skin looked gray and dry like that of a corpse, and there were crusted lines of brown blood on his bare back. But it seemed that his injuries had healed while he'd been in stasis.

At the sound of her voice, Dalhu turned his head and smiled, his dry, chapped lips cracking.

She ran to him and wrapped her arms around him, burying her nose in the crook of his neck. The tears came next, then the sobs, and soon her whole body was quaking. She sobbed even harder when Dalhu's once powerful arms hugged her limply.

"It's okay, don't cry, my love," he rasped in her ear. "I'm fine, just a little weak, it will pass."

Dear, merciful Fates, she loved this man. Even barely alive he was comforting her, putting her needs before his— always and without fail.

"I love you," she sobbed into his neck.

As if her words had given him strength, she felt his arms tighten around her. "Say it again," he whispered.

Amanda lifted her head and kissed his cheek. "I love you," she said aloud. "I love you," she repeated even louder. "And I'm so sorry for putting you through this," she added quietly.

"It was all worth it, and I'd do it again tonight, and tomorrow, and the day after that, just to hear you say you love me."

There were tears in his eyes, and she quickly kissed each one to hide it from the guys. "I promise to say it over and over again, so many times that you'll grow sick of hearing it."

He smiled, the sparkle in his eyes infusing life into his cadaverous visage. "Not going to happen, I'll never tire of hearing the woman I love say it back to me, never."

The sound of clapping reminded Amanda that they were not alone, and with one last kiss to Dalhu's forehead, she retreated a step.

Anandur's grin was so wide that his face looked like it was going to split in half. He went on clapping for a few more seconds. "This must be what true love is. Dude, you look like a corpse and stink like one too, and she kisses you and tells you she loves you. Damn." He shook his head.

Brundar opened the box of saltines and handed Dalhu a few. "Eat, you need the carbs and the salt."

Dalhu chewed obediently but refused more. "Help me get out of here, would you?"

The brothers assisted Dalhu, practically lifting him out, and Anandur held on while Brundar produced a folded white sheet from inside the folds of his robe, flopped it out of its square, and wrapped it around Dalhu's naked body. He tied it like a toga so it wouldn't unravel.

"Thank you," Dalhu murmured.

"No problem. Can you walk?"

"Not on my own, I need your help."

"That's what I'm here for. Lean on me, brother."

Wow, did Anandur just call Dalhu "brother"? Was it a joke?

From the expression on Dalhu's face, he wasn't sure either. "Thanks, you're the man, Anandur."

Brundar got on Dalhu's other side and wrapped his arm around his middle. "Put your arms on our shoulders, you need to distribute your weight between us."

Dalhu did as he was told. "I'm sorry for the stink, guys," he said as the three of them shuffled slowly toward the exit.

"Yeah, you owe us for this, big time. I think a nude of me in full color would do. What about you, Brundar, what would make you happy?"

"To burn it?"

"What? My nude? Why? I want to hang it in our living room."

"That's why."

Their banter continued as they made their way down the corridor at a snail's pace with Dalhu's feet dragging on the floor between them.

Walking behind the men, she felt her heart breaking at the sight of Dalhu's poor back. A week in stasis had taken care of his wounds, and even the scars were barely visible, though it was hard to tell under the layer of crusted brown blood.

"We are not going to the cell. I'm taking Dalhu up to my penthouse," she announced.

The procession halted, and both Anandur and Dalhu turned their heads to look at her.

"Kian would have our heads," Anandur said.

"He is not here. I'll deal with him when he returns."

"All I need is you, a shower, and a bed. I don't care where," Dalhu croaked through his dried out throat.

She put her palm on his sunken cheek. "I know, my love, but I will no longer tolerate anyone doubting the value and loyalty of my fated mate."

Dalhu nodded. "As you wish, my princess."

She smiled. Her guy was so smart. In a matter of mere weeks, Dalhu had figured out the key to a successful marriage—the three little words every male should know and use—

As you wish.

Michael & Kri's story
The Children of the Gods book 6.5
<u>My Dark Amazon</u>

READY FOR ANDREW'S STORY?
THE CHILDREN OF THE GODS BOOK 7
DARK WARRIOR MINE
TURN THE PAGE TO READ THE EXCERPT.

DARK WARRIOR MINE

When Andrew is forced to retire from active duty, he believes that a boring desk job is all he has to look forward to. His glory days in special ops are over. But as it turns out, his thrill ride has just begun. Andrew discovers not only that immortals exist and have been manipulating global affairs since antiquity, but that he and his sister are rare possessors of the immortal genes.

Problem is, Andrew might be too old to attempt the activation process. His sister, who is fourteen years his junior, barely makes it through the transition, so the odds of him coming out of it alive, let alone immortal, are slim.

But fate may force his hand.

Nathalie

Harvard-Westlake High school

Studio City, California

13 years ago.

"Hi, Nathalie." Leaning his hip against the metal door of his locker, Luke Bruoker produced his seductive smile. For her.

Walk away, the voice in her head commanded.

Shut up, Nathalie thought back.

Just do it. You know what he's thinking.

As if she needed Tut to freaking tell her what was on Luke's mind as he flashed her, *Nutty Nattie,* the perfect set of teeth that had all the other girls wetting their designer panties. With his good looks and rich daddy, Luke was one of the most popular guys in school, and for giving her the time of day, he probably expected her to fall at his feet in gratitude.

Not this girl, not going to happen, buddy.

Trying to ignore her too handsome and too full of himself locker neighbor, Nathalie stuffed the books she came to retrieve in her backpack.

But what if she was wrong? What if Luke was just being nice? And anyway, even if he wasn't, she didn't want to be rude.

"Hi, Luke." Nathalie lifted the corners of her lips in a tight smile and waved goodbye.

You're not wrong, Tut snickered. *But if it's any consolation, he thinks you're hot.*

It's not.

Unfortunately, there was no way to hide things from the stowaway sharing her cranium space.

You're such a liar. Tut's laugh echoed in her head before slowly fading away.

Well, what did he expect? She was only human and couldn't help but feel flattered.

He was such a pain, but if she was lucky, for the next few hours he'd leave her alone. Tut, or *tutor*, as he'd introduced himself after chasing all the other voices away, hated math class. In fact, the ghost in her head didn't like school, or homework, or tests—which was probably the main reason she was such a good student. The only time

Nathalie could be alone in her own skull was while studying.

Tut claimed to be teaching her about life.

Yeah, right, more like ruining it.

Watching TV with him was a nightmare. He wouldn't shut up for a moment with his nonstop derisive commentary about everyone and everything. And hanging out with friends or going to the mall was more of the same.

Who was she kidding? As if anyone wanted to hang out with Nutty Nattie—the girl who talked to herself.

Nathalie pulled on the straps of her heavy backpack, hitching it higher on her back as she walked faster—pretending to rush so no one would notice that she always walked alone.

Mostly, she felt invisible. No one would look at her, except maybe for some of the nicer girls who would occasionally give her a pitying smile—as if she was retarded or deformed. The best she could hope for was to be regarded as the crazy genius. Unfortunately, even though she was smart and worked harder than most, she deserved only the first part of the title.

But at least her hard work had gotten her accepted into this overpriced private high school. Trouble was, her parents couldn't really afford it—not even with the generous financial aid they'd been awarded—and she knew for a fact that they were dipping into their equity line to finance the difference. The school called the discount a scholarship, but it wasn't. None of the rich kids were getting it, not even those who were excellent students.

Still, it wasn't as if anyone was privy to that information, but it wasn't hard to guess either. Her classmates arrived at school in Mercedes and BMWs while she drove a three-year-old Toyota Corolla hatchback.

Not that she was complaining, her car was great—the previous owner had hardly driven her, and she was almost as good as new. Besides, this was the best her parents could afford. God knew they had always given her everything they could, and probably more than they should—spoiling their only child.

When she was younger, she'd thought it was her due, but lately, it was making her feel guilty. It seemed as if by giving her all of their love, her parents were left with nothing for each other.

In fact, this morning, her mother told her that she'd filed for a divorce.

Oh, God, what is Papi going to do?

The coffee shop wasn't making much, and they would not have been able to afford much of anything without her mother's government pension.

How is Papi going to survive without it?

Thank God, it was her last year of high school, so at least this expense would be gone. And since she'd gotten a full-ride scholarship to the University of Virginia, college wouldn't cost her parents anything.

But savings aside, it meant that her father would be all alone once she left.

At sixty, her mother was still a knockout, while Papi, two years her junior, looked like a grandpa. It had to do with his love of baking—and eating. He was at least fifty pounds overweight and almost bald. But he was the sweetest guy. Which was probably why his business wasn't doing so well. He had never turned away anyone who was hungry, regardless of their ability to pay.

Not fair.

The God her father believed in so earnestly should've smiled upon a man like him, rewarded him for his good heart and generosity. But instead, his beloved coffee shop was barely staying afloat, and his beautiful wife was leaving him.

Nathalie had a feeling that her mother had just been waiting for her to finish school and go to college to make her move. Eva hadn't been happy for years—even when Papi had been much thinner and still had hair. She always looked troubled, almost fearful, though Nathalie couldn't figure out why.

Maybe her mother suffered from some mental disease—like Nathalie did. Though instead of hearing voices of dead people in her head, Eva might've been anxious or depressed.

It was about time she talked with her mother and cleared things up. She was definitely old enough for a grownup conversation. Perhaps they both could benefit from psychiatric help. And maybe, just maybe, with treatment, Eva might change her mind about leaving.

But even if she wouldn't, to be rid of Tut, it was worth a try.

Problem was, psychiatrists were expensive.

Maybe that was why her parents had never taken her to one, even though they must've known that her so-called imaginary friends had been very different than those of other kids.

But Papi had said that it was harmless, nothing to worry about, and her mother had agreed. They'd cautioned her that it was okay to play pretend at home, but she shouldn't be talking to herself in public.

Nathalie had tried.

As she had grown older, she'd realized that it wasn't normal and that the people talking to her in her head were probably just elaborate hallucinations. A mental disorder and not ghosts. She'd stopped telling even her parents about it.

But here and there, she would forget herself and respond out loud—hence the damn nickname. *Nutty Nattie*.

Andrew

I've just landed, taxiing in, I can be at your place in an hour. Andrew texted Bridget as soon as it was okay to turn cell phones on.

She answered. *Waiting impatiently* ('}~{')

It took him a few seconds to decipher the meaning.

Cute.

For an immortal, who was born God knew when, she was surprisingly well versed in current texting lingo and etiquette. Better than he was. He'd never asked Bridget how old she was, in part because he felt it was impolite, and in part because he was afraid to find out. For a forty-year-old man, it would've been beyond weird to know that his girlfriend was hundreds of years old.

Andrew wondered how Syssi dealt with her husband's age. His baby sister, thirteen years his junior, had fallen in love with Kian before finding out that her Greek-god-lookalike boyfriend was so ancient.

The few clan members Andrew had gotten to know since he'd been sucked into their world ranged in age from nearly two thousand, like his new brother-in-law, to Amanda, who was over two hundred. Not to mention their mother, the goddess, who was over five thousand years old or more.

This was another lady who Andrew would never dare ask for her age. He was an adrenaline junkie, but he wasn't stupid enough to court certain death.

After a day of endless meetings, followed by a five-hour flight from Washington back to L.A., Andrew would've preferred for Bridget to come over to his place. Trouble was, whatever was in the fridge had probably spoiled over the two weeks he'd been gone.

True, he could've ordered takeout, but there was also the issue of his bed being messy, and probably not quite fresh smelling. He couldn't remember the last time he'd changed the linens. Not that they were all the way into the gross category, but Bridget deserved better.

He'd thought about buying her a present in D.C. but eventually had given up on the idea. First of all, Bridget was loaded, just like all other clan members, and what Andrew defined as a reasonably-priced gift, she might consider trash. Secondly, he had no idea what to buy for a woman in general and for this one in particular. Dr. Bridget's tastes gravitated toward the practical.

Except, she had a thing for red.

Damn, just thinking about those spiky red heels of hers was enough to get him hard. But it wasn't as if he could buy her shoes. And even if he were one of those guys who could guess a woman's shoe size, hers were probably the kind that cost over a thousand bucks—not something he could afford on his government salary.

So yeah, the only things he felt confident buying for a woman were chocolates and flowers.

But at least he wasn't as clueless as Bhathian, who didn't even know how to behave around one, or what to say.

The guy had been terrified of going to see the long-lost daughter Andrew had found for him. So much so that he'd asked Andrew to accompany him to her coffee shop, just so they could sit there, pretending to be customers. It hadn't been a good feeling to bail on the guy, but Andrew had had no choice. Her place had been closed on the evening he'd delivered the news of her existence, and the next day he'd been told to pack up a suitcase and hop on a plane to Washington.

The trip had been a total waste of time. He'd spent two fucking weeks in Homeland Security headquarters—stuck in boring meetings, listening to bureaucrats who believed they knew best how to devise a plan of action that could've been condensed into five paragraphs on one yellow-pad page. Actually, it was exactly what he'd brought back.

One fucking page.

They could've bloody emailed him. Anyway, no one had listened to what he'd had to say.

Fuck, he hoped Bhathian hadn't waited for him to go see the girl—correction, woman; earlier this year the guy's daughter had turned thirty.

An hour later, Andrew knocked on Bridget's door. Luckily, no one had hitched a ride with him on the elevator that had taken him from the clan's private parking level up to her floor. And by no one he meant Bhathian.

He planned to call the guy after his reunion with Bridget.

Andrew and the doctor had a lot of steam to release. The entire time he'd been away, he'd been preserving his energy for the insatiable immortal.

Today, he would show her staying power.

She opened the door, wearing a long white T-shirt, spiky red heels, and nothing else. "Andrew, you have no idea how happy I am to see you," she purred.

"Not as happy as I am." He lifted her up for a kiss, kicking the door closed behind him. She wrapped her legs around his hips.

Bridget was naked under that semi-sheer thing, every curve and shade of her generous breasts and aroused nipples clearly visible, and the bedroom was too far away.

Turning around, he pinned her against the nearest wall. "I can't wait," he groaned, holding her up with one hand and going for his belt buckle with the other.

"Let me." She pushed his hand away and opened things up for him. Freeing his shaft, she guided it into her moist heat. Bridget was drenched. He hesitated, but only for a split second, before ramming inside her with one powerful thrust.

On a groan, her head hit the wall behind her.

With the wall holding part of her weight and her thighs locked in a tight grip around his hips, he needed only one hand on her ass to keep going, and he put the other one to good use, pushing her shirt up and palming a breast.

Bridget did one better, pulling the thing over her head and tossing it on the floor. Now, she was completely bare save for the shoes.

They could stay on.

Damn, this was so fucking hot.

Thumbing one perky nipple, he pinched and tugged, taking turns and giving each the same loving attention.

Bridget's hands shot into his short hair, and she gripped his skull, bringing his head closer for a hungry kiss. As their tongues and teeth dueled, her sharp incisors were winning, and as she bit down on his lower lip, she drew blood.

Feisty immortal.

He brought his hand down on her butt with a loud slap, then gripped both cheeks and began pounding with gusto.

"Yes! Oh, dear Fates, yes!" Bridget seemed oblivious to the fact that she was being banged into the wall with such force that the plaster was cracking, and small particles of paint were flying in the air.

If she were mortal, she would've bruised badly.

Liberated by her resilience, Andrew kept going hard.

It was so fucking good to feel vital, strong, male. But as he neared his completion, Andrew had the passing thought that as amazing as this was, something was still missing.

"Now," Bridget hissed.

He obeyed her command, synchronizing his climax with hers and coming hard inside her—his shaft milked by the convulsing muscles in her sheath gripping him harder than any fist.

"God, Bridget..." He fumbled for words as he lowered her.

Her thighs trembled a little, but as her feet touched the floor, she was steady. "Come to bed." She bent and pulled his pants up but left them unzipped. "I don't want you to trip on the way. I still have a use for you." She winked and walked away.

To his relief, he saw that although her back was slightly reddened, the skin looked intact. But as she sauntered ahead of him, he noticed that one of her curvy butt cheeks still bore a faint outline of his handprint. That one, he didn't mind. Not at all.

In fact, he felt his shaft give a twitch. Good, the abstinence was paying off. Tonight, he would be able to last, hopefully for as long as it would take to satisfy the lustful immortal.

Two hours later, a Victoria's Secret lineup naked parade wouldn't have gotten a rise out of him. And if tongues could get sprains, his would've been sporting a brace.

The merry tune Bridget was whistling in the kitchen was like a slap to his manhood. She was going to kill him, pleasurably, but he'd be dead nonetheless.

Andrew closed his eyes and inhaled deeply. One didn't need an immortal's superior nose to smell the thick scent of sex on the bedding, and if he had an ounce of energy left in him, he would've gotten all domestic and taken them off for her.

Still naked, Bridget sauntered into the bedroom with a loaded tray and placed it on the side table. "Sit up. I'm going to nourish you. You look pale."

"I wonder why?" he said as he propped himself up on the pillows and took the coffee mug she'd handed him.

"Poor baby. Too much for you?"

Now, that was mean.

"Not at all. Give me an hour and I'm back up." *Not if my life depended on it...*

"Aha. Sure. Whatever you say." She handed him a pastry.

As he chewed, he was reminded of the call he still owed Bhathian. It would have to wait until he could move.

"This is good. Where did you get it?"

"I was on Fairfax earlier today, and the smells lured me into this new bakery. I don't remember the name, but it's on the box if you want to write it down. I bought an assortment to try it out, but I'm afraid this is the only one left." She smiled sheepishly.

"Oh, yeah? Who ate all the rest?"

"I did."

"How many?"

"Eleven. There were twelve in the box."

And here he'd thought that Bridget only ate veggies. With an appetite like this for baked goods, it was a miracle she wasn't fat.

He appraised her lean midsection. "Where do you pack it all?"

"Breasts and butt." She patted the aforementioned parts.

"Then by all means, eat more. I love your curves."

A sad shadow clouded her eyes, but only momentarily. She shook it off so fast Andrew wasn't sure if it had really been there or if he'd just imagined it.

She grinned. "You and the construction workers renovating that old office building on Olive. Every time I pass by, they whistle and comment."

"Want me to beat them up for you?"

She laughed. "Why on earth would I want that?"

"Some women find it offensive." He shrugged.

"I don't mind the whistling, but the comments they think I can't hear..."

"My offer is still on the table."

She leaned and kissed his cheek. "You're so sweet."

"What is it with immortal females and calling me sweet? Even my own mother never called me that."

She kissed him again, on the lips this time. "What's the matter? Your machismo got hurt?"

He crossed his arms over his chest. "Yes."

Bridget refilled his coffee mug and handed him a piece of an apple as a peace offering.

"Can you stay the night?"

And prove himself a liar when even three hours later he would remain as limp as a noodle? No way. "I wish I could, but I need to talk to Bhathian. There is something I'd promised him to do, and I didn't have a chance because of that damn useless conference my boss sent me on with barely any notice."

"You could come back later...I'm flying out to Baltimore tomorrow..."

"I thought Julian's graduation was next week."

"It is, but I wanted to spend some time with him, and he made plans with his roommates for a road trip after the graduation."

Damn, he hated to disappoint her, but he hated the prospect of staying even more. His suitcase was still in his car because he'd come here straight from the airport, and tomorrow was another long workday. He needed to go home.

Andrew pulled her into his arms and kissed her lips gently. "I'm sorry, but I just have to go home and unpack, check what alien life forms are growing in my fridge..." He tried for humor, and it worked.

She smiled. "Fascinating, save some samples for me."

"I promise to save something better than disgusting growth for you to play with."

"And what might that be?"

"Life force? Energy?" He made a face.

Bridget laughed. "After another ten days of nada, you'll need it."

"I know."

Sebastian

Standing on top of the old monastery's newly added third-floor balcony, Sebastian leaned over the railing and glared at the cars parked outside. A damned parking lot was one more thing Sebastian realized he had neglected to plan for his new base of operation in the picturesque Ojai.

The front of the building looked like a junkyard, and in the daytime it was even worse.

From his balcony, he should be gazing at a grassy lawn and flowerbeds, not a bunch of used cars scattered on top of packed dirt.

A paved circular driveway and a fountain with a statue at its center, surrounded by rose bushes, would have made the place look grand.

But hiring workers now that the warriors were all in residence was problematic. Training would have to be suspended, and the guys would have to make themselves scarce.

The men hardly matched what one would expect of those visiting a restful *spiritual retreat*.

There was no helping the cars, though. The men needed vehicles to transport themselves to and from the clubs they were now scoping nightly in search of male clan members. Tom and Robert had gone shopping, and in a few days had managed to fill the lot with a bunch of used cars. Sebastian would've preferred to go into a dealership and lease a fleet, but Tom had insisted that buying from private owners was more discreet.

All in all, they now had twenty-nine vehicles at their disposal.

One was a big truck, for just in case, and the rest an assortment of minivans and SUVs. While the troops shared the used cars at a ratio of three to one, Sebastian had insisted that he and his two assistants each had their own brand new vehicle.

For obvious reasons, all had darkened windows.

The cars were serving dual purposes. The obvious one was transportation, but also, when needed, the back seats could be folded to provide a place for a quick fuck.

With his basement brothel's low occupancy rate, his troop's needs had to be satisfied off base.

Over the last two weeks, Sebastian had been able to find only five girls for his brothel. Not enough to take care of seventy-five immortal warriors, two assistants, and one sadist. But there was only so much he could do in a day, and snagging the right females required investigative work that took time.

Most hadn't been the right fit.

Which reminded him that there was another issue he hadn't accounted for. Human females required sunlight and fresh air to stay healthy and in a good mood. Thralling was not enough to counteract the underlying depression the lack of natural light and tiny jail rooms were causing.

He'd come to the conclusion that he couldn't keep them cooped up in the basement twenty-four hours a day.

On Pleasure Island, the women enjoyed several swimming pools, above-ground bars and restaurants, and the beautiful, tropical ocean. It was a gross oversight on his part to not realize the importance of those amenities.

Sebastian should have known that the exalted leader of *The Devout Order Of Mordth*, Lord Navuh, never did anything without a good reason. If Navuh had chosen to provide his whores with outdoor recreation, it had been only because it was crucial for the women's health and their ability to provide the exceptional services his secret island was known for.

Sebastian pulled out his phone and selected Robert's number. "Grab Tom and meet me outside."

"Yes, sir."

Sebastian rolled his eyes but didn't say anything. Robert was a lost cause. Jogging down the stairs, he glanced at the spacious recreation room. The men were done with their chores for the day, and several were taking a break playing pool or watching a movie before going to their rooms to get ready for the nightly club patrols.

There had been a lot of grumbling about the domestic chores they'd been assigned, but he had no intention of getting more humans on the premises to perform the cooking and housekeeping duties. Perhaps once the basement rooms were all filled, he would divert his attention to finding at least a decent cook. He was sick of the barbecued steaks and hamburgers the men were taking turns preparing.

Other than that, the lazy fuckers could keep on doing laundry, sweeping floors, and cleaning toilets. It wasn't as if they had that much to do during the day. Five hours of training was enough to keep them in shape, and the rest of their work was done at night.

Outside, the mountain air was crisp and cool, and other than the rumbling voices of the men inside, he could hear only the chirping of crickets and the hooting of the occasional owl. Even the coyotes didn't dare go anywhere near the compound.

"You wanted to see us, boss?" Tom said from behind him.

"Yes, I want to do something about the grounds." He waved his hand at the vehicles. In the weak moonlight, their colors were faded, all looking like different shades of gray and black. "I don't want to see this out of my window."

Robert glanced around at the gentle hills surrounding the former monastery. "This is the only flat area."

The problem with subordinates who were good at taking orders was that they didn't think independently, you had to chew everything for them.

"What do you have in mind?" Tom asked.

"I want the parking lot to be moved over there." Sebastian pointed to the side of the building. "And I want a circular driveway with a fountain in the center. The rest of the grounds need planting; grass, flowers, trees, the works." Sebastian began walking. "Come with me." He motioned for them to follow.

At some point, the back of the property had had grassy lawns with gravel paths meandering through them, but now there was nothing besides overgrown weeds and construction debris that hadn't been taken care of yet.

"I'm thinking of putting in a swimming pool over there, and an outdoor bar with shaded trellises on that side. We'll need to bring in large, mature trees to create a green canopy around the whole thing. Girls lounging in bikinis are not exactly what one expects to find in an 'Interfaith Spiritual Retreat'."

Robert looked intrigued.

"And how do you suggest we do it?" Tom asked.

"That's what I need to figure out. If it were only planting, I would've had the men do it, but for the pool and hardscaping we need a contractor with heavy equipment."

Robert crossed his arms over his chest and started pacing back and forth. "Curfew," he uttered a few moments later. "We need to coordinate several contractors with large crews to come and be done in a few hours. We'll have the men on lockdown in the house while the construction is going on."

"What about the cars?" Tom asked.

"We park them in a line on the side of the road, one behind the other."

Sebastian clapped Robert's back. "Great idea, Robert. We could tell the contractors that there are guests in the retreat and work needs to be confined to a predetermined number of hours a day. This will also explain the cars."

The guy, who was tall to begin with, seemed to grow a few inches. "Thank you, Sebastian," he said without stuttering or mumbling for the first time.

Clap, clap, clap. "Finally," Tom said.

Andrew

I'm back and here in the building. Want to meet me downstairs? Andrew texted Bhathian.

Come to my place. 37 floor, #4.

I'm on my way.

Bridget's apartment was just one floor above Bhathian's, and Andrew opted to take the emergency stairs down.

They had already said their goodbyes. He'd offered to come get her and drive her to the airport, but she'd declined. Her flight was leaving in the afternoon, and she'd said that she saw no reason for him to take time off work. A taxi would do.

To his shame, he'd felt relieved. There was a big pile of files waiting for him in the office, and to catch up, he would need to not only work through his lunch break but stay overtime. His damn bosses still expected him to deliver a report despite sending him on that useless trip.

Andrew rapped his knuckles on the door and waited.

After a moment, Bhathian opened it. "Hey, my man, come in. How was your trip?" He clasped Andrew's hand.

"A waste of time." Andrew shook it then followed him inside.

The layout and furnishings were similar to Bridget's. But where hers had been personalized with all kinds of knick-knacks, and everything was nice and tidy, the guy's place was typical of what one would expect to find in a bachelor's apartment.

There was an opened box of pizza on the dining table, and empty beer bottles littered every surface. It seemed that Bhathian had appropriated all that had been left from Kian's bachelor party because most of them were Snake's Venom, the expensive, super potent Scottish beer Anandur had bought for the occasion.

Bhathian followed his gaze. "Want one? I have plenty."

"Sure, why not?'

The guy ducked into the kitchen and returned with two cold ones.

Andrew took one. "I'm surprised so many were left. I thought we demolished all of them."

"There were none. But they were good, so the next day I went and bought two cases for myself."

"I thought they were pricey."

Bhathian shrugged his massive shoulders and planted his butt in a chair across from Andrew. "I have plenty of money and nothing to spend it on."

"You didn't go to see her." There was no need to specify which her he was talking about.

Bhathian winced. "The farthest I got was to stand outside her shop, but I didn't have the guts to go in."

"I'm sorry that I bailed on you."

"Not your fault."

"Do you want to go tomorrow?"

"If you can come, then yes."

"So, did you get a peek?"

Bhathian nodded. "She looks like her mother."

"Oh, yeah?"

"Beautiful." There was a definite note of pride in Bhathian's voice.

"Does she have anything from you?"

"Luckily for her, not much." Bhathian grimaced. "She has my thick eyebrows. Though, hers are pretty, not bushy like mine."

Andrew tried to picture a woman with Eva's exotic beauty and Bhathian's surly expression and came up blank.

Bhathian took a swig from his beer. "I need to find out what happened to Eva. Any idea how?"

Good question. The fact that the police hadn't found anything didn't mean much. Their investigation had probably been superficial at best.

"We can start by following the money trail. The government is still depositing her monthly pension checks into her bank account, and if she's still alive, I'm sure she is accessing it."

"And you can find out where she's making withdrawals?"

"Not easily, but yes. Unless the money is funneled through a Swiss bank. Then it's next to impossible."

Bhathian shook his head. "Just so you know, I'm forever in your debt. Whatever you need, whenever, just say the word."

"I appreciate it, but save your gratitude for when I actually find something."

"You already found my daughter, and for this alone I owe you big time. I'm not just blowing smoke up your ass, I mean it. Whatever, whenever."

"Okay, I got it, but it's really not necessary. If the roles were reversed, I'm sure you would've done the same for me." It seemed like the right thing to say, even though Andrew wasn't sure it was true. He was an outsider, tolerated only because his sister was married to the regent.

But Bhathian nodded solemnly, and leaned forward, extending his hand with the bottle. "That's what family is for."

Okay, so he might have been wrong. It seemed that Bhathian had really accepted Andrew as one of the clan. "To family." He clinked bottles with the guy.

"To family," Bhathian echoed.

Andrew emptied his bottle of Snake's Venom and put the empty on the coffee table before pushing up to his feet.

Damn, the thing must've gone to his head because he had a moment of vertigo. But it passed almost as soon as it started. It was probably only the fatigue catching up to him. "Tomorrow after work I'll come to get you, and we'll drive to Glendale. Seven okay?"

Bhathian got up and escorted him to the door. "Whatever works for you." The guy pulled Andrew into a crushing bear hug and clapped his back.

"Careful, my man. I'm still only a fragile human."

A rare smile brightening his gloomy features, Bhathian let go. "You might be a human, but from what I hear there is nothing fragile about you, tough guy."

And wasn't that good to hear.

On his way home, as he drove through the deserted streets of downtown L.A., Andrew reflected on his conversation with Bhathian.

Family.

For better or worse, the clan was now his family—independent of his decision regarding chancing the transition or not. They'd accepted him as is—the first human ever to be admitted into their tight, secret community.

He wondered if things would've been different if he hadn't brought all that he had to the table. If he were just an average Joe, with an average job, would they have entrusted him with their secrets?

Probably not.

The truth was that the clan needed him. Not that it was a bad thing necessarily, being needed was just as important as being accepted, maybe even more. Especially for a proud son-of-a-gun like him.

Which made him think of Dalhu.

The dude had done the impossible. His acceptance by the clan, however, had come at an unimaginable price. Andrew could not think of a single male that could've taken the torment Dalhu had gone through—not with the dignity and unparalleled willpower the guy had displayed.

One thing was for sure, if Andrew ever needed someone to fight by his side, Dalhu would be his first choice. Not that there was a chance the guy would be allowed to fight anytime soon. For all intents and purposes, Dalhu was still under house arrest—during his probation period as Kian had called it. True, he was no longer confined to the dungeon, and was sharing Amanda's spacious penthouse, but he wasn't allowed to leave.

The guy must be going crazy.

For a warrior to be cooped up in an apartment without the ability to release some steam must be hard. And it didn't matter that he was living in the lap of luxury with the love of his life.

Maybe Andrew should go spend some time with the dude, invite him for a sparring contest down in the gym.

Right.

Who was he kidding? As if he could offer any kind of a challenge to the powerful immortal. Even among the Guardians, Andrew suspected that only Anandur, or perhaps Yamanu, stood a chance against the ex-Doomer.

Amanda had gotten herself one hell of a protector.

Damn, it still stung.

Losing to the other guy hadn't been good for Andrew's ego. But he had to concede that despite his initial opinion of the guy, Dalhu had turned out to be the better man for Amanda.

God knew that with the kind of trouble the woman courted, Dalhu was probably the only male on earth capable of keeping her safe.

Order Dark Warrior Mine Today!

Join the VIP Club
To find out what's included in your free membership, flip to the last page.

The Children of the Gods Series

Reading Order

THE CHILDREN OF THE GODS ORIGINS

1: Goddess's Choice

When gods and immortals still ruled the ancient world, one young goddess risked everything for love.

2: Goddess's Hope

Hungry for power and infatuated with the beautiful Areana, Navuh plots his father's demise. After all, by getting rid of the insane god he would be doing the world a favor. Except, when gods and immortals conspire against each other, humanity pays the price.

But things are not what they seem, and prophecies should not to be trusted...

THE CHILDREN OF THE GODS

Dark Stranger

1: Dark Stranger The Dream

2: Dark Stranger Revealed

3: Dark Stranger Immortal

Dark Enemy

4: Dark Enemy Taken

5: Dark Enemy Captive

6: Dark Enemy Redeemed

Kri & Michael's Story

6.5: My Dark Amazon

When Michael and Kri fight off a gang of humans, Michael gets stabbed. The injury to his immortal body recovers fast, but the one to his ego takes longer, putting a strain on his relationship with Kri.

DARK WARRIOR

7: Dark Warrior Mine

8: Dark Warrior's Promise

Andrew and Nathalie's love flourishes, but the secrets they keep from each other taint their relationship with doubts and suspicions. In the meantime, Sebastian and his men are getting bolder, and the storm that's brewing will shift the balance of power in the millennia-old conflict between Annani's clan and its enemies.

9: Dark Warrior's Destiny

The new ghost in Nathalie's head remembers who he was in life, providing Andrew and her with indisputable proof that he is real and not a figment of her imagination.

Convinced that she is a Dormant, Andrew decides to go forward with his transition immediately after the rescue mission at the Doomers' HQ.

Fearing for his life, Nathalie pleads with him to reconsider. She'd rather spend the rest of her mortal days with Andrew than risk what they have for the fickle promise of immortality.

While the clan gets ready for battle, Carol gets help from an unlikely ally. Sebastian's second-in-command can no longer ignore the torment she suffers at the hands of his commander and offers to help her, but only if she agrees to his terms.

10: Dark Warrior's Legacy

Andrew's acclimation to his post-transition body isn't easy. His senses are sharper, he's bigger, stronger, and hungrier. Nathalie fears that the changes in the man she loves are more than physical. Measuring up to this new version of him is going to be a challenge.

Carol and Robert are disillusioned with each other. They are not destined mates, and love is not on the horizon. When Robert's three months are up, he might be left with nothing to show for his sacrifice.

Lana contacts Anandur with disturbing news; the yacht and its human cargo are in Mexico. Kian must find a way to apprehend Alex and rescue the women on board without causing an international incident.

Dark Guardian

11: Dark Guardian Found

12: Dark Guardian Craved

13: Dark Guardian's Mate

Dark Angel

14: Dark Angel's Obsession

15: Dark Angel's Seduction

16: Dark Angel's Surrender

Dark Operative

17: Dark Operative: A Shadow of Death

18: Dark Operative: A Glimmer of Hope

19: Dark Operative: The Dawn of Love

Dark Survivor

20: Dark Survivor Awakened
21: Dark Survivor Echoes of Love
22: Dark Survivor Reunited

Dark Widow

23: Dark Widow's Secret
24: Dark Widow's Curse
25: Dark Widow's Blessing

Dark Dream

26: Dark Dream's Temptation
27: Dark Dream's Unraveling
28: Dark Dream's Trap

Dark Prince

29: Dark Prince's Enigma
30: Dark Prince's Dilemma
31: Dark Prince's Agenda

Dark Queen

32: Dark Queen's Quest
33: Dark Queen's Knight
34: Dark Queen's Army

Dark Spy

35: Dark Spy Conscripted
36: Dark Spy's Mission
37: Dark Spy's Resolution

Dark Overlord
38: Dark Overlord New Horizon
39: Dark Overlord's Wife
40: Dark Overlord's Clan

Dark Choices
41: Dark Choices The Quandary
42: Dark Choices Paradigm Shift
43: Dark Choices The Accord

Dark Secrets
44: Dark Secrets Resurgence
45: Dark Secrets Unveiled
46: Dark Secrets Absolved

Dark Haven
47: Dark Haven Illusion
48: Dark Haven Unmasked
49: Dark Haven Found

Dark Power
50: Dark Power Untamed
51: Dark Power Unleashed
52: Dark Power Convergence

Dark Memories
53: Dark Memories Submerged
54: Dark Memories Emerge

55: Dark Memories Restored

Dark Hunter
56: Dark Hunter's Query
57: Dark Hunter's Prey
58: <u>Dark Hunter's Boon</u>

Dark God
59: Dark God's Avatar
60: Dark God's Reviviscence
61: Dark God Destinies Converge

Dark Whispers
62: Dark Whispers From The Past
63: Dark Whispers From Afar
64: Dark Whispers From Beyond

Dark Gambit
65: Dark Gambit The Pawn
66: Dark Gambit The Play
67: Dark Gambit Reliance

Dark Alliance
68: Dark Alliance Kindred Souls
69: Dark Alliance Turbulent Waters
70: Dark Alliance Perfect Storm

Dark Healing

71: Dark Healing Blind Justice

72: Dark Healing Blind Trust

73: Dark healing Blind Curve

Dark Encounters

74: Dark Encounters of the Close Kind

75: Dark Encounters of the Unexpected Kind

76: Dark Encounters of the Fated Kind

The Children of the Gods Series Sets

Books 1-3: Dark Stranger trilogy—Includes a bonus short story: **The Fates take a Vacation**

Books 4-6: Dark Enemy Trilogy —Includes a bonus short story—**The Fates' Post-Wedding Celebration**

Books 7-10: Dark Warrior Tetralogy

Books 11-13: Dark Guardian Trilogy

Books 14-16: Dark Angel Trilogy

Books 17-19: Dark Operative Trilogy

Books 20-22: Dark Survivor Trilogy

Books 23-25: Dark Widow Trilogy

Books 26-28: Dark Dream Trilogy

Books 29-31: Dark Prince Trilogy

Books 32-34: Dark Queen Trilogy

Books 35-37: Dark Spy Trilogy

Books 38-40: Dark Overlord Trilogy
Books 41-43: Dark Choices Trilogy
Books 44-46: Dark Secrets Trilogy
Books 47-49: Dark Haven Trilogy
Books 50-52: Dark Power Trilogy
Books 53-55: Dark Memories Trilogy
Books 56-58: Dark Hunter Trilogy
Books 59-61: Dark God Trilogy
Books 62-64: Dark Whispers Trilogy
Books 65-67: Dark Gambit Trilogy
Books 68-70: Dark Alliance Trilogy
Books 71-73: Dark healing Trilogy

MEGA SETS

INCLUDE CHARACTER LISTS

The Children of the Gods: Books 1-6
The Children of the Gods: Books 6.5-10

TRY THE SERIES ON

AUDIBLE

2 FREE audiobooks with your new Audible subscription!

PERFECT MATCH SERIES

Vampire's Consort

When Gabriel's company is ready to start beta testing, he invites his old crush to inspect its medical safety protocol.

Curious about the revolutionary technology of the *Perfect Match Virtual Fantasy-Fulfillment studios*, Brenna agrees.

Neither expects to end up partnering for its first fully immersive test run.

King's Chosen

When Lisa's nutty friends get her a gift certificate to *Perfect Match Virtual Fantasy Studios*, she has no intentions of using it. But since the only way to get a refund is if no partner can be found for her, she makes sure to request a fantasy so girly and over the top that no sane guy will pick it up.

Except, someone does.

> **Warning:** This fantasy contains a hot, domineering crown prince, sweet insta-love, steamy love scenes painted with light shades of gray, a wedding, and a HEA in both the virtual and real worlds.
>
> Intended for mature audience.

Captain's Conquest

Working as a Starbucks barista, Alicia fends off flirting all day long, but none of the guys are as charming and sexy as Gregg. His frequent visits are the highlight of her day, but since he's never asked her out, she assumes he's taken. Besides, between a day job and a budding music career, she has no time to start a new relationship.

That is until Gregg makes her an offer she can't refuse—a gift certificate to the virtual fantasy fulfillment service everyone is talking about. As a huge Star Trek fan, Alicia has a perfect match in mind—the captain of the Starship Enterprise.

The Thief Who Loved Me

When Marian splurges on a Perfect Match Virtual adventure as a world infamous jewel thief, she expects high-wire fun with a hot partner who she will never have to see again in real life.

A virtual encounter seems like the perfect answer to Marcus's string of dating disasters. No strings attached, no drama, and definitely no love. As a die-hard James Bond fan, he chooses as his avatar a dashing MI6 operative, and to complement his adventure, a dangerously seductive partner.

Neither expects to find their forever Perfect Match.

My Merman Prince

The beautiful architect working late on the twelfth floor of my building thinks that I'm just the maintenance guy. She's also under the impression that I'm not interested.

Nothing could be further from the truth.

I want her like I've never wanted a woman before, but I don't play where I work.

I don't need the complications.

When she tells me about living out her mermaid fantasy with a stranger in a Perfect Match virtual adventure, I decide to do everything possible to ensure that the stranger is me.

THE DRAGON KING

To save his beloved kingdom from a devastating war, the Crown Prince of Trieste makes a deal with a witch that costs him half of his humanity and dooms him to an eternity of loneliness.

Now king, he's a fearsome cobalt-winged dragon by day and a short-tempered monarch by night. Not many are brave enough to serve in the palace of the brooding and volatile ruler, but Charlotte ignores the rumors and accepts a scribe position in court.

As the young scribe reawakens Bruce's frozen heart, all that stands in the way of their happiness is the witch's bargain. Outsmarting the evil hag will take cunning and courage, and Charlotte is just the right woman for the job.

My Werewolf Romeo

The father of my star student is a big-shot screenwriter and the patron of the drama department who thinks he can dictate what production I should put on. The principal makes it very clear that I need to cooperate with the opinionated asshat or walk away from my dream job at the exclusive private high school.

It doesn't help matters that the guy is single, hot, charming, creative, and seems to like me despite my thinly-veiled hostility.

When he invites me to a custom-tailored Perfect Match virtual adventure to prove that his screenplay is perfect for my production, I accept, intending to have fun while proving that messing with the classics is a foolish idea.

I don't expect to be wowed by his werewolf adaptation of Red Riding Hood mesh-up with Romeo and Juliet, and I certainly don't expect to fall in love with the virtual fantasy's leading man.

The Channeler's Companion

A treat for fans of *The Wheel of Time*.

When Erika hires Rand to assist in her pediatric clinic, she does so despite his good looks and irresistible charm, not because of them.

He's empathic, adores children, and has the patience of a saint.

He's also all she can think about, but he's off limits.

What's a doctor to do to scratch that irresistible itch without risking workplace complications?

A shared adventure in the Perfect Match Virtual Studios seems like the solution, but instead of letting the algorithm choose a partner for her, Erika can try to influence it to select the one she wants. Awarding Rand a gift certificate to the service will get him into their database, but unless Erika can tip the odds in her favor, getting paired with him is a long shot.

Hopefully, a virtual adventure based on her and Rand's favorite series will do the trick.

Note

I hope my stories have added a little joy to your day. If you have a moment to add some to mine, you can help spread the word about the Children Of The Gods series by telling your friends and penning a review. Your recommendations are the most powerful way to inspire new readers to explore the series.

Thank you,

Isabell

Copyright © 2016 by I. T. Lucas

All rights reserved.
No part of this book may be reproduced in any form or by any electronic or mechanical means, including information storage and retrieval systems, without written permission from the author, except for the use of brief quotations in a book review.

NOTE FROM THE AUTHOR:
Dark Enemy Redeemed is a work of fiction!

Names, characters, places and incidents are products of the author's imagination or are used fictitiously and are not to be construed as real. Any similarity to actual persons, organizations and/or events is purely coincidental.

FOR EXCLUSIVE PEEKS AT UPCOMING RELEASES &
A FREE COMPANION BOOK

Join my *VIP Club* and gain access to the VIP portal at itlucas.com
To Join, go to:
http://eepurl.com/blMTpD

INCLUDED IN YOUR FREE MEMBERSHIP:

YOUR VIP PORTAL

- Read preview chapters of upcoming releases.
- Listen to Goddess's Choice narration by Charles Lawrence
- Exclusive content offered only to my VIPs.

FREE I.T. LUCAS COMPANION INCLUDES:

- Goddess's Choice Part 1
- Perfect Match: Vampire's Consort (A standalone Novella)
- Interview Q & A
- Character Charts

If you're already a subscriber, and you are not getting my emails, your provider is sending them to your junk folder, and you are missing out on **important updates, side characters' portraits, additional content, and other goodies.** To fix that, add isabell@itlucas.com to your email contacts or your email VIP list.

Manufactured by Amazon.ca
Bolton, ON